PRAISE FOR THE LIMITS OF LIMELIGHT

"An engrossing glimpse into a bygone era and the forces affecting a young woman's evolution into her own abilities and adulthood . . . vigorous and involving to the end."

—*Midwest Book Review*

"Based on a true story . . . a witty and meticulously researched treat."

—*Kirkus Reviews*

"A biographical novel as bright as the Golden Era . . . A lovely tribute to the larger-than-life celebrities of early Hollywood . . . a glitz and glamour novel that shines brighter the deeper you go."

—*Independent Book Review*

"A time capsule of Hollywood's Golden Era . . . a captivating novel of Tinsel Town's perils and pitfalls, trade-offs and triumphs!"

—*Leslie Carroll, author of American Princess*

"Porter's elegant, warm and well-researched novel is a joy to read! Perfect for lovers of historical fiction and tales of remarkable women. 5 of 5 Stars."

—*Literary Redhead, Goodreads*

PRAISE FOR *A PLEDGE OF BETTER TIMES*

"Porter's ambitious novel of 17th-century England is brimming with vivid historical figures and events . . . rigorously researched and faithfully portrayed."

—*Publishers Weekly*

"A true delight for fans of monarchy . . . Porter does a sensational job portraying the time period."

—*The Examiner*

"Porter winningly captures both the dramatic societal upheavals and the sparkling wit and court life of the time . . . A very rewarding reading experience—I highly recommend it."

—*Historical Novels Review*

"A richly evocative peek into a world long gone, with political and ideological maneuvering and romantic entanglements . . . Porter explores friendship, marriage, parenthood, and loyalty as she tells the story of people who were celebrities in their time."

—*New Hampshire Sunday News*

PRAISE FOR BEAUTIFUL INVENTION: A NOVEL OF HEDY LAMARR

"Hedy Lamarr is feted as much for her intellect as for her beauty in this captivating novel . . . Porter's insightful account of a gifted yet often misunderstood inventor and movie star makes for a winning novel."

—*Publishers Weekly*

"*Beautiful Invention* deftly weaves Hedwig Kiesler's life as an intelligent, daring woman with the seductive, exotic Hedy Lamarr MGM invented and displayed to a fascinated public. It's fast, fun, fascinating, enjoyable, intriguing, and recommended."

—*Historical Novels Review*

"The terror felt by Lamarr, who was Jewish . . . is brilliantly conveyed by Porter, whose empathy for Lamarr and historical knowledge brings danger to the plot . . . Resonating with the modern reader are Lamarr's struggles within her career and private life . . . A revealing look at Lamarr's life . . ."

—*The Lady Magazine (UK)*

"*Beautiful Invention* swept me into Hedy's life from the first page, so captivated was I by this incredible woman, fleshed out in the most compelling fashion by the author's very assured prose, plotting and execution . . . *Beautiful Invention* surpasses every expectation."

—*Literary Soirée*

THE LIMITS OF LIMELIGHT

Cover by Tugboat Design

Interior formatting by Melissa Williams Design

Published by Gallica Press

The Limits of Limelight/Margaret Porter—1st Edition

ISBN 13: 978-0-9907420-1-2

To Tina,
Thanks for being a great friend + inspiration on my journey(s).

THE LIMITS OF LIMELIGHT

A NOVEL

MARGARET PORTER

GALLICA PRESS

For my husband, the best possible companion for viewing black and white movies from Hollywood's Golden Age.

PART 1: 1931-1934

So it was that she came to talkie town, to visit her cousin, Ginger Rogers.

–New Movie Magazine, 1932

CHAPTER 1

An unshaded railway platform was the worst place to be on a searing July afternoon. Helen felt sure that everybody else waiting for the train shared her hope that it would arrive on time. Although her dimity dress was lightweight, its short, puffed sleeves exposed her arms to the merciless sun. Baked into a melting state by the heat radiating up from the platform, she longed to remove her summer hat and strip off her white gloves and be free of the silk chiffon stockings sticking to her skin.

To take her mind off these discomforts, she turned away from her mother and sister to study the people fortunate enough to be going on a journey. Ordinary folks carried plain cowhide grips. Others had stuffed their belongings into cheap cardboard suitcases held together with rope. She amused herself by guessing their destinations—any of which had to be more interesting and exciting than Oklahoma City. And less hot.

Matched suitcases of polished leather surrounded one prosperous-looking traveler. He wore a three-piece suit and fanned his face with his fedora while examining Sunday's edition of *The Daily Oklahoman.* An oilman, Helen guessed. He probably wouldn't notice the society page advertisement, inviting the public to meet a special celebrity guest at Classique Beauty Salon tomorrow.

Her sister Jean studied him, too, but with a different sort of interest and a great deal more intensity. Fully absorbed in his reading, he failed to notice.

He'll look up quick enough, thought Helen, when our cousin arrives.

Mama pressed a handkerchief against her temple to absorb a bead of perspiration. The slender hand, so steady when wielding comb or brush to beautify her clients, quivered from nerves. "I don't hear anything yet. Do you?"

"Yes." The blast of the whistle confirmed the train's approach. Helen focused half-shuttered eyes on the shimmering parallel ribbons of track. The engine came thundering along the sun-scorched rails and slid to a stop with a deafening shriek from the brakes.

Her mother pointed at a middle carriage. "I see them." Waving frantically, she called, "Lela, over here!"

A smile stretched the short woman's crimson lips as she marched briskly to meet them. Placing both gloved hands on Mama's shoulders, she kissed each powdered cheek. "How well you're looking, Virginia. And your girls."

"Ginger!" Helen rushed to meet her auburn-haired cousin. Suddenly self-conscious, she took a backward step, tightly gripping her purse. "Welcome to Oklahoma City!"

"Oh, my word," Ginger gasped. "Sweet little Helen—all grown up." She set down her vanity case and delivered a hearty hug. "Gosh, you're pretty!" She reached out to straighten Helen's straw hat, dislodged during their embrace. "What a long time it's been since we saw each other. Do you remember me?"

Too emotional to voice her reply, Helen nodded.

"Come along, girls," Lela Rogers called, taking charge of the situation. "Let's not stand about in this scorching weather a moment longer." She directed a porter to bring the suitcases.

"Can I drive?" Jean asked.

"No." Mama's tone indicated that any argument would be useless. She led the procession to the car, her gait more uneven than usual in her highest heels.

Helen spent the journey squeezed between her pouting sister and her cheerful, chattering aunt. She tugged off her gloves, damp from perspiration, and flattened them across her lap to prevent wrinkles.

Ginger sat in front, gazing at the streetscape. Turning her coppery head in Mama's direction, she said, "A Dallas judge made me a single woman again, not that I've felt like a wife since I ran away from Jack. Who, apparently, still exists—otherwise, I'd be a widow. A more dignified and respectable term than 'divorcee.'"

"You ought to pray you're never widowed. It's much worse than getting a divorce. I know, because I've suffered through both."

Ginger's hand flew to her mouth. "Sorry," she muttered. Swift to make amends, she added, "We look forward to meeting Mr. Nichols. We've seen how handsome he is in the photographs Helen sends us."

Helen, silent since leaving the train station, spoke up. "Aunt Lela, do you want to marry again?"

"Two matrimonial adventures were enough for me. My first marriage was a disaster. The second one wasn't worth saving, even if Ginger did adore her Daddy John. I'm too independent-minded to replace him."

"No man could keep up with you anyway," Ginger commented. "She's the busiest—and bossiest—woman in Hollywood."

Lela broke in on the laughter to offer her defense,

saying, "I'm managing your career, dearie. Always looking out for your interests. You'll never believe this, Virginia. After all the effort I put into choosing the perfect shade of red for her hair, so it would look just right on film, those idiots at Pathé decided to turn her into a blonde. The studio hairdresser went ahead and applied the bleach without any warning! Or asking permission."

"It burned my scalp," her daughter volunteered.

"I threatened to sue the company."

"I don't doubt it," Mama commented, sticking her arm through the open window to signal a turn onto an unpaved street. "Don't they know better than to risk the wrath of the first female Marine sergeant?"

"Once a Leatherneck, always a Leatherneck," her sister replied.

Aunt Lela's wartime service fascinated Helen. An early volunteer, one of the first females to join the armed forces, she'd edited a newspaper and a military magazine and produced newsreels and training films and sold Liberty Bonds. She'd also written movie scripts out in Hollywood, and from there had gone to New York to work for Radio Pictures. Last month, she'd moved back to California after Ginger, veteran of the vaudeville circuit and the Broadway stage and a supporting player in talkies, accepted a studio contract. Helen suspected her strong-willed aunt enjoyed bullying powerful motion picture men. They probably hadn't realized what Lela's relatives had always known, that her bark was more fearsome than her bite.

Listening to the mother and daughter, she noted the similarities and faint difference in their warm, well-modulated tones, devoid of any regional accent. Lela spoke with a ladylike refinement, choosing each word with care, whereas Ginger peppered her wry comments with slang.

Normally on a day this searing, Helen would change

her crumpled dress for a swimsuit and go with Jean to a friend's pool. But if she remained at home, Ginger and Aunt Lela might invite her to accompany them to the radio station—a favor she was reluctant to request. She carried her cousin's suitcase upstairs to her bedroom, surrendered to the house guests for their overnight stay.

"What a delightful color," Ginger commented, taking in the robin's-egg blue bedspread and matching tie-back curtains. "Look at all the books! You must be quite a reader."

"I like writing, too. I won an essay contest, and the newspaper published my entry." Going to the bookcase, Helen picked up her wooden pencil box. "Here's my prize."

Ginger removed her brown hat and placed it on the bedpost. "Advise me, please, about tomorrow. What will the ladies at the beauty shop expect me to say? Or do? I doubt Aunt Virginia wants me breaking into a tap dance routine."

Helen smiled. "I wish you would!"

"Didn't bring my dancing shoes."

"Classique is Oklahoma City's most elegant salon," she explained. "Many of the customers are rich oilmen's wives, who want beauty advice and new skin treatments and the very best cosmetics. They'll ask you what they can do to look as glamorous as a film star. And they're curious about the famous Hollywood people you know. Like Claudette Colbert."

"Is she your favorite?"

"You are, of course. On my birthday we hosted a cinema party—Mama and Jean and I. We invited my guests to a fancy supper here, and then we all went to watch you in *Honor Among Lovers.*"

"You didn't see much of me. My part was minuscule." Ginger sprawled out on the bed.

"If you want to rest, I'll go."

She was halfway to the door when her cousin called her back. "I'm not sleepy, just feeling lazy. Sit down, tell me about yourself. How old are you now?"

"Fifteen." Helen perched on the dressing table chair.

"Boyfriend?"

"I study with Vinnie Greiner. He's Cherokee. We sit together at the same lunch table. But usually Jean and I go out with a group. To the pictures, or to a dance. Football games, during the season. Classen High has a winning team."

"Sounds like fun. I missed out on all that. If it's possible to miss what you never had." Ginger concluded her wistful comment with a gusty sigh. "I remember the swell time we had as kids, living with our grandparents in Kansas City. You were a tiny tot, with those adorable dimples. My very own living, laughing dolly. You gave me my name."

A familiar story, and a point of pride. As a toddler, her attempts to pronounce all the syllables in her cousin's full name, Virginia, resulted in the nickname that stuck.

"And it's where I made my cinematic debut—in a local optician's advertisement that ran before the newsreel and main feature. No talkies back then, so the dialogue was printed across the screen. Nowadays I have lines to memorize. Mother drills me hard, I get them right on the first take." Ginger's rosy lips parted in a gaping yawn. "Guess I need a nap after all."

Creeping around the room, Helen pulled down the window shades. By the time she closed the door behind her, her cousin was sound asleep.

At the end of this unbearably hot and unusually busy Sunday, Helen welcomed the quiet and privacy of the

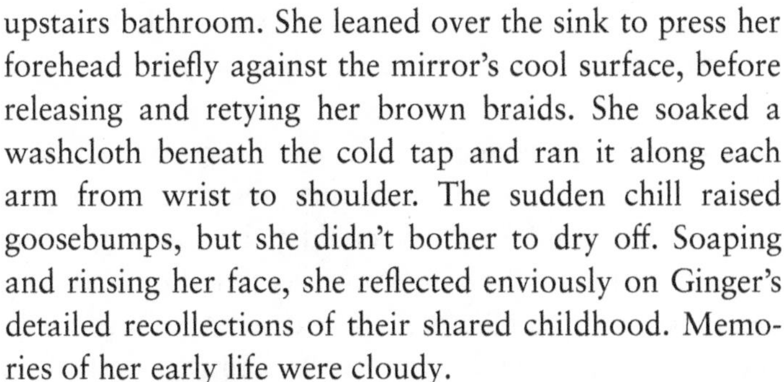

upstairs bathroom. She leaned over the sink to press her forehead briefly against the mirror's cool surface, before releasing and retying her brown braids. She soaked a washcloth beneath the cold tap and ran it along each arm from wrist to shoulder. The sudden chill raised goosebumps, but she didn't bother to dry off. Soaping and rinsing her face, she reflected enviously on Ginger's detailed recollections of their shared childhood. Memories of her early life were cloudy.

"When your poor mother takes you back, you must behave all the time and never be naughty," Grandmother Owens had often told her. "She's suffered so much."

"Don't cry," Aunt Genevieve said, whenever some childhood accident or sisterly slight brought on tears. "Be cheerful. When Mama feels sad, your smiling face will comfort her. You're a lucky little girl, you know."

Many years passed before Helen understood why.

Two months before her first birthday, her father was killed by a gas explosion in the cellar of their apartment house. Mama inhaled so much smoke and dust that her lungs were permanently weakened, she suffered a partial hearing loss, and she received the leg injury responsible for her enduring limp. Jean, knocked unconscious, recovered from a severe concussion but it, too, had lasting effects. A flying shard of glass pierced Helen's right cheek, leaving a half-moon scar that she could adequately conceal with foundation and powder.

Nobody had ever explained how she was rescued from the rubble of the flattened building.

Although Mama didn't speak of the accident, the whole family knew about the monetary settlement she received from the Kansas City gas company, deemed culpable for failing to repair a reported leak. This "fortune," as they called it, enabled a young widow to provide for her fatherless girls when between jobs and acquire a few luxuries—a nice automobile and the stylish clothing and accessories necessary for the manager of a beauty business.

When quite young, Helen and Jean—and Cousin Ginger—were deposited with their maternal grandparents so Mama and Aunt Lela could make their way in the world. Eventually the sisters found second husbands and reclaimed their daughters. Lela married Mr. Rogers and took Ginger to Fort Worth. Mr. Williams left less of an imprint on Helen's memory than his Wichita drugstore, and after a speedy divorce Mama resumed the responsibilities of breadwinner. To preserve what remained of her nest egg, she took a job at an Oklahoma City beauty shop and boarded Helen and Jean with a middle-aged lady and her elderly mother. Helen recalled her as a fleeting, floral-scented Sunday visitor. And she could never forget those dreaded nighttime journeys to the dank privy behind the lodging house and creeping alone through the darkness because Jean refused to venture outside.

I wonder how long we'd have stayed there, thought Helen, if I hadn't been run over by a laundry van.

When sunk in one of her gloomy moods, her sister would moan, "We're children of tragedy."

Jean, stubborn and often sullen, had a habit of stealing small and easily pocketed items. Loose change from Mama's top bureau drawer. A sterling silver compact. She'd purloined their parents' wedding portrait from a shelf in the parlor and concealed it in a shoebox that she kept in her closet. Helen had to pay a penny whenever she wanted to look at it. Jean had inherited Percy Brown's olive skin and dark eyes and hair, which could explain her possessiveness about the photograph. Her capacity for learning was limited, and she resented the fact that Helen, two years her junior, had skipped past her in school.

Loving Jean was her duty, Helen accepted that,

although it was impossible when her sister was disagreeable or misbehaved. This shameful truth could be mentioned only during confession, to the shadowy priest on the other side of the grille. He listened in silence, and then doled out "Our Fathers" and "Hail Marys" as penance for her transgression.

Mama, a fixture at an exclusive beauty emporium and increasingly active in local society, was seldom at home. Helen, left to her devices, devoted herself to her academic subjects and extracurricular activities. Through literature, she explored distant places and encountered fascinating people. And in the privacy of her room, she wrote in her diary and covered sheets of paper with the stories and poems she sent to Lela, who provided literary advice and light editing.

For comfort and companionship, she relied on the family's black maid. Clara Willingham and her husband Mort, a Pullman porter, lived down in the basement. Helen helped her make sandwiches for the vagrants who wandered up to the back door, begging for money but no less thankful for food. Whenever she handed one of them a bowl of washing water and a rag, she almost recoiled from the pungent odor of sweat and the bootleg liquor fumes. Clara, devoutly Christian and devoted to her church, always reminded Helen to count her blessings and thank the Lord that in these hard times, she had a comfortable house, working parents, plenty to eat, and nice dresses.

A soft knock drew her to the door.

Ginger, wrapped in a chenille robe, waved her toothbrush. "Mind if I join you?"

"Come on in. I'm finished." Stepping away from the washbasin, she said, "You were terrific during the broadcast. The radio man thought so, too. I could tell."

"I was worried I'd mess up the interview and embarrass you. And your family."

Helen was startled by this display of vulnerability in an ascendant performer of the screen and a featured star on the Broadway stage. Ginger's effervescence had charmed the program host at WKY, and she'd responded to his questions with verve and wit. Throughout their dialogue, Aunt Lela had nodded her bright head in encouragement, and she tapped her feet in time when Ginger sang a song from one of her New York shows, *a cappella.*

Ginger rinsed her mouth and emptied it in the basin. "Mother and Aunt Virginia are still jabbering downstairs. Let's go to your room for another chat. I want to know everything about you."

"Okay. But you'll be bored stiff." Her usual activities, and what passed for entertainment and excitement in Oklahoma surely paled in comparison to the delights of Hollywood and New York City. "If you didn't have to leave us tomorrow night, we'd take you to the Spring Lake amusement park. Or we could go to an air-conditioned cinema. The Liberty is showing *Up for Murder,* starring Lew Ayres."

"He's absolutely dreamy," her cousin gushed. "I fell for him really hard when I saw *All Quiet on the Western Front.*"

"This time he plays a baddie. 'A kiss that she meant as a joke caused him to kill!'" she quoted. "That's what the newspaper advertisement says."

CHAPTER 2

Striding along the dim hallway from bathroom to bedroom, Lela Rogers couldn't help comparing Virginia's circumstances with her own. She'd always been aware of their differences—in looks, in desires, in personalities—and tonight she recognized them with greater clarity.

After everything she's endured, my sister deserves to be happy and comfortable. But I wouldn't relish her humdrum existence, Lela acknowledged. I'm a born vagabond. An adventurer, an achiever. Ginger takes after me.

Lela, loving her daughter so intensely, had rejoiced at the arrival of each of Virginia's girls. But her greater affinity for Helen dated from that horrific road accident. When her niece's shattered leg became infected, Lela argued against amputation. Constant prayer, she insisted to Virginia, could ward off gangrene, and bring forth healing and wellness. Faithfully she entreated God to intervene and save Helen's tiny, broken limb. Her sister placed her trust in the medical men, but she did return to church to pray novenas and even attended mass, although her divorce barred her from receiving communion. These combined acts of faith, Lela was positive, wrought the miracle. Helen spent almost a year as a bedridden invalid, repeatedly admitted and discharged from the hospital. But today she walked on two legs, with perfect steadiness.

From their regular correspondence, Lela recognized her niece's flair for writing, and her ability to convey emotion and thoughts and observations with ease and effectiveness. Most of Helen's letters contained a poem or two, or an essay clipped from her school newspaper. Lela responded with praise or suggestions for improvement as warranted, offering encouragement that she doubted was forthcoming here on the home front. Whenever Ginger's feathery, sequined dance costumes began showing sign of wear, Lela would carefully wrap them in tissue paper and pack them into a box to send to Helen for dress-up games or to show her friends.

Entering her niece's bedroom, she was relieved to see an oscillating fan on the dressing table, pointed at the bed. Ginger leaned against the headboard, a photograph album propped on her bent knees.

"I thought you'd be fast asleep, after the day we've had. From Dallas to here, and a big dinner, then on to the radio station. In this stifling weather." Thankfully, she began to peel off each constricting garment, layer by layer—dress and slip and girdle and stockings. Her thoughtful daughter had laid out her cotton nightgown. "My ankles are more swollen here than they were in Texas," she said, settling onto the bed.

"No turban? Your hair will get mussed."

"Too hot. Might as well take advantage of having hairdressers in the family. Before I leave the house, Virginia or her husband will repair the damage."

She'd intended to review the Christian Science tract received from a Los Angeles practitioner. Instead, she took up her Bible and thumbed through until she came to the chapter in The Book of Judges about Deborah, the prophetess, and Jael, wife of Heber the Kenite, who dispatched an enemy by driving a nail into his head. She read aloud several passages.

"A gruesome scene," Ginger commented.

"But an inspiring one. The act was done for the glory of God." Lela peered over the top edge of her spectacles. "For females, there's no sin in strength. 'Blessed above women shall Jael be . . . blessed shall she be above all women in the tent.'" She placed her Bible on the bedside table. "I'm glad we came. Are you?"

Her daughter nodded. "Helen's a charmer. What do you think of dashing Uncle Nick?"

"He's good to my sister and treats Jean and Helen well. An improvement on her second husband."

"You knew him?"

"In high school. Like all the boys, Roy Williams had his eye on Virginia. Soon as she buried what was left of poor Percy Brown, he started courting her again. And after he returned from the war, he convinced her to marry him. I suppose she accepted for the sake of her girls. A pity that none of them benefitted. This time she did all right, as far as I can tell. Five marriages between us, Virginia and me."

"Counting mine, it makes six. Even more, if you add grandmother's two."

"Girls shouldn't marry till they're out of their teens. I hope my nieces have more sense."

"Lots of boys must like Helen. She's a darling little thing. Soft brown hair. Porcelain complexion. Straight teeth. Bright and merry and full of life. I recognize that spark. Granddaddy Owens has it, and he passed it on to you."

"You've got it, too." Lela plumped her pillow. "Enough chitchat. High time we extinguish our sparks and get some sleep. Big day tomorrow." She switched off the light and let the fan's persistent hum lull her into slumber.

In the morning, Lela rose early. Washed and dressed, she went down to the kitchen to give instructions about what Ginger liked for breakfast.

"Eggs sunny-side up, bacon fried to a nice crisp, and orange juice. No toast—she can't dance it off while we're traveling."

"Helen will take care of it," her sister said. "Jean and I have to get everything ready at the shop. Nick went in early to turn on all our fans, and the extra ones he borrowed. Ninety-nine degrees yesterday, and today the mercury could reach one hundred. We ordered a taxicab for you and our movie star."

Ginger wasn't a star in Hollywood—not yet—but in Oklahoma City she passed for one. "What about Helen?" Lela asked.

"She can ride with you."

Helen cracked eggs and seared bacon and poured the orange juice and coffee. She removed her bib apron and handed it to Ginger to protect her suit from any spills. After seeing to the guests' needs, she excused herself to finish dressing.

Ginger leaned across the table. "She's cute enough to be in pictures, isn't she? And photographs well, judging by the snapshots in her album. I just finished playing a character called Baby Face, and she's got a real one. Mother, I'm making a plan."

Lela put down her cup. "Oh?"

"Let's take Helen back to California. I'm positive I can get her into the movies."

CHAPTER 3

Ginger's notion was intriguing, but pragmatism ruled Lela. "Not every girl dreams of being a film actress."

"It's a lost cause, for most of them. But not Helen."

"I daresay she possesses sufficient imagination to envision a more exciting future than Oklahoma City offers her. And if she's with us, that's one less person for her parents to support on their income. Before telling them about your plan, I need to know whether Helen's interested. Talk it over with her."

"She'll be interested." Ginger flashed the perky smile that had enchanted theatrical producers and film directors, and countless members of the public.

"Be completely honest about what she can expect. Don't lead her on by pretending it's easy work and fast money. Without any theatrical experience—school plays don't count—she'll have a lot to learn."

"I'll give her dancing lessons. And you know everything about negotiating a contract. And publicity."

"I'm happy to do what I can to help her, but your career is paramount. After you've finished your three-picture commitment to Pathé, we won't waste your talents in any more B movies. Now that the Hollywood press is taking notice, it's time to raise your profile."

"With a singing role, like I had on Broadway." Her daughter's eyes glistened like aquamarines. "And if I'm cast in a musical, I'll get to dance again!"

The newspaper advertisement about Ginger's appearance, combined with Classique Beauty Salon's proximity to a Main Street department store, ensured a constant flow of customers. Some of Helen's Classen High friends brought their mothers, and a group of senior boys showed up to see a glamorous Hollywood star in the flesh. She enjoyed her role as her cousin's assistant, replenishing the stack of paper slips to be autographed, refilling the glass of iced cola, and standing close by in case anything else was needed. Jean handled telephone inquiries. Mama's staff of half a dozen women and men tended regular clients who arrived for previously scheduled appointments.

Twice before the lunchtime closing, Ginger rose from her chair to address the crowd. She described the difference between the thick makeup she wore when filming and products she relied on for daily use. This brand of "Ginger Rogers Cosmetics" would be offered as a special purchase for the rest of the week, and sales were so brisk that before midday Daddy was phoning his supplier to re-order. Helen overheard him telling Mama that they ought to extend the promotion for the rest of the month.

"Do it," she replied breezily, ushering the next lady to the waiting manicurist.

During the lunch break, her cousin and aunt complimented her parents on their employees' professionalism. The salon, they declared, offered a menu of services that rivaled any New York or Hollywood establishment.

"Is there a soda fountain nearby?" Ginger asked Helen. "You fed me plenty of breakfast, but I'd love a milkshake or a sundae. You can order whatever you like. My treat."

"There's one around the block. Air conditioned," she added.

"We need emery boards," Jean said, handing over some change.

"Won't you come with us?" she asked, despite her reluctance to have her older sister tagging along.

"Nope. Too many things to do before we re-open. There goes the phone again." Jean rushed to the reception desk to pick up.

At the drugstore, Ginger let Helen place their order at the counter while she claimed a booth at the back. Plunging their paper straws into the frothy shakes, they sipped greedily. An avalanche of icy liquid slid down Helen's parched throat.

"All day I've wanted to talk to you in private," Ginger told her. "Mother and I agree that you're exactly the type of girl who could work in pictures."

"Doing what?"

"Acting, of course. Maybe dancing and singing, if you have a knack for it. Don't look so surprised. I'm serious. You can live with us at the Garden of Allah—it's a residential hotel on Sunset Boulevard. A swell place, popular with actors and actresses and musicians. You'll have the twin bed in Mother's room, or else we'll set up a daybed in mine. There's a fountain full of goldfish right outside our door. And just steps away, a swimming pool like you've never seen, shaped like the Black Sea—or so everybody says. We want to prepare you for a film career." Ginger paused to take a breath. "Provided you'd like to go back with us. On the train."

Helen stared at her. "Leave Oklahoma City?" She swallowed. "Tonight?"

"Why not? It's summertime. You're not in school.

We'll be stopping in Denver to spend a couple of days with Granddad Owens, so we can meet his new wife. What a grand surprise for him if you're with us."

"That sounds terrific. But . . . Hollywood . . ." The suggestion was staggering.

"Every single day, girls who aren't half as pretty as you arrive in Los Angeles, convinced they'll be discovered instantly and become stars overnight. You've got Owens blood, which gives you plenty of smarts and the tenacity to succeed at anything."

"That won't be enough, will it? Winning that Charleston dance contest started you off in vaudeville. Then you appeared in Ziegfeld shows and Broadway musicals. You were a professional before you appeared in any movies."

"Experience doesn't matter as much as you think. Hollywood likes newcomers. In New York, showbiz is so clique-ish. I was lucky, because of Lela's connections. I got to know George and Ira Gershwin. Adele and Fred Astaire. Harold Ross took me to parties at the Mayfair Club, and lots of places. He's editor of *The New Yorker* magazine, which is quite influential, and he hangs out with all those Algonquin Round Table literary folks." Redirecting herself to her subject, she went on, "People in the picture business are fascinating, too, in different ways. You'll see. But if you're going with us tonight, we have to persuade Aunt Virginia to give her permission."

Yesterday, while wilting from heat at the railroad station, Helen had envied all the people with suitcases for being lucky enough to leave Oklahoma City. Now, with her cousin's unexpected invitation, she had a chance to do the same.

Thrilled by the prospect of living in Hollywood with Ginger and Aunt Lela, possibly becoming a motion picture actress, she said decisively, "If Mama says I can go with you, I will." With her limp straw, she stirred the diluted remains of her milkshake. "I need to get those emery boards Jean asked for. Go on back to the shop. I won't be long."

She found the narrow aisle containing nail care products and plucked two packets from the display. Motionless, she stared down at them, her mind a tangle of questions.

Why would Mama object to Ginger's plan? For years she relied on other people to look after me—her parents when Jean and I were small, then those two ladies we boarded with for six whole years. I don't think Daddy would mind. Jean either, though she might be annoyed that I'm being singled out. Clara's sure to miss me. But will anybody else?

She returned to find the salon busier than it had been in the morning. Ginger signed her name to another stack of paper slips and delivered her spiel twice. Helen noticed that Mama and Aunt Lela had withdrawn to the stockroom. Her heart thudded with the realization that they must be discussing her.

The phone was silent for the first time all day. Jean sat at the reception desk paging through a ladies' magazine. Helen joined her, intending to forewarn her about what might transpire before the day was over but didn't get the chance.

Mama emerged from the back regions, her expression revealing nothing. Not pride or displeasure or approval.

"Helen, come with me."

Ginger glanced up and grinned as Helen passed her table.

Mama pulled her into the claustrophobic room of shelving and stacked boxes. Aunt Lela, her lips pressed together, shut the door.

Before either of them could speak, she turned pleading eyes upon her mother. "Can I go to California? Please let me."

"Their train leaves in a few hours, and this is no decision to be made in a rush. Besides, you're too young to live so far away. Too pretty. And innocent."

"We all start out that way," Lela commented.

With a sharp glance at her sister, Mama said, "You were utterly idiotic about Ed McMath. Your first baby would've been born alive, if not for him and that brute of a doctor he called in. At least you'd wised up enough to get away from him after the second time you got pregnant. And when Ginger was scarcely older than Helen, and acting foolish about Jack Culpepper, you didn't stop her from marrying him."

"I tried. I failed. Like me, she learned hard lessons from her wretched mistake," Aunt Lela said soberly. "Infatuation blinded her to every one of Jack's numerous defects, and my opposition drove her into an elopement. He was a heavy drinker and turned violent towards her. And me."

This monologue revealed a portion of family history previously unknown to Helen. Never had she heard that note of remorse and humility from a woman who was, as Ginger often said, always correct about everything all the time.

Facing her mother, she declared, "I won't run off with a man. I promise."

"You won't have the chance," Mama answered tartly. "You'll stay and finish your education. You attend an excellent school with fine teachers. They've told us that after you graduate from Classen, you could get a college degree, something nobody else in the Owens family ever did. Daddy Nick and I put off moving into a bigger house in order to save up tuition money."

Helen hadn't known that, either.

"Ginger earns a thousand dollars a week," Lela declared. "As an untried beginner, Helen wouldn't make that much. But if any studio offered a reasonable contract, she could set aside her earnings to pay for college. That would allow you and Nick to buy that dream house now. You won't be paying Helen's room and board. She'll be our guest."

"So you said." Mama's top teeth grazed her lower lip, a sign of distress.

In a soothing tone, Lela said, "Let it be a summer vacation. If she goes with us to Denver tonight, she'll see her grandfather again. She can spend enough time in California to find out how she likes it. Ginger will take her to the studio and show her all that movie work entails. And we'll send her home in time for the start of classes. Remind me of your birthday, dear?"

"April thirteenth."

"Then you've got many months to consider whether you want to become a professional actress. I maintain that schooling is just training kids how to study. I never got past the eighth grade and always managed to provide for myself and for Ginger. She left school at fourteen and now supports both of us. Next year, when Helen is sixteen, we'll re-open this discussion. What do you say to that, Virginia?"

"You have to send her home before the fall term starts."

Nodding, Lela smiled at Helen. "There, dearie, it's settled. With this compromise Ginger gets her way, and you'll have a holiday out West. In the meantime, Virginia, if you and Nick need a larger house, I'll lend you the down payment money. Interest free. After spending the day at your salon, I've no concerns about your ability to repay me."

"That's generous of you, Lela. But I can't accept an offer like that without talking to my husband."

"Yes, you can. You should." Lela looped her pocketbook over her forearm. "I'm taking Helen to the department store to pick out some new shoes and dresses. We'll return before you close up the shop."

During their impromptu trip to Rorabaugh-Brown, Lela selected two expensive-looking garments, warning Helen not to inspect the price tags. She waited outside the dressing room and carefully checked the fit of each garment.

"They're long, but I can hem them while we're on the train. Your size and shape are close enough to Ginger's that you'll be able to borrow from her. If you don't object to all the bows and ruffles and frills she can't do without."

Helen was in a state of excited exhaustion when they returned to Classique, laden with shopping bags and shoe boxes. On the way home Mama decided to stop at the Pig Stand for food to take home, then fretted that a hasty and informal meal was an inappropriate farewell dinner.

Helen volunteered to wash and dry the dishes. After Ginger helped her put them away, they hurried upstairs to pack.

CHAPTER 4

Helen rushed to the parlor window of the luxury Pullman compartment and raised the shade so she could wave goodbye to her grandfather and his wife.

Ginger leaned over to blow them a kiss. "Maude was sweet to bake that scrumptious cake for my birthday. I like her, don't you?"

"She doesn't get a chance to say much. Granddaddy takes over every conversation."

"Larger than life, that's Smokey. Such a show-off. Summoning all the neighbors to meet his movie actress granddaughter. How many autographs did I sign for his friends? And I had to answer all those questions about Hollywood."

"He was awfully interested in Rin-Tin-Tin. I thought Maude would cry when you told her you're not best friends with Greta Garbo, and never had a date with Gary Cooper."

"He's in Europe, recovering his health after starring in ten pictures in two years. Moviemaking is tough, I tell you. By the end of a working day, I'm too tired to go out at night. And I don't touch alcohol, so the speakeasies and bootleg booze parties have no appeal for me."

"I wish we could've stayed longer," Helen said. She

hadn't seen her grandfather since her toddler years, and she would have liked to know him better.

"Me, too. But I've got to get to San Francisco to meet a theatre manager. He's considering me for a stage production."

Thrown off balance by the sudden forward motion, the cousins fell backwards onto the velvet-upholstered sofa.

Concluding her conference with the porter, Lela watched closely as he stowed their luggage. As a career woman and during her military service and when following the vaudeville circuit as her daughter's guardian, costumer, and dresser, she'd crisscrossed the country by train. For their overnight journey to Salt Lake City, she'd booked this deluxe drawing room, with bunks for three, a wardrobe, and access to private washbasin and toilet.

The train rolled out of Union Station, leaving the city behind. With dismay, Helen noted the sagging tents hobos had set up close to the tracks, and the feeble streaks of smoke rising from their campfires. Every city and town had its Hooverville, she'd discovered, a large encampment of rough lean-tos or flimsy wooden cabins occupied by those unfortunates impoverished and displaced by the Depression. A little while later, she spied rugged Pikes Peak, majestic in its height and breadth, looming over Colorado Springs. The air must be very thin on the summit, she thought. Yesterday, when her grandfather took everyone to the foothills to fish a rocky stream, she'd grown lightheaded from the sudden change in altitude.

She politely declined the offer of Christian Science literature, having promised Mama to resist any attempt at conversion. Her aunt didn't press her. Before their fifteen-minute stop in Pueblo, she handed out nickels and dimes so the girls could purchase movie magazines. The train veered west, carrying them through winding river valleys cutting through the mountain landscape. Towns were sparse and small—mining and logging communities, according to Lela. Following the direction of a sinking sun, they dined at dusk.

After dark, their porter returned to prepare their compartments for sleeping. He carried out his responsibilities with practiced efficiency and evident pride. When asked, he told Helen that he wasn't acquainted with Mort Willingham. She supposed he must have a wife like Clara, who meticulously pressed his uniform before every trip and kept the metal band on his cap bright and shiny.

Tucked in her bunk, barreling through the black night, Helen lost all sense of her location. Before dawn, the horn blasted at a railway crossing, startling her into wakefulness. Pressing her cheek into the shallow pillow, she wondered where she was. In the morning, when the porter arrived with fresh towels, he announced that they had crossed into Utah.

A well-worn deck of cards provided Helen and Ginger with endless amusement. They played acrostics and competed to finish newspaper crossword puzzles. Backgammon was another mutual passion, and the compact traveling board was in frequent use. They carried on extended conversations in pig Latin, at which Ginger was proficient. Her throaty laugh, a contrast to Helen's high-pitched giggle, rang out at intervals, incurring smiles or glares from others in the lounge car—which they preferred to their private sitting room.

"We've been studying our fellow passengers," Ginger explained to her mother. "There's one lady who wears a monocle and carries a tiny dog and speaks with a veddy, veddy affected accent. We're convinced she's pretending to be English."

She plopped onto the narrow sofa that opened into

a bed, clutching pen and paper, and crooked a finger. "Come here. I've got a present for you, but not one I can put in a ribbon-wrapped box. You're getting a new name. To use professionally."

Helen cast a questioning look at Lela.

"There's nothing wrong with Helen Nichols," her aunt declared. "It's elegant and refined, and easy to pronounce. Four syllables, like Ginger Rogers." With a smile for Helen, she added, "That nickname you gave her when you were a tot turned out to be perfect for show business. Spicy and strong, that's my girl."

With a twitch of her auburn head, Ginger opined, "Helen is pretty enough, but not unique or memorable. If she dislikes what I came up with, I'll keep thinking."

"What is it?" Helen wanted to know.

"Phyllis. Fraser—with an 's.'" Ginger handed over the paper. "It has alliteration. You're an English scholar, you know what that means. I think it suits you. We'll try it out when I introduce you to people at RKO-Pathé. When you go home, you can be Helen again. Write it out. An actress has to practice her autograph."

She followed instructions. Dissatisfied with the plain P and F, she tried a more graceful, flowing version. "How's this?"

"Perfect!" Ginger placed a beautifully manicured finger on the paper. "Write it again. And again. I want that whole sheet covered—front and back—before we get to Salt Lake City." With a glance at her mother, she added, "We're calling her Phyllis from now on, so she'll get used to it."

That night when she settled into her bunk, the new name echoed in her mind, keeping time with the steel wheels pounding the steel rails.

Phyl-lis Fras-er. Phyl-lis Fras-er. Phyl-lis Fras-er.

After twelve hours aboard Union Pacific's Daylight Limited, covering hundreds of miles of coastal and mountainous terrain separating San Francisco from Los Angeles, Phyllis stepped out of Central Station's magnificent lobby into the soft light of early evening. Her pulses thrummed with the thrill of arriving in a city she'd never imagined she would visit, bearing a name different from the one she'd received at birth. Hoping to spot a famous face, she cast expectant glances at every passer-by.

Lela immediately commandeered the services of a uniformed porter to trundle their luggage to the electric railway stop. From the heart of downtown, the streetcar clattered northward along roadways jammed with automobiles, occasionally halting to let off and take on passengers. A setting sun cast a golden glow over the imposing buildings and the occasional lush park.

Eyeing the layers of hills visible in the distance, Phyllis noticed a row of white letters stretching across one unobstructed summit. She interrupted Ginger, indicating nearer landmarks, to ask, "What's Hollywoodland?"

"A residential neighborhood in Beachwood Canyon. After dark, three sections of the sign light up and flash in sequence. Holly. Wood. Land. Then all at once."

"It's an eyesore," Lela declared.

A lowering sun in the west cast the mountains into darker relief, and the cloudless azure sky was splashed with vibrant orange streaks, like horizontal flames.

They got off at Sunset Boulevard, and a taxi delivered them to an oasis of tropical trees.

"Welcome to the Garden of Allah," Ginger said.

"This used to be the old Hayvenhurst estate," Lela explained, leading the way into the complex of pink stucco buildings, some connected and others detached, all with red tile rooftops. "Alla Nazimova, a very fine actress on stage and in silent pictures, bought the property and lived in the mansion. After she turned it into a hotel, she built all these rental bungalows—or villas, to use the grander term."

Clutching her pocketbook and her single suitcase, Phyllis trailed her aunt and cousin along the broad flagstone walkways that meandered between the residences, past large ferns with curving fronds. Palm trees of different varieties and sizes surrounded the main house. The outline of the swimming pool reminded her of the amoeba illustration in her biology textbook, although according to Ginger, Madame Nazimova had it designed to match the shape of the Black Sea. Men and women in colorful bathing suits sat on the edge, legs submerged to the kneecaps, or they lounged in canvas chairs. Discreetly, she scanned the group for screen stars, but their dark glasses and sunhats and swimming caps concealed their identities.

An archway marked a narrow passage between two large buildings. Passing beneath it, they encountered a casually dressed man with a folded easel under one arm and a tricolor cat under the other. His brown hair was slicked back from his forehead and his eyebrows were peculiarly curved.

"Good afternoon, Harpo," Aunt Lela greeted him, receiving a smile and a nod in reply. "Elmer escaped again?"

"Tomcats. Always chasing women." His mobile face stretched in a grin.

Ginger put down her suitcases and stroked the animal's furry head.

Phyllis recognized the owner's bulbous nose and lively eyes despite the absence of the curly wig he'd sported in

Animal Crackers and *Cocoanuts*. She'd just crossed paths with a famous person who wasn't a blood relative.

"Wasn't that—" she stopped before uttering the name. Mentally she began to compose a letter to her family, informing them that Harpo Marx was a near neighbor.

"Two of his brothers live here, too," Ginger told her. "Another one has an apartment nearby. That's ours, beyond the fountain."

Water shot up from the spout, filling a circular upper basin and flowing into a lower one containing a school of goldfish. Evergreens shaded four attached bungalows, and pots of flowering plants were arranged in wall niches. A lantern on a pole cast faint light on Lela as she inserted a key in the door lock and pushed it open.

The Rogers women occupied a compact living space—sitting room, tiny dining room, small but serviceable kitchen, and two bedrooms.

"We're renting it furnished," Lela said, "but added some pieces to suit our tastes. I hope you won't mind sharing my room. It's the one with twin beds. I'll make space in the closet so you can hang your things."

The newly purchased dresses required pressing before she could wear them again, but that task could wait. She was dazed by the realization that she was here, at the Garden of Allah, one week after Ginger had described it to her.

"The icebox is empty. I'm afraid the food in the hotel restaurant is merely adequate, but it's the best we can do. Tomorrow we'll celebrate your arrival at a suitable establishment."

"The Brown Derby," her cousin piped up. "My favorite."

Phyllis didn't much care what she was being fed for her first Hollywood meal, or where she ate it.

She'd covered approximately two thousand miles since Ginger sat across from her in that Oklahoma City drugstore and invited her to California. In Denver she'd been reunited with Granddad Owens and had caught a rainbow trout in a mountain stream. From the train window she'd marveled at the Rocky Mountains and the sight of snow-topped peaks in the middle of summer. Bustling San Francisco had afforded her a view of the Pacific Ocean, and such a crowd of Asian people that she wondered whether any remained in China and Japan. After all those detours, her adventure in filmland had begun.

CHAPTER 5

While the performers who occupied the scattered dwellings in Garden of Allah were confined to studio soundstages or on location, musicians and composers and screenwriters idled away the morning and afternoon, waiting until nighttime to continue their notation and practice their instruments and pound their typewriters. Before an audience of poolside regulars, Phyllis received her first lessons from her cousin, and they were unrelated to acting or tap-dancing. She was learning the backstroke.

Ginger propelled herself through the water with a dolphin's grace, slipping beneath the surface and floating back up.

"Ginger, your mother wants you." A woman was waving at them. "Phone call from your studio."

Breathing hard, her leg muscles jittery from constant kicking, Phyllis swam after her cousin and gripped the edge of the pool.

Miss Hellman smiled down at her. "You're improving, kid."

The sharp-featured literary scout for Metro-Goldwyn-Mayer was also an author of short stories, and her lover, Dashiell Hammett, was famous for his detective novels. Intimidated by Miss Hellman's literary stature,

Phyllis was too shy to ask what book she was currently reviewing. To her, it sounded like a dream job—getting paid to read novels before they were published. And after.

She and Ginger pulled off their swim caps and wrapped towels around their dripping bodies. Lela met them as they were rounding the fountain.

"Hurry inside and get dressed," she told Ginger. "Don't worry about your hair and face. Pathé wants you for publicity photos. It's their job to fix you up."

Ginger turned to Phyllis. "Come along to Culver City. I'll find somebody to give you a tour."

Phyllis changed her damp suit for a lightweight summer dress and hastily wound her hair into a chignon and pinned it in place. She envied the California girls their stylish marcel waves and bobbed hair but was prevented from chopping hers by Lela's decree that she must get her mother's permission.

Within half an hour, the boxy secondhand car Ginger and her mother used was headed downtown. Phyllis studied the large, pale buildings jammed together, and marveled at the multitude of automobiles moving every which way. The electric railway was powered by a web of black wires strung above the busy street. Beyond the congested city, she spied distant oil derricks—a familiar sight to an Oklahoma girl—and modest rural dwellings.

At an intersection, Ginger pressed the brake pedal. "Anybody coming from your side?"

"No."

The car eased forward, emitting an ominous chug. "Don't stall, please don't stall," Ginger pleaded, gripping the steering wheel for dear life.

Their destination turned out to be an elongated white building of Colonial design with an extended colonnade. Ginger bypassed the curving front drive and continued to the employees' parking area. A series of enormous buildings that looked like warehouses covered the property. An orange grove bordered it on one side, ripening fruit barely visible beneath glossy green leaves.

"Thomas Ince founded this studio. After him, it was De Mille's. Now RKO owns it," Ginger explained before getting out. "Oh, look, it's Eddie Quillan. We worked together in *The Tip-Off*. He's got eight sisters and brothers. Can you imagine? Like me, he started out on the vaudeville stage and ended up in the flickers." When she waved, the dark-haired actor waved back.

"Ginger!" he called out as she approached him. "Thought you were having a vacation."

"All good things must end. Soon I'm joining Bill Boyd in a picture. Don't ask me what it's called, nobody seems to know. It might be *Mystery Ship*. Or *Suicide Fleet*. The title keeps changing."

"I was s'posed to do that one, but they put me in *Auto Camp* instead."

Even cuter in person than on the screen, he was only a few inches taller than Phyllis and Ginger. His brown eyes glinted with mischief.

"Meet my cousin, Phyllis Fraser."

Phyllis smiled back at him. "You were terrific in *The Sophomore*. And *Big Money*."

"Phyllis is an actress," Ginger announced.

"Not yet." She didn't want to give him a false impression. To prevent the breeze from whipping off her hat, she placed one hand on its crown.

Eddie flashed his boyish grin. "How'd you like to start acting next week?"

Ginger's eyes widened. "Could she?"

"They rarely ever cast the minor parts till right before the cameras roll, you know. Miss Fraser, I'll put in a special word with Ralph. He's just been promoted from dialogue writer to director." Turning back to Ginger, he asked, "Are you here for a photo session, too?" After she nodded, "Come along, ladies!" Grabbing each by the hand, he half-marched, half-skipped towards the main building.

He might be a film star, Phyllis mused as the cinema comedian swung her hand back and forth, but he's no different from the goofy boys at Classen High.

While observing Eddie mugging for the camera, she couldn't stifle her giggles. Ginger, in her form-fitting black gown, struck elegant poses as instructed and suggested some herself.

"Want me to give you a trim?" the hairdresser asked Phyllis.

"Let her," Ginger urged. "If you don't like it shorter, it'll grow back."

Disregarding Lela's edict about asking Mama, Phyllis sat down in the chair her cousin had vacated. As the shears snipped along her shoulders, she watched in the mirror as inches of brown hair drifted down her cape to the floor. After cutting, the hairdresser used the hot tongs to create a cloud of curls. Ginger suggested that Mr. Collins, the makeup man, work on Phyllis. He was using his dark pencil, feathering across her eyebrow, when the photographer came over and took a picture.

"You're really getting the star treatment," Eddie told her. "Before you know it, we'll have you under the big lights." He tweaked his lapel and cocked a grin. "Gotta free myself from this monkey suit. I expect I'll see you again before long."

After Ginger changed into her regular clothes, she took Phyllis on the promised tour of the lot. They followed a broad alley that separated rows of soundstages.

"If that red light up there is turned on, it means the cameras are rolling inside," she explained. "It's the signal to keep out and be quiet. For outdoor scenes, we go to

Forty Acre Ranch, where Eddie and I shot *The Tip Off*. I'm not sure why they call it that, because the property isn't quite that large. Years ago, it was DeMille's backlot. The Temple of Jerusalem from his *King of Kings* is still standing. There's an exotic Middle Eastern city. And the French town from *All Quiet on the Western Front*. As well as city streets and houses and a creek and woods and meadows. And plenty of room to construct whatever is needed, although sometimes we're sent to an authentic location. The battleship scenes in the Navy picture will take place on a real destroyer berthed in San Diego Harbor."

"Sounds exciting."

"For the guys. Not for me. I play a seaside taffy seller, the girl back home that the hero and his buddies adore. For my scenes, I'll go to Warner Brothers' Coney Island set."

Within days, Ginger returned to Culver City for her wardrobe fitting and again invited Phyllis to go with her. This time Lela accompanied them, determined to seize the opportunity Eddie Quillan had presented.

She took Phyllis to the production office, and asked the receptionist if Ralph Murphy was on the lot.

"He's rehearsing Miss O'Sullivan and Mr. Quillan right now."

"Is it a closed set?" Lela persisted.

"Nobody said so."

"Then it's not. Where can we find them?"

Bowing to superior force, the woman told her the number of the soundstage.

Satisfied, Lela softened her tone. "When Miss Rogers finishes in wardrobe, please tell her where we've gone."

"Yes, ma'am."

Off they went through the warren of huge buildings, like warehouses, each bearing a number. They located the one they were seeking at the same moment Eddie Quillan was leaving with another man and a petite, dark-haired lady.

"What do you know, Ralph—here's that darling girl I told you about. Miss Fraser. And Ginger's mother."

Lela beamed. "I'm pleased you remember me. And my niece."

The director was studying Phyllis from top to toe. "Eddie tells me you want to be an actress."

Heart pounding, she replied, "That's why I left Oklahoma City."

Eddie punched the man in the arm. "Hey, isn't that a coincidence? A family of Okies stops at my gas station. Typecasting!"

"How about it, Miss Fraser? It's a brief scene, but we'll give you some lines."

Before she could answer, Lela inquired, "What's the rate of pay? Hourly or weekly?"

"Day rate. I can stretch it to ten dollars. With lunch. And that's generous."

Eddie nodded. "You'd better be. Her cousin's a member of our RKO-Pathé family." He winked at Phyllis.

"But you can't tell the folks we bring in from Central Casting," the director warned. "I don't want any ill feelings on my set."

"I won't," she assured him, scarcely believing her luck.

Phyllis, seated in an open-top motorcar parked beneath a stand of tall trees, tried not to crowd the blonde girl squeezed between her and a heavyset female holding a small boy on her ample lap. The older man behind the wheel removed his spectacles and whipped off his battered fedora to fan his face. The boy on the seat beside him tugged off his beanie and twirled it on one finger.

A breeze rustled the leaves overhead, and they all sighed in relief.

Her debut as a professional actress resembled a summertime excursion with her family, apart from the film crew and stars' trailers. Workmen darted here and there, tugging cables and positioning light stands. The wardrobe woman had provided her with a sleeveless cotton dress, and a stylist had pinned back her shoulder-length brown hair and attached false braids to match.

Eddie Quillan, in casual shirt and trousers, listened carefully to the director's instructions. They stood near a ramshackle service station bearing the sign GAS OIL & ACCESSORIES. Ralph Murphy sent Eddie inside and came over to address the car's occupants.

"This time we'll shoot your arrival from a different angle," he informed them, "Remember, you've been on the road for days. You're weary and hungry and hot. Boys, you can't wait to get out and run around."

"Ain't that the truth," the kid with the beanie muttered.

"Bill, we want a two-shot of you and Eddie, when you ask him about that bad smell. Then, after Phyllis says her final line, a three-shot of you ladies in the backseat. Make sure you speak up, honey, it's real windy. Ready for another go?"

Everyone nodded.

Phyllis stole a glance at Lela, her on-set chaperone, seated with the children's mothers. She received an encouraging smile.

The older actor cranked up the engine and put a foot on the pedal. The car shot forward and abruptly halted at the gasoline pump. The boys scrambled out, and Phyllis called them back—Eddie's cue to rush out of the garage.

"Cut!"

The director asked the script girl a question. The clapper loader stepped in front of the camera. On his slate the film's new title, *The Big Shot,* had been printed with chalk.

Untying the baggage lashed to the car, Bill informed Eddie that his family would rest up at the auto camp two or three days. Lifting his head, he wrinkled up his face and asked suspiciously, "What's that?"

Phyllis leaned forward to speak her second line. "It's the swamp over there, Papa!"

"Cut!" Ralph Murphy shouted.

The cameraman positioned his equipment closer to the vehicle. Phyllis and the younger girl pinched their noses and made faces.

Gesturing towards the row of cabins, the woman playing their mother said, "There's a swamp over there."

The older actor and the boys raced to the car and jumped in. The vehicle sped away from the gas station, until the director shouted a command to stop.

Moviemaking isn't as hard as Ginger said, Phyllis thought. Nothing to it.

A sack lunch of sandwiches and pickles and fruit salad was ready in the cabin serving as an on-set commissary.

"You acquitted yourself well," Lela praised her. "We're fortunate that your scene establishes the campground's proximity to a malodorous bog. It won't be edited out."

"How long until the picture is released?" she wondered.

"No more than a couple of months, I expect. These Quillan comedies are concocted in haste and put before the public quite quickly."

Before supper that night, Ginger and Lela toasted Phyllis with glasses of ginger ale, assuring her that the day's activities had transformed her from schoolgirl to professional actress. By bedtime, she was almost convinced.

Lela began intensive instruction in diction and voice modulation. From the bookcase she removed a slim volume.

"I gave this to Ginger when she started out with the Orpheum Circuit—I had a feeling she was destined to work in pictures. It was published before talkies existed, so some studios mentioned have changed hands or ceased to exist, and others came into being. But the advice to aspirants is still sound."

Written for an earlier generation, *What Chance Have I In Hollywood? Intimate Information Concerning the Movie Capital of the World* contained practical advice. It informed her: *Work as an "extra" for a beginner is the only rational introduction to the picture game.* Reading cautionary tales of the girls who sought fame and fortune but ended up as prostitutes, dope fiends, or dead, she was increasingly thankful for the assistance and protection of aunt and cousin.

Never one to idle away spare time, Ginger took up tennis. On Sunday and days off she trained with the professional at the Havenhurst apartment building adjacent to the Garden of Allah. At lunchtime one day she returned from the courts in a particularly cheery mood.

"After I finished my lesson with Mr. Larson, the nicest gentleman challenged me to a match. Turns out he's with RKO—the main studio, not Pathé. He directed Edward G. Robinson's *Little Caesar* and is currently shooting a Gloria Swanson picture. He asked me for a date, but instead I invited him to the poolside cocktail party."

That evening Mervyn LeRoy, handsome and dark-haired, pleasant and well-spoken, joined them for the popular social hour.

Even in their casual clothes, the starry residents impressed Phyllis. She was flattered by their questions about how she'd been spending her time and received congratulations on her appearance in *The Big Shot*. A few admitted that they'd come from places more obscure and far duller than Oklahoma City. They certainly had adopted the wilder ways of Hollywood, drinking quantities of bootleg liquor, and carrying on wildly and noisily late into the night and through the early morning hours.

All too soon Phyllis was boarding the first of a succession of trains that would transport her back to her family. During her outbound journey she'd grown accustomed to the plushness of the superior Pullman compartment. Now she found herself in a cramped and shabby single, seated on scuffed leather upholstery, a reminder of the ordinariness of her life as Helen Nichols.

Resigned, she opened her diary to record the events of those final, fleeting days in Hollywood.

CHAPTER 6

"I can't believe she's going to do it." Ginger lowered the newspaper, revealing her shocked face.

"Who's doing what, dearie?" Lela inquired absently. They sat under a broad umbrella near the Garden of Allah pool, recovering from their cross-country railway journey. She was reading a letter from Phyllis, one of three delivered during a month spent elsewhere.

"Adele Astaire is marrying her English lord. Their romance was a hot topic in New York."

"When Harold Ross took us to the Astaires' revue, he predicted it would be the last time they performed as a team."

"The songs in *Band Wagon* were divine." Ginger hummed one of them.

"That's nice. Which is it?"

"'Dancing in the Dark.' Gershwin. Whenever I switch on the radio, it's playing Bing Crosby's version."

With time to fill between pictures, Ginger had performed her song-and-dance production at the Ambassador Theatre in St. Louis. After a brief run in that city, she'd joined a cast of fifty as a featured performer in a musical variety show in New York. During their weeks on the road, she and Lela lived out of suitcases and stayed in hotels far superior to those of the vaudeville years. Ginger pocketed a tidy two thousand dollars for her Broadway appearances, which would amply cover living expenses and secure them against the hardships the Depression had inflicted on those less fortunate.

"Adele's wedding is in January," Ginger reported. "After that, she'll live with her duke's son in Ireland. What on earth will Fred do without her?"

"Find another partner. His career won't suffer, and it could improve. Dancing with his sister prevented him from performing in romantic roles."

Ginger left her chair. "In his dance number with Tilly Losch, he was plenty lover-like. When Harold took me to the 21 Club, we ran into Adele. She told us she was tired of show business, but I never imagined she meant to quit."

"She's not getting any younger. Well into her thirties, I should think."

"As a ladyship, she'll have servants waiting on her hand and foot." Shaking her bright head, Ginger added, "Wouldn't suit me. I'd be bored all the time."

Removing her glasses, Lela said, "You must be eager to get back to work."

"I am. When I report to the studio, I'll be rehearsing my songs for the riverboat scenes. Day after tomorrow, we head to Fresno, I think, or near there. Some place with trees big enough to pass for logging territory." She raised her arms high and rose onto her toes. "What's the news from our girl?"

"She was rushed by several social clubs and pledged the best one. Her friends are treating her like a movie star."

"It was swell having her here. The minute her school term is over, she's got to come back to us."

"I've no doubt she will," Lela replied, opening the

remaining envelope. "Now that she's with her family, she's Helen Nichols again. But she signs all her letters as Phyllis."

When *The Big Shot* opened at the Liberty Theatre, Helen waited nervously for her scene. Her breath was suspended as her section of celluloid spooled through the booth projector. Her shrillness when uttering her two lines troubled her, but her fleeting appearance thrilled her friend Doris White. At school the next day, she dispensed Phyllis Fraser autographs with the humility appropriate to a bit player.

She was investing a substantial portion of her weekly allowance in fan magazines. With her fingernail scissors she removed Ginger's photos and the gossip about her—what she wore, who she went out with, which pictures she was making. Carefully she glued each cutting into a special scrapbook. Her sister Jean, marginally interested in their cousin's exploits, tolerated her passionate interest in the movie business.

In mid-April, the long-awaited birthday festivities doubled as her farewell party. The cake her parents ordered from the Old Mill Bakery was inscribed with *Happy 16th Birthday to Our Star!* in sugar icing. Her presents included a set of luggage and a pocket diary for recording appointments with casting directors. She received a gift voucher for a facial at Classique Beauty Salon, and either a Pure Steam permanent wave or a Eugene Push Wave. Aunt Lela sent a check to cover her train fare to Los Angeles, and a box from Ginger contained two smart suits to wear during her journey. One had a short-waisted plaid jacket paired with a green skirt, and the red one had a peplumed jacket that flared over Helen's narrow hips.

She was touched by Jean's offer to shorten the cuffs and raise the hems an inch.

It's really happening.

That refrain repeated in her head throughout the final days of her term at Classen High, whether studying for final exams or watching Jean compete on the swim team. Yearbooks arrived, a sure sign that the term was nearing its inevitable end, and she paged through until she found her image on the Student Council page and in the Pep Club's group photo.

I'm not glamorous, she fretted as she passed around her book to be signed. *Not like Clara Bow or Greta Garbo. But nobody would call Claudette Colbert a classic beauty. Or Ginger, and she's just about the hottest thing in the movies right now.* Liberated from RKO-Pathé, her cousin could work for any studio that wanted her. According to Aunt Lela, plenty of them did—First National, Monogram, Fox.

On the day Helen left the house with her suitcases, gray clouds, low and heavy, darkened the sky.

"Tornado weather." Her mother paused on the porch.

"Ginny, you signed that document. You promised Lela we'd send Helen off today."

Document? Nobody had mentioned this to her.

Avoiding her curious gaze, Mama said, "A twister can tip over a passenger bus. Or push a railway car right off the tracks. It's too dangerous to travel."

"You're being fanciful." Daddy's tone was the one he always used to soothe her fretting. Hat in hand, he craned his neck to study the sky. "Thunderstorm clouds. There'll be rain, nothing worse."

"Check the barometer," Mama pleaded.

"All right." He went back inside.

Heaving an impatient sigh, Jean sat on the top step, elbows on her knees.

Unwilling to dirty her new green skirt, Helen remained standing, uncomfortably aware that she was still a minor. Whatever document Mama signed hadn't nullified her role as legal guardian. If she changed her mind and rescinded permission to travel, Helen would be stuck in Oklahoma City. Possibly for two years, until emancipated by her eighteenth birthday.

I won't beg, she vowed.

Daddy stepped onto the porch and planted his hat back on his head. "No cause for concern. Come on, ladies."

For the entire drive to the bus station, Mama was quiet. But when Daddy left them and went over to the window to purchase the ticket, a torrent of advice poured from her carmine lips.

"Don't talk to strangers—men or women. Keep enough coins handy, in case something goes wrong along the way and you need to telephone us."

"Yes, Mama. I won't. I mean, I will." She'd heard it all before—every day for the past week—and again this morning at the breakfast table.

Let me go, she pleaded silently. Don't send me away under the heavy burden of your anxieties. I'll be as careful as I always have been. I got used to your leaving me behind, again and again, for much of my life, so you could work. Now it's my turn to do the same.

"Tell Lela to send us a telegram when you arrive," Mama went on. "And don't let her make you do anything you don't want to do. She's my oldest sister, and all my life I've had to put up with her know-it-all ways. So will you. It's a credit to Ginger that she never rebelled—much. Not that her mother was around during her growing up years. If you fall sick, they're supposed to send for a real doctor and get you proper medical treatment. I insist on that, and Lela knows it. She and her daughter can practice their Christian Science if they must, but it's nothing to do with you. Understand?"

"Yes, ma'am."

Daddy rejoined them and handed her a slip of paper. "Your ticket to stardom. Ginny, honey, time to say goodbye. We've got a full schedule of appointments at Classique. You wait here with Jean, and I'll walk Helen to the bus."

"Don't cry, Mama, or I will, too. So long," she said to her sister. They hugged briefly, awkwardly. "Good luck in your championship swim meet."

When she and her stepfather approached the bus, a porter took her suitcases and thrust them into the baggage compartment.

"Don't worry about your mama. She'll calm down after you're on your way. She doesn't know it yet, but Jean and I are taking her to a nice restaurant tonight. I ordered an orchid corsage from Batten's." Daddy placed a hand on her shoulder. "Remember, you can come home to us at any time. As long as we haven't rented out your room." He was trying to cheer her with a joke.

"Nobody'd want it," she replied, blinking back tears. "Too small."

Within minutes, she was seated on the bus that would shuttle her to the train. On leaving the depot, she opened her book. *Flappers and Philosophers,* F. Scott Fitzgerald's collection of short stories, was a necessary diversion from the volatile mixture of emotions she'd been struggling to contain.

Before nightfall she was surrounded by soaring mountain peaks frosted with spring snow. In the morning, the train passed through seemingly endless miles of desert terrain. With every stop, she was conscious of a shift in her perception of herself. With her Oklahoma City identity rapidly receding, likely vanishing forever, she wondered what would replace it when she reached California, where citrus flowers scented the air and the palm fronds seemed to rake the broad blue sky. For the entirety of this journey she existed in a state of limbo. She was no longer Helen Nichols but not entirely Phyllis Fraser, the successful movie actress of her hopes and of Lela's and Ginger's high expectations.

CHAPTER 7

Lela met Phyllis at the train station. "Ginger couldn't come," she explained, "she has an important screen test. Now that she freelances, we can't turn down any offer. A pity you didn't arrive in time to see *Girl Crazy*. She's quite the trouper, that girl of mine. Four stage shows a day, singing and dancing—as big a hit here as it was on Broadway. No tickets to be had in San Francisco or in Oakland."

"Are she and Mr. LeRoy still dating?" Phyllis asked.

"They're inseparable. She hopes he'll put you in one of his movies. I wish he'd give *her* a part—or even better, a contract. To celebrate your return, he's taking the three of us to an opening at the Belasco. A tryout play, with Billie Burke and New York actors. And you're invited to the party he's planning."

Arriving at the Garden of Allah, they followed the familiar paths between the trees and under the arches to the bungalow by the fountain. The interior was unchanged, apart from different pictures on the walls and floral pillows on the sofa. This was now her home—after all those months of waiting and wishing, she was a Hollywood resident.

Guiding Phyllis into the room with twin beds, Lela

said, "We found this bureau at a secondhand shop. You have a full set of drawers for yourself."

"I brought only the clothes as I could fit into my grips," she replied. "I don't have money for new things."

"That will change, once you're working," Lela replied with characteristic confidence. "I've got fruit juice. If you're hungry, I can make a sandwich while you unpack. We'll eat at home tonight, but tomorrow Ginger wants to treat you to dinner at the Brown Derby."

She was nibbling a celery stick when Ginger returned, brimming with energy and sporting red hair several shades lighter than it was last summer.

"I'm unemployed at the moment, so I'll be showing you all the sights you missed when you were here before. I've become acquainted with important movie people I can introduce you to."

Within days of her arrival, Phyllis was making the rounds of the studios, usually with Lela, occasionally Ginger. In the mornings, they put on their summery suits and flattering hats and set out in search of employment. They spent afternoons lounging by the Garden of Allah swimming pool, sipping cool drinks while Ginger shared anecdotes from her years on the vaudeville circuit. At night they either stayed in, listening to the radio, or ventured out with Mr. LeRoy to one of his favorite restaurants. The couple never made Phyllis feel unwelcome, but she sometimes chose to stay home with Lela so they could have privacy.

One day when she and her cousin were swimming, Phyllis said, "Maybe I should look for another job."

"Like what?"

"I can operate a cash register. After school I sometimes filled in for Jean at the beauty salon."

"We brought you out here to work in pictures."

"I could be a ticket seller at the cinema," she said, only partly in jest. "Or an usherette."

"Never," Ginger declared. "Don't get discouraged."

"I'm not. But I want to earn my keep."

"You're a family member, not a lodger. Take it from me, that lucky break will come when you least expect it. Probably sooner than you think!"

Ginger's beau, a former actor turned director, frequently entertained in his fine apartment in the Havenhurst building, adjacent to the Garden of Allah. In his early thirties, Mervyn LeRoy was popular enough to draw an array of famous people to his party. Phyllis, by far the lowliest of his guests, was grateful for his attentiveness.

When he introduced her to Carole Lombard, the beautiful blonde drawled, "Are you a hoofer, too?"

"Ginger's teaching me her old routines," she replied. The simplest ones.

"Bill, darling," said the actress to a tall, dark-haired bystander. "Say hello to Ginger's kid cousin. What's your name again, honey?"

"Phyllis Fraser." She smiled up at William Powell, debonair in his evening clothes.

"I'm Mr. Carole Lombard," he volunteered, his teeth flashing beneath the thin moustache. His wife barked out a laugh.

Lela came over, accompanied by a gentleman whose swarthy complexion and black hair gave him a distinctly foreign look. "Phyllis, Frank Capra asked to meet you. Columbia Pictures."

While Lela cited his directing credits, he scrutinized Phyllis. "I'm on the look for fresh faces, Miss Fraser. Would you be available for a test this week?"

She glanced over at Lela, who inclined her head.

"I am." In her excitement, she didn't fully absorb what Mr. Capra was telling her about his current project. Sipping her orange juice, she nodded politely and marveled at the speed with which Hollywood people made decisions. A screen test was a crucial prerequisite to employment.

Lela took her by streetcar to a part of Los Angeles referred to as Poverty Row, where the minor studios were located.

Pausing at the junction of Sunset Boulevard and Gower Street, she reached out to straighten Phyllis's hat. "Never come here unchaperoned. Harry Cohn, like so many men in the picture business—executives, producers, directors—can't be trusted around pretty actresses. He's also highly temperamental, and his language is the foulest. Columbia's players don't get much rehearsal, and their scenes are shot at breakneck pace. But we have to start somewhere. Casting directors from any studio can request your test. I'll see that they do."

The building was as unimposing inside as out. Leaving the shabby reception area, they went into a darkened room containing a camera on a tripod and stands with large lights attached. Frank Capra invited them to sit. He presented Phyllis with a page of dialogue, a lighthearted conversation between a girl and her father.

"Read through it with me."

She invested each phrase with what she hoped was the correct intonation.

"That's fine. You have five minutes to memorize your part."

"Are you putting her in makeup?" Lela inquired. "Or a costume?"

"No. But she has to take off that hat, so we can see her face. And the gloves."

Insistent on quality sound recording, Lela conferred with the man in charge of the boom microphone. While Phyllis waited, she committed her words to memory.

She moved onto the makeshift set, recalling Ginger's advice just in time.

Breathe naturally.

Remember to smile.

Don't blink, no matter how bright the glare.

Capra pointed out the marks on the floor as he blocked the scene for her. "Any questions?"

"I can't think of any." Hurry up, she pleaded silently. Before I forget everything.

"Quiet on set," the assistant director called out. "Roll sound."

"Rolling."

"Roll camera."

"Camera rolling."

The clapper loader held up a slate with her name printed on it. "Phyllis Fraser test. Take One."

Hearing the loud click, she flinched.

"Action."

Phyllis beamed at Frank Capra and recited her opening line. Perfectly.

A succession of glowing neon signs marked the movie palaces and theatres stretched along South Broadway. The Belasco and the Mayan, both operated by Edward Belasco—brother of David, a New York acquaintance of Lela's—vied with their near neighbors for grandiosity. She was grateful to Mervyn LeRoy for planning this special treat for Phyllis, who looked charming in a gown purchased yesterday at the May Company department store. Columbia and RKO were considering her for productions that would start within a few weeks.

Her niece's blue eyes widened when they entered the opulent lobby.

"I know what my cousin is thinking," Ginger said to Mervyn. "'There's nothing like this in Oklahoma City!'"

"I've stopped saying that," Phyllis replied. "But it's true."

The Mad Hopes, a comic play, was having an extensive West Coast tryout before transferring to Broadway. Successful runs in San Diego and Santa Barbara whetted the appetites of Los Angeles theatregoers, guaranteeing a sellout crowd for the premiere performance. Everyone wore formal attire—the powerful and prominent men and their wives. Or their mistresses. Matinee idols and glamor queens, paired with their co-stars for publicity purposes, posed for photographers and promenaded ostentatiously. Some of the stars escorted spouses who, if not also celebrities, were anonymous, shadowy figures relegated to the background.

The demand for tickets exceeded the auditorium's capacity. Extra chairs accommodated the overflow, and the standing section was packed. A hush fell as the curtain slowly lifted.

At her entrance, the lengthy ovation that greeted the legendary actress delayed the start of her first scene.

In Lela's opinion, the script was shallow and lacking in substance but redeemed by its performers. Billie Burke portrayed Clytie Hope, a capricious, spendthrift mother of a grown daughter and two sons. With her finances in disarray, she was in danger of losing her beautiful villa on the Riviera.

"The woman is ageless," Lela commented during an intermission. "Makeup and lighting help, of course, but she moves like a someone half her age. She must be close to fifty." Having passed her fortieth birthday, she was determined to preserve her own youthful looks and her vibrancy.

"When we lived in New York," Ginger murmured, "I always thought of her as Flo's wife. Mrs. Ziegfeld. The lead actor looks familiar. I believe he's married to Mary Philips. Or was."

Phyllis consulted the program they shared because the ushers' supply had run out. "Humphrey Bogart."

Lela grimaced. "Terrible name. He should change it."

Her niece said merrily, "Ginger could make one up. Like she did for me."

"Who's the blonde playing Geneva, the daughter?"

Phyllis pointed to the name near the top of the cast list. "Peg Entwistle."

"In her way, she's as talented as Billie. I've rarely seen an ingenue receive applause after her exit line. She deserved it. And her English accent is perfect."

"The ladies' clothes are gorgeous," Ginger gushed. "The embroidery on the pale blue velvet negligee was exquisite. Trust Adrian to design flattering costumes."

"If you had a contract with Metro-Goldwyn-Mayer," Lela pointed out, "he'd be making them for you, as well as Greta Garbo and Joan Crawford."

"I object," Mervyn LeRoy stated. "Ginger is supposed to give Warner Brothers another chance." Turning to his date, he added pensively, "I can't believe you went dancing over to Monogram, of all places."

"I won't be dancing in *The Thirteenth Guest,* more's the pity. It's a murder mystery. I'm proving my versatility."

The overhead lights and the wall sconces dimmed, and the curtain rose on the final act.

Mervyn swept them from the theatre to an opening night party. The hour was late, but Lela wouldn't turn down an opportunity for her girls to mix with prominent people.

"My first limousine ride," Phyllis confided as they glided through the city streets, still clogged with traffic.

"Get used to it." Ginger patted her arm, then turned to her date. "Columbia wants her. And RKO tested her for—what's it called?"

"*Fraternity House.*"

"Good part?" Mervyn quizzed her.

"A few lines," Phyllis answered. "Funny ones."

He nodded. "People notice the comic players. Who's the director?"

"Greg LaCava," Lela told him. "With David Selznick producing. Or Pandro Berman."

Mervyn tipped his head to one side. "I need lots of girls her age for *Three on a Match*. Either in a reform school or an exclusive boarding school for young ladies."

Ever protective, Lela said decisively, "The latter, if you please. She accepts only respectable parts."

The party venue was less crowded than the Belasco but no less noisy. Tagging along so often with Ginger and Mervyn, and with Lela, Phyllis was used to being the youngest person at social gatherings.

"I'd like to meet Miss Entwistle," she whispered to her cousin, whose hand was entwined with Mervyn's.

The petite blonde actress conversed with Miss Burke, her beaming face reflective of her triumph on the stage that night. The saturnine Mr. Bogart stood close by, regarding his pretty castmate with a fond and possibly proprietary smile. Were they an item?

Ginger waved and went to meet him, taking Phyllis with her.

He lifted his glass in welcome. "Well, well, here's Broadway's lost soubrette. Are you missing the Great White Way like Peg and I do?"

"I definitely would be, if not constantly busy chasing after my next job."

"Look, Peg, here's Ginger Rogers."

The other actress turned around. She and Phyllis were the same height.

"And my cousin," Ginger said. "Phyllis Fraser."

"Peg's counting the days till she returns to Maine for the summer stock season. Aren't you, hon? Hollywood won't keep her away from the Lakewood Players."

Smiling, the girl replied, "That's where Humphrey and I met." Her voice was musical, flavored with an English accent less pronounced than her stage character's. "But in a way, I'm a Californian. During my school years I lived here, and this is where I received my earliest theatre training." One pale hand drifted in the direction of a silver-haired gentleman across the room. "My uncle works in pictures. We're an acting family."

"So are we," Ginger told her.

"You're an actress, too?" Peg asked Phyllis.

"I'll be in *Fraternity House,* at RKO." Until that moment, she hadn't absolutely committed herself. "It's based on the play *Crossroads.*"

"That's grand," Peg responded with genuine enthusiasm. "Sylvia Sidney played the heroine in the Broadway production. Is that your role?"

"Oh, no, I'm in just one or two scenes. I might be in another picture soon, at Warner Brothers, if Mr. LeRoy casts me. But my Aunt Lela says I shouldn't accept parts until I find out what I'll get paid."

"Not enough," Humphrey said wryly. "You can be sure of that."

CHAPTER 8

Phyllis knelt beside the narrow, fourposter bed. She secured her nightgown's lacy strap so it wouldn't slip down her shoulder to reveal an inappropriate amount of skin. Careful not to jostle star Ann Dvorak, leaning back against the pillows, she propped her elbows on the mattress. Other actresses, similarly clad, scrambled into position around her. When the boom microphone was in place, and after satisfactory checks of the lighting, Mervyn, the director, called for action. They erupted in a chorus of giggles.

"Go on, Vivian," Phyllis said. "Read us some more."

Mervyn had given her two lines of dialogue. She looked forward to the day she'd get three lines. Or four.

And eventually, if I'm lucky, an entire speech.

"All right, ladies," he called, "consider yourselves released from Miss Jason's School."

As the cast dispersed, he took her aside. "I want you back for the playground scene and the elementary school commencement ceremony. Soon as we find the right kids to play Ann and Joan Blondell and Bette Davis as youngsters, we'll schedule the shoot."

Lela, overhearing this, shifted from chaperone to

manager and promptly opened a discussion about remuneration.

She must have been satisfied with the terms, because Phyllis joined the dozens of boys and girls who spent an entire morning cavorting on the grounds of Hollywood High School. In the afternoon she and her aunt returned to the Warner Brothers-First National lot. She was told to put on a simple dress cut in the style of a decade past and to wear a dark wig of trailing curls. At Lela's insistence, the wardrobe woman pinned on a large, white bow.

"So you'll stand out from the rest of the girls," she murmured to Phyllis on their way to the soundstage where the school auditorium had been set up.

Demonstrating his habitual favoritism, Mervyn placed her in the front row of graduates. He also instructed the elderly actor playing the principal to insert her name into his opening announcement.

"The first diploma tonight will be awarded to Miss Phyllis Fraser."

Rising, she moved forward to accept the roll of paper and returned to her chair.

Dawn O'Day, appearing as the youthful version of Ann Dvorak's character, chatted to her in the dressing room.

"I saw you earlier, when we were shooting outdoors. The sun was so hot, I thought I'd melt during my scene with Frankie Darro." She swiped a tissue across her face to remove the layer of foundation.

"I wondered who he was," Phyllis admitted. "He's cute."

"And nice as can be," Dawn said. "Are you under contract here?"

She shook her head. "Mr. Leroy hired me for the day, because he's my cousin's beau. She's Ginger Rogers. I'm still waiting to find out if RKO will sign me. What about you?"

"I've worked at Fox, Paramount, and now Warner Brothers. Or is this a First National picture? I don't keep up with the details like Mother does. I started in movies when I was four. Shorts, mostly. Uncredited." When Phyllis asked her age, Dawn replied, "I turned fourteen on the seventeenth of April."

"My birthday's the thirteenth! I'm sixteen."

"Let's celebrate together next year. Won't that be fun? A boy-girl party, so we can invite Frankie Darro, and his friends. Here comes Mother. She'll be wanting to get home for tea—she has to have it, she's English. I hope I see you again soon. Good luck with RKO!"

Because Phyllis was legally a minor, Lela had to secure power of attorney from Mama and Daddy before finalizing her studio contract. Telegrams zipped between Los Angeles and Oklahoma City, followed by a lengthy telephone discussion delineating terms and the renewal options. Shortly thereafter a cable arrived, granting parental permission to proceed with the signing. A judge's assent was also required, but Phyllis could begin work on her two films before her assigned court date. Her salary was thirty dollars a week.

On her first day as an employee of RKO Radio Pictures, Inc., Lela went with her. A giant globe topped the administration building on Gower Street, adorned with the company name in stylized letters. Never missing an opportunity to instruct, her aunt explained the significance.

"When Mr. Sarnoff of the Radio Corporation of America purchased Radio-Keith-Orpheum, he retained the initials. His firm manufactures microphones, so this studio made talkies from the start. After the Pathé merger, it acquired the Culver City soundstages and the backlot where we went for your Eddie Quillan picture."

A woman from the casting office took them to a room where half a dozen girls were corralled.

"Welcome to the club!" a pretty brunette cried out, the only other accompanied by an adult. "I'm Betty Furness and this is Harriet Hagman and that's Dorothy Wilson. What's your name?"

"Phyllis Fraser."

"I moved here from New York. Harriet's from Finland—by way of New York."

Lela introduced herself to the chatty girl's mother. "When did you arrive?"

"A few weeks ago," Mrs. Furness replied. "The photographer who took Millbrook School's graduation portraits also worked at RKO's East Coast office. He showed Betty's picture to somebody, who sent it to someone out here. All of a sudden, she has a contract, and we're boarding a westbound train."

"I started at RKO in the stenographer pool," dark-haired Dorothy confessed, "handling correspondence for the actors and actresses. Then I was Mr. LaCava's secretary. Now he's put me in a picture. Even though I've never acted in my life, he gave me a lead role in *Fraternity House.*"

"Sylvia Sidney played it on Broadway," Phyllis volunteered. "Peg Entwistle told me."

"Her name's on our group sheet," Betty said. "Is she nice?"

She nodded. "She's an experienced stage actress. Extremely talented."

"This isn't so important," Harriet said dismissively. "Any girl can be in a movie."

"Did any of you get a call for the giant gorilla picture?" Dorothy asked.

Betty stared at her. "The what?"

"*Kong*. The studio's most important production this year, so big it has two directors. Jean Harlow and at least twenty girls tested for the love interest."

"Who she is loving?" Harriet wondered. "The gorilla?"

"It falls in love with her," Dorothy answered. "I learned all about it when I was taking Mr. Selznick's dictation and typing up his long, long memos."

An assistant ushered each girl into the executive office, one by one. When Phyllis's turn came, Lela went with her. After her contract review, they were shunted over to the Publicity Department to provide personal information and schedule a photography session.

Before they went inside, Peg Entwistle came to meet them.

"Oh, good, a familiar face," she said in obvious relief. "You're Phyllis."

Flattered that her idol remembered her name, she congratulated Peg on being signed.

"Nothing's settled yet. I'd tell you more, but I've got to find a way to get home. My uncle meant to collect me, but he rang the office to let me know one of his tires has a puncture. I need to figure out which streetcar to take."

"I can drive you," Lela offered. "If you don't mind waiting until Phyllis finishes her interview."

"Really? I'd be so grateful."

The head publicist's female assistant called them into the room.

"We'll promote our new girls all together, as a group," she said. "And break you into threesomes. Or pairs. You're short, Phyllis, but your figure is ideal for fashion work. The wardrobe department is going to record your height, weight, and bust and waist measurements. You're how old? Sixteen? Teenage girls love their movie magazines—and stories about actresses of similar age. We'll work up topics you can address. Beauty hints. Party themes. Do you cook? Doesn't matter. We can provide recipes. Unless you want to get some from your aunt. Or your mother."

"She makes our breakfast," Lela said, "and helps me with lunch and dinner when we take our meals at home. She's also a fine baker."

"Wonderful," the woman said, making notes. She posed additional questions before handing over a studio map. She pointed out the commissary, the soundstages, wardrobe, and makeup departments. "You'll soon learn your way around."

Returning to the reception area, where Peg lingered, Lela told her, "It's well past noontime. Let's dine at Al Levy's Tavern, over on Vine. If you haven't met him, Miss Entwistle, you should. He's an Englishman, from the northern regions."

Lela knows everybody, Phyllis thought. And everything.

Over lunch, they learned that Peg was twenty-four years old and had spent the past eight years as a professional actress in Boston, in New York, and touring the country with the Theatre Guild company.

"*The Mad Hopes* was transferring to Broadway this autumn, without Humphrey and without me—I'd already agreed to do summer stock in Maine. But our producer was so pleased with my performance that he begged me to break my prior commitment to the Lakewood Playhouse so I could continue playing Geneva Hope in New York. I've idolized Miss Burke since I was a kid, and I did it as favor to her. Unfortunately, she abandoned the play when Mr. Selznick offered her the mother in *A Bill of*

Divorcement, her first talkie. That's how I lost two jobs in a row."

"But it doesn't matter," Phyllis observed, "now that you've signed with RKO."

"Well, that didn't end as expected, either," Peg said. "When George Cukor rang, inviting me to test for Miss Burke's daughter, Sydney Fairfield, I suspected it was Humphrey playing a prank and almost put down the phone. Maybe I should have." She shoved her hat brim back from her face. "Mr. Selznick preferred Jill Esmond's test to mine and offered her the part. But she turned it down on advice from her husband—Laurence Olivier, a London stage actor. And now Mr. Cukor's keen to cast Katharine Hepburn, who came out from New York. Today Mr. Selznick tried to make amends by offering me a one-picture contract and a part in *Thirteen Women,* his pet project."

"Everything worked out well," Lela observed.

"I want to see his script before I agree." Peg raised her startlingly blue eyes. "He warned me that I'd be playing a scandalous woman in a troubled marriage."

"She has an affair?" Lela asked.

Peg nodded. "But not the kind you mean."

"Ah. I see."

Phyllis didn't.

From Gower Street they drove north to Beachwood Canyon. The Entwistle family lived within sight of the mountain upon which the Hollywoodland sign was prominently planted. Their house had a low-pitched peaked rooftop and a front porch flanked on each side by sentinel cedar trees.

When Lela's car pulled up at the curb, two boys dashed outside.

"My brothers, Milton and Bobby. Our aunt and uncle took us in when we were orphaned." Before leaving the car, Peg thanked Lela for the lunch and the lift. "If I sign the RKO contract, I'll see you soon," she told Phyllis.

"Interesting girl," Lela commented. "She ought to accept that part David Selznick offered. He can put her on the path to stardom."

In addition to appearing as college students in *Fraternity House,* Phyllis and Betty Furness were assigned to *Thirteen Women.* They went to the courthouse on the same day to have their contracts approved by the judge. While waiting to enter his chambers, Phyllis overheard Lela pouring advice into Mrs. Furness's receptive ears.

Mr. Selznick had undertaken an extensively publicized search for the thirteen women who would fill out his cast. When Phyllis and Betty and the rest of the recently contracted girls gathered for a class in makeup techniques, she assumed all the others would be joining her and Betty—and possibly Peg—in the production. Wrapped in their beauty parlor capes with heads covered by white coifs, she thought they resembled Dominican postulants—something she'd briefly aspired to be during an early adolescent phase of intense Catholic devotion. Mr. Westmore demonstrated on each girl in turn, describing his method of coloring lips and cheeks and eyebrows. Because Phyllis had a broad mouth, he showed her how to fill the center with a deep red lipstick and swipe a lighter shade at the corners.

Two rows of chairs were arranged on a tiered platform. A photographer positioned the girls so each face was visible. Phyllis was placed on the top row, in the middle, between her fellow Oklahoman Rochelle Hudson and Harriet Hagman.

"Our Radio Pictures Starlets," the publicist dubbed them.

Six of the nine were already assigned to *Thirteen Women*. They clustered together, exchanging gossip.

"Myrna Loy plays the scheming murderess," Betty announced. "She's replacing an actress who dropped out. Never in my life did I imagine I'd meet her. Or Miss Dunne." Turning to Harriet, she asked, "What's your role?"

"An aerialist. One of the Raskob sisters."

Phyllis raised her freshly shaped brows. "The one who falls off the trapeze?"

The Finnish actress shrugged. "I'm to perform in the circus tent, is all I know."

"We can practice our dialogue together," Peg said. "And develop the interaction between our characters to make it believable."

"You think I am needing your help?" Harriet asked derisively. "Because you are the so great Broadway star, and me the showgirl from the *Vanities* burlesque?"

The blondes faced each another unsmilingly.

Don't rise to the challenge, Phyllis silently cautioned Peg. Ignore her. You're the professional. She's practically an amateur.

Harriet continued, "You look down on me, I see. Maybe you are jealous?" She inflated her well-developed chest. "Mr. Earl Carroll would never want a skinny stick of a creature like you in his revue. And I will steal from you our scene. You'll see."

In a calm, measured voice, Peg replied, "You can try to. But you'll have to be quick—you've got scarcely a whole minute of screen time." She stepped away, pausing in front of Phyllis to say quite audibly, "Let's hope she's the Raskob sister who plunges to her death."

CHAPTER 9

What foul luck, Phyllis realized in dismay when she saw the label bearing her name attached to the back of the makeup chair beside Harriet Hagman's. Ginger had warned her that posing for the still photographer, changing into and out of clothes for hours on end, was more exhausting than it sounded. Harriet's cattiness would make a tedious session even worse.

As requested, each of the RKO Baby Stars, as the studio dubbed them, brought with her a plain bathing suit or shorts and a top. Before being photographed at play, they were told, they would pose in formal gowns. Phyllis accompanied the girls to the hanging rack. The rich fabrics and plunging necklines and flashing sequins prompted a crescendo of joyful squeals, but Phyllis was afraid the styles were completely wrong for her.

"Try this." The wardrobe assistant removed a flowing creation of layered chiffon. "If not fitting perfect, I will pin in back and tape hem." Her accent was noticeably foreign and not Irish, although she'd introduced herself as Mrs. O'Connor.

The thin, clinging fabric complimented her figure, but its pale color did her no favors. Returning to the rack, she searched until she found a short, velvet jacket.

When she slipped it on, the woman bobbed her dark head. "Is good."

"You're lucky, working with all these pretty clothes."

"For now, is all right. I am writer—screenplays and novels—using name of Ayn Rand. Nothing produced yet. Or published. But always I work at it hard."

"My aunt is a screenwriter," Phyllis told her. "She tells me I should try writing a script someday. Or a book." Latent dreams of authorship would have to wait, until she'd accumulated enough knowledge and experience, both of which Lela possessed in abundance.

When it was her turn to pose in front of the backdrop, she just saved herself from stepping on the trailing fabric at her feet.

"Hello, honey," the photographer greeted her. "Can you give me a Clara Bow pose? Hold your right arm high and place your hand on your head to fluff up your hair. Left hand on your hip. Terrific! Lower your chin—not so much. That's right. Perfect! Don't blink."

The bulb's flash was bright and hot and blinding.

"I doubt we can improve on that, but let's see." After one more shot, he sent her off to change again.

The wardrobe lady gave her a satin shirt and matching pair of shorts, a large cap, and a long-handled polo mallet. "Keep your stockings on. And wear these." She handed over a pair of pumps with a high heel.

"Nobody would ride a horse in these shoes," Phyllis said, laughing.

She'd always enjoyed dressing up games with her sister and their friends, but her patience had limits. She put on formal garments, smiled or didn't, as the photographer directed her, and longed for the ordeal to end. She posed in countless dresses and skirts and blouses, with changes of hats and accessories. Eventually Ayn O'Connor presented her with a full bridal ensemble: shimmering satin gown, gauzy veil, floral bouquet.

In the changing room, she climbed into a green bathing suit. With regret she eyed her clothing, wishing she was daring enough to make a run for it.

"Phyl?"

She parted the curtain to find a fully dressed Betty Furness, wearing her hat and holding her pocketbook.

"You're leaving?"

"Mother says I can't do swimsuit pictures. I wanted to tell you Peg Entwistle showed me the *Thirteen Women* script. We'll be in a sorority house flashback scene. One of us insults Myrna Loy for being a half-caste from India, and that's why she takes revenge on everyone. She mails scary horoscopes to her former classmates, describing terrible tragedies that will happen to them, and the power of suggestion is enough to make them come true. Peg stabs her husband and goes insane. Or was it the other way around? Oh, and if we want to, we can fill out the circus crowd as extras."

With a wicked grin, Phyllis said, "Let's do it. I'd enjoy watching Harriet Hagman fall off the trapeze!"

The publicity department distributed a lengthy and detailed questionnaire to Phyllis and Betty and the large group of young people working on *Fraternity House,* to determine their various likes, dislikes, and habits.

Before they turned in their responses, she asked Betty, "How did you answer the question about smoking and drinking?"

"Truthfully," her friend replied. "We weren't told to write our names on the questionnaire, so my mother will never know."

Sensitive about her unworldliness, Phyllis shielded her survey paper. "It's unfair, asking us if we like to neck with boys." She hadn't had the chance to find out whether she did or not.

In the newspaper article that summarized the tabulated results, she was embarrassed to discover that she was the only respondent who wasn't a smoker or a drinker. Dreading exposure as the goody-goody, she joined her peers in speculating about the identity of that pitifully uncorrupted individual.

What difference did it make if she didn't puff cigarettes or swill liquor? She'd been cast as the Twelfth Woman in *Thirteen Women*. As one of the Kappa sorority girls, she spent several hours shooting a scene with Irene Dunne and Myrna Loy.

Before the actresses were dismissed, the indefatigably inventive studio publicist presented a special guest, the president of the National Astrological Association. He looked appropriately macabre, with stark black hair, bushy brows, thick moustache, and a pointy nose that supported a pince-nez.

"I will cast each of your horoscopes," he intoned, distributing a printed form. In a professorial tone, he instructed them to record the month and date and time of their birth.

When the illustrious prognosticator carried their papers away, Irene Dunne turned to Myrna Loy. "It's hokum, this astrology business. Nobody but the gullible believe in it."

Myrna responded with the same feral smile that she used to great effect as the exotic and evil Ursula Georgi. "Whether the results are accurate or not, they'll be interesting."

Miss Dunne rose to her full height. "Ladies, I hereby offer a wager. Five years from today, I want each of you to inform me about the accuracy of the doctor's predictions. If you can prove it, I'll pay you one hundred dollars."

"That's madness," Jill Esmond, the English actress, declared. "There are a dozen of us. If just some of his horoscopes come true, you'll be giving away loads of money."

"I'll be astonished if I have to pay a cent," the star replied, and her castmates laughed.

Peg, svelte and sophisticated in a light-colored duster with broad shawl collar, placed a jaunty cloche on her bright head. She sat still while Ayn O'Connor pinned a large corsage of fabric flowers onto her chest. "What does your horoscope say?"

"I haven't had time to read it yet." Phyllis scanned all the curious symbols and indecipherable numbers and unfamiliar terms, until she found paragraphs of descriptive text. "You who have the Sun in Aries are direct, straightforward, and uncomplicated. Some are bold, but even the quieter ones can be brave and plucky. Nothing stirs you like a clean slate, the promise of a new day, and a fresh start."

"And that's why you came to Hollywood. Right?"

"Aries Suns are happiest when their lives are moving forward and active." She glanced at Peg. "Isn't everybody?"

"Go on."

"You are personally popular and attractive to people. Your relaxed, easygoing disposition puts others at ease."

"Also true," Peg affirmed, standing up so Ayn could smooth the fabric of her calf-length car coat.

Preferring to study the remainder in private, Phyllis folded the sheet.

"Don't stop! There must be more." Peg pulled the paper from her grasp. "Endowed with generosity and friendliness, in some ways you appear to be lucky in life. You are good-hearted, possessing strong morals. You find the positive in situations. People can turn to you for a dose of faith and optimism. You are creative." She stopped reading. "I want to be you!"

Phyllis shook her head. "These are personality traits. Not predictions."

"Oh—listen to this! You are amorous, demonstrative in love. You really enjoy sex."

"I'm a nympho?" Appalled, Phyllis seized the page and tugged at it, tearing the edge in her haste to prevent further exposure. She folded it and stuffed it into her purse. "What does yours say?"

"Don't ask." Peg blew a kiss, saying airily, "See you on the set."

Ayn handed Phyllis a red beret and horn-rimmed spectacles with circular lenses. "To make you not look like your character in girls' school."

"Thanks. I think."

She and Betty went with dozens of extras of all ages to the soundstage, draped with swags of canvas to replicate the inside of a circus tent. They crammed themselves into a rear section populated by women in hats and gents wearing straw boaters or fedoras. Two equestriennes guided their gray ponies around the enclosure at a trot, then sped into a canter. During a series of bareback acrobatics, the animals' hooves stirred sawdust spread over the floor. Phyllis and Betty clapped appreciatively along with the spectators.

The camera and sound crews shifted their equipment. The ringmaster stepped forward to announce the Raskob sisters' act. After another break for set-up, Peg appeared, blue eyed and fair-haired, like a storybook princess, wearing a dreamy expression.

"Who's that with her?" Phyllis wondered when a mature actress sat down on the bleachers next to Peg.

"Marjorie Gateson. Gosh, her hair is cropped short. How unflattering."

George Archainbaud, the director, was calling out instructions to Mary Duncan and Harriet Hagman, standing on their elevated perches.

"I adore his French accent," Betty murmured.

The director called for the camera to roll. While the empty trapeze bar was swinging back and forth between them, Mary and Harriet mimed their communications. They abandoned their separate perches, making way for a quartet of stuntmen who would perform the aerial sequence. These professionals wore ladies' wigs and sequined costumes, identical to those of the actresses they personified, and flesh-colored tights.

"We won't see Harriet die after all," Betty complained.

Mattresses had been stacked beneath the trapeze to cushion the slender fellow impersonating Harriet. Both stuntmen repeated the ill-fated routine, and when the deadly sequence ended the audience sent them off with applause.

The director called for shots of the crowd, reminding everyone to look happy and excited about the famously daring circus act. Then he told them to make horrified faces in response to a dangerous feat gone wrong. Betty and Phyllis competed to out-shriek the extras.

Back in the communal dressing room, Peg chatted with Ayn O'Connor. She came over to Phyllis, saying, "I've got my uncle's car today. If you're able to come home with me, I certainly could use your help running lines for my big scene. We're shooting tomorrow. Stay to supper, if you don't mind warmed-over soup. And a slice of my Aunt Jane's bread, toasted."

Phyllis had spent much of her free time with Betty, on and off the lot, and never enough with Peg. "I have to let Mrs. Furness know I won't need a ride. And I've got to phone Aunt Lela."

"Tell her she won't have to collect you. You can catch the bus that goes back and forth between Hollywoodland and the Franklin Avenue trolley stop."

Phyllis surrendered the spectacles and red beret to Ayn, who stood by with hands impatiently extended. "That'll be swell. Good to know you don't mind associating with a nympho like me."

CHAPTER 10

Peg's apartment building was a short walk from her relatives' house on North Beachwood Drive and nearby homes of various aunts and uncles and cousins. She liked living within easy reach of her tight-knit family while at the same time maintaining independence.

She removed books from one side of her sagging sofa to make space for Phyllis. "If you want to borrow any, help yourself." Plopping into an armchair, she put her feet on a worn footstool. "The studio got its money's worth out of me today. I did a short scene with both Raskob sisters, answering their prying questions. Then I had to listen to Mary Duncan describe the creepy horoscope she got from the swami, prophesying a fatal accident. She was overacting, and the director let her get away with it. So I deliberately underplayed my response."

"Was Harriet Hagman unpleasant?" Tension inevitably surfaced whenever the two actresses met.

"Not today. I won't have to see her again, now that she's dead." With a sly smile, Peg clarified, "Her character, I should say. Tomorrow I have to pretend to be devastated by her fall from the trapeze. And right after that, I film my major scenes. The ones you're about to help me with." Peg dug into her oversized handbag and removed the script. "Hazel Cousins and her friend Martha have a particularly close relationship. Did you read the novel?"

"Nope."

"Take my copy, if you like. I hoped it might help me understand Hazel, why she chose to preserve her virginity after she got married. My husband never gave me a choice about going to bed with him."

This was another unexpected turn into personal—and sexual—territory. "You're a widow?"

"Divorced. From an actor who didn't bother telling me before our wedding that I'd be his second wife and that he and his first had a six-year-old son. He got me pregnant. I didn't want children, and Bob couldn't afford to raise another one. Leaving me to do the only thing a woman in that situation can do."

"It must feel awful, giving up your baby for adoption."

"No baby. I visited a doctor. He took care of things." Peg pressed her thin lips together. After a silent moment she said, "Horrid, I know, and it's illegal. Please don't think badly of me. Bob said he was taking my earnings to keep up his alimony, but he lied. And he landed in jail for failure to pay. To cover his debt, I had to borrow from my employers. He was arrested—twice—for drunken driving. He got sloshed before rehearsals. And after performances. Occasionally he would yank my hair and knock me around. When I was touring in a play, he followed me from city to city, creating disturbances. I considered killing myself, but I had a responsibility to go onstage every night. Divorce was an absolute necessity. Three years ago, a judge set me free."

Awed by Peg's acting abilities and her attractiveness, Phyllis never imagined the betrayals and tragedy concealed by her placidity.

"Let's get on with it, shall we?" Peg passed her pages

to Phyllis. "You'll read the husband. He's about to leave for a business trip." She stood up. "I'm anxious, pacing. I study my horoscope. Tom knocks at my bedroom door."

As they worked their way through the scene, Peg exhibited perfect recall.

The couple's interaction puzzled Phyllis, and she was confused by Hazel's firm rejection of Tom when he reached out to her. "He's so affectionate," she commented, looking up. "Why is she cold and hateful?"

"She wants to get him out of the way before her secret lover arrives."

She stared at Peg. "You mean it's Martha? The lady who sat with you at the circus?"

"That's right. They're lesbians. Females who have sex with females." Peg's eyebrows jutted upward. "Surely you've heard about them."

"We don't have any in Oklahoma City."

"Yes, you do. They've existed down the ages, as far back as the ancient Greeks. I've met women like that. I think one wanted to seduce me." With an understanding smile, Peg told her, "You look like you need a strong drink."

"Just a glass of water, please."

While Peg was running the tap, Phyllis studied the rest of the scene. Hazel and Martha on a sofa, cuddling and talking. Fade to black. The husband's unexpected return. His confrontation with Hazel. Martha's intrusion. Recriminations, angry accusations. Hazel wielding a knife. Tom's blood seeping into the bedcovers.

Peg returned with a water glass. "Mr. Selznick doesn't want anybody to find out we're portraying Hazel and Martha as lovers. You can't tell a soul."

"I won't." She'd be too embarrassed.

CHAPTER 11

Lela felt sure she was quite the busiest starlet chaperone in Hollywood. Phyllis was a popular model for images the studio supplied to newspapers and magazines. Her trim figure, like Ginger's, suited the newest fashions in formal and casual wear, and her bright eyes and dimpled smile were appealing and extremely photogenic. To everyone's disappointment, her speaking role in *The Age of Consent,* formerly *Fraternity House,* had been edited down to a glimpse in the opening, when she amorously cuddled with a young man, and few frames during a college dance. The newspaper review had not been kind.

"At least I couldn't be singled out for criticism," Phyllis said. "I'm barely visible."

They were on their way to Culver City's newly popular Frolics Garden to celebrate Ginger's twenty-first birthday. After wrapping *Three on a Match,* Mervyn LeRoy had sailed to Hawaii for his vacation, leaving the honoree dateless. The mild summer evening had drawn a stellar crowd to the picturesque indoor-outdoor café, attractively illuminated with swags of miniature lights. Movie people flocked there for the food, the song and dance revue, and music performed by Irving Aaronson and his Commanders.

Lela had invited the castmates Ginger considered friends, and Betty and Florence Furness. She secured a large table in a section of flowering shrubs that didn't impede her view of the celebrities who were present. She spotted the Bing Crosbys near the bandstand, Barbara Stanwyck, and an actor whose matinee idol looks were familiar, although she couldn't recall his name.

"Ricardo Cortez," Phyllis said. "He's the detective in *Thirteen Women.* He tries to stop Myrna from killing Irene."

"Listen to you," Ginger teased. "No more *Miss* Loy and *Miss* Dunne."

"He's not Spanish or Mexican," Betty reported. "A girl in publicity told me his real name is Jacob Krantz."

They had just finished their main course when a birthday cake appeared, drawing diners to their table to offer best wishes. When the bandleader and his musicians began playing, Ginger and a male acquaintance made their way onto the floor.

A good-looking stranger walked up to Phyllis. "I'm Buddy Parsons, and I've had my eye on you all night. Of all the lovelies I've seen here, you're the loveliest. Care to dance?"

Phyllis went with him, her chiffon overskirt billowing with her movement.

Far from feeling slighted, Betty clapped her hands softly. "What a charming thing to say. Don't they make a cute pair?"

When Phyllis and her partner returned, he boldly appropriated the chair Ginger vacated—she wasn't one to sit down after a single dance. Relying on skills honed during her years as a newspaperwoman, Lela extracted a considerable amount of personal information from her niece's admirer. A stockbroker working in his father's firm, Arthur Parsons, Junior, lived with his parents in Los

Angeles. He had one sister. When not at the office, his activities included going out on the town and singing and dancing in amateur theatricals to raise funds for charity. He was quick to declare that he harbored no professional ambitions whatsoever.

"After the crash, nobody could guess whether investment jobs would be secure, or if people would trust the markets ever again. Or the banks. Nowadays it's a different scenario for profits."

"My father says that," Betty said. "He's a company executive."

"I went into business after the worst of it was past." Buddy offered Phyllis a rueful smile. "My sister Daisy tells me girls don't like fellows who talk about themselves too much. She does keep me in line. If I strike out with any of her friends, I hear about it."

"Do you strike out often?" Phyllis inquired.

"If I say yes, you'll think I'm a skirt-chaser. And denying it would make me sound conceited. So instead of answering, I'll ask you for another dance."

Ginger reappeared, her face a-glow. "Who's the smooth operator giving our Phyllis the rush?"

"Buddy Parsons," Betty said. "Isn't he a doll? He's smitten."

"Is she?"

"Time will tell." Lela shook her head. "I'm not looking forward to this aspect of guardianship."

"If she wants to go out with a boy," Ginger said, "why shouldn't she?"

"She can. If social activities don't distract her from work."

"She's plenty dedicated. An Owens woman, through and through."

That may be, thought Lela. But inevitably we attract the wrong kind of man. I'm not letting Phyllis repeat the mistakes her mother and Ginger and I made. Hasty marriages end in heartbreak, desertion, and divorce.

Ginger sang and shimmied to the music booming from the phonograph. She didn't miss a beat when the telephone rang and Phyllis raced past her to pick up.

"Hello, Peg," she greeted her friend, with no hint of disappointment in her voice. She was expecting a call from Buddy Parsons.

"Care to spend the day with me? Now that *Thirteen Women* has wrapped, I'm a lady of leisure. My brothers are begging me to take them on a picnic."

Bored from sitting at home, waiting for her handsome dancing partner to contact her, she readily agreed.

"Come over as soon as you can. I'll be at my aunt and uncle's."

Phyllis crossed to the Victrola and turned down the volume before Ginger could launch into the next song.

"Hey, I was just getting warmed up."

"You're beyond warm, you're red hot. Listen, I'm spending the afternoon with my friend Peg Entwistle. If anybody phones me, write down the message."

"I always do."

"May I borrow your hat with the wide brim? I don't dare get a sunburn—I'm booked for fashion pictures this week."

"Okay. And you should tie a hankie around your neck. Like a cowboy."

The electric tram delivered her to the bus that traveled up Beachwood Drive to the Hollywoodland gates, and from there she walked in the opposite direction to the Entwistle home.

Peg, watching from the front porch, called. "You can't ride a horse in those slacks."

"Is that what we're doing? You said we'd have a picnic."

"The boys wandered off with their friends, and I've no idea when they'll return. I'd rather go riding anyway. I'll find some clothes for you. Milton's might be baggy, but they'll do. Aunt Jane's boots won't fit your little feet, but you'll be all right in those oxfords."

Mrs. Entwistle, a sturdy middle-aged woman seated at a wooden desk, looked up from writing. "You're a godsend," she told Phyllis. "Our Babs is suffering from the restlessness that comes after wrapping a picture. Or a play. Something her uncle and I know all too well."

"Aunt Jane used to be an actress," Peg said.

"Before I had a houseful of kids and a pair of lodgers keeping me busy. Don't bother rummaging through Miltie's bureau. His dungarees are on the wash line, clean and dry. If I didn't have so much to do, I'd go with you. I've not been on a horse for at least a week."

The boy's denims didn't quite fit Phyllis, and she needed a leather belt to keep them from drooping. Rolling up the fabric above her ankles, she asked, "Why does your aunt call you Babs?"

"That's the nickname my family and friends have always used. I'm not Peg, either. My parents christened me Millicent Lillian. Quite a mouthful, isn't it?"

As they trudged along the avenue, Phyllis confided, "I've got two first names and three last names. I started out as Helen Maurine Brown. After Mama married my second stepfather, we decided I should be a Nichols like him. Then Ginger gave me a stage name. If I go home for Christmas, I guess I'll be Helen again."

"I wish I could spend the holidays in New York, with Mari and Marta. We share an apartment in Tudor City.

But with money so tight, I've got to work. Mr. Selznick is so pleased with the rushes of my murder scene that he's putting me in another picture." Peg kicked at a stone in her path and sent it tumbling down the ridge.

"Don't start an avalanche."

"I'm scaring rattlesnakes. They cool off in the shade of the boulders, or lurk under sagebrush, waiting for a rabbit to hop by. You've got to watch your step in these hills."

A pair of stone towers marked the entrance to Hollywoodland, one taller than the other. Both had arches with space for pedestrian walkways leading to the village shopping area, which consisted of a market, butcher shop, greengrocer, drugstore, beauty parlor, barber shop, and laundry.

Peg paused. "When I was a kid and came to live in the canyon, none of these buildings and houses existed."

The residential enclave was lush with greenery, its slopes covered with trees and shrubbery and bordered by retaining walls of locally quarried rock. At intervals, steep stone stairways rose to the streets higher up. Ordinary dwellings were outnumbered by grander, multilevel mansions that mimicked foreign styles. Half-timbered small-scale manor houses abutted others that replicated the Spanish hacienda design so prevalent in California. Some of the architects had favored Italian or French or Moorish styles. Ornamental trees and topiary added to the formality, and flowering vines clambered up pale stucco walls. This peaceful neighborhood seemed far removed from the bustle of the vast city in the basin below.

"Mr. Baum, author of all the Oz books, lived on Cherokee Avenue," Peg told Phyllis. "He died before Enty and Jane moved here. As kids, we used to watch Mack Sennett and his actors and actresses filming scenes. He wanted to create an estate way up there on the mountaintop, above the sign. But building a roadway to reach it was too expensive, and that's all he could afford to do."

The office at the riding stables had closed for the day. Peering through a gap in the exercise ring, they enviously watched equestrians and their mounts leaping over a series of jumps.

"We'll come back another time," Peg said. "There are hacking trails all around here, and over in Griffith Park. Bobby and I have covered every one of them." She released the fence rail. "If you want a different kind of adventure, we can climb onto the Hollywoodland sign."

Phyllis regarded the distant landmark uncertainly. "You've done that?"

"Lots of times. Miltie and Bobby started scaling it right after it was built, about ten years ago. There's a ladder behind each letter, for the man who replaces the lightbulbs when they burn out. You'll love the view from up there."

Peg's enthusiasm was irresistible. She marched on. Phyllis followed.

CHAPTER 12

Leaving the road, they hiked up a rocky incline thick with vegetation. Phyllis brushed against bushes of satiny green leaves, heavy with tiny, unripe berries.

"Wild holly," Peg said. "Poisonous."

She hadn't realized the possible dangers posed by this hilltop ramble. Rattlesnakes. Deadly plants. She paused to cinch the belt tighter around the waist of her borrowed dungarees. Bending down to re-tie the laces of her oxfords, she saw the layer of red dust smudging the white portions. The flat, smooth soles provided no traction, hampering her progress.

Each of the sign's thirteen letters was formed by panels fitted together, and an incalculable number of lightbulbs studded the edges. When Phyllis saw that the flat surfaces were perforated, she asked why.

"Those holes let the wind pass through," Peg explained, "so the sections don't get blown down. Especially in Santa Ana season."

Their trail was now reduced to a deep gulley cut into the earth by rain runoff, somewhat straighter but trickier to navigate. They continued their ascent to the uneven ridge where the massive structure was planted, supported at the rear by an array of telephone poles and metal girders running crossways. Nearby was a toolshed for storing the replacement bulbs.

Peg strode past the giant H and stopped at the O. "Follow me. Go slow. You don't want to slip." A narrow ladder stuck out at a right angle, and she gripped the rails to pull herself up. Stopping at the letter's opening, she crawled along the crossbeam and perched there as if sitting on a sidesaddle. Her athleticism was impressive for such a small-boned, petite creature.

Phyllis went after her, halting at each rung. She recalled the time her sister dared her to climb the tallest cottonwood tree on their street. Lacking the courage to refuse, she'd crawled up only to learn that getting herself back on the ground was a far greater challenge.

"Never look down. Keep your eyes on me," Peg called.

Her breath came in gusts, and her mouth was parched. She continued her slow progress to the crossbeam and reached it. Hand over hand, inch by inch, she scooted herself towards Peg.

"Did you ever see such a sight?"

She clutched the hot metal for dear life and scanned the landscape. Sunlight glinted on the waters of Lake Hollywood. Her gaze traced the rippling mountains to the east and west. Los Angeles lay spread out before her, a carpet of civilization.

Tipping her head back, Phyllis asked, "Have you been all the way to the top?"

"As far as the middle of the H—once. I'd be afraid to go higher."

A gust of wind flowing from higher elevations swept under the brim of her hat. Fearful of losing her balance, she couldn't reach up to hold it on her head. It tumbled forward, ricocheting off a boulder, and rolled out of sight.

"Forever lost," Peg said sympathetically.

"It's Ginger's."

After an extended silence, Peg commented, "I never noticed that scar on your cheek."

"Because it was covered by makeup."

"What happened?"

Still winded from exertion, Phyllis sucked in air before answering. "I was a baby. The furnace in our apartment wasn't working properly, but the gas company wouldn't send someone to fix it. My father and another man—the landlord, or a friend—went down to the cellar to try and re-light it. There was a gas leak. When he struck the match, it caused an explosion. He was killed right away. The entire building came down. My mother and my two-year-old sister and baby me were taken to the hospital. The company had to pay Mama a lot of money because of their negligence."

"That's terrible." Peg brushed back a windblown lock of cornsilk hair. "I can't remember my mother. My papa divorced her, and nobody ever explained why. For years we floated from England to America and back again, wherever he could find theatre work. My Aunt Jane had a sister, and she and Enty—my Uncle Charles—played matchmakers. I adored my stepmother. She died before Miltie was four years old. Bobby had turned two. A year later, when we lived in New York, a speeding motor car knocked Papa down in the street. He was supposed to recover, but he didn't. And suddenly the three of us were orphans."

Phyllis had never known anybody who had lost a mother, a stepmother, and a father.

"I don't know whether Enty and Jane wanted children, but they became our parents." Eyes fixed on the horizon, Peg reflected, "I had the advantage of being raised by a working actor-manager and an excellent actress. And because Jane is so passionate about women's rights, she wasn't sanctimonious or judgmental when I had to end my pregnancy and decided to divorce my husband. I'm always able to confide in her without fear of losing her affection. My grandmother, on the other hand . . ." Grimacing, she shook her bright head.

"Lela and Ginger are my fairy godmothers. I'm not sure their faith in my acting ability is justified. Whether I succeed or not depends on producers and directors and the casting office."

"It is frustrating," Peg agreed, "our inability to control our destiny, no matter how dedicated we might be."

"Lela's worried I'll be distracted by a boy I danced with at the Garden Frolics. Buddy Parsons. Making movies and posing for photographers is all right, but going on dates would be a lot more fun."

"If you two become a regular thing, we could make a foursome. You and him and Humphrey and me."

"Is he your B-E-A-U-gart?"

"No, because he's got a wife. He's off to New York after he finishes his Warner Brothers picture with Ann Dvorak. The one you were in. I'm planning to do the same, after I achieve solvency. Film acting is simply a means to an end." Peg's expression grew pensive and her voice husky when she added, "Dr. Gordon the astrologer would say that my faults and shortcomings were pre-ordained. But I put my faith in Shakespeare. 'The fault, dear Brutus, is not in our stars, but in ourselves.'" She stroked her throat. "I'm parched. Let's go home, shall we?"

Phyllis preceded Peg down the ladder, her anxiety easing with every rung that took her nearer to the dusty, solid earth. Before hopping off, she surveyed the ground below her feet, in case a vicious rattlesnake was coiled and ready to sink poisoned fangs into her flesh.

Her friend descended as nimbly and speedily as she'd gone up. "Sorry about your cousin's hat."

"I'll buy her another. A small price to pay for my adventure."

During their absence, Peg's brothers had returned to the Entwistle house. Milton, a year younger than Phyllis, laughed to see her in his dungarees. After she changed clothes in the boys' bedroom, she stood before the age-speckled mirror above the bureau and dragged her pocket comb through her wind-tousled hair. Her face was noticeably pinker than when she'd arrived, but not red enough to indicate sunburn.

Milton was impressed that she'd scaled the Hollywoodland sign. "I want to do it at night," he declared, "when all those lightbulbs are flashing on and off."

Peg looked up from a letter she'd received and said with unaccustomed severity, "You could get electrocuted. Where's Bobby?"

"Dining room. Working on his model airplane. Can't you smell the glue?" He wrinkled his nose.

She folded her letter and said to Phyllis, "When you finish your lemonade, let's go over to my lair."

A frown creased Peg's brow as they walked in the direction of her apartment building.

"Bad news?"

"One of my flat mates is broke, and the other one moved out. I have to cover all the rent on my own, in addition to paying what I owe on this place." She inserted her key into the door of her apartment and swung it open.

To cheer her, Phyllis said, "You'll be all right. Mr. Selznick likes you."

The glass-topped table in the dining alcove was covered with loose papers and books. Peg took up a single page and offered it to Phyllis.

"My horoscope. Read it if you dare."

The sheets were covered with the familiar zodiac

symbols and perplexing numerical calculations. Phyllis looked past these to the personality analysis.

You have intense emotions and passionate feelings.

You fear the loss of control in emotional and domestic matters.

You are tormented and will cause torment to others.

Bypassing the darker qualities, Phyllis searched for positive ones. "You're gentle, warm, humorous, and artistic. You should enjoy a substantial measure of popularity and success in life."

"Perhaps I've already had my full share. My future might contain unmitigated sadness and bad luck and failure."

"Look on the bright side. If time proves Dr. Gordon wrong, tell Irene Dunne. She'll pay you one hundred dollars."

CHAPTER 13

After Phyllis signed her RKO contract in Judge Parker Wood's chambers, she had an interview with Albert Lovejoy, who doubled as the studio's drama coach and talent scout. The script he handed her lacked a title, but the characters in the opening scene were Meg, Jo, Beth, and Amy—the March sisters of *Little Women.*

"You'll read Beth." Mr. Lovejoy granted her several minutes to review the dialogue.

He must have been satisfied, because he also asked her to perform a sentimental sickbed scene featuring Beth and Jo. She began to experience the intoxicating effect of genuine and intense ambition.

Swayed by curiosity, she disregarded Lela's advice never to ask studio people nosy questions. "When does production begin?"

"Whenever we put together a cast and get a final draft. Later this year, or early next." Mr. Lovejoy placed the script on his desk and placed his hand reverently upon it. "This picture will prove to Will Hays that RKO is capable of producing wholesome, quality stories. Selznick has a gift for putting great literature on the screen. We'll leave it to our competitors—like Warner Brothers—to traffic in gangsters and gun molls and loose women and simple comedies for sapheads."

On leaving his office, she went looking for Lela, no doubt gathering intelligence from secretaries and publicists. As she followed the dim corridor, she peeked into every open door—and almost careened into someone.

It was Peg, whose red and swollen eyes were evidence of a sustained bout of weeping.

"What's wrong?"

"Everything."

She seized one slender arm. "Tell me."

Leaning against the wall for support, Peg's forefinger wiped a tear running alongside her pointed nose. "A man named Joy made me the opposite of joyful."

"Do you mean Mr. Lovejoy?"

"Not him. Colonel Joy. He's the censorship board's Hollywood representative, and reviews all the scripts at all the studios to decide which ones breach the morality code. He objected to the lesbians in *Thirteen Women.* But because the rules don't explicitly prohibit them, my Hazel-with-Martha scenes were filmed as written. And now Mr. Selznick has to tidy them up. Mr. Hays, the big watchdog, is coming from Washington for the Olympic Games and to meet with all the movie executives. All morning Archainbaud rehearsed me for re-takes of the murder scene, and we're shooting it this afternoon. Ayn O'Connor is hunting for an evening gown that fits me." Peg's hands fluttered down her waist to her hips. "No negligee. Or rumpled bedclothes. Or Martha."

"That's too bad," Phyllis sympathized.

"Mr. Selznick is paying me well for today's work, even though he means to toss it all. He's determined to include the original footage in the final cut. But that's risky, because the theatre owners can refuse to show the picture. And I'll have wasted my time at RKO." Peg's balled fist struck the doorframe. "If only Cukor had cast me as Sydney Fairfield in *Bill of Divorcement* instead of Katharine Hepburn." Peg raised her drooping head to ask, "Are you still seeing the handsome businessman?"

"Buddy has tickets to all the Olympics tennis competitions and takes me whenever I'm free. His sister serves on the junior hospitality committee, and I'll be his date for her fancy dinner before the Ball of All Nations. And afterwards, we're going to the dance at the Cocoanut Grove. If you'd like to join us, I'll ask Daisy to fix you up."

"With a society boy?" Peg produced a fleeting smile. "I'd bore him to death with theatre talk."

After a night of uninterrupted sleep, Phyllis joined Ginger for her morning swim. On leaving the pool, she picked up a discarded section of the newspaper her aunt was reading. Her eye fell on an article about the important visitor from Washington.

"Why is everyone at the studio so afraid of this Mr. Hays?" she asked Lela.

"Because he has the authority to prevent distribution of movies with scandalous and salacious content. Cinemas across the country rely on the endorsements from the National Board of Review and the Catholic League of Decency. Will Hays is a fine, upstanding Republican, although in my opinion, he ought to more stringently enforce his Production Code. Too much unsavory material gets past Colonel Joy of the Studio Relations Committee."

"They're the reason Peg Entwistle had to re-shoot her biggest scene yesterday."

"What was wrong with it?" asked Ginger, emerging from the pool.

"A man's wife has an affair with another woman. They're lesbians." She'd never spoken the word aloud.

"That," Lela said, "is precisely what the code is supposed to keep off the screen. Along with fornication and rape and illegitimacy. Abortion. Miscegenation."

Ginger expanded on this recitation of vices, chanting, "Nudity. Profanity. Alcoholism. Drug addiction."

"Treason," Lela added darkly. "What's more, when actors and actresses are careless in their private lives, they run the risk of making themselves unemployable—even the big names. Executives can't afford to offend the public by overlooking promiscuity or criminality."

Swinging her bathing cap by its chin strap, Ginger said, "They should make stars out of decent girls like Phyl and me. We don't drink or smoke or wager on racehorses. We have no social diseases. We're athletic and healthy. Maybe we should promote our purity on a billboard."

Phyllis grinned, spreading her arms out wide. "As big as the Hollywoodland sign!"

After Ginger finished her secondary role in *Hat Check Girl,* she was scheduled to begin work on Joe E. Brown's *You Said a Mouthful.* She departed for her Catalina Island location with Mervyn LeRoy, leaving Phyllis to wonder whether the purity she'd espoused would survive their time away.

Although RKO hadn't yet offered her the part in *Little Women,* the publicity department expected her to be productive during this fallow period.

With her pencil poised, an assistant publicist said encouragingly, "Tell me whatever could be considered interesting or unusual about you. Betty Furness talked about her love of knitting, and the thirty sweaters she's made. You must have a special skill, or some kind of useful knowledge you could impart to female film fans."

"My mother and my stepfather operate a popular beauty salon. She taught me about arranging hair and applying makeup and giving facials."

"Wonderful! I can put together a column of your best beauty hints and send it out to one of the movie magazines and maybe the newspapers. With one of your lovely photographs, of course. What would you like to tell the readers?"

Delving into her store of tips passed on by Mama, she replied, "For softer hands, at bedtime rub on lotion, instead of a heavy cream, and apply it lightly. That way it will absorb into the skin, and you won't have to wear gloves overnight."

The publicist's pencil moved swiftly across her pad as she jotted down this tidbit. She looked up with an expectant face, obviously wanting more.

"Using tomato juice as a face wash will soften and lighten the complexion."

"I had no idea. Go on."

"Rubbing a pumice stone gently over the legs will make them smooth. I showed Ginger Rogers—she's my cousin—how to do that. Oh, if you bend over and brush your hair backwards, it stimulates the scalp. To make your hair extra healthy, give it a short sunbath a few times a week. And regularly sterilize your brushes and combs and hairpins."

"What advice do you have about makeup?"

"When powdering your face, always move the puff in a downward direction—never up or across." She took her compact out of her purse to illustrate the technique. "If you wear nail polish, choose a color to harmonize with your lipstick. Red with red. Rose with rose. Pink with pink."

"I'm going to incorporate your suggestions into my

routine. And I'll type them up and submit the piece to a movie magazine."

"If it's all right, I can write the article myself."

"Are you sure?"

"I've been published in a newspaper," she stated, in case the woman doubted her abilities. She'd didn't want anyone else pretending to be her, and she aspired to get her own words into print—with her byline attached. "My aunt has a typewriter I can use."

The publicist closed her notepad. Without looking up, she said regretfully, "The audience response cards we collected at the *Thirteen Women* preview weren't as complimentary as we'd hoped. Mr. Selznick and Mr. Archainbaud sent it back to editing. I'm afraid your sorority house scene had to go."

"Not again," Phyllis groaned. Her funny dialogue had been cut from *The Age of Consent.*

"There will be other pictures."

When? But she knew better than to ask. A publicist wouldn't know what decisions had been made about a future production. Lela had warned against seeking information from studio personnel, as she routinely did herself, to gather information that might prove helpful to Ginger or Phyllis.

How will I sustain a career, Phyllis wondered, when I'm getting no more time on the screen than a dress extra?

"We can schedule another picture session," the woman continued. "Different types of photos than the fashion ones. I'll talk to Mr. Bachrach about setting aside an afternoon for you."

When posing for the studio's foremost creator of glamor images, she wore a pale, peach-colored lace teddy and skimpy tap pants that revealed a considerable expanse of bare flesh. Her All-American Girl image was being replaced by that of a junior *femme fatale.* Perched on a block-shaped dais, she tried to produce the come-hither expressions perfected by Garbo and Dietrich. She widened her eyes, and pursed her carmined lips in a Clara Bow pout. And the whole time she felt like laughing at this ridiculous and, she hoped, temporary transformation.

"Lie on your back," the photographer instructed. "Place your arm behind your head. Cross one leg over the other. Now hold still and stare straight ahead. No smiling."

Gazing soulfully at the void above, her mind busily concocted beauty advice and makeup tricks to include in her article.

On the day she turned it in to her publicist, she was shown the photo proofs. Unsure what to think, she handed back the glossy images, saying, "Greta and Marlene won't be worried about losing any roles to me."

"They turned out very well. After retouching, we'll send them out to newspapers and magazines with some flattering copy. And when the people in our casting department see these, you can expect plenty of scripts to come your way."

Buddy's socialite sister stepped in to fill her idle days. Daisy took her shopping at Bullock's, invited her to fancy tea parties or picnics, and enlisted her as a participant in charity fashion shows.

Many days went by before Phyllis found a moment to contact Peg. The person who picked up the phone announced that her friend had given up the apartment and moved in with family. When the operator connected her to the Entwistle residence, Miltie explained that his sister was living above their uncle's garage.

"Hold on, I'll get her," he offered. "She's in the kitchen with Aunt Jane."

Peg came on the line. "I can't talk right now. Come over tomorrow, and I'll catch you up."

Mentally reviewing her commitments, Phyllis suggested, "How about the day after?"

"I'll be here." Peg's tone was forlorn as she added, "Nowhere else to go."

CHAPTER 14

On prior visits to the Entwistle house, Phyllis hadn't noticed their outbuilding. She discovered that it had space enough for a single automobile and various gardening implements, and the set of wooden steps that led her to Peg's living quarters. A tiny window admitted enough sunlight to reveal a double-cushioned sofa and worn armchair and a small table with two chairs. A single-ring electric burner sat on a shelf beside a basin with a pitcher. The place smelled of stale cigarettes.

"Primitive," Peg acknowledged. "But the lodger before me didn't mind a bedroom only slightly larger than a closet. I eat with the family, and if I want a bath, I go to the house and wait my turn. Mustn't moan, though, because this place costs me nothing. I'm flat broke."

"Last month you were paid three hundred dollars for a single day of work. Betty Furness told me."

"I spent it all. On clothes and outings and fine dinners and presents for the family. Paying some of their household bills. Tires for Enty's car. Hiring horses for the boys and Jane and me at the stables. How could I know I was about to lose my RKO salary?"

Phyllis stared at her, shocked into speechlessness.

"Haven't you heard? The studio dropped me the minute my contract option came up."

"But why? You and Dorothy Wilson are the best of the actresses they signed this summer. You've got heaps more experience than the rest of us—and a bigger chance at starring roles."

"If I ever did, I don't any longer. I'm mostly chopped out of *Thirteen Women*. Bits of the circus scenes remain, but none of the husband-stabbing."

"At least you'll be seen. I was eliminated." She shook her head. "I can't believe RKO let you go."

"Mr. Selznick spent a lot money on *Thirteen Women,* with no hope of earning it back. He's tightening budgets across the board. Payroll is the first and easiest item to cut."

"But he hasn't stopped making pictures." She perched on the sofa arm and clasped her hands on her lap. "He commissioned a script for *Little Women*. The Louisa May Alcott novel."

"I'm familiar with it," Peg said wearily. "I played Amy March on the New York stage."

"Tell the casting department. Even better, prove to them you could do Jo—you'd make a terrific tomboy. Wouldn't it be swell if we played sisters? I had my screen test yesterday."

"For which part?"

"Mr. Robertson was testing Dorothy Wilson for Meg and wanted to see me as Beth. Ginger went with me and made sure my hair and makeup and costume looked all right. Ayn O'Connor, the Russian lady, gave me one of the pretty gowns Ann Harding wore in *The Conquerors*. I'm the same height—five feet, two inches."

"So am I. They'd want somebody taller for Jo. I hope you get the part. In Beth's dying scene, you'll bring the audience to tears. Everybody's handkerchief will be soaked."

"RKO owes you another chance. Their financial losses aren't your fault."

Peg's blue eyes bored into her. "I'm finished with movies. And I can't stand being stuck here without work. All I want right now is cross-country train fare to New York—even if I don't have anywhere to live. When I couldn't cover the overdue rent on my Tudor City apartment, I lost it." Her voice wavered when she said, "The landlord evicted my roommate and seized all my belongings in lieu of payment. Jewelry. Clothing. The furniture."

Phyllis, struck by the enormity of her friend's losses, couldn't summon a single comforting platitude.

"This run of foul luck started when I agreed to do the play with Billie Burke and broke my agreement with the Lakewood Playhouse in Maine. Then I stupidly dropped out of the Broadway production of *The Mad Hopes* to make the RKO picture. According to Humphrey, I've become *persona non grata*—every stage director in New York has heard how unreliable I am. I wish he were still here to take my mind off my problems. Which multiply daily." Peg gnawed at her thumb. "Worse, I've passed along my misfortune to others. Not just Mari, my roommate. My aunt's dear friend and lodger, an elderly actress, had to give up this room so I could have it. Jane and Enty depended on that income."

Striving to instill confidence, Phyllis pointed out, "If you don't have a contract, you can freelance at other studios. Like Ginger."

"Any director would be thrilled to hire Ginger Rogers. None of them ever heard of me."

"I'm sure you could find a different job, to tide you over."

"Doing what? I've only ever been an actress. I doubt

if any city in America has as many unemployed people as Los Angeles. Even before the Depression, hordes of the desperate came here—and discovered there's simply not enough work for everyone who needs it. You've seen the street corner beggars. The old people and men and women and their kids picking fruit in the orchards. And all those depressing Hooverville camps around the city."

"Aunt Lela knows just about all the managers of the playhouses. If she persuaded them to give you an audition, maybe Mr. Selznick would write a letter of recommendation. He owes you that much."

"The professional theatre is just as competitive as the picture business. But I suppose it's worth a try."

Relieved to see that Peg was surfacing from her pool of despondency, Phyllis continued cheerfully, "We'll figure out a way to make you stand out. I've got so many stylish clothes—Ginger shops all the time but won't wear anything twice. She lets me have whatever I want. And I've just bought a lovely new coat and matching handbag that you can borrow. I'll even arrange your hair and make up your face."

"If I land an interview or an audition, you can primp me to your heart's content."

"I'll do more than that. Aunt Lela and Ginger won't let me pay them for my room and board. I have a savings account for the money I've earned modeling and making movies. I'm sure I can cover your travel expenses. How much do you need?"

"I don't really know. When I performed with touring companies, the producer's office handled everything—train tickets, hotel rooms, meals."

"Just let me know the amount. Whenever you're ready."

Visibly moved by this offer, Peg said "I couldn't let you do that."

"You can pay me back after you land a part in a play."

"That might never happen. And it would break my heart—in a way losing a film role like Sydney Fairfield didn't do. I don't much like working in pictures. There's barely any rehearsal before a scene is shot, and everybody's so concerned with perfecting camera angles and positioning the lights and microphones. That narrow strip of celluloid is a permanent record of a performance. For a stage play, I have weeks of preparation. I live inside my character and she in me. I develop her style of speech and her mannerisms. I put on her personality with my costumes and makeup. The set becomes my home. My fellow players are like family. We share jokes and meals, and we squabble and console each other. And when the show opens, the presence of an audience gives life to our performances. I'll never stop craving all of that."

Phyllis envied her powerful sense of purpose. Ginger had it, too. So did Lela.

It'll come, she assured herself. *I've been a professional actress for just a few months.*

Casting aside self-doubt, she suggested, "Let's walk to the village drugstore. I'll buy your lunch, and we can make a plan for your triumphant return to the New York stage."

Lela's fingertips tingled after a solid two hours of pounding the typewriter keys. She paused to massage each aching wrist, determined to complete another scene before leaving her desk. But the decision about a break was made for her, by whoever was knocking on the door. She got up and crossed the living room on legs cramped and stiff from inaction.

A familiar young blue-eyed blonde stood on the threshold.

"Miss Entwistle. Was Phyllis expecting you?"

"No. I was hoping she might be at home."

"She went with Ginger to the Havenhurst tennis courts, but they'll be back any time now. Come in and wait. I've been busy with my screenplay since lunchtime, with no one but my characters for company."

Peg crossed the threshold, saying, "Till now I've never been inside the Garden of Allah. Doesn't Clara Bow live here?"

"Sometimes. If she needs a bolt hole."

"When she was the biggest star in Hollywood, she lived in Beachwood Canyon, not far from my uncle's house. If the It Girl's luck can run out, I guess anybody's can."

"Good fortune ebbs and flows, like an ocean tide. I've got fresh lemonade cooling in the icebox. Can I pour some for you?"

Peg tugged off her gloves and tucked them into her cloth purse. "Thank you. That sounds refreshing."

Lela returned with two glasses. "I'm giving my script a final polish," she explained. "It's the story of a destitute woman who supports herself by selling the items she gathers from the city dump. One day she finds an abandoned infant, a girl, lying among the rubbish and decides to keep it. After the death of a rich man, who left his entire fortune to his wife, the poor woman comes forward to claim it as his widow. She's convicted of perjury and false impersonation and sent to jail. But she's telling the truth. I won't give away the ending."

"Does it have a title?"

"Today, I'm calling it *The Woman Nobody Knows*. George Batcheller at Chesterfield Productions wants to have a look. He's got Nancy Carroll in mind for the lead."

"Could you please let me know when he begins casting? Like Phyllis, I'm no longer employed at RKO." Peg reached into her pocketbook and took out a newspaper clipping. "I saw this announcement in the *Examiner.* 'Three of RKO's eleven Baby Stars have been dropped already. Harriet Hagman, Phyllis Fraser . . . Peg Entwistle.'"

"Oh, that." Lela waved a dismissive hand. "Mr. Hearst's reporters should check and double check their facts. Yesterday, Phyllis received the happy news that the studio picked up her option. We sent a wire to the paper, requesting an immediate retraction for the afternoon edition. Tomorrow we meet with Judge Wood again so he can approve the new term contract." Shaking her head, she commented, "David Selznick showed terrible judgment in releasing you. I'll be saying special prayers on your behalf. So will Ginger. The Book of Romans tells us 'all things work together for good to them that love God, to them who are the called according to his purpose.' I know the truth of it—faith has sustained me through every difficulty. If you like, I can introduce you to an excellent Christian Science practitioner."

"I was raised Anglican. My relatives sent me the Episcopal boarding school for girls in La Jolla."

Lela nodded. "We all need religion. A great comfort, in times of distress."

The chatter of voices from the courtyard heralded the cousins' return. Ginger and Phyllis bounded through the door, their rosy, smiling faces and liveliness contrasting with Peg's drooping shoulders and despondency.

CHAPTER 15

"What a surprise! We've been talking about you," Phyllis told Peg. "Ginger was curious about our brave climb up the Hollywoodland sign."

Her cousin grabbed a glass of lemonade from Lela's tray. "I'd do it at night. When the lights are flashing on and off."

"That's what my brothers say," Peg told her.

"But after dark you wouldn't be able to see the view of the hills and the city and the sea." Phyllis pointed her racquet to the ceiling. "From the summit, you can see for miles and miles." She sat down beside Peg and guzzled her drink.

"Not so fast," Lela cautioned. "You'll get stomach cramp."

"Mrs. Rogers told me the studio picked up your option."

Sensitive to Peg's plight, she merely nodded. "How do you feel about your audition at Pasadena Playhouse?"

"Hard to say. I haven't heard from the director. Sorry, but I forgot to bring the dress and coat you loaned me. I'm so absentminded these days."

"I can get them next time I visit you."

Ginger said, "I'll ask Mervyn LeRoy to talk you up at

Warner Brothers. And I can, too. I've got a featured role in *Forty-second Street.*" She excused herself to change out of her tennis clothes.

Phyllis was glad to see her go. Ginger was trying to be helpful but hearing about her success in the movies must be agony for Peg.

Returning to the living room, Ginger announced, "I'm going out with Mervyn tonight, Phyl. Sorry I won't be here for the eight o'clock radio show."

"What's the program?" Peg inquired.

"Nothing important," Phyllis said quickly. The *Thirteen Women* actresses were being interviewed on KGO.

Peg rose and hooked her pocketbook handle over her arm. "If I don't get home soon, my aunt and uncle will wonder what's become of me. Or maybe they won't. I have a habit of missing meals when I visit the girls at the Hollywood Studio Club. A few of them invited me to help them stage their skits, even though I don't live there."

Phyllis followed her friend outside and accompanied her as far as the fountain, where the goldfish swam in infinite circles.

"You're the one person I haven't let down," Peg said. "Not yet. Promise you won't squander your chance of success the way I did."

"Stop blaming yourself," she protested. "True talent is a rare commodity, Lela says. And you've got plenty. I mean to send you back to Broadway, where you can put it to good use."

"I told you, that's another dead end."

"You can't be sure."

"I'm positive."

Through the shimmering arc of rising water, Phyllis watched Peg drift away into the deep, black shadows formed by low-hanging branches.

Phyllis followed Lela into Judge Parker Wood's chambers. At their approach, his stern features relaxed, as invariably happened when a starlet made her entrance.

Lela handed over the contract. "It's boilerplate, identical to the previous version. And I'm still her guardian, while she's in California. Her mother and I are sisters."

After he reviewed the clauses, he glanced up at Phyllis. "Are you satisfied with your working conditions, Miss Fraser?"

"Yes, sir."

"How about your education? California requires motion picture companies to provide teachers and an approved curriculum for younger players."

"She's enrolled in the studio school." Lela answered for her. "And does plenty of reading on her own. Books of all kinds. Literary magazines."

"I plan to earn my high school diploma," Phyllis told him. "I've been saving up my salary so I can go to college." Last night she'd gone through her account book, calculating the amount of money she could give to Peg without entirely depleting her hoard.

"A bright young lady like you should seize every opportunity for learning. What will you study?"

The question stumped her. "I'm not sure."

"You're sixteen, there's no need to decide just yet." He smiled. "Excuse me for running out on you, but today's docket is full and so is my courtroom. I assure you I prefer these visits to custody suits and forgery cases. Or the Chaplin divorce. I expect we'll meet again in three months." He returned the document to Lela and addressed his secretary. "The photographer can come in."

"Two of them today, Your Honor."

With a smile for Phyllis, he said, "And they aren't here to shoot me."

The man from the Associated Press asked her to pose in the still-warm chair the judge had vacated. Folding her hands in her lap, she looked at the camera and smiled broadly. He asked for some particulars—her name, her age, her hometown—and left.

The second photographer wanted her to sit on top of the judge's desk. "Cross your legs and hitch your dress. Higher than that. Past your knees."

Lela glared at him. "Who do you work for?"

"National Enterprise Association." Raising his camera, he pointed it at Phyllis and the shutter clicked. When she told him her age, his gaze roamed from her face and along her chest to her waist to her black leather shoes. He whistled through his teeth. "Jailbait."

She felt Lela's gloved fingers curling over her wrist, pulling her down from her perch. "Let's go."

Ginger insisted that they celebrate the contract renewal. Despite Mervyn LeRoy 's best efforts to enhance her visibility, she was a homebody rather than a social butterfly, but did like going out for special occasions.

"Your choice," she told Phyllis. "And if you say Schwab's, I'll ignore you."

"The Brown Derby," she replied, knowing it was her cousin's favorite.

"Done!"

"Let's dress like twins. I have a jade-green dress, and you can wear your new crepe in the same shade."

"Peg borrowed it. We'll have to go in blue."

Because the Rogers ladies didn't consume alcohol, they were unaffected by Prohibition, and Phyllis had no interest in the concoctions that club and restaurant bartenders surreptitiously enhanced with bootleg liquor. They could choose from the array of drinks mixed from fresh juices and soda water and non-stimulating cordials like grenadine or maraschino juice.

While she sipped her fizzy fruit drink and Ginger and Lela debated the merits of Busby Berkeley's style of dance direction, Phyllis considered Peg's plight. And Mr. Selznick's culpability, for tossing nearly all the Hazel Cousins footage and then callously dropping the actress who'd performed the role to his and everyone's satisfaction. She knew he was still testing girls for *Little Women,* because his publicists were releasing their names to the press. Peg should've been included.

But it doesn't matter now. Her heart is set on New York. Tomorrow, or the day after, definitely before the weekend, I'll make a cash withdrawal from my bank account. If I give her a check, she might tear it up for the sake of her pride.

The next evening, as she was dressing for a dinner date with Buddy Parsons, Lela called her to the telephone.

"For you." Her aunt lowered her voice to a whisper, "A man."

Buddy, who habitually ignored his wristwatch, must be calling to say he'd be late.

"Miss Fraser? Charles Entwistle. Peg's uncle. Did you happen to be with her last evening? Or today?"

"No, sir. She paid me a visit on Thursday, but I haven't seen her since then."

"Yesterday after supper she decided to walk over to the drugstore to buy a book, but she didn't turn up for breakfast this morning. Miltie went over to the flat and saw that she hadn't slept there. Could be she's off on a lark with her mates and didn't bother to tell us where they were going, or how long she'd be away. She's grown rather unpredictable."

Phyllis was unable to supply him with names or telephone numbers of his niece's so-called mates. She had the impression that Peg, who had so eagerly befriended her, was almost entirely friendless.

"If she gets in touch today, do tell her to ring us."

"I will," she promised.

CHAPTER 16

Lela devoted Sunday afternoon to her screenplay, determined to make the most of her solitude. Phyllis had taken the streetcar to an RKO starlet's apartment to cook a holiday meal for a *Photoplay* magazine feature. Ginger, dressed like a vagabond and jingling the car keys, left after lunch for an unspecified destination. She hoped one of them would proofread the stack of completed pages before they tuned in to the evening radio programs. With luck, she could finish revising before the nightly bacchanal began. In advance of the sun's descent, their neighbors would congregate around the swimming pool, cocktails—or liquor flasks—in hand.

She was replacing the typewriter ribbon when Ginger reappeared, her face glistening with perspiration, strands of rusty hair slipping from beneath her straw hat. Lela couldn't comprehend why she carried her cousin's new black and tan coat over one arm and clutched a black leather handbag. After she placed the items on the sofa, her denim-clad legs gave way and she sank down beside them. Clutching a high-heeled shoe to her chest, she sobbed.

Nothing made Lela more wretched than seeing her daughter overcome by distress. "Are you in pain? Did you hurt yourself?" She perched on the armrest and stroked the damp forehead. "Tell Mother what's wrong."

"Phyllis loaned her coat to Peg Entwistle. It was lying on the ground under the Hollywoodland sign. With the handbag." Ginger choked on an indrawn breath. "I found this note inside." Her hand trembled when she displayed a scrap of paper.

Lela put on her glasses to read.

I am afraid. I am a coward. I am sorry for everything. If I had done this a long time ago it would have saved a lot of pain. P.E.

"I was shaking all over from shock, and my legs were already wobbly after my hike up the mountain path. I crept all around looking for—for her. And then I saw, a long way down, that blonde head. Her body was bent and all twisted, and she was lying so still." Ginger leaned over, elbows on her knees and her head in her hands. "Mother, Peg killed herself. She jumped."

Lela put her arms around her daughter. "Dear heaven. That poor child." Shuddering at the recollection, she said, "She sat right here, days ago, while I told her the plot of my script."

"I carried everything to the riding stables, where I parked the car. Her family lives on Beachwood Drive, but I was too upset to go knocking on doors to ask people where I could find them. Phyllis has their telephone number, so we can call them as soon as she comes home."

"No!"

Ginger sat up. "Why not?"

Lela went to the kitchen and opened the icebox, her mind moving as swiftly as her limbs. She reached for the pitcher. One thing was certain. She mustn't allow her daughter, or her niece, to become mixed up in this tragedy.

Offering Ginger a glass of cold water, she stated firmly,

"It is essential that you avoid bad publicity. If your name is in any way associated with that unfortunate girl, your career will suffer. I can't—I will *not* let that happen. Is that clear? Do you understand what I'm telling you? And why?"

After a long silence, Ginger nodded.

"When it's dark, I'll take these things to the police station, the one here in Hollywood. I'll take care that I'm not seen, and I won't go inside. I'll leave everything on the front steps. Are you listening?"

"Yes."

"When I return, you'll telephone the Central Office downtown and tell the desk clerk what you've told me. You won't identify Peg by name, or acknowledge your acquaintance with her. Let him know the dead person's belongings—and suicide note—were left outside the Hollywood precinct. Is that clear?"

"Won't you place the call? Please."

"I didn't see the body, so I can't give a statement. Lying to a law enforcement officer is a crime."

"We should contact her relatives, too."

"I've no doubt the Entwistles have reported their niece as a missing person. When the police examine her note, they'll make the connection. They're trained to deliver a notification of death to next of kin."

"But we'll tell Phyllis."

"Absolutely not. It's also for her benefit, her future, that we're keeping silent."

Ginger fingered the decorative brooch attached to the coat lapel. "I got kind of jealous when she became so friendly with Peg, which makes me feel even worse. What made her do it—end her life that way? I can't believe she wanted to die because RKO dropped her."

"An unwed female can feel quite hopeless when she discovers she's going to have a baby."

"She wasn't that sort of girl. I'm certain."

"I suppose not. Try not to dwell on it, dearie. Pray for the Lord to comfort those she left behind. All too soon they'll be burdened by a very heavy grief." She picked up her niece's leather and suede coat and folded it around the purse and the shoe. "I'll take these to the car so Phyllis won't see them, and lock them in the trunk. Help me come up with a reason to go driving at night. And check the newspaper for a cheerful program we can listen to after supper."

"How can you be so calm?" Ginger marveled.

"I'm not. Far from it. But certain steps must be taken, immediately, for your protection. And to safeguard Phyllis. Trust me, it's for the best."

While performing her assigned tasks of measuring out the rice and slicing the carrots, Phyllis also monitored the Kook-Kwik pressure cooker wobbling on the stovetop, watching for the right moment to open its valve and release the pent-up steam.

"I appreciate your help with supper," Lela said, "after you spent all day cooking with your friends."

During their meal Ginger was remarkably subdued, excusing herself from the table without having her nightly bowl of chocolate ice cream. Phyllis cleared the table and volunteered to wash and dry the dishes.

"Is Ginger coming down with something?" she asked Lela.

"It's leg cramps, she says. I haven't found our hot water bottle, and no drugstore will be open on Sunday night. I'll have to borrow one from a neighbor."

Phyllis was tempted to check on Ginger, whose bedroom door was closed, but was reluctant to barge in and

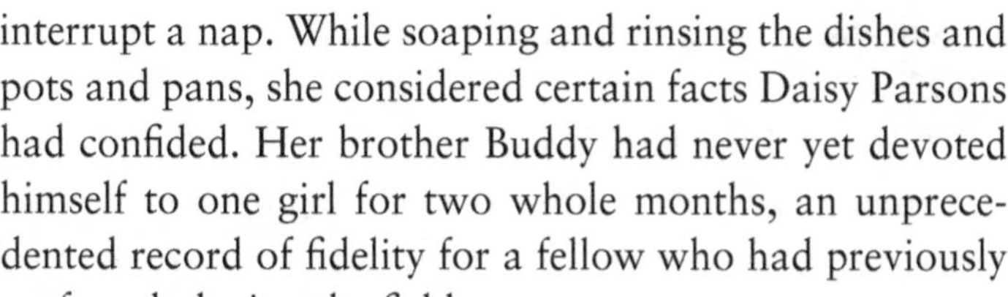

interrupt a nap. While soaping and rinsing the dishes and pots and pans, she considered certain facts Daisy Parsons had confided. Her brother Buddy had never yet devoted himself to one girl for two whole months, an unprecedented record of fidelity for a fellow who had previously preferred playing the field.

He was fun to be with and a splendid dancer, whether the music was slow or fast. He liked singing, and could accompany himself on any available piano or the ukulele he'd brought back from his Hawaii vacation. The girls Daisy pointed out as Buddy's former flames had been wary of her, the movie actress and model, but their apparent envy receded somewhat on learning she wasn't allowed to keep any of the stylish clothes she wore in photos. Phyllis was aware that she had little in common with her boyfriend and his circle apart from their affinity for sports—tennis, croquet, ping-pong, bowling. If she asked about his work as a stockbroker, he spoke of the income-producing investments he sought for clients and the necessity of adhering to state and federal regulations. It sounded dull and dry and uncreative.

She finished tidying the kitchen and gathered up her knitting basket to add more rows to the hat she was giving Jean for Christmas. The front window was partly open, admitting occasional bursts of laughter from the poolside revelers, and the resounding splash each time someone jumped—or was pushed—into the water.

When Ginger, in robe and pajamas, joined her in the living room, Phyllis asked how she was feeling.

"The same," was her cryptic response. She turned on the radio console and increased the volume to drown out the festive sounds flowing in from outdoors. "Sunday night hijinks is underway." She stretched out on the sofa, one arm flung over her head. Her right foot tapped against the armrest, up and down, up and down. "Easy to tell which people don't have an early morning studio call."

"Wish I did," Phyllis said.

Ginger typically offered an encouraging and optimistic reply to that sort of comment. Surprisingly, she said nothing.

"Why don't you go to bed?"

"I'm waiting up for Mother."

The program ended and another was starting when Lela returned, empty-handed.

"I couldn't locate a hot water bottle," she told Ginger. "I ran into Clara Bow. You know how she is, chatting on and on about this and that. She's making her comeback in a dramatic role in *Call Her Savage,* based on yet another Tiffany Thayer novel. May it serve her better than *Thirteen Women* did Irene Dunne and Myrna Loy. And Phyllis."

"And Peg," Phyllis added. Her mouth stretched wide in a yawn. She stuffed the hat and her yarn ball and knitting needles in her basket. "I'll finish up in the bathroom now, so I won't be in your way later."

She went through the usual evening rituals, washing her face and brushing her teeth. By the time she turned off the taps, the radio had gone silent. But she heard her cousin's voice, followed by the sound of the phone receiver being set down. Awfully late to place a call—it was after nine o'clock.

She got into bed. Shutting her eyes, she wondered fleetingly how Peg had explained her night away from home.

Tomorrow, she vowed, pressing her cheek into the pillow, I'll give her the money.

CHAPTER 17

Lela found it impossible to drop off to sleep, even after the nightly revels subsided and the Garden of Allah inhabitants dispersed, and her bedroom was shadowy and silent.

For hours she lay wakeful, questioning the plausibility of the errand she'd concocted. She'd taken the precaution of removing the hot water bottle from its place in the bathroom cupboard, concealing it in the back of a dresser drawer so Phyllis couldn't discover her subterfuge.

I didn't bear false witness. I never expressly said my conversation with Clara Bow occurred tonight. God understands that my every misleading word and secret action was on behalf of my precious daughter and my dearest niece.

Across the room, Phyllis slept soundly, oblivious to her agonizing and not yet aware of her friend's gruesome demise.

Lela's expectation that police would swiftly identify Peg was dashed by the headline on the front page of the *Los Angeles Times*: GIRL LEAPS TO DEATH FROM SIGN. Below it was a highly sensationalized article.

She carried the paper to her daughter's room. "Read this."

Blinking hard to clear her eyes, Ginger obeyed. "A blonde. Crumpled body found by the police on the mountainside. Unidentified? That means there was never a missing person's report. We're still the only people who know who she is." She continued to scan the article. "The officer on the phone is a good note taker. This is what I told him, word for word." She looked up. "What are we going to do?"

"Nothing."

"But the family—"

"The suicide note is printed in full, and the Entwistles will see it. They'll collect the body from the morgue. And the victim's name will be released to the press. I'll hide this from Phyllis."

"It still feels so wrong not to tell her. What about the radio? If she hears a news bulletin, she's going to figure out that the dead girl is her friend."

Lela hadn't thought of that. "I'll unplug it. Keep her occupied. Take her to the tennis courts over at Havenhurst. Afterwards, you can go to Schwab's Pharmacy."

"I'm too achy—my muscles are sore from hill climbing yesterday. And all the Monday regulars at Schwab's will be talking about the same thing we are."

"I'll figure out a diversion."

She left the room and went into their kitchen to start breakfast. The strangely murky morning sky increased her foreboding. The strain of concealment wouldn't let up until public notification that the nameless young woman in the city morgue was the celebrated stage actress Peg Entwistle. Only then would she be able to comfort Phyllis, and preach hopefulness in the face of adversity, and impart her hard-won wisdom.

In retrospect, she regretted not offering enough of it to poor Peg.

Don't permit deep despair to overcome your good

judgment, she should've said. A female has unlimited reserves of strength and stamina. Optimism can change bad luck into good. Put your trust in God, and you will prosper.

Lela had prayed her way through each cruel blow fate had delivered. And by enduring them, she'd discovered her invincibility. Delivering a dead infant. Escaping her first marriage during her second pregnancy. Her daughter's kidnapping by her vengeful ex-husband. Her dread of never again seeing her only child.

We'll spend the day at the beach, she decided. Phyllis enjoys swimming and fishing. We'll find a bait shop where she can rent a rod and tackle.

Ginger made the sandwiches and packed the picnic basket. Phyllis carried their towels and swimsuits and bathing caps to the car, placing them where her dead friend's effects had been hidden.

"Where to?" Lela asked when they exited the bungalow.

Phyllis laughed. "You're the one who always has a plan."

Ginger said darkly, "Or a scheme."

Discerning this comment as a criticism of her actions last night, she delivered a chastening frown.

"Santa Monica." Ginger gripped the handles of the picnic basket and stalked toward the car.

Phyllis hugged her inflated beach ball. "Miss Rogers got up on the wrong side of the bed."

"She needs a day of sunshine and sea. We all do." The looming cloud cover had evaporated, exposing a serene blue sky. "You girls will swim. We'll eat. If we get too hot, we'll visit the bingo hall." By playing a succession of cards, listening for the caller to announce the combinations of letters and numbers, she could set aside her anxiety. Temporarily.

The familiar view of curving bay and layered mountains lifted her low spirits. The shoreline wasn't entirely deserted, but they had their choice of striped canvas lounge chairs.

Phyllis waded deep into the water, up to her narrow waist. While she bobbed and leaped to meet incoming waves, Lela and Ginger sat silently, both of them fixated on the cap-covered head. Phyllis ended her swim and returned, dripping saltwater. Ginger picked up a towel and went to meet her. Lela opened the picnic basket.

Phyllis accepted a peanut butter sandwich. "I should've invited Peg to come with us."

Lela took a bite and slowly chewed. Ginger drank her cola.

Phyllis wiped her mouth with a napkin. "I need to tell you something important."

Ginger smirked. "Does it involve Buddy Parsons?"

"No. It's about the money I've saved up."

"We've already talked about that," Lela reminded her. "What you earn is yours to keep. For clothes. Singing lessons. Streetcar fares."

"Peg Entwistle wants to return to New York, but she can't afford to. I told her I'd pay her way."

Ginger stared at the lettuce leaf she'd pulled out of her ham sandwich.

"If we stop at the bank on the way home," Phyllis continued, "I can withdraw the cash."

Lela's throat tightened. She should say something, anything, to curtail this discussion. "All right."

"I need to stretch my legs," Ginger announced, wincing as she stood up.

"Want some company?" Phyllis asked.

"Stay here. I won't be gone long."

Lela placed their napkins and the empty soda bottles in the picnic basket, struggling to find a harmless topic of conversation. "I forgot to ask about your *Photoplay* shoot." Yesterday she'd been too preoccupied with what Ginger had discovered on Mount Hollywood.

"The magazine challenged Dorothy Wilson and Mary Mason and me to create a complete Thanksgiving dinner and serve it to our boyfriends. We chose the menu, and the men brought the ingredients. Our decorations were red and white—table linens, flowers. We all sat down to a roast turkey feast on a hot September day, while palm fronds tapped against the windows." Dimples crimped the pink cheeks. "You can read about it in the November issue."

"What dish did you contribute?"

"Pumpkin tarts. Jean and I always bake them at holiday time."

"You'll have to make some for us." Shielding her eyes, Lela watched Ginger skirt an abandoned sandcastle.

"I want an ice cream cone." Phyllis searched the depths of her beach bag for loose change. "I've got enough coins here to buy one for you and one for Ginger."

"No, thank you."

Ginger also declined the treat, saying the studio expected her to keep her weight stable. When Phyllis scooted up to the snack stand, she muttered, "She has a generous heart, that kid."

Another lengthy, awkward silence descended. High time, Lela decided, to leave the beach and head for the bingo parlor.

Ginger ripped off her sunglasses. "Here she comes. Oh, dear. Look at her face. She must have heard something."

She swiveled around and saw her niece running, stumbling towards them, her bare feet sending up sprays of sand.

"Peg Entwistle," Phyllis gasped. "She's dead! She

climbed the sign and she—she jumped." Her bare knees buckled, and she sank to the ground. Kneeling in the sand, she swiped at her face, wiping away tears.

"Who told you?" Lela asked.

"The man on the radio."

Ginger leaned down, her ruddy head touching the brown one. "I'm so sorry."

"It's my fault," Phyllis sobbed. "She wouldn't have done it if she'd had the money I meant to give her."

"You mustn't think that."

Lela, silently watching, could find no words to stem the tide of grief battering the girl she loved like a daughter, whose trust she and Ginger were betraying.

CHAPTER 18

Phyllis learned every agonizing detail of the Mount Hollywood tragedy from Tuesday's newspapers, in their graphic description of Peg's voluntary plunge from a fifty-foot height. Her delicate body, battered by rocks and scraped by sagebrush, had rolled a further one hundred feet to the place where it rested from Friday night until late Sunday evening. The police, alerted by the unnamed female hiker who found her discarded possessions and spotted the corpse, arrived after dark. Armed with flashlights, they searched until they located the lifeless body in the shallow ravine. They delivered it to the morgue where it remained, unidentified and unclaimed, until the Entwistles saw the suicide note printed in the *Examiner.*

In the photographs that accompanied each devastating article, Peg looked so pretty, her lips curved in that familiar half-smile. The writers described her as a "jinxed" actress, the increasingly despondent victim of blasted hopes and bad luck. Her uncle confirmed that Peg had fruitlessly sought the funds she needed for traveling back to New York, where she could resume her stage career.

You are tormented and will cause torment to others.

The memorable line from Peg's horoscope haunted Phyllis.

She stared at the photo portrait taken weeks ago, when her friend had been a hopeful starlet. "It's a miracle that the mystery woman came along and discovered her." After Lela tugged the paper from her slack fingers, she added, "The funeral is at one o'clock."

"I'll take you. I can pay my respects and represent Ginger. Why look," Lela said brightly. "Dorothy Wilson, the former studio stenographer, will be in *Little Women*. 'And Phyllis Fraser is also assigned to the production.' Did you know?"

"No." The juxtaposition of her improving prospects and the description of Peg's gruesome death added to her pain and regret.

She picked out the one dress that seemed suitable for the service, a simple black gabardine with scalloped trim along the hem. Her black velvet beret had a nose-length veil that impaired her vision but successfully obscured tearful eyes. She placed two handkerchiefs in her handbag.

Ginger had driven herself to Warner Brothers, so Phyllis and Lela rode the streetcar to Hollywood and Vine. Phyllis didn't recognize any of the mourners gathered in the small chapel at W. M. Strother Mortuary. She searched in vain for representatives of RKO, disappointed to be the sole member of the original Baby Stars group in attendance. A white silk pall embroidered with gold thread covered the coffin, which was flanked by tall candle stands with lit tapers. The floral arrangements, all white, were sparse.

Jane and Charles Entwistle, and Peg's other relatives, were escorted to the front row. Her brothers hadn't come with them.

The officiant, an Episcopal priest in clerical robes and

collar, opened his prayer book and intoned, "I am the resurrection and the life, saith the Lord. He that believeth in me, though he were dead, yet shall he live. And whosoever liveth and believeth in me shall never die."

Had Peg been a believer? They had never discussed religion. Because her final days had been a living Purgatory, perhaps she'd swiftly attained her heavenly rest.

"I know that my redeemer liveth, and that he shall stand at the latter day upon the earth. And though this body be destroyed, yet shall I see God, whom I shall see for myself."

Solid earth and hard rocks had destroyed her body.

"I will lift up mine eyes unto the hills, from when cometh my help." The minister broke off, as if belatedly aware that the psalm would remind his listeners of the deceased's manner of dying. He moved on to a lengthy passage from First Corinthians, and a series of prayers.

The funeral director accompanied the grieving Entwistles and the priest from the chapel. The mortuary staff extinguished the candles and rolled the bier behind the black curtain.

Goodbye, Peg.

"A dignified rite," Lela murmured when they followed the mourners towards the door.

The woman exiting ahead of them said to her companion, "They're having her cremated. Jane and Charles arranged for the ashes to be interred with her father and stepmother, in their family plot in Ohio."

"Too much suffering in that girl's short life," her companion commented.

Young women of twenty-four didn't make burial plans for themselves. Would Peg have wanted her remains to be deposited halfway between Hollywood and Broadway?

Wordlessly Phyllis accompanied Lela to the intersection, making the sign of the cross when the black hearse passed. Cars on both sides of Vine Street respectfully pulled aside and halted as the vehicle slowly proceeded to the crematorium.

Phyllis pasted on a false smile and pretended not to have a single care as she marched down the strip of Persian carpet. Hand on hip, she turned to one side, then the other, gazing over the hatted heads of her audience, seated in a semi-circle of chairs in the Ladies Department of the Wilshire Boulevard Bullock's. Turning, she glided back towards the curtain, which parted for Betty Furness. At the conclusion of the fashion show, they circulated among the customers, allowing them to admire their dresses and stroke the fabric and place their orders. When they were free to go, they went to the elegant Tea Room.

"Mother and I are going to the Roxy tonight to see *Thirteen Women,*" Betty told her, spreading a napkin across her lap. "Care to join us?"

"I'll never watch it," she declared.

"I understand. Honestly, I do. How's Buddy?"

"I haven't seen him this week."

"Did you hear anything about Peg's funeral?".

"I was there."

"Mr. Selznick and Mr. Robertson wanted her for Amy March in *Little Women,* but they didn't send their letter till Monday. Imagine how awful they must feel. If she'd received it sooner, she'd still be alive."

Phyllis didn't need to imagine, she knew exactly how they felt. Too many 'what ifs.' "Can we please not talk about her?"

Betty paused for a sip of tea and placed her cup in

its saucer. "I expect Dorothy Wilson will get Meg. And you'll be Beth."

"It's not definite. The director says if I want the part, I have to lose ten pounds. I look too healthy to play a sickly, dying girl."

"Constance Bennett is tipped for Amy, now that Peg is—that she—oh. Sorry. Nobody knows who's playing Jo."

When Phyllis was assigned to a film with a starring role for Dorothy, she suspected it was Mr. Selznick's method of testing their abilities before making his final *Little Women* casting decisions. Then she and Betty learned they would appear in the new Irene Dunne picture.

"You'll be so busy, you won't have time for meals," Ginger teased.

"That's not funny," she retorted. "I'm always starving. I eat like a rabbit and exercise every single day. All afternoon I played doubles with Buddy and his sister and her boyfriend."

"If I become a big enough star, I'll have my own tennis court. And a swimming pool."

"If you marry Mervyn, you could have them now."

"He hasn't asked."

"I bet he does."

"How much?"

"Ten dollars."

"Why not double it? Twenty dollars says Buddy proposes to you before Mervyn proposes to me."

"Done!"

They shook hands.

CHAPTER 19

"Tell Mr. Robinson of RKO that Buddy Parsons thinks Miss Phyllis Fraser is perfect. Just as she is."

Phyllis felt the pressure of his hand on her waist, skillfully guiding her around another pair of dancers. Talking during the foxtrot was risky, but nevertheless she replied, "He's the director, so his opinion matters a lot. If he wants me to slim down, I have to do it."

"I say he should cast you in that picture you want because you are such a *little* woman. Like the gal in the song. You're five foot two. And your eyes are blue."

The musicians finished the dance tune with a flourish. Buddy and Phyllis returned to their table.

Reaching for her tumbler of ginger ale, she asked, "What's Daisy doing tonight?"

"Not sure. But I'm glad she's not here. I wanted you all to myself. You're about to be so busy making movies that I need to get everything settled now."

"Like what?"

"Our future. Phyl, sweetie, I'm crazy about you. Have been since we met at the Garden Frolics. You're my forever girl, because I intend to marry you." He smiled across the table, waiting for her to respond.

She very nearly retorted that he was definitely crazy but didn't want to be rude. "Buddy, I'm sixteen."

"We can wait till you're seventeen. Or eighteen. When we're together, the time flies by."

Increasingly uncomfortable, she asked, "Does your family know?"

"Mother's thrilled. She wants you to have the diamond ring that belonged to her grandma. Daisy is over the moon. You know she adores you. And she can't wait to take you shopping for your trousseau."

"What if I want to go to college?" She wasn't sure she did, but she hoped mentioning the possibility would make him see reason.

His brows jutted down. "This conversation isn't going the way I expected."

"You're sweet to propose. But it'll be best—for both of us—if I don't say yes."

She could've reminded him that there was greater significance to marriage than restaurant dining and dancing in nightclubs and debutante parties and partnering one another at tennis. Why hadn't that occurred to him? She couldn't guess what future he envisioned for himself, apart from buying and selling all the stocks and bonds he could. Her prospects might be murky, but she didn't intend to spend a year and a half engaged to a rich pleasure-seeker she'd dated for three months.

"Well, kid," Ginger said two days later, "I owe you that twenty bucks."

"You're wrong," she contradicted.

"Not according to this."

Accepting the newspaper, she found a grainy picture of herself above an item stating that RKO actress Phyllis Fraser was engaged to businessman Buddy Parsons.

"It's not true," she insisted. "He proposed but I didn't

accept. I thought we were having fun together, I never guessed he was that serious."

"This is a wire report," Lela fumed, "from the Associated Press. Practically every newspaper in the country will run it. You must cable your parents right away and let them know there's no truth to the story. I'll help you write a statement of denial to submit to tomorrow's editions."

Later that day Buddy called her, profusely apologetic.

"I swear I never spoke to any reporters. Just my parents and Daisy. And her friends. I suppose one of them spilled the beans. My tux is back from the cleaners in the nick of time. When should I pick you up?"

She'd forgotten their double date with Ginger and Mervyn LeRoy. RKO was celebrating the release of *A Bill of Divorcement* with a formal gala and benefit for the Motion Picture Relief Fund. Phyllis hadn't yet attended a film premiere, and she couldn't bear to miss it. And she'd planned to wear the outfit purchased with her Bullock's employee discount—a tight-fitting blue gown with a crossover bodice and a sheared and undyed mouton jacket almost as luxurious as genuine mink. Showing up with Buddy immediately after repudiating their engagement might cause tongues to wag, but that couldn't dissuade her.

The giant spotlights planted outside RKO's Hillstreet cinema cast their rotating beams skyward. Ginger inscribed her name in the guest book, Phyllis did the same. She waved to Betty Furness, hostess for the radio broadcast of the festivities. Her friend gestured towards the microphone stand, a tacit invitation to an interview.

Mr. Selznick, ever the showman, treated his star-studded audience to music composed by Max Steiner and performed by the studio's orchestra. Throughout the concert, Phyllis fancied that Peg's unhappy spirit was haunting the cinema. Katharine Hepburn, who had supplanted her as Sydney Fairfield, was a reed-thin creature with a decidedly bony face and a jutting jaw and a singular, affected way of speaking. Attractive, but no beauty.

I'm not being fair, Phyllis chided herself. Miss Hepburn didn't cause Peg's death.

And I didn't either.

Instead of accepting my help, Peg chose to martyr herself. She knew I promised to pay her way to New York, but it didn't stop her from climbing that ladder.

When Buddy sought her hand, she pulled it away. As the credits scrolled over the screen, he suggested that they go dancing. She pleaded weariness.

"You don't have to take me home," she added when the lights came up. "Mervyn lives so close to the Garden of Allah."

After she evaded his goodnight kiss, Buddy backed away. Wearing an expression that was equally pained and perceptive, he said, "This must be the only time a girl dropped someone for having honorable intentions. I'm so sorry, Phyllis."

"I know. But my aunt is worried about the bad publicity, and she says I shouldn't go out with you anymore." This truth was useful cover for the fact that Phyllis was no longer comfortable being seen with him.

Her first romance had ended, and her relief was far greater than her regret.

CHAPTER 20

Arriving at RKO's wardrobe department to try on her *Lucky Devils* costume, the label attached to it informed her that her character's name was Toots. She also found out that Ayn O'Connor would resign from her job because another studio had purchased her screenplay.

Dorothy Wilson, preparing for her fourth leading role since her departure from the studio typing pool, shared her concerns about her initial scene. "I'm playing an out-of-work actress, cut from her latest picture, who plans to commit suicide—by jumping from a high balcony. Worse, the script indicates that the Hollywoodland sign is flashing in the background. One of my rescuers warns me not to go through with it, in case something swell happens later, 'and you won't be here to celebrate.' Which is exactly what happened to Peg—she could've played Amy March. Should I refuse to play the scene as written? It seems so disrespectful."

To soothe Dorothy's conscience, Phyllis answered, "Think of it as a tribute. She wouldn't want you to risk your starring role by making a fuss. Have you heard anything else about *Little Women?*"

"Not a word."

"I've lost five pounds since the director told me I'm not thin enough for Beth. Another five to go."

"Gosh, you'll be a skeleton! I'm counting on you to eat at my Halloween party. I've invited some of our *Lucky Devils* castmates. Richard Cromwell is bringing some fellows he knows from Universal—Ben Alexander, who's in practically everything, and Tom Brown. I hope I'll have enough food for everyone."

"I could make stuffed eggs. Half regular, half tuna. We'll call them Lucky Deviled Eggs."

"What a great idea! Oh, and tell your cousin she's invited."

Ginger, who complained mightily about the sulfuric aroma of boiling eggs that permeated the bungalow, couldn't decide what to wear.

Holding up a pair of castanets, she said, "Maybe I should go as a flamenco dancer. I've got a Mexican shawl and a ruffled skirt. What about you?"

"Ayn, the Russian lady in wardrobe, let me borrow this tinsel hula-hula skirt I wore for a Halloween promotion."

After Phyllis put on the costume, her cousin eyed her critically. "It sure shows plenty of leg."

"I'm used to it. I've posed for publicity photos in my bathing suit. In shorts. And for Mr. Bachrach, in a pink silk teddy and step-ins. Don't forget, you've also worn your scanties in sexy sheba pictures."

"Tap pants," Ginger said defensively. "Professional attire."

With two trays of deviled eggs carefully packed in the trunk, they drove to Dorothy's apartment. Ginger, recognizing the pair of actors who accompanied Richard Cromwell, hurried to greet them.

"Ben was in *Suicide Fleet,*" she told Phyllis. "Tom and I made a picture together in New York."

"I'm surprised you remember." The dark-haired actor turned to Phyllis. "Dorothy says you're the one who brought the tastiest stuffed eggs I've ever had. I'm guessing you're an actress, like Ginger."

"Not quite like her. I'm contracted to RKO, working on my fourth picture, and I've been assigned to a fifth. When did you start acting?"

"About nineteen years ago."

Her eyes widened. "You're joshing."

"Nope. You're even cuter when you're confused." When she gave him a playful shove, he held up his hands in mock surrender. "Okay, okay. I was six months old when I made my stage debut. My parents were vaudevillians. They enrolled me in the Professional Children's School. By age ten, I was making silent flickers. And doing radio shows. After I started in talkies, I met Ginger. A triple threat, that girl. She acts, she sings, she dances. What's your line?"

"Not sure I've got one," she confessed.

His hand cupped her elbow. "How about I judge your dancing ability?"

She fluffed the silvery tinsel hanging from her waist. "I'm afraid if I move too fast, I'll lose some of my skirt."

Grinning, he scanned her legs. "Fine by me."

Phyllis went out with Tom Brown so often that the show business columnists routinely coupled their names. Like Ginger, he was a valuable source of professional advice. He was serious about his work but could also show a girl a good time. And he looked dashing when picking her up in his gleaming Ford. Aware that he'd previously dated Rochelle Hudson and Anita Louise and any number of actresses before her, she doubted she'd remain his steady for long. But she sensed they could remain friends even after he moved on to the next girl.

In *Lucky Devils* she had a small role as a movie extra, appearing in the staged bank robbery performed by the titular stuntmen. On her second day of filming, she perched on a desk, holding up her pocket mirror as she combed her hair, drawing admiring males like Lorelei on her rock.

"Let's take that again," director Thomas Ince boomed through his megaphone. "You need to show us a lot more leg, honey."

She crossed her left knee over her right and reached over to raise a few inches of polka dot fabric. Her lower limbs, she reflected, invariably received more attention and comments than her performances.

"I scream during the robbery," she informed Ginger when they were lounging by the swimming pool. "At the tavern, I laugh a lot and join in the group sing. But I'm the dumbbell who asks why the men get so upset when one of them drops a wine bottle. Breaking glass is a bad omen for the stuntmen. It's a prediction that one of them is going to die on his next job."

"I never heard that."

"They're very superstitious. And even though the fellows knew it would happen, they flinched when they heard that bottle shatter. Bill Boyd knew a man so unnerved by a broken beer bottle that he quit his assignment on the spot and left the profession."

"Good grief."

"I love watching them work. The bank robbery stunts were choreographed like a ballet—but with gunfire. They were shooting blanks, of course. One stuntman came crashing through a skylight. Another tumbled from the top of a stairway all the way down to the bottom. Everything went according to plan. Because of the budget cuts at RKO, the directors are expected to get a scene in a single take."

"That's pressure," Ginger commented.

"For everybody," Phyllis agreed. "Even bit players like me."

Ginger pushed her tinted glasses lower on her nose and peered over the rims. "Remember when we were on the train last summer, watching that odd lady who wore a monocle and spoke with a fake British accent?"

"And carried her dog everywhere."

"I'm using her as the model for Anytime Annie in *Forty-second Street*. My doggie is even cuter than hers."

"When we move into your movie star mansion, with the pool and the tennis court, can we please get a dog?"

"Sweetie, if I make it that big, we'll have a whole pack of them."

CHAPTER 21

In early December, the Western Association of Motion Picture Advertisers announced their list of Baby Stars. Ginger was among the actresses designated as candidates for stardom. Lela, brimming with satisfaction, declared that she deserved the honor more than any other in the group. She had extensive experience and was an extremely versatile performer, and her popularity with audiences was rising.

"Next year, they might pick you," Ginger told Phyllis.

Knowing the unlikelihood, she responded, "Only if they create an award for the actresses who are frequently removed from a picture. You could make a hilarious film short by splicing together the miles of my discarded celluloid."

Lela had been working for Universal Pictures as a continuity writer while her script was in production. With filming and editing completed, *Women Won't Tell* would soon be released to East Coast theatres.

"After Christmas, when you return from Oklahoma," she told Phyllis, "I'll have extra time to devote to your training. It's a shame that RKO doesn't school their young players as rigorously as Metro-Goldwyn-Mayer. It's not enough, showing you how to apply makeup and trotting you in front of photographers wearing next to nothing. They rely on that superficial sort of publicity at the expense of making you into a genuine actress. You need to work at diction and movement, scene study and character analysis."

"Careful," Ginger warned. "You'll scare her into staying with her family."

"She can't," Phyllis contradicted. "Nothing will."

"It's necessary to refine your identity," Lela maintained, "or you'll never break out of party scenes in college pictures. We mustn't pin our hopes on *Little Women.* Selznick is wrangling with RKO's New York executives for greater control or bigger budgets, if not both. I can't imagine they'll give in to his demands. Not after *Thirteen Women.* It was a disaster financially and a serious setback for Irene Dunne and Myrna Loy."

"And for me," she sighed, still regretting the loss of her single scene with the female stars.

The Baby Stars assembled at Paramount Studios for a group photo. Chattering in excitement, they lined up to have their corsages pinned on before being placed in rows. After counting the yellow and platinum heads—nine out of fifteen—Lela said regretfully that Ginger should have deepened her red highlights so she'd stand out more.

Press reports about her cousin's achievement prompted a congratulatory telegram from Ginger's great admirer Harold Ross, founder and chief editor of *The New Yorker*. He provided the Rogers household with a complimentary subscription to his magazine, and Phyllis always read the weekly issue from cover to cover before passing it on.

"When you get to Manhattan," Lela observed, "you'll be more informed about the best plays and the finest restaurants and the choice nightclubs than its residents."

Phyllis was sorry to miss the dinner at the Biltmore

Hotel, where the Baby Stars would be feted. Mervyn LeRoy, a victim of influenza, was permitting another man to stand in for him as Ginger's date, a substitution that Lela deplored.

"I'll be chaperoning her," she told Phyllis when driving her to the train station, "so I can keep my eye on that Howard Hughes. He's by far the biggest wolf in town, and before his divorce committed adultery with countless females. His affair with Billie Dove was quite the scandal. Oh, he wasn't in love with her—men like him can love only themselves. He bought out her studio contract, lavished her with luxuries, and cast her in his pictures. He had to know she was also involved with George Raft. All of a sudden, she goes to the hospital to have surgery for 'appendicitis.' Mind you, no respectable doctor would perform an illegal procedure. Might have been a clean-up operation."

During her months in California, Phyllis had acquired a great deal of worldly knowledge, much of it unsavory. She'd learned about lesbians, abortions, extramarital affairs, and predatory producers. At the Garden of Allah, she had witnessed displays of drunkenness and occasional nudity—certain male and female residents preferred to sunbathe in their birthday suits. At night, returning home from a date, she occasionally spotted a trysting couple not entirely concealed by darkness and shrubbery and oversized ferns.

I prefer realism, even if not pure or pretty, to illusion, she realized. But I can't let on to Mama and Daddy and Jean that my Hollywood education wasn't restricted to making a few movies for RKO, and one for Mervyn LeRoy, and having school lessons with my studio tutor.

In the house that was supposed to be her home, Phyllis felt like a guest. During the day, Mama and Daddy worked at the salon, and Jean was in school. She passed the time helping Clara Willingham clean and cook and prepare meals, re-read the favorite books she'd left behind, and scribbled stories about Hollywood.

She'd missed the maid's sonorous hymn-humming and her way of dispensing wisdom, either gleaned directly from the Bible or her preacher's interpretation of it.

"Can I go to church with you this Sunday?" Phyllis asked.

"Goodness, no, Miss Helen. You're a young lady now, for all you still look like a child to me. Your mama won't be wanting you in the pew with black folks."

But here she sat in the kitchen with one of them, their hands touching every time she passed a peeled potato.

Reluctant to shatter her Classen friends' belief that her Hollywood life was all glamor and glory, she didn't mention those dull hours spent with her head bowed over her knitting, waiting to flit past the camera. When asked about the movies she'd made, she rattled off five of her six credits, leaving out the ill-fated *Thirteen Women.* Nobody had heard of Peg Entwistle, or remembered—if they'd ever known about—the lovely actress who had thrown herself off the Hollywoodland sign.

She was using some of her savings to purchase presents for her family. Each time she stood at a cash register, counting out bills and handing over coins, she thought about Peg.

Her letters to Lela and Ginger were effusive and cheery, describing the search for the perfect Christmas tree, drives downtown to see holiday decorations, and the dance to be held in her honor.

"I'm the local version of a WAMPAS Baby Star," she wrote. "I've been featured in the *Oklahoma News*. When a lady from the *Daily Oklahoman* interviewed me, I had to convince her that my 'fame,' as she called it, hasn't spoiled me. Too funny!"

She combed Mollie Merrick's "Hollywood in Person" column in the newspaper for familiar names. Speculation that RKO wouldn't re-sign minor contracted players made her wonder about her prospects. She was captivated by the columnist's style, and her manner of describing the stars' personalities, fashions, events, and industry developments. She found none of the faintly malicious innuendo employed by Louella Parsons and Walter Winchell. There was, she realized, an art to composing show business gossip.

After Christmas she received a chatty letter from Ginger, illustrated with pencil sketches of neighbors gathered around the Garden of Allah pool at cocktail hour on a chilly night, bundled in their furs and overcoats. Beneath a line drawing of Mervyn LeRoy's profile was the caption: *He wants to marry me!* Hands hovering gracefully over typewriter keys must mean her aunt was working on another screenplay.

"Did Lela's picture, *Women Won't Tell,* play in Oklahoma City?" she asked her mother.

Mama shrugged. "I wouldn't know. Does she earn much money from her writing?"

"She doesn't have to. Ginger makes plenty."

"Then they ought to get a bigger place. You shouldn't be sharing a bedroom with your aunt. Does she have a gentleman friend?"

"Mr. LeRoy, a director at Warner Brothers. He's crazy about Ginger."

"I meant Lela."

"No time for that. She has to supervise Ginger's

career. Her contracts. Her shooting schedules. The banking. Everything except her choice of clothes."

"Has to?" Mama repeated, choking on her cinnamon toast. "She *wants* to. Of all the Owens women, my sister is the most managing." She plucked the napkin from her lap, folded it neatly and laid it beside her empty plate. "Stop by the salon at lunchtime. One of my girls will wash and set your hair so you'll look like a film star for your party. And you can wear my silver fox throw."

This brief visit to her hometown reminded Phyllis of all the reasons she preferred Los Angeles. Hovering gray clouds and the occasional wet snow, always embedded with the reddish dust that blew about, made her miss serene blue skies and seemingly constant sunshine. The flat cityscape, punctuated here and there with oil derricks, inspired longing for mountains and ocean. She yearned to see searchlights crisscrossing a black sky on premiere nights, and the multicolored neon signs that transformed city streets into a carnival midway.

Boarding her train, she was thankful to leave Oklahoma and thoroughly convinced that she would never again live there.

CHAPTER 22

Ginger's engagement was the talk of Hollywood.

"Mervyn and I can't go anywhere without being swarmed by photographers." Ginger reached out to shut the gaping suitcase. "You can unpack later. Come see what he gave me for Christmas."

They went to her bedroom, where she showed Phyllis a full-length coat of luxurious ermine, with numerous, black-tipped tails dangling from its broad collar and cuffs.

"Beautiful." She trailed her hand along the white fur sleeve. "Lucky girl."

"In all kinds of ways," Ginger acknowledged, flopping onto her bed. "Mervyn is so attentive. And he's a wonderful dancer."

"Have you set the date?"

Ginger, bending over to brush her russet hair, replied, "We will after his New York trip. Mr. Zanuck is sending him there to meet with the bigwigs and work out his contract with the studio. Mother and I told him to get in touch with our friend Harold Ross, who knows all the best restaurants. If Mother and I go there to order my trousseau, we're taking you with us. But Mr. Zanuck wants me for the next big musical, so I'll have to beg him for time off."

During her fiancé's absence, Ginger reverted to her former habit of staying in at night, apart from an occasional foray to the Brown Derby.

Phyllis, helping her draw up a preliminary list of wedding guests, eagerly picked up the ringing phone in hopes that it might be RKO's casting office.

"For you," she mouthed to Ginger, holding up the receiver. Returning to the column of names they'd written down, she half-listened to Ginger.

"No, I don't have plans this evening."

Looking up, Phyllis stuck out her tongue. They were supposed to see *A Farewell to Arms* at the United Artists cinema.

Ginger returned her derisive gesture. "The Biltmore ballroom?" She was quiet for a short time, then said, "That sounds lovely. I'm at the Garden of Allah." She provided the number of the bungalow.

"Who was he?"

"Howard Hughes."

"You're a bad girl, stepping out on Mervyn when he's thousands of miles away."

"He won't mind. When he had the flu, he let Howard escort me to the WAMPAS party. We had a swell time."

"You know how desperate I am to see that movie."

"You will. Meanwhile, why not read the novel?"

"I *have* read it. More than once."

Phyllis couldn't understand why Ginger wanted to go out with Howard Hughes when she was engaged to Mervyn LeRoy. Retreating to the bedroom she and Lela shared, she shut the door with sufficient force to communicate extreme displeasure at missing her cinema night.

A Farewell to Arms was popular enough to be held over a second week. On a day when Ginger was working, Betty Furness joined Phyllis for an afternoon screening. When they emerged from the cinema, clutching tear-dampened handkerchiefs, the line of people waiting outside angled around the corner of Broadway and extended along Tenth Street. At Schwab's they discussed at length Helen Hayes's affecting performance, and Gary Cooper's good looks.

As usual, Betty had a wealth of studio gossip to share.

"George Cukor's favorite, Katharine Hepburn, will play Jo March. They'll make an announcement soon."

"What about the other sisters?"

"I haven't heard anything more. Don't lose hope."

Lela blamed Howard Hughes for the shocking breach between Ginger and Mervyn LeRoy. She was so furious that she refused to utter his hated name.

Mervyn was handsome and personable, a skillful young director with potential. He was well-placed to support Ginger's career at Warner Brothers, and their marriage would have ensured favorable, even preferential treatment. He could make her queen of the studio. Norma Shearer, married to MGM producer Irving Thalberg, received starring roles in top-budget pictures. Ginger had ten times her talent.

While her fiancé was in New York, Ginger had occasionally gone out with the millionaire—and she'd done it once more since Mervyn's return. Leading gossip columnists, detecting a rift, posed their questions in print, speculating on the cause of the broken engagement. Mervyn was directing Ginger in *Gold Diggers of 1933,* but his involvement with Doris Warner, the boss's daughter, crushed Lela's hopes for a reconciliation.

Ginger, wounded by his defection, put on a brave face.

"She's his New York souvenir. A good thing for us

both that his change of heart came before our wedding instead of after."

"He turned out to be as great an opportunist as David Selznick," Lela grumbled, "who supposedly deserted RKO so he could start his own production company. Now he's working for his wife's father. And we all know L.B. took David under his wing because he didn't want him as a competitor."

"Nobody will be making pictures if the labor union disputes aren't resolved," Phyllis reminded her.

"The workers can't afford to strike," Lela declared.

Warner Brothers planned to send Ginger and an assortment of stars across the country to President-Elect Roosevelt's inauguration on a train dubbed the "Forty-second Street Special." Lela, grateful that her daughter was being detached from Howard Hughes, trusted that she was too faithful a Republican to be infected by the Democratic idealism of the incoming administration. She very much doubted that Roosevelt's much ballyhooed New Deal would cure the nation's financial ills.

Preparing to do battle with RKO on her niece's behalf, she arranged a meeting with Mr. Stockton in the Casting Department.

"We're determined to maintain our project schedule," he told them, "but we operate in the midst of uncertainty. Even before the craft unions threatened a work stoppage, our industry was in decline. Two studios have already shut down production."

Carrying out her planned strategy, Lela said, "If you've got nothing to offer Phyllis, she'll seek work elsewhere. She'd benefit greatly by doing a stage play. If not for her years in the theatre, my Ginger wouldn't be the success she's become—a Baby Star and a leading actress on a national tour to the White House."

"Warners is lucky to have her. We could use a performer like that here."

"This studio signed her first," she reminded him.

"RKO-Pathé, wasn't it?"

"Same initials," she shot back. "Come along, dearie. We mustn't keep Mr. Stockton from whatever he does to pass the time."

As they made their way through the alley between two soundstages, Phyllis waved down a gray-haired gentleman. While they conversed, Lela eyed the doorways, counting the number of illuminated red warning lights—far fewer than during Selznick's heyday. A large number of RKO-owned cinemas were in receivership, and union employees were aggrieved by stalled contract negotiations.

"Who is he?" she inquired when Phyllis parted from her acquaintance. "I can't place him."

"Peg Entwistle's uncle. He has a bit part in *Little Women,* as old Mr. Laurence's butler."

"I'm glad." Lela walked on, digging in her pocketbook for change to pay for the streetcar, shoving away intrusive memories of a late-night drive to a police station to drop off the dead girl's clothing.

In her campaign to turn Phyllis into a stage actress, Lela arranged meetings with theatre managers and took her to every available performance. They saw Sylvia Sidney perform in *Liliom* at the Pasadena Playhouse, and went backstage to congratulate the director and cast. Phyllis was an amused witness to her aunt's interaction with actor Earl Eby, whose role was small but whose physique and attractiveness had obviously made a big impression.

Ginger returned from her East Coast adventures in

time for the Los Angeles premiere of *Forty-second Street.* She attended the gala event with Howard Hughes, and Lela made no secret of her disapproval.

On a Friday afternoon when her cousin was free, Phyllis suggested a movie matinee.

"What's playing?"

"*No Other Woman.* Irene Dunne. And me—maybe." So many of her scenes had been removed from her films, she had no expectation of making the final cut.

"Rain check? I thought I'd go shopping."

"You have plenty of clothes already, and you don't wear half of them."

"Which is why I need more. And I've already made an appointment at my salon."

"There's nothing wrong with your hair."

"Maybe not. But here's something I know that you don't. At Una Merkel's party, Lew Ayres lured me away from Howard to get my phone number. I've got to look my absolute best, in case he asks me out."

"Suit yourself."

About an hour after Ginger departed, the telephone rang.

"Lew Ayres here, calling for Miss Rogers. Is she available?"

"By now she'll be at her hairdresser's."

"Do you know which one?"

His persistence impressed her. "Oddie's, on Sunset."

"Got it. Thanks."

She went alone to the imposing motion picture palace at the corner of South Broadway and Eighth Street. The audience, seated in twos and threes, chatted while waiting for the double feature. Phyllis was dismayed, but not surprised, by her fleeting appearance as Irene Dunne's maidservant. The second picture, *Employees' Entrance,* featured Marjorie Gateson as the lady accused of shoplifting in a department store. In *Thirteen Women,* she'd been cast as Peg's character's lesbian lover.

The floor beneath her feet lifted and sank. Her seat shifted sideways. Queasy from the abrupt loss of equilibrium, she gripped the armrests.

"Earthquake!"

A roar of panic erupted throughout the auditorium, and the din was deafening.

The projected image was frozen and blurry, until the screen went black.

"Turn on the lights!"

Phyllis heard an ominous creaking.

"Get out from under the balcony. Hurry!"

CHAPTER 23

Phyllis joined the mass of desperate humanity stampeding up the dark tunnel of an aisle. Someone stepped on her toes. A sharp elbow connected with her ribcage. A heavy woman leaned against her for support.

Phyllis gripped the plump arm. "Keep moving!" she cried. "If you fall, they'll crush you."

They were carried with the wave of people streaming from the movie house out into the contrasting daylight.

Disoriented, Phyllis struggled to get her bearings. A motorcar had jumped the curb, its front tire flattened by the impact. The driver, shaken and stunned, gripped the wheel. A broken electrical wire dangled above the roof of the vehicle, sparking and hissing.

The clock crowning the Tower Theatre showed six minutes to six, but a glance at her wristwatch told her the actual time was five past. Along Broadway, poles leaned precariously, their cables ripped away by the earth's movement, but the ornate iron lampposts were still standing. Large chunks of rubble and shattered bricks littered the sidewalks and had spilled into the street.

She had to get herself to the Garden of Allah. But how? It was miles from downtown.

Dozens of people waited at the streetcar stop, in

unthinking expectation that the transit system could operate in spite of the obvious damage to its rails and overhead lines. A double decker bus rumbled past—crammed with passengers, many standing in the aisle. The workday had just ended, and the great migration from the heart of the city was underway.

I'll have to walk, she realized.

Crossing over to Wilshire Boulevard, she found a similar scene of destruction. She tried to keep her distance from broken structures. Pieces of stone and concrete continued to tumble, thudding and cracking as they hit the ground. Sidewalks had heaved up, creating gaps. She avoided them, fearful of twisting an ankle.

As she placed one foot in front of the other, she prayed that Ginger and Lela were at home and in no danger. The faces of some pedestrians were bleeding from scrapes and cuts. Coats and shirts had become makeshift slings for broken arms. People walked down the middle of the street, dodging stalled automobiles and debris. Sirens clanged as the police cars and ambulances and fire engines responded to an unknown number of injuries.

She estimated she was half an hour into her journey when the ground beneath her weary legs trembled. Cutting through Westlake Park, she stepped around toppled pepper trees, their roots ripped from the earth. She made her way to a bench at the edge of the lake and sat down to catch her breath. Her shoes had rubbed blisters on her heels and toes. When she used her hankie to wipe perspiration from her forehead and upper lip, she dirtied the fabric. Examining her face in the mirror of her compact, she scrubbed away a layer of accumulated dust and grime. Removing her hat, she let the late afternoon breeze cool her head. Seeking to impose a semblance of order in the midst of chaos, she applied her pocket comb to her tangled hair.

She was still a long, long way from West Hollywood.

Trudging along Wilshire, she remembered the 3rd Street bus shelter. Maybe this far from downtown, she could catch a ride. She was unnerved by the prospect of continuing her journey alone and on foot, after darkness fell. Looters were out in force, and the authorities would be too busy dealing with emergencies to uphold the law while the shuddering city continued to crumble.

She squeezed onto a bus that carried her northward along Crescent Heights Boulevard to Sunset. Hobbled by sore feet and aching arches, she limped along the Garden of Allah's pathways, stepping around the flagstones pushed out of place by the powerful tremor. Puddles surrounded the swimming pool where its contents had swept over the edge. But the fountain in front of the Rogers bungalow was intact, spouting as usual, and its goldfish still darted about in their watery world.

"Thank God." Lela hugged her tight. "Our prayers are answered."

"I'm all right." She gazed at Ginger, impeccably dressed and coiffed. "You look beautiful," she croaked.

In the kitchen she opened an upper cabinet. Two beakers tumbled to the floor, scattering shards of glass and shattering her fragile composure. She knelt to pick up the broken pieces, and her tears dripped onto the linoleum.

She filled an intact glass with water and soothed her parched throat. Taking it to the living room, she intruded upon a tense discussion between mother and daughter.

"You're not going out tonight, it's too dangerous. These aftershocks could go on for hours. There may well be another quake."

"I don't care. He wants to take me out. I want him to."

"On this, of all nights."

"Oh, for goodness sake, Mother." Ginger was barely

keeping her exasperation in check. "He's already on his way."

Phyllis slipped away to run a bath. She removed her dusty clothing, piece by piece, and climbed into the tub. Hot water seeped into her blisters, making her cry out. She scrubbed every inch of her body. She soaped her hair and rinsed it. She wished she could soak her strained and throbbing legs all night long, but the water was rapidly cooling.

When Lew Ayres arrived, Lela invited him in and asked about the road conditions.

"Passable," he replied, "around here. Long Beach got the worst of it."

Phyllis and Lela followed the couple to Lew's Packard. Along Sunset, the streetlamps and signs were shining as though nothing catastrophic had occurred.

When Ginger and her date drove away, Phyllis said, "He seems pleasant. And he's not Howard Hughes."

"Neither is he Mervyn LeRoy. I prefer a movie director to an actor. Come along, let's get you fed. You must be starving."

Hours later, her cousin returned wearing a dreamy expression. Her lipstick was smudged at the corners.

"Kissing on the first date?" Phyllis teased, when they were out of Lela's earshot.

"What if I was? When a girl's dream man wants to smooch, she doesn't say no."

"You've turned into a real-life Anytime Annie." She held a finger to her brow. "She only said 'no' once, and that's because she didn't hear the question."

Ginger pinched her arm. "When Lew Ayres asks, I'm always going to say 'yes!'"

The earthquake's effects on the region were devastating. Thousands had been seriously hurt and dozens were dead. The film studios had expected a shutdown forced by union opposition to wage cuts, and now a natural disaster had abruptly curtailed production. Motion picture companies provided their portable light units and studio electricians at no cost, to undertake night repairs throughout the city. All branches of the Armed Forces had mobilized, providing manpower and supplying medical facilities with additional staff to deal with casualties.

At breakfast on Sunday morning, Ginger glanced up from the newspaper, saying, "The studios are shutting down tomorrow, just as the banks are reopening on President Roosevelt's orders. Not that we'll have any money to deposit, if the union strike happens."

"Look on the bright side," Phyllis commented. "You and Mr. Ayres will have plenty of free time for canoodling."

Lela spent hours on the telephone, drumming up assistance for earthquake relief and relaying the information scrawled on her notepad to friends. Concluding one conversation, she hung up the phone. Before she could pick up again, it began to ring.

Ginger looked up expectantly.

"Yes, I'll accept the charges," Lela said. "Hello, Virginia. She's fine. We all are." She fell quiet for a moment. "Quite right, Helen should have been in touch. Things have been unsettled, you understand." Again, she listened. "No, the phone service wasn't out, yesterday or today. I've been making lots of calls. Yes, she's here. Just a minute." She extended the receiver towards Phyllis.

"Mama. You heard about the earthquake?"

"I've been so worried! Every time I tried this number,

it was engaged. Why didn't Lela let us know you're all right? Why didn't you?"

"I'm sorry."

"Your stepfather and I want you to come home. Right away."

"Why?"

"Never you mind why. I'm your mother. I've decided it's best that you leave California. Ginger's getting married. She won't be around to keep you company, and—"

"She and Mr. LeRoy broke it off."

"Did they? That's too bad. Do you have a job?"

Reluctantly, Phyllis admitted that she did not. "But Lela says RKO will renew my three-month option. And I might be auditioning for a play."

There was a long silence. "Put her back on."

Phyllis handed the phone to her aunt. Steeping in disappointment and dread, she listened closely to Lela's side of the conversation, desperate for clues.

"Don't even bother showing that document to a lawyer, Virginia, it's not necessary. It wasn't notarized, and I don't claim that it's legally binding."

Last year when Phyllis left Oklahoma City, her stepfather had referred to a document. Since then she'd heard nothing about it, and its contents were a complete mystery.

"Please calm down. I told you then, and I tell you now, while your daughter's underage I won't contest your right to make decisions. I'm a mother too, remember."

After Lela hung up, Phyllis clutched her arm. "Don't make me go. Please!"

"Dearie, it's not up to me. You're a minor, and your mother is your legal guardian. She'd have to give permission for another contract extension, and I doubt we can convince her to. I'm supposed to send you back before your birthday. You'll return to your high school and finish the term."

"Nobody ever told me about the signed document. What does it say?"

"Virginia granted me authority to act on your behalf with regard to your professional activities. I committed to housing and feeding you, and enrolling you in the studio's academic program, and generally acting in *loco parentis*." Lela flipped the page of her notebook and reached for her pencil. "Lots to do in a short time. Travel arrangements. Packing up your things. Oh, and we'll need to request a record of the school credits you've earned working with your tutor. That might take time, but I'll hurry things along. What else?"

"I can't understand why she wants me back."

"I suppose the quake revived her memories of the gas explosion when you were a baby. She almost lost you and Jean. A person doesn't ever recover from that kind of fear. I still have nightmares about Ed McMath stealing Ginger from me when she was a toddler."

"I'm going to miss you so much, Phyl," Ginger said. "Just remember, after you turn eighteen you can come back to us. Your parents can't stop you."

"That's a whole year from now. Plus one month. RKO will forget all about me."

"We won't let them. Anyway, they signed you to a seven-year contract, and they might not terminate it. Even if they do, you'll be all right. Trust me, starting over in show business isn't impossible. I've done it lots of times. From vaudeville to Broadway to making those early pictures in New York to singing and dancing in Hollywood. Isn't that right, Mother?"

Lela glanced up from her jottings. "Hmmm?"

"She shouldn't worry about her future. When she returns, she'll be older, and have a chance at bigger roles.

She won't need a chaperone on the set, or any schooling." Turning to Phyllis, Ginger added, "While you're away, we'll write to each other. Like we did when I toured all around the country on the circuit."

Lela had written most of those letters.

Ginger, on the threshold of major stardom, was already so entranced by Lew Ayres that she couldn't stand being apart from him. When would she have time to correspond with her kid cousin?

CHAPTER 24

Phyllis hated leaving California in this season when opening citrus blooms perfumed the breeze, and apple and pear orchards blanketed the landscape with their pink and white blossoms. As her departure date loomed, she helped Lela gather clothing and necessities for people left homeless by the earthquake. At RKO, they obtained a letter suspending her contract—temporarily, Lela had emphasized. When told that the person who could provide documentation of earned academic credits was at lunch, Lela parked herself in the office to wait. Phyllis decided to look around the lot for former castmates.

A production secretary confirmed that Betty Furness had clocked in that morning.

"I know she's assigned to a hospital picture," Phyllis said.

"*Emergency Call* should be on lunch break. You might try the Commissary. Or wardrobe."

She didn't find her friend in the crowded dining room, so she went to the building where costumes were created and stored. The female smoker standing outside was recognizable from her shoulder-length cinnamon bob and willowy figure.

"I do like your hat," Katharine Hepburn told her.

"Doug Fairbanks wore a similar one in his Robin Hood picture, and I think the style might suit me. I'm waiting for Mr. Plunkett, who's showing me sketches for my *Morning Glory* costumes. Are you here for a fitting?" Her manner of speech was unique, each word emerging with staccato force.

"I'm looking for someone. I wanted to say goodbye to her before I leave town."

"Where are you headed?"

"Oklahoma City. My parents want me to finish high school. I don't want to go. But I have to, because I'm underage."

The actress sat on the bottom step. After expelling a cloud of smoke, she gazed up at Phyllis. "Might as well take your time to develop, as a person and as a performer. At twenty-five, I'm just beginning to hit my stride. This work demands toughness, in body and in mind, and an independent spirit. We have a motto in my family, 'Listen to the song of life.' There's a tune specially composed for you, that's certain. Eventually you'll hear it—loud and clear."

"You're a lot like Jo March," Phyllis realized.

Katharine bowed her head. "I consider that a great compliment."

"Your family didn't object to your becoming an actress?"

"Mother is a progressive, not the sort of woman who wants her daughter confined to the drawing room, dispensing tea. If this acting business leads me to a dead end, and my song of life changes to a different key, I'll cultivate my other skills. I might become a championship golfer. Or an Olympic swimmer. To be weak, to give up, is to be doomed—I learned that at an early age." Katharine inspected the stub of her cigarette. "I'm the one who found my poor brother after he hanged himself.

The memory haunts me, always will. But it solidified my determination to stand strong, no matter what befalls me, or batters me. We must never let setbacks defeat us."

"A good friend of mine committed suicide." Phyllis swallowed. "Peg Entwistle. Compared to her, I wasn't very ambitious. Now I am, even though I'm about to leave Hollywood."

"What's your name?"

"Phyllis Fraser."

The actress extended a long, slim hand. "I'm Kath. Best of luck to you, Phyllis. I hope you'll come back. And don't forget to bring that ambition along with you!"

When Lela took Phyllis to La Grande railway station, they discovered that its Moorish dome had tumbled down during the earthquake. Her niece's departure was depriving her of a confidante with whom she could share her opinions of Ginger's admirers, or talk over the plots of her scripts, or discuss articles in *The New Yorker,* or take to the Santa Monica beach bingo hall. No longer a chaperone, she lacked a reason to visit RKO.

Ginger found a remedy for her restlessness.

"When I was a kid in Fort Worth, you directed plays for the community theatre. I read in the paper that the Spotlight will mount a full season. Why not get involved?"

Lela wasted no time following this timely suggestion. She met with Mr. Edward Kay, and his cohort Mr. Russell, at their playhouse on Cole Avenue. She touted her credentials in community theatre and shamelessly dropped the names of her valuable film industry connections. Recognizing that she could be an asset to their enterprise, they invited her to direct a play. She left their office with *The Funnyman* tucked under her arm. Before the week was out, she'd arranged for auditions and devised a rehearsal schedule.

Earl Eby, the handsome actor from the Pasadena Playhouse, came to the tryouts. She doubted he was ready for a leading role, but she offered him a minor one and he accepted it.

Gathering her cast for a read-through of the script—which she'd altered extensively, with the playwright's permission—she reminded them that Los Angeles and surrounding areas still reeled from the earthquake. It was their civic responsibility to provide the theatre-going public with light-hearted, professionally presented entertainment. And she pointed out that if her players hoped to capture the attention of agents and movie producers and directors interested in fresh, undiscovered performers, they must apply themselves.

Back at home, Ginger was bursting with news.

"I'm lucky I wasn't fired today. It's possible I wrecked any hope of ever being taken seriously as an actress. I did something very silly."

Lela, tugging her script from her briefcase, prepared herself for the worst. "Go on."

"When I reported to the *Gold Diggers* soundstage, I received music for a song—the opener. I was having trouble learning the words. So I skipped lunch to work on it with our rehearsal pianist. For a lark, I started singing the chorus in pig Latin. Malcolm thought it was funny and had me do it again. Halfway through he stopped playing. He looked like he'd had the shock of his life. I turned around and found Darryl Zanuck standing right behind me!"

"He heard you," Lela groaned.

"After I apologized for joking around, he asked me to sing my nutty pig Latin version again, all the way through. He wants me to do it that way when we shoot the number tomorrow." Ginger sat down and removed her shoes. "Mervyn thought it was a great idea."

"Your clowning could've gotten you in big trouble. Here's a letter from Phyllis." Lela handed it over.

"Oh, how nice! Aunt Virginia and Uncle Nick hosted a welcome home dinner and a dance in her honor at the country club."

Lela settled at her desk to make notes in her script. "Are you going out tonight?"

"Lew is picking me up at eight."

"Don't stay out late. You need to be in excellent voice when you record your song track tomorrow."

"Today I tried on my dance costume for 'We're in the Money,' the big opening number. The chorus girls and I really will be 'in the money.' We're wearing it. And not much else. Our outfits are made out of coins. Big ones, little ones. Very shimmery."

Word of Ginger's vibrancy and verve had filtered out to the major studios. Harry Cohn of Columbia invited her to make a screen test, and after reviewing it with his executives, he called her in to a private meeting.

Huffing with indignation, Ginger described her ordeal. "He chased me around his desk. He never got his hands on me, but he sure tried."

"How did you keep him off?"

"I reminded him that I'm acquainted with his *wife*, and I threatened to tell her. Then he turned mean. Said he wouldn't sign me because my mouth is too big and my smile too broad and I'm not a beauty. I told him that great beauty doesn't always equate with great talent. Then I stormed out." Ginger shook her head, no longer strawberry blonde but dyed a shade akin to platinum, because every studio wanted its copy of Jean Harlow. "If I'd let him paw me, he would've given me a contract."

"Maybe. Maybe not. Next time a studio boss sends for you, I'm going along."

Ginger's alarming encounter at Columbia paid an unexpected dividend. RKO requested her test and promptly offered her a three-picture deal. She needed to complete a one-film commitment to Universal, in a starring role opposite Lew Ayres in *Don't Bet on Love*. Lela suspected a lot of billing and cooing would take place on the set. She wouldn't mind if their mutual infatuation outlasted the production, she was so grateful to the actor for pushing Howard Hughes out of the frame.

On opening night of *The Funnyman,* the crowd outside Lela's theatre spilled into the street. She called in the police to control the motor traffic and maintain order—and as a calculated publicity stunt. She was delighted to see all the celebrities in the audience.

She couldn't recall the last time she'd blushed, but when Earl Eby presented her with a corsage, her cheeks blazed with pleasure. There was also a note in which he expressed his hope that after their professional relationship ended, they might achieve a closer friendship. With a rush of giddiness, she tucked it in her handbag.

Positive reviews reinforced her determination to make her mark in local theatre. When not devoting her time to directorial duties, she would oversee the competing project that her daughter thrust upon her.

"There's no reason to keep this poky bungalow," Ginger declared. "I've had enough of our rambunctious neighbors and their noisy pool parties. At day's end I prefer relaxation and quiet. With RKO paying me a crazy amount of money, I'm buying a house for us. Somewhere in the hills, with a view, but not too far from the studio. Wouldn't you like that?"

"Very much. As soon as my play closes, I'll look around."

Lela's extensive search led her to Dundee Drive and a three-bedroom, two-bath Spanish-style residence. Set within a velvety green lawn and surrounded by trees and flowering shrubs, it had the requisite panoramic view.

Ginger approved her choice. She was willing to pay the shipping of Lela's custom-designed furniture, languishing in a New York warehouse.

"It would cost as much, if not more, to buy what we need," she said. "You know what I like best about the house? Phyllis can have her own room when she returns."

CHAPTER 25

Ginger's costume, what there was of it, consisted of shining coins of various sizes. Hundreds, maybe thousands formed the cape draped over her shoulders. A string of them circled her neck.

"She's hardly wearing any clothes!" Phyllis whispered to her friend Doris. "Neither are the dancers."

Ginger reprised her song—in pig Latin—and the camera zoomed in, framing her face in an ever-tightening close-up until it filled the giant screen. Phyllis grinned at this exemplary demonstration of one of her cousin's greatest, but least known gifts, now revealed to the film-going public.

Gold Diggers of 1933 was a movie about making a musical about the Depression. The humor was sharp and witty, the situations gritty, and the grim concluding number was heavy with social commentary.

"When I go to a picture," Doris said as they were leaving, "I don't like to be reminded of hard times."

At Kerr's department store they looked over the summer frocks. Made of inexpensive, lightweight fabrics—organdy and voile and dotted swiss—the sleeves were short and fluttery, and the skirts were long and flowing. Phyllis chose one in a lime sherbet color and bought matching pumps that cost less than two dollars. Spotting a Father's Day sale table, she picked out a beautiful silk tie to give her stepdad on Sunday and had it boxed and gift-wrapped.

From there she walked to the Classique Salon, to help her parents tidy up at the end of the workday. Perplexed by the *Closed* sign facing the street and drawn window shades, she tapped on the glass portion of the door.

Miss Florence, the senior beauty operator, opened it. "Helen! I wasn't expecting to see you this afternoon. One of the girls gave your mama a ride home."

"Is Daddy here?"

"There's no telling where *he* is." Venom poured from that tiny pronoun. "Do you have change for bus fare? I can give you some."

"I've got it, thanks."

"Tell Virginia if there's any way I can help her out, she must let me know."

What's wrong with Mama, she wondered as her bus lumbered along the dusty streets. If she's sick, Miss Florence should've said so.

She got off at the stop nearest her house and walked the rest of the way, as quickly as she could in heeled shoes. Bounding up the concrete front steps, she hurried inside and flung her shopping bags and pocketbook onto the sofa.

"Mama? Jean? Clara?"

She heard the maid's heavy tread coming up the basement steps.

"Miss Florence said my mother left the shop early."

"Lordy, she forgot you'd be going over there after your picture show. She come back over an hour ago. By herself." The final two words received ominous emphasis. "Go on up to her. I need to start supper. She might not want any, but you and Miss Jean will."

Phyllis rushed up the narrow staircase and made her way to her parents' bedroom. The chenille coverlet was obscured by all the clothing spread across it. Daddy's bureau drawers were gaping open, empty of all contents. Mama sat in the corner rocker, staring bleakly at a jumble of shoes on the floor.

Looking up, she said flatly, "I can't do any more."

"Do what?"

"Pack his things. I won't have him coming here to fetch them. I'll need to call a taxi to deliver all this to the hotel."

Phyllis knelt beside her. "What happened?"

"I might as well tell you everything—by morning it'll be all over town. Your stepfather is carrying on with one of the Classique girls behind my back. I caught them. I reckon she wanted me to, the shameless, sneaky little slut. I kicked over his desk chair—bruised my good leg." She rubbed the mark on her shin. "And I chased her out of the storeroom. Then I fired her, right in front of the staff and all our customers. She ran off. I told him to get lost."

"How do you know he's at a hotel?"

"He telephoned. All apologetic, saying it wasn't fair to you girls to break up our family and destroy our business because he made a silly mistake." Mama's pale hand swept at the tears sliding down her mournful face. "With so many divorces in the Owens family, nobody will care if there's another one."

"I don't understand men."

"Oh, there's no mystery about them. A man will take whatever he can get, whenever he wants it. Never thinking how his stupidity will hurt the poor foolish woman who believes in him. I might have known a man that handsome, with all the charm in the world, would show his true colors one day."

When Jean returned from a swim meet, eager to share

news of her win, Phyllis informed her about the sudden rupture in their household. While Mama was in the bath, they bundled their stepfather's clothing and hats and shoes into dust sheets, and placed his cufflinks in a cigar box.

"I bought a tie for us to give him on Sunday," Phyllis remembered, placing the ones he already owned on a stack of handkerchiefs and undershirts.

"Return it," Jean said waspishly.

Their mother had to unravel her business relationship with her husband, as well as their marriage. She'd invested a significant portion of her gas company settlement, that legendary "fortune," in the Classique, and was determined to withdraw as large a sum as she could. She offered to sell it to Miss Florence, an arrangement that would permit her to stay on as stylist and cosmetic consultant.

"Mr. Nichols will take nothing out of the place but his scissors," Mama declared. "He's supposed to provide maintenance for you, Helen, while you're a minor, but I doubt he will. When you go back to California, Lela and Ginger will have to support you."

Phyllis suspected Mama would put her on the westbound train straightaway if she didn't have an entire year of high school to finish. Her eventual return to Hollywood was an economic necessity, and there she would be wholly dependent on Lela and Ginger unless she found work. Not for her those lofty artistic ambitions Katharine Hepburn had espoused—she had to pursue the acting profession to avoid becoming a charity case.

Whenever she felt blue about her prospects, she studied the snapshots Ginger sent of her lovely house in the hills. The one she liked best showed the bedroom that was allotted to her. When Lela wasn't at her theatre, she was decorating. RKO had given Ginger a secondary role in a musical, *Flying Down to Rio*. But she didn't mind, she wrote, because it paired her with an acquaintance from her Broadway days.

> Fred Astaire and I haven't danced together since he helped me out with the *Girl Crazy* choreography. My New York pal Harold Ross used to take me to see Fred and his sister Adele in their revues. Back then, Fred and I dated a few times. His act with Adele broke up when she got hitched to the son of an English duke. Then he married a society gal—named Phyllis! They've moved out here so he can dance in pictures. When I said I'd be glad to help him out, he said, "You can start by not stepping on my toes!" Our dance coordinator, Hermes Pan, has terrific ideas for us. This funny flight down to Rio will be a fun journey. I hoped RKO might use me in a dramatic picture, but you know me, I can have a good time whatever I'm doing.

The postman brought her no more letters from Ginger or Lela, even though she sent them her new address. She and Mama and Jean moved to an apartment building on North Robinson Avenue, yellowish brick with a red tile rooftop that reminded Phyllis of California. It was an equal ten-minute drive to the Classique salon and Classen High. She and her sister had to share a bedroom and help out in the kitchen, now that Clara Willingham came only twice a week to clean and cook. One benefit of the family crisis was an improving sibling relationship. Phyllis cheered for Jean as she competed for the state swimming championship. Jean volunteered to fix her hair before parties and dances. They went to the cinema together.

When their stepfather returned from New York, where he'd explored the latest techniques in hairdressing and permanent wave applications, he opened the Nichols

Salon. An active promoter, his newspaper ads described his skills and featured his photograph. Whenever Mama turned to her favorite page in the *Daily Oklahoman,* she saw her estranged husband's handsome, smiling face inserted among notices of engagements and weddings and parties and out of town visitors.

The letter Lela tucked in with her Christmas card announced her acquisition of an unused church building as her personal playhouse, with funds provided by Ginger. She was forming a repertory company and wanted to audition Betty Furness for the inaugural production. Her Hollytown Theatre would serve as a training ground and a showcase for the undiscovered. One day, she declared, Phyllis would tread the boards that Earl Eby had been scrubbing and shining.

Phyllis took solace in her studies and school activities. She was a member of the yearbook staff and edited the school paper. She and her friend Doris wrote a gossip column. One frigid January night, at a gala honoring local girls' clubs, she was crowned Queen—undoubtedly due to her status as Oklahoma City's resident movie actress. Nearly a year had passed since her return, and nowadays hardly anybody wanted to hear about her months in Hollywood, or the celebrities she'd encountered there.

On her eighteenth birthday, her stepfather telephoned.

"Watch the mail for a check," he told her. "Use it for your train fare to Los Angeles. Anything left over is spending money for when you get there."

"That's not necessary," she told him, speaking softly so Mama wouldn't overhear.

"Sure it is," he insisted. "I set aside money for Jean, too, so she can train as a beautician. You'll always be my daughters. I'm not likely to have more."

As the last week of term sped by, her classmates had difficulty concentrating on their studies. With the approach of commencement, those who would graduate talked excitedly about their chosen colleges or the jobs they had accepted, conversations from which Phyllis felt excluded.

After lengthy, long-distance discussions with her sister, Mama received another document to sign, paragraphs of legalese granting Lela and Ginger authority over Phyllis's career and prohibiting interference. Phyllis, recovering from an untimely bout of the measles, didn't understand the necessity, but it was additional proof that her future was wholly entrusted to the Rogers women. With undisguised relief, Mama folded the pages and placed them in an envelope.

In contrast to the tears and anxiety her mother had displayed at their parting two years ago, she was calm and dry-eyed when the taxicab arrived. After hugs and kisses, Phyllis handed her suitcases to the driver.

From behind the steering wheel, he asked, "Where you headed, Miss?"

"The train station."

"Travelin' far?"

"All the way to Los Angeles," Phyllis told him.

"You're goin' out there to be a movie star, aren't-cha? Well, good luck to you."

"Thanks. I need it."

But not as much as other girls do. I've got Ginger and Lela on my side.

PART II: 1934-1936

Ginger has no real intimate friends, outside of her cousin, Phyllis Fraser.

–Photoplay, 1935

CHAPTER 26

From the largest balcony of Ginger's hilltop home, Phyllis simultaneously felt separated from Los Angeles while also knowing herself to be embedded in it. She always ate her breakfast there, when morning's pastel glow colored the distant expanse of the city. Within hours the midday blaze would arrive, and the summer heat would make it shimmer. Later, the landscape would absorb sunset hues of gold and orange and blue and purple. Lastly, after nightfall, she would gaze upon a vast constellation of tiny lights.

Dragging her attention from the perpetually entrancing vista, she picked up her plate and empty coffee cup and went inside. Like the outside stucco walls, all the interior ones were painted white. Contrasting wood beams and clay tile flooring gave the house color and character, and its rooms had arched doorways. Lela's elegant Art Deco furniture didn't quite the fill the spaces, but the absence of clutter lent a refinement that other homes lacked. Ginger had acquired a player piano, a popular feature at the parties and game nights she hosted for her closest friends and colleagues.

In the kitchen, the housemaid was taking stock of the larder's contents. Phyllis rinsed her plate and cup and dried them. The silence was broken by the repetitive clack of clippers slicing through greenery. The German gardener came weekly to mow the lawn and douse the flowering plants in the large terracotta pots on the patio and the landing of each outdoor stairway.

Ginger was officially a resident but rarely present, spending her spare time—and her nights—with Lew Ayres. Although Lela voiced no objection, knowing it would go unheeded, she reminded her daughter of the dire consequences for the couple if the press discovered they cohabited, and toppled them from the lofty pedestal of respectability. Ginger's lover wouldn't suffer greatly from exposure, but any hint of scandal would destroy her wholesome appeal.

Lew preferred the privacy of his bachelor home to the clubs and restaurants that exerted magnetic appeal for attention-seeking performers. When he ventured out with Ginger, his close-lipped smile indicated amusement at the Hollywood social scene. An enthusiastic musician, he played banjo and guitar and keyboards, and he composed rhapsodies for the piano. He was passionate about astronomy and had corresponded with Albert Einstein. His devotion to tennis matched Ginger's. They spent hours on the court, in friendly competition or battling another couple as a formidable doubles partnership.

No longer a contract player, Phyllis served as Ginger's unpaid personal assistant and live-in secretary, supporting the efforts of Patty Dubuis, official holder of those titles. She routinely visited the publicity departments at RKO and Warner Brothers to collect an ever-increasing accumulation of fan letters, or to return stacks of autographed photos. If asked, she accompanied the star on personal appearances at film premieres, ribbon cuttings, and other events. Ginger earned less money than her dancing partner, but her latest contract tripled her salary. After the runaway success of *Flying Down to Rio*, and with high expectations for *The Gay Divorcee,* the studio would pair her with Fred Astaire in *Roberta,* a third musical production.

Phyllis had purchased a new typewriter and a secondhand car, both necessary for performing her assigned duties. Pooling birthday money from her stepfather and a sum borrowed from Ginger, she'd bought herself a five-year old Ford coupe for one hundred and twenty-five dollars—cash—after Lela persuaded the seller to cut thirty bucks from his asking price.

She selected a hat from the half-dozen lined up on her closet's top shelf. Grabbing her keys from the dresser, she gathered up her handbag and her satchel and quickly slipped out through her private door before the household dogs could follow. Hooligan, the trained police shepherd, was wonderfully obedient—unlike Yankee, the fluffy mongrel. Phyllis sometimes delivered one or the other to Ginger's dressing room or soundstage, to keep her company between takes.

Her journey down from the hills carried her along green, shadowy canyons to the main thoroughfares of Los Feliz and Franklin, and along Gower Street to RKO's complex. A secretary in the publicity offices handed over several manila envelopes filled with letters from Ginger's legion of fans. With no urgent responsibilities, Phyllis went in search of friends who might be in the adjacent building housing the wardrobe and makeup departments.

Peering into the first suite, she spied a tawny head and a russet one. The mirror reflected two familiar faces.

"Phyllis!" Katharine greeted her. "Had a feeling you'd come back."

Their single fleeting conversation had taken place over a year ago, before her departure for Oklahoma City. Since then, the star had won the Best Actress Oscar for

Morning Glory, and according to Ginger, was already vying with veteran Irene Dunne for title of RKO's reigning queen.

Dawn O'Day jumped up to hug her but was hampered by the cape protecting her gingham dress. "You went away before we could celebrate our birthdays together."

"We will next April," Phyllis assured her. "I thought you belonged to Warner Brothers."

"I did one picture here—*Finishing School.* Your cousin was in it, too. Hardly anyone will see us, though. The League of Decency condemned it."

"Not surprised," Katharine drawled. "Those boarding school girls really know how to cut loose. I met plenty of them at Bryn Mawr." To the woman rolling a section of her thick hair onto a curling wand, she said, "Don't fry me."

"I'm here to test," Dawn continued, "for *Anne of Green Gables.* Tom Brown is Gilbert. Do you know him?"

"We used to date. Casually," she added, in case the other girl was interested in him.

Dawn's stylist finished braiding her pigtails. "You're ready for makeup."

"My mother says I'll look younger without it." Sliding out of her chair, she beamed at Phyllis. "Hope I see you again soon."

When the younger girl was gone, Katharine commented, "Dawn O'Day. Dawn of the day. Ridiculous. She says she's been in the business since she was a tot. Why didn't anybody tell her to ditch that dreadful stage name?" The dark eyes shifted from the mirror to Phyllis. "Are you glad to be back in lotus land?"

"I'm here to stay," she replied. "I have no other home. While I was away, my best friend and I saw *Little Women* three times. Doris would love to have your autograph."

She felt around inside her purse for the notebook she carried to track her daily errands.

Turning back to her reflection, the actress said flatly, "I never do that."

"I didn't know."

"No reason you should." Katharine glanced at the stylist. "Are we finished? If you keep curling my crop, I'll look like Shirley Temple instead of a hillbilly woman."

The woman consulted the sketch she'd worked from. "I've done what I'm supposed to do, Miss Hepburn."

The actress got up and headed for the door. Halting, she turned back and told Phyllis, "Oh, very well. Give me a piece of paper and something to write with."

Phyllis handed over her pad and fished a pencil stub from the depths of her pocketbook.

Katharine signed her name, crossing the H and the T's with a long, straight line. "All righty. Here you are."

"Thanks, Miss Hepburn."

"Kath, to you. Don't go telling people, now."

"I won't. And I'll swear Doris to secrecy."

"Much appreciated. You're a good egg."

As assistant to the star, Phyllis attended rehearsals for *The Gay Divorcee.* Hermes Pan, who collaborated with Fred Astaire on the choreography, taught it to Ginger. The dance studio was off-limits to all observers when Fred practiced, either with Hermes standing in for Ginger or with Ginger herself. Guards stationed outside the door stopped people from entering—curious executives, the director, the cameraman, or an errand girl like Phyllis.

An unlikely heartthrob, Fred had prominent ears and a jutting chin and spindly limbs, and the extent of his baldness was concealed by a well-anchored hairpiece.

Gregarious and amusing on screen, he was deadly serious and observed strict privacy when developing a routine. He and Ginger and Hermes worked together from morning till late into the evening, and on weekends as well.

"What I like most about those two," Ginger confided, "is the way the dances they create always develop the romance plot and reveal character traits."

"Do you offer suggestions?" Phyllis asked.

"Sometimes. Hermes knows I want my steps to be every bit as complex as Fred's. But I don't complain or make waves—no matter how much I'm tempted."

Phyllis witnessed the preparation of the athletic routine that would close the picture. A speeded-up version of "The Continental" started in waltz-time, and concluded with a swinging beat. Hermes vaulted Ginger onto tabletops and swung her over the furniture, while Fred stood in front of them to judge the view from a cameraman's vantage.

Her favorite number was the deliciously lyrical "Night and Day," the only Cole Porter tune retained from the original Broadway and London stage productions. She and her cousin arrived at the studio early on the day it was filmed. Phyllis handed Ginger the plate of buttered toast while a hairdresser curled the strawberry blonde hair and wound a false braid around her cousin's head. A wardrobe woman helped Ginger into a pale silk chiffon evening gown, lightly embellished with ruffles, held up by narrow sequined straps and plunging behind to expose the tapering bare back.

They found Fred, supremely dapper in his tuxedo, waiting in the section of the soundstage where the terrace restaurant set had been constructed. A beach with waves in motion would be projected on a screen behind them—Santa Monica standing in for Brighton, England.

"Ready, Ginge?" he asked, shortening her name as he always did.

"I'd better be, after all our weeks of preparation."

The camera tracked the couple as they sparred, and gradually the playback music came in under their dialogue. Fred began crooning along with the pre-recorded track of "Night and Day." When the song concluded, he approached Ginger, who avoided him, until she was reluctantly drawn into their dance duet. The rhinestones in her necklace glittered under the lights, and ruffles at the bottom of her gown swept the floor as she circled around in Fred's arms. His coat tails whipped about. Together they covered every inch of the space, their romantic clinches interspersed with spirited tap steps, and their synchronous movements were as mesmerizing on the first take as on the twelfth.

Phyllis stood with Hermes Pan, who swayed in time with the music, unable to keep still while watching dips and swirls he'd devised and had often performed in rehearsals. She envied future cinema audiences, who hadn't witnessed all the practice and pain and sweat. They would be captivated by the gracefulness and charm of the elegant couple in constant motion. The movie screen would reveal a gorgeous, atmospherically lit ballroom, not the rough carpentry at the edges or the lighting rig or the camera's bulk.

During a break, Hermes turned to her. "Ginger says you're still contracted to RKO."

"Not that anyone else remembers," she replied. "Or cares."

"I can change that, with a word to Mark Sandrich. You should be there in the nightclub when Fred performs his opening number to 'Don't Let it Bother You.' Where you'll be seen."

Grateful for this kind suggestion, she didn't admit that

visibility on the screen mattered less to her than returning to the studio's payroll.

When her big day arrived, wardrobe put her in a black gown and handed her a pair of dangling drop earrings. She was sent to one of the tables on the riser overlooking the cabaret stage. Her table mates, two older male day players and a blonde woman, were experienced background performers. A property man handed out finger puppet dolls like the ones manipulated by Fred and the French-accented chorus girls.

"You can walk them across the tabletop while Fred and Ed talk to each other," Sandrich informed the extras. "But when he's dancing keep your attention on him and refrain from creating distractions. After he finishes, give him a standing ovation."

Hermes stood close to the dolly operator, nudging him to indicate a shift in the choreography that required the camera to move closer or farther back. Each time Fred completed his routine, he conferred with Hermes or Dave Gould, the dance director.

Phyllis sat through multiple takes, no hardship at all, the action was so entertaining. When the director called a halt, she carefully descended the steps to the stage level.

Katharine Hepburn, a sideline spectator, gave her a jaunty wave and then came over, saying, "My, what a treat that was! Simply fascinating. Mr. Astaire's footwork looks positively effortless. He inspires me to take up tap dancing." She indicated Hermes, enthusiastically thumping Fred's shoulder. "I'll ask the production department to send that fellow to my house to give me some lessons."

When Ginger found out the studio had fulfilled this request, she groused to Phyllis, "Of all the nerve! She must've heard *Flying Down to Rio* brought bigger box office to RKO than *Little Women.* Well, if Miss Hepburn means to replace me in musicals, I'm going to compete for the dramatic parts they're handing out to her like Halloween treats."

"She only took up tap dancing for the exercise," Phyllis consoled her. "That's what she told me. Hermes visits her every Saturday."

"And the studio pays him to do it, I bet."

Because Ginger's next picture wasn't a musical, her schedule was less hectic than it had been during the summer, and her secretary Patty Dubuis required no more help with errands, phone calls, and correspondence. When Phyllis bemoaned her idleness, her aunt proposed an activity that would fill her free time.

Lela's catlike smile narrowed her eyes. "You can play the ingenue in my Hollytown production. Provided you don't mind curbing your social life for a while."

"If I'm cast, I wouldn't."

"Don't worry about that, dearie."

"What's the play?"

"*A Man of Ideas*. A satire on the advertising business."

Phyllis attended auditions, along with a host of hopeful actresses, and won the role. Not because her abilities exceeded theirs, she suspected, but due to blatant nepotism.

"You're perfect for the role," Lela assured her. "We'll polish your performance in rehearsals, and you'll feel quite confident by opening night."

Earl Eby received the minor but showy role of a radio executive. A veteran of the Pasadena Playhouse, he was a fixture at Lela's upstart theatre on North New Hampshire Street, barely a ten-minute drive from the Rogers house on Dundee. In addition to performing, he handled basic carpentry and served as caretaker of the facility.

According to local legend, the deconsecrated Episcopal church that housed the Hollytown players had been built in one day. The single interesting feature of its plain exterior was an extremely narrow, stone-clad bell tower. The spacious former sanctuary was windowless, making it an ideal venue for plays and concerts. Performances always sold out, Earl told Phyllis, because there were just ninety seats—fewer than in the Classen High School auditorium. A modestly sized stage accommodated simple sets. Actresses and actors had separate dressing rooms. Lela had demonstrated her flair for decorating in an entrance lobby that doubled as a reception room for coffee service during intermission.

Phyllis looked forward to the green room camaraderie Peg Entwistle had relished. But as the youngest person in an ensemble that was primarily male, and known to be the director's niece, forming friendships proved tricky. She was surprised to discover how much she enjoyed performing on the stage—a great deal more engaging and demanding than loitering on a film set, waiting for the camera to roll.

Lela conducted rehearsals with her customary firmness and efficiency, and her cast responded to her painstaking direction. Occasionally the playwright, Dore Schary, sat in. A former actor who had appeared in summer stock back East and on Broadway, he reminisced with Lela during breaks, and they traded names of show business acquaintances. Phyllis overheard her aunt telling him of her desire to direct a play in New York.

Phyllis played the young inventor's girlfriend, an aspiring actress. Dim-witted and clumsy, Judy was willing to do anything to further her career and naively trusted the businessmen who readily exploited her ambition and her sweetheart's creations. Her one astute comment was a reference to theatrical producers who invariably wanted something from a girl before offering her a part.

"Is the line supposed to be funny?" she asked Dore Schary. "Or is it a criticism?"

"In this town, it'll get a laugh. The men who routinely

prey on starlets won't even recognize themselves. Or if they do, they haven't shame enough to squirm." He gave her a sympathetic smile. "Does Judy's misfortune match your experiences?"

"Not at all," she assured him. "Lela and Ginger watch out for me. They told me all the cautionary tales about Hollywood predators, and I heard even more from other actresses." She knew she was fortunate not to have worked for the most notorious, Harry Cohn at Columbia and L. B. Mayer of MGM.

After inquiring about his conversion from performer to playwright, she admitted her hope of writing a script.

He regarded her with heightened interest. "You've got literary talent, too?"

"Lela thinks so. I've been showing her my scribbles since I was kid. I mess around with short fiction, stories with quirky or unexpected endings. I'm thinking about writing a full-length novel. Or a three-act drama, for the stage or the screen. I've got lots of ideas. But not quite enough time to develop them."

"Find it," he advised.

She combined the return of Ginger's signed publicity stills and a lunch date with Dawn O'Day in the RKO dining room. Phyllis told her about the conversation with Dore Schary.

"He says I should make up my mind about whether to concentrate on a novel or a screenplay."

"I know what you can write about." Dawn brandished her fork. "A pretty Oklahoma girl who comes to Hollywood and makes it big in pictures."

Phyllis laughed. "That would be a fairy tale."

Polishing off her apple pie, Dawn heaved a satisfied sigh. "I've never been so thankful for cafeteria food. What we had in Santa Cruz was terrible." After relating incidents from her days on location shooting *Anne of Green Gables,* she asked, "Have you met Henry Willson?"

"Occasionally. He's one of Tom Brown's pals. I've read his articles in a motion picture magazine."

Dawn's red-gold head bobbed up and down. "He's also an agent. He's helped me so much, and he even promotes actors and actresses he doesn't represent. He was a founder of the Puppets Club and was involved in getting them a clubhouse where they host teas and parties and charity fundraisers. It sounds like fun. I bet Henry would let us join. Or we could ask Tom to take us."

Detecting the wistfulness in her friend's voice, Phyllis said, "I'm game, if it's not a night when I've got rehearsal at Hollytown."

"Henry's after me to change my name. For the second time."

"What was it before?"

"My birth name is Dawn Evelyn Paris. When I started in theatre, Mother decided I should be Dawn O'Day. Henry says I should be Anne Shirley, that it'll make a great story and get me lots of publicity. My mother is already talking to the legal department about it. What do you think?"

"Perfect! You're so much like her." Cheerful and chatty, but with an endearing sensitivity.

"'Anne with an e' kept me company backstage, when I was younger. I used to borrow a stagehand's flashlight so I could read those books between scenes. These days my time is taken up with reading scripts." Grinning, she added, "And fan magazines."

"I'm halfway through F. Scott Fitzgerald's *Tender is the Night.* Ginger's friend Harold Ross sent it to us. One of the characters is a young film actress."

"I hope she gets a happy ending."

Phyllis smiled across the table. "Let's hope we do, too."

CHAPTER 27

The proximity of the Puppets' Beachwood Canyon clubhouse to the Entwistle residence dredged up memories of Peg. Driving along the familiar stretch of road on a Saturday night, Phyllis confronted the looming Hollywoodland sign, that shrine to ambition upon which her distraught friend sacrificed herself. Watching each section flash in sequence, then all together, she fancied Peg was communicating from the beyond.

Have faith in yourself. Never lose hope, like I did.

Alternatively, it might be a warning.

Unfulfilled dreams of success will end in disappointment and despair.

She and the newly-christened Anne Shirley received a hearty welcome from Henry Willson, agent to some party attendees and advisor to others. Both were well acquainted with handsome Tom Brown and a number of the other hardworking, fun-loving actors—Ben Alexander, Junior Durkin, and Jackie Coogan. A vivacious blonde introduced herself as Mary Blackford before she was absorbed into a cluster of actresses. As the exodus began, the first ones to depart grumbled about having to clock in at their respective studios at an early hour.

When putting on her coat, Phyllis dropped her purse.

The contents scattered across the floor, and she knelt to retrieve her compact, car keys, and comb.

Henry Willson held up her notepad. "Why do you carry this around?"

Taking it from him, she explained, "Out of habit. When I wrote the gossip column for my high school newspaper, I could record any interesting information I dug up about students and teachers. Now it's handy for keeping track of Ginger's schedule and my play rehearsals. Shopping lists. Telephone numbers."

Mary Blackford, pursuing a lipstick tube as it rolled across the floorboards, looked up. "Henry writes for *The Hollywood Reporter* and *New Movie.*"

His dark eyes remained fixed on Phyllis, and his forefinger stroked his receding chin. "I've seen you in the clubs and restaurants along the Strip, with your cousin. Maybe I should use you as a stringer."

She stood up. "I'm not ratting on Ginger. Or anybody else."

"I'll pay."

"Nope. Even as a lowly bit player, I got stung by the innuendo and exaggerations printed about me in your fan rags."

He acknowledged the truth of it with a self-conscious laugh. "Our readers are insatiable, and they like knowing that the stars aren't immune to conflict and drama in their private lives. Instead of feeding me information, how about writing an article? Everybody longs to know whether Ginger and Fred are pals in real life. And we're desperate to find out when she and Lew Ayres are tying the knot. And what that bossy mother of hers thinks about their romance."

"Not interested. You gossip columnists are constantly urging stars to marry each other. After they do, you start counting the days till they announce their divorce." She turned to go.

"I'm an agent, I've got clout with the studios. All of them. I'll get you a role in a good picture. Credited."

Mary handed over the lipstick. "You might ask Ginger's permission to write about her personal life," she suggested. "That way she's assured of an honest and positive story instead of a hatchet job."

Henry nodded. "Your cousin understands the value of favorable publicity. I get Junior's okay before I put him in my columns."

Junior Durkin, his housemate, had twice portrayed Huckleberry Finn on screen. He was buddies with Jackie Coogan, the equally popular and perennial Tom Sawyer.

"Think it over," Henry urged, his voice as silky as his elegant necktie. He eschewed the casual California attire adopted by his fellow East Coast transplants.

Eager to wrap up this conversation, she replied, "I will."

Tom Brown, Anne's co-star, walked them to the car. "Persistent as the devil, isn't he? But it serves us well. He devotes time and effort to promoting us and our careers."

Maintaining a neutral tone, Phyllis replied, "I've noticed."

"Here's a fresh gossip item," Tom went on. "One that hasn't appeared in Henry's column—not yet. Ben Alexander has a crush on you. He wants to ask you out."

Like Anne and Tom, Ben had performed since childhood and freelanced at many studios. Lela couldn't hear his name without recalling that she'd known him since he was four years old. Pleasant company, easy to be with, devoted to his friends, fond of sports, he was exactly the sort of fellow Phyllis preferred. After appearing with Lew in *All Quiet on the Western Front,* the pair had become great chums, and he'd also worked on Ginger's pictures.

"If he asks, I'd accept," she told Tom.

"Great! I'll let him know." He flashed his impish grin at Anne. "See you on the set tomorrow, kiddo. And make sure you know your lines."

"I already do," she shot back. "Can you say the same?"

Phyllis disliked Henry Willson's tactics, but his offer was undeniably tempting. By writing for a motion picture magazine with mass circulation and a national readership, she could justifiably claim to be a professional writer. Provided her cousin was willing to cooperate. She'd always refrained from asking favors, except for the occasional request to borrow a hat or a dress or a fur coat.

Ginger was devoting her half-hour lunch breaks to preparing Phyllis for a screen test, assisted by Hermes Pan. In the empty rehearsal hall, they took turns drilling her in a complicated dance routine until her soles were sore and her back ached from strain and she was dizzy from the sight of her bouncing reflection in the mirrored wall.

Completing a particularly demanding and exhausting session, she sat down on the floor to remove her tap shoes. As she recovered her breath, she asked Ginger's opinion of Henry Willson.

"Can't say I've formed one."

"He wants me to submit an article for his magazine. About you. And Lew. But I'm not doing it unless it's okay with you, and you tell me exactly what I can and can't say. And I'd make Henry swear he won't embellish my copy after I turn it in."

"The RKO publicists are constantly churning out items about me, and they're only superficially connected to the truth. I can trust you be accurate. Let's talk it over with Mother."

Lela's view coincided with her daughter's, and she

concurred with Henry Willson's assertion that the publicity would be beneficial. Phyllis posed a series of questions to Ginger and incorporated the responses into her piece. After polishing the text to her satisfaction, she read it aloud to her aunt and cousin, who expressed approval.

"Lew won't take issue with anything you've written," Ginger assured her.

"Your style is distinctive," Lela commented. "Breezy and lively, yet insightful. Not easy to pull off."

"I'm no rival to Louella Parsons," she acknowledged.

Ginger patted her shoulder. "You don't have a mean streak. She and her kind play favorites. And after they've built up their pet actors and actresses, they shred them into bits, to prove how powerful and important they are."

Lela frowned. "I'm not convinced this Willson character's magazine is worthy of you."

"The article was his idea. He commissioned it."

"I'm glad you have a chance to earn money with your writing, but I'd rather see you contributing to a quality publication."

"Like *The New Yorker*? I'm hardly as sophisticated and erudite as the writers edited by your friend Mr. Ross."

"Always set your sights high, dearie."

When Phyllis accepted a dinner invitation from Ben Alexander, they double dated with Ginger and Lew. At a popular restaurant on Sunset, the foursome encountered Henry Willson at a nearby table, encircled by Junior Durkin, Tom Brown, Mary Blackford, and Will Rogers's daughter.

Excusing herself, Phyllis went over to present the article she'd been carrying around in her handbag.

Henry unfolded the pages and held them up to the candlelight. "Your opening paragraph is fantastic. I can't wait to read the rest. Where should I send your check? It'll be our standard fee."

"My address is printed at the end."

"Terrific. So, how soon will wedding bells chime for the lovebirds over there?"

"I haven't heard a thing about it."

"When you do, I'm the first person you tell. I can make it worth your while."

Lela watched with pride as her daughter and her niece crossed the dining room: a striking, blonde movie star and a pretty, clever brunette.

"Sorry we're late," Ginger said, seating herself.

"Autograph seekers," Phyllis explained, stripping off her gloves. "They waylaid Ginger."

"They asked for your signature, too."

"Even though they'd never heard of me."

"Someday they will."

After they finished the main course, Ginger ordered an ice cream sundae. Phyllis and Lela had coffee.

"I didn't want to spoil our lunch with bad news," Ginger said, blotting her lips with her napkin, "but I can't put if off any longer."

Lela folded her hands in her lap. "Go on."

"Our Hollytown Theatre is operating with a significant deficit, and I'm afraid the receipts for your play won't cover rent and all the expenses of running the place. I can't keep it going for you indefinitely. It pains me to say so, but it's time to close down."

This was an unexpected development, and a hard blow to her pride. "I see," she responded, and was impressed by her ability to appear stoic and unconcerned.

"You should congratulate yourself on your artistic successes, even if they weren't profitable. Your productions drew lots of movie producers and casting directors, and the studios are offering contracts to your players. And wasn't Earl Eby approached for a Broadway show? The playwrights you've presented are screenwriters now or having their works staged in New York. Because he's lost Betty Furness to MGM, RKO's main casting man wants to see Phyllis in *Man of Ideas.*"

"Won't you let me mount one more show?" Lela bargained. "I promised Earl he could direct *Strangers All.*" She'd done so in order to keep him in California. With her.

"I suppose so. You'll be too busy to do it yourself."

She lifted her brows. "Doing what?"

"I didn't intend to tell you today," Ginger hedged. "Lew and I have decided to get married. You've got a wedding to plan."

Lela reached across the table to grip her daughter's hands. "Oh, my dearest girl. Are you quite sure?"

"Absolutely. We aren't making a public announcement yet," Ginger declared, "so neither of you can tell a soul. Re-takes for *Divorcee* are finished. Fred and I haven't yet heard how soon *Roberta* starts production. Lew and I hope we'll be married before it does. You know how he likes to study astronomy and astrology. He says he can determine the luckiest date for our ceremony."

Accept it, Lela told herself.

She had to maintain outward complacency and conceal her inner turmoil. After years of diligent labor and plenty of luck, Ginger had achieved top billing and real stardom. This was no time to retreat into domesticity. And she was concerned about her effervescent, easygoing girl's devotion to a deeply serious introvert with the habits of a recluse. True, they each had a sense of humor, and were eminent performers in their separate spheres. But if they shared a burning passion for anything but tennis, Lela hadn't detected what it might be. Lew was a good hearted, generous, and sympathetic soul. He'd traded in his expensive motorcar for a cheaper model to avoid ostentation at a time when other people were suffering from financial reverses and outright poverty. Lela hoped he could accept her daughter's occasionally lavish tastes and wouldn't feel diminished by her exorbitant salary.

Exchanging vows, she acknowledged, was an improvement over secretly living together as an unwed couple. That harpy, Louella Parsons, had spies all over town and would eventually discover the truth—if she hadn't already done so.

Ginger broke the silence, saying, "We want a simple, intimate service. Just family and friends."

"The Little Church of the Flowers would be ideal," she decreed.

"Whatever you think best."

"And for the reception, the Ambassador Hotel. You're too prominent to exclude all the important people you've worked with since we came to Hollywood. Or the ones who might be interested in employing you in future. The guest list will be at least two hundred. If not three. We'll buy your trousseau in New York. Now, about the engagement party—"

"We don't need one, Mother. A notice to the press, shortly before the event, will suffice. You know how carefully Lew and I guard our privacy."

"Have you decided on your attendants?"

"Phyllis will be my maid of honor. For bridesmaids, I'll ask Janet Gaynor and Mary Brian. I expect Lew will want Ben Alexander for a groomsman," she added with a conspiratorial nod at her cousin.

"Someone has to give you away," Lela reminded her. "It's part of the ritual. Not Leland Hayward. It's best to keep your relationship with your agent strictly professional. Earl could do it. I'll ask him tonight. He's coming to the house for dinner and to run lines with Phyllis."

Swift to perceive the connection between the engagement and Hollytown's impending closure, Lela believed Ginger's claim that the decision had been a difficult one. That's why she'd sugarcoated her unpleasant announcement with a happier second one. Only a selfish and unchristian mother would begrudge her daughter's desire to spend her money setting up household with her new husband. But losing her little theatre was a personal as well as a professional hardship, because it had allowed her to be with Earl by day and at night. Even though she had no intention of following Ginger and Lew down the aisle, having a man in her life was proof—though she needed none—that an independent female of forty-two was entitled to a romance. Every aspect of one, emotional and physical.

Nonetheless, her conscience whispered, even after my daughter's marriage I will be financially dependent upon her. She purchased the house I live in. The car I drive. She pays the servants. And she's supporting Phyllis and me in the high style and comfort to which we've grown accustomed.

Ginger folded her napkin. "We've got to be on our way. Hermes Pan is teaching Phyllis a tap routine this afternoon. When the studio agrees to give her that screen test, she'll be ready."

Their protégée's dubious expression indicated uncertainty on that point.

CHAPTER 28

"Another Hollytown sell-out," Earl Eby whispered to Phyllis as they waited for the curtain to part.

Lela's productions always drew a crowd, and all week long the newspapers had touted this opening night.

Peering through a gap in the fabric she saw Ginger, swathed in furs and every inch the rising star, flanked by Lew and Lela. Ben Alexander and Anne Shirley, recipients of her complimentary tickets, sat in the same row. Phyllis tried not to think about the casting directors who had been invited and had come to assess her performance. She was nervous enough.

She drew laughs in all the right places, and her confidence grew as each of her scenes unfolded. Immediately after she delivered her final line, the curtain fell and the cast members lined up to take their bows. The auditorium's compact size amplified the applause, and it was decidedly appreciative.

In the morning she found a telegram from her mother and sister beside her breakfast plate, offering best wishes. She tucked it into her neglected diary for safekeeping, thankful to be remembered.

Not many days into the run, RKO contacted her to schedule a screen test. Despite her cousin's insistence that favorable reviews were responsible, she knew where credit was due.

"You convinced them to give me another chance."

"I didn't have to. You impressed the studio scout, just like I knew you would."

On the appointed day, she was pleased to encounter familiar faces in wardrobe and the makeup room. She was slightly acquainted with the director. Bolstered by her past experience as a bit player, she felt more comfortable and confident in the presence of the camera than she'd been as a novice. Stepping away from the bright light, she felt she'd acquitted herself as the professional actress that she was.

Evidently RKO agreed, unearthing her dormant contract and renewing their option. The executives had a vested interest in keeping Miss Rogers happy—the highly profitable *Flying Down to Rio* had staved off financial disaster, and the release of *The Gay Divorcee* would create a surplus. Employing their newest star's cousin was a low-cost investment that would pay a large dividend in goodwill.

Phyllis harbored no illusions about her abilities as an actress and doubted she'd ever be more than competent. Film work was generally dull, but pleasant enough, and provided her with an income while she pursued more meaningful credits as a professional writer and photographer. Because she was of legal age, she no longer had to obtain a judge's approval to accept employment. Ginger asked her agent Leland Hayward to review the terms stipulated in each wordy clause. Compared to the sum her cousin received, a salary of seventy dollars a week was a pittance, but Phyllis regarded it as a fortune.

After the paperwork was signed and submitted, Ben Alexander took her to the Trocadero for a festive dinner. They joined Henry Willson, seated with Junior Durkin and Anne Shirley and Tom Brown and Mary Blackford, the lively satellites who orbited him. Mary introduced her date as Michael.

"Love your dress," she told Phyllis. "What we girls wouldn't give to have the clothes you wear."

"Mostly Ginger's castoffs, or loans she never takes back," she admitted. "Even though her closets are stuffed with the latest fashions, she prefers slacks or shorts or her tennis whites."

"She looks lovely in anything. So do you." The blonde patted the empty chair between hers and Henry's. "Sit here, and let's get to know each other."

Mary, she quickly learned, was a native of Philadelphia but grew up in Kansas City, Missouri.

"That's where I was born," Phyllis told her. "My sister and I lived with my grandparents after my father died, because my mother was working in another town."

"There's a coincidence! I lived with my grandparents, too. A pity we didn't meet back then."

"Maybe we would have, if Mama hadn't taken Jean and me to Oklahoma City. I'd probably still be there, only Ginger and her mother decided I should come here and try my luck in show business. How did you start out?"

"After my mother, brother, and I came to Los Angeles, a man from Warner Brothers saw my class play and encouraged me to enroll in their studio school. I got nice notices in a stage production of *Ah, Wilderness* with Mr. Will Rogers—your fellow Oklahoman. Warners cast me in *Sweetheart of Sigma Chi* after your cousin went over to RKO, because they thought I resembled her. But when it comes to dancing and singing, I'm no substitute for Ginger Rogers."

"Are you working on something now?"

"Developing patience," Mary said with a laugh. "Fox

borrowed me for *Love Time,* the Franz Schubert story. A glorified bit part. And you?"

"I'm waiting to find out." With a nod towards her date, she added, "Ben and I are celebrating my RKO contract. I passed my screen test."

Phyllis spent the morning on the balcony with Ginger's script for *Romance in Manhattan,* her latest RKO assignment. She'd reached the halfway point when she heard the telephone.

"It's for you," Lela called from the living room. "Anne Shirley."

Anne interrupted her greeting with the frantic question, "Have you heard the awful news? About Mary Blackford?"

"No." Phyllis steeled herself for an announcement.

"After she left the Troc last night, she was in a terrible car crash."

CHAPTER 29

In a quavering voice, Phyllis asked, "Is Mary dead?"

"No. Her date is. He was so drunk that he drove into a telephone pole on Santa Monica Boulevard. A witness called for an ambulance to take Mary to the nearest emergency room. This morning she was transferred to Methodist Hospital. Her skull was fractured, her neck is broken, and she can't move any of her limbs. The doctors told Mrs. Blackford that if she survives—they think she will—her paralysis may be permanent."

"How did you find out?"

"Henry Willson phoned me. I want to be there for her, but Mother can't take me, and I don't drive. Even if I did, I'm too upset. That's why I'm asking you. You're always so calm and collected."

Phyllis didn't feel that way after learning that the cheerful, lively girl who had chatted with her hours ago was lying motionless in a hospital bed.

"We might not be allowed to see her," she told Anne.

"I don't care. We can leave notes. I've already written one."

She hurried to her room to remove her shorts and blouse. Dress, stockings, hat, gloves—she went through the dressing ritual, scarcely aware of what she was doing. This was the second time her professional prospects improved at the same time tragedy befell an actress friend. Two years ago, shortly after RKO informed Phyllis that her contract option would be renewed, Peg Entwistle decided to jump to her death.

But Mary's still alive, she told herself.

When Lela heard where she was going, and why, she said, "I'll order an arrangement from Flossie Selznick's flower shop and have it delivered to the poor girl's room. With all our names on the card."

She hugged her aunt. "I should've thought of that myself. Thank you."

"And I'll say plenty of prayers. God's powers are infinite, far greater than those of medical men."

Phyllis had no time or patience for a dissertation on Christian Science beliefs. In childhood her injured leg was saved by her doctors' expertise, and the nurses had been so kind to her. At the moment, her prayers were chaotic but constant. If she weren't in such a hurry to collect Anne, she'd stop at a Catholic parish to light lots of candles for Mary.

Anne scarcely spoke during their drive, apart from admitting her anxiety about being in an automobile so soon after their friend's accident. Phyllis cautiously navigated the busy thoroughfares leading to South Hope Street.

"I'll drop you at the door," she offered. "Go inside and inquire about Mary while I park. I'll find you."

When she entered the building, the stark white walls and pervasive silence and distinctive smell carried her back to her long-ago hospitalization, and those days and weeks and months as an invalid.

"You're a family member?" the woman at the reception desk wanted to know.

"A friend. I'm looking for the blonde girl who recently came in. Miss Shirley."

"I sent her to the lounge. There's a large group in there. Down the corridor and to the left."

The waiting room was crowded with Puppet Club members and permeated with smoke from their cigarettes. Those who spoke did so in hushed, concerned tones.

Anne came over, saying mournfully, "Nobody's allowed in Mary's room except her mother. The x-rays showed that her spine is shattered. Her head is all wrapped in bandages and her neck is in a cast. The rest of her is attached to a body brace. She's starting to come out of the sedation they gave her. Because she's paralyzed, she's not feeling any pain at all, except for a bad headache."

"When she's well enough," Phyllis said, "she'll receive physical therapy. Like the polio patients."

"The doctors were frank with Mrs. Blackford. She told us Mary might be bedridden for the rest of her life. She won't walk or play tennis or—or feed herself. Can you imagine living like that?" Tears welled in Anne's brown eyes.

Phyllis pulled her close. "Look how many of her friends are here. She won't have to endure it alone."

Ben Alexander came to stand with them. "Mrs. Blackford is a widow. It's unlikely she can pay the hospital bills, or the costs of Mary's care after she's released. They have little enough to live on without losing Mary's Warner Brothers salary."

"We'll help them," Phyllis said.

"How?" Anne wondered.

"When I was a kid in Oklahoma City and got run over by a laundry truck, the newspapers wrote about it. Department stores sent me clothing. Grocers extended credit to my mother and never sent her their bills. The toyshops emptied their shelves to provide me with games and puzzles—enough to share with everyone else in the children's ward. Local businessmen took up a collection to pay for my treatment. Think of all the money in Hollywood—all over Los Angeles. Studio bosses. Bankers. Agents. Lawyers. Every day, we're surrounded by famous actors and actresses. We'll ask them for donations. We can stage a benefit show, and sell tickets, and give the proceeds to Mary. Henry Willson's a publicity man. If he's as well-connected as he claims, he'll convince the biggest names to perform for free."

A faint smile was replacing Ben's glum expression. "I'll talk to him. We'll start organizing right away." He bent to kiss her cheek—his first overtly affectionate act in view of their friends. "We won't help Mary by loitering here, feeling sorry for her. She'd hate that."

"She needs more than money," Phyllis continued. "It's lonely, being an invalid. We have to provide companionship. I'll inquire about visitor hours," she volunteered, "and draw up a rota so we can take turns coming to see her."

"That's a great idea." Anne blotted her face with her handkerchief.

Ben clapped his hands together. "Attention, everybody. On Sunday night we're meeting at the Puppets' clubhouse. Come one, come all, and help us plan how we can best support Mary and Mrs. Blackford. Spread the word to the folks who aren't here."

On leaving the hospital, Anne said to Phyllis, "I'm so glad you thought of things we can do for Mary. Her life—if she lives—will be miserable."

"Not when we're around to cheer her up. And we will."

For so long September had been her favorite time of year. It marked the beginning of the school term, and the purchase of clothes and shoes and pristine composition books to be filled. The seasonal aroma of freshly sharpened pencils was firmly imprinted. She clearly recalled the sound of unused chalk squeaking across a blackboard. And the class bell signaling the great shift of humanity from room to room. But two years ago, Peg's suicidal leap had tainted this month, and Mary's misfortune increased her aversion.

As she and Anne left the hospital, Phyllis longed to slip into the unscarred days of October.

When selling war bonds as a Marine and while touring with Ginger on the vaudeville circuit, Lela had visited every sizeable United States city during every season of the year, and no place she'd seen compared with New York during autumn. Most of the tourists had returned to their towns and hamlets, leaving Manhattan to its residents, and the heat that rendered it so oppressive in summertime had vanished with them. The air was pleasantly sharp, and Central Park's trees showed faint color.

She and Ginger occupied a suite at the Waldorf Astoria that increasingly resembled a florist's shop, with arrangements arriving hourly from acquaintances and strangers. They were seldom able to enjoy the flowers. The bride-to-be had wedding gown fittings at the couturier's salon and shopped for her trousseau at department stores and exclusive boutiques. Milliner Lily Daché would create a hat for Ginger and her attendants, and a theatrical costumer would sew custom dresses in different pastel colors for all three attendants.

"Aqua for Phyllis," Lela decided after a close study of fabric swatches the designer brought to the hotel. "It complements her coloring. Janet Gaynor will look lovely in yellow. And this periwinkle for Mary Brian. "

"That's 'Eleanor blue.' At the President's inauguration, Mrs. Roosevelt wore that color." The dressmaker smoothed the square of crepe.

"Oh." Because so notable a Democrat had worn it, Lela said, "Maybe we should reconsider."

"Let's not," Ginger objected. She was admiring an array of gauntlet style kid gloves, stamped with her initials.

"You've got all the necessary measurements?"

"My seamstresses are standing by to complete your order, Mrs. Rogers."

"Is there anything else, dearie?"

"I'm satisfied. If we're late, Harold will fuss at us."

They took the elevator down to the ornate lobby. Their friend sat stiffly on a sofa, his hat on his knees. He stood up, tall and lanky, then had to bend over to kiss Ginger's cheek and shake hands with Lela. In appearance and manner, he reminded her of certain untamed animals. His bushy hair stuck upright like a porcupine's quills. He moved with a lumbering, bear-like gait. A badger's gruffness overlaid the doe-like gentleness that he occasionally revealed to his intimates.

His eyes, set beneath caterpillar brows of charcoal gray, settled on Ginger. "You're determined to marry that matinee idol?"

"I couldn't remain a spinster forever after losing you to that Frenchwoman you eloped with."

"Don't tease. You were never serious about me, I accepted it years ago. Don't think I blame you." Bony fingers ploughed the thatch bristling atop his head. "I'm an ignoramus. No education. No wit. No polish. The antithesis of Mr. Eustace Tilley, my magazine's effete, top-hatted cover caricature."

"That's why we're so fond of you."

Spreading her napkin across her gabardine skirt, Lela inquired about the state of the magazine.

"Revenues are up. Thanks to the Prohibition repeal, ad dollars from the distilling industry are flowing our way. I was able to restore the staff salaries we had to cut back a year ago. I'm still the scariest editor in the business, male variety. Katharine White is terrifying in her own particular fashion, and keeps me in line—or tries to. Next year *The New Yorker* will be ten years old. Who thought it would last so long? God knows I didn't."

"My niece Phyllis reads it cover to cover."

"Glad somebody does. A lot of people merely glance at Thurber's cartoons before throwing the damned thing out with the rubbish." He stuck a cigarette between his thick rubbery lips and slowly drew his lighter from his inside coat pocket.

Despite his dismissive tone, Lela knew he took pride in his achievement. She admired his commitment to producing a publication worthy of its finest writers—E.B. White, Alexander Woollcott, James Thurber, F. Scott Fitzgerald, Dorothy Parker, and all the rest in his stable.

Ginger said, "We're longing to meet your new wife."

His shoulders lurched in a shrug. "Marie Francoise isn't yet proficient in English. You don't speak French."

"That doesn't matter. Why don't the two of you join us at the Starlight nightclub on the top floor? She'll enjoy the music and the dancing."

"Can't," he replied with characteristic brusqueness. "It's my poker night with Bennett Cerf. The bastard will fleece me, as usual, but his liquor and cigars are the best."

"Why play with him," Ginger asked, "if you always lose? I prefer games I can win."

"Which is all of them," Lela commented.

Occasionally pausing to insert a forkful of food into his mouth, Harold flung questions at Ginger. He wanted to know if the studio treated her well and how she liked being a star and whether Astaire was a pansy. Then he asked about earthquakes.

"Nothing as bad as the one last year," Ginger assured him.

"Dangerous place, California." He wagged his head. "Raging wildfires. That big mudslide at New Year's. Why don't you come back to Manhattan?"

"I just might," Lela volunteered.

He regarded her incredulously. "Leave Ginger? I'll believe that when I see it."

"Why not? She's leaving me to get married."

"That's not true," her daughter protested. "Anyway, Lew and I hope to set up house not too far from you and Phyllis. And after I'm out of your way, you'll be able to spend more time with Earl."

"Earl? Who's he?"

"Mother's beau. She's written him at least three letters since we've been here and has his framed photograph in our hotel room."

"It's not going to be a double wedding, is it?"

Lela held up her hand as if taking an oath. "I'll never marry again." She was relieved that her daughter hadn't mentioned that Earl was twelve years her junior. Eleven and a half, she amended. Everyone said she looked nearly as young as Ginger, and her outlook was just as youthful. So why not enjoy the attentions and company of a man who was thirty-one?

When the waiters removed their dessert plates, Harold glanced at his wristwatch. Cursing, he declared that he'd been absent from his office too long. "I appreciate your choice of hotel—it's an easy ten-minute walk from my lair."

Lela stopped at the front desk, saying she had to

check for any phone messages but hoping she'd received another letter from Earl.

"Is this all?" she asked the clerk who handed her a single air mail envelope.

"Yes, Madam."

Ginger came up beside her. "From Phyllis. What does she say?"

Lela pulled the flap open. "My goodness," she breathed after scanning the even lines of handwriting. "RKO is loaning her to Mascot Pictures for *Little Men*. Production starts in a couple of weeks. Listen to this: 'Henry Willson owed me a favor for my Ginger article, and I've received my just reward. He represents Junior Durkin, who's cast as one of Jo's boys. I'm playing Mary Anne, his sweetheart.'"

"Good for her. Even better for RKO. They'll pay her usual weekly salary and pocket a larger sum from Mascot."

"Mustn't look a gift horse in the mouth. She hoped to play Beth March in RKO's *Little Women*. Instead, she'll be in its sequel."

"At a Poverty Row studio."

"Makes no difference. We'll cable our congratulations straight away. And arrange a special treat for her once we're home again."

Home. For a short while longer, until the wedding of the year, that was the Dundee Drive house. But she and Phyllis could manage perfectly well in a smaller place, one that was closer to the studios. Eventually, whenever her niece decided to move out, it would become a love nest for her and Earl.

CHAPTER 30

Four days before her cousin's happy event, Phyllis received a telegram from Mama, announcing that Jean had become Mrs. Robert Sylvester.

"Do you know this man?" Lela asked.

Staring at the cable in disbelief, she admitted, "Never heard of him."

"Surely there's no urgency to your sister's marriage?"

If so, Phyllis supposed time would reveal it. "I've got to buy a wedding present."

"Not until you finish recording the ones that arrived today for Ginger. I had to send Patty out to take care of my errands. Oh, and you can telephone everybody in the wedding party to let them know the rehearsal time at Forest Lawn."

Two days later, the participants assembled at Little Church of the Flowers, a suitably picturesque setting for a candlelit ceremony at twilight. On either side of the chapel, broad open arches revealed deep stone troughs planted with evergreens and blossoming plants. Phyllis repeated her solo stroll down the central aisle, pretending to hold an invisible bouquet. Lela required the bridesmaids and Ginger to practice until even-tempered Lew grew impatient.

"You're the director of this show," he told Reverend Huber, the Lutheran minister. "It's time for you to say 'That's a wrap!' Otherwise, I'll be late for my bachelor party."

"Couldn't we work on the kiss again?" Ginger asked, tugging his sleeve. He gave her a quick peck on the lips. "Now you can go. I'll meet you tomorrow evening—at the altar."

Phyllis and Lela had invited a select group of her friends to the Rogers house for hot chocolate and a marshmallow roast in front of the fireplace. The actresses took out their knitting, and late into the night the married ones reminisced about their own weddings—single or multiple.

Ginger got up at dawn. She was too distracted for solitaire or piano playing or any other distraction Phyllis suggested before departing for Mascot Pictures. The studio had chosen a highly inconvenient day for her wardrobe and makeup tests and wig fitting.

In the middle of the afternoon, a production assistant sidled up to her. "Miss Fraser, you need to go now. A police car is waiting for you in the parking lot. Miss Rogers sent it to escort you to her house."

Phyllis suspected it was Mrs. Rogers who had called the cops. Lela's long-ago war service as a lady Marine had lasting effects, and she typically relied on military sergeant tactics.

Driving at high speed, she tried to keep up with the black and white police sedan as it raced along the city streets, lights flashing and siren blaring. By the time they reached the Los Feliz intersection, she was the most conspicuous and embarrassed motorist in all Los Angeles. A cadre of reporters had converged on Dundee Drive. The photographers' lenses were pointed at the house but abruptly shifted in her direction when she pulled in behind the Buick sedan, Ginger's engagement gift from Lew. Holding her purse against her face, she dashed inside.

Ginger circled the dining room table, wearing a shirt so large it had to be her fiancé's, and her sloppiest dungarees. Lela, her golden head bowed over a checklist, calmly sipped from her teacup.

"Thank goodness you're here. But your hair's a rat's nest," her cousin wailed.

Without looking up, Lela said, "It's two hours before we leave for the church. Plenty of time to fix it."

At her cousin's urging, Phyllis changed into her sea-blue coat dress. She and Lela helped Ginger put on the pale green Chantilly lace bridal gown and arranged her matching picture hat. On their way to the limousine parked in the street, Lela thanked the police for removing the newspapermen.

"They didn't have to," Ginger's agent said. "They're already heading for Glendale. You look gorgeous, gorgeous," he said before helping her into the vehicle.

Phyllis sat sandwiched between them. She couldn't imagine why Leland Hayward, who had no role in the ceremony, was riding with them. Or why he felt it necessary to discuss business, citing publicity plans for *Roberta,* in pre-production, and tossing out titles of pictures the studio was considering for their popular dancing couple.

Ginger interrupted him, saying, "After all those years performing with his sister, Fred dislikes being half of a team. As you know, I'm ready to take a break from musicals. Too time-consuming for a married lady. I want a meaty dramatic role."

"You always say that. You're well on your way to the top of the RKO heap. When you get there, you can pick and choose."

"Wrong," she retorted. "They'll keep me singing and

dancing until I'm wrinkled and creaky. *Roberta* requires weeks of rehearsal with Hermes and Fred. When it's in the can, I mean to devote my time to my new husband. So you can tell Merian Cooper and Pan Berman and Mark Sandrich and anyone else you can buttonhole that in the future I want less demanding pictures."

"All right." He leaned across Phyllis, saying grimly, "Listen to me. It doesn't have to be like this. Don't do it."

"Do what?"

"Get married. This is a huge mistake."

"You picked a strange time to give your opinion. Did Mother put you up to this?" Ginger asked crossly.

"She didn't have to. It's obvious to me that your desire for this marriage exceeds Lew's. You're ashamed about living with a man who isn't your husband and afraid that if you're found out, you'll suffer the consequences."

Shocked by his bluntness, Phyllis stared down at her handful of sweetheart roses and feathery fern leaves.

"Lew proposed to me, I'll have you know. He loves me. I love him. It'll be happy ever after for both of us. He was always my dream man. Ask Phyllis. She knows."

"According to your mother, he insisted on a pre-marriage contract. Separate banking accounts. No merging of possessions. Equal division of household bills. He's not willing to take care of you the way you deserve."

Ginger turned her face to the window. Phyllis adjusted her gardenia wrist corsage, hoping that the slowing of the vehicle meant they were approaching their destination.

"Well, well," Leland said. "There's a fine spectacle." He pointed to a roadside hamburger and hot dog stand.

A pair of men in formal cutaway coats and black trousers stood in the parking lot, stuffing their faces.

"It's Lew. With Ben, his best man."

Her agent asked, "What kind of fellow grabs a hamburger before marrying a movie star?"

"One who knows he won't have a chance to eat much—if any—of the food at his wedding reception."

"You know it's bad luck for a groom to see his bride before she enters the church."

"She believes only in the good omens," Phyllis told him. But Ginger refuted this claim by ducking down so her head was below the window.

The vehicle was passing between the Forest Lawn entrance gates. Their chauffeur halted before the stone chapel that could have been uprooted from rural England and planted among the sheltering trees, if not for that single, soaring, incongruous palm.

Ginger handed Phyllis her flowers, a mix of rare long-stemmed orchids and fragrant gardenias, and clutched the crown of her pale green crepe hat to hold it in place. Phyllis climbed out after her and returned the bouquet.

Leland Hayward strolled over to the photographers. Spreading his arms wide, palms open, he shouted, "No pictures yet, boys. You'll get your chance after she leaves the chapel."

"When *we* leave," Ginger muttered. "Lew and me. Together."

Phyllis twitched the back of the wedding gown, smoothing the spots where the starched lace had crumpled. She tweaked her cousin's golden-red curls and arranged the chin-length veil. With a catch in her throat, she said, "You've never looked so beautiful. Or happier."

Lela, elegant in her blue suit trimmed in silver, adjusted the boutonnière in Earl Eby's jacket lapel. Janet Gaynor and Mary Brian blew kisses to Ginger. The setting sun bathed everyone in soft, golden light as they proceeded towards the building, followed by Ginger and Earl. As they waited in the vestibule, soloist Walter Woolf sang the final stanza of "Drink to Me Only with Thine Eyes."

Lela positioned the bridal attendants in their correct

order before she let the best man take her to the front pew. Woolf then started his rendition of "Those Endearing Young Charms." When he finished, the organist plunged into Franz Liszt's "Liebestraum," Lew's choice for the processional.

Phyllis waited for the two actress bridesmaids to finish their stroll down the aisle before beginning her sedate journey past the congregation. Louella Parsons craned her plump neck, absorbing every detail worth sharing with readers of Mr. Hearst's newspapers.

Ginger, her hand resting on Earl's forearm, entered to the familiar strains of the "Wedding March." Her smile was radiant as she glided towards her bridegroom.

When Reverend Huber and Lew glanced at Ben, he thrust one hand into his breast pocket. Frowning, he tugged off his glove and delved deeper, but failed to produce the bride's gold band. A flush stained his cheeks.

"Oh!" Lew gasped. "I forgot to give it to you!" Reaching into his waistcoat, he held up the ring.

The couple spoke their vows and signed the register and received a blessing from the minister. The organist pounded out the traditional Mendelssohn recessional as they paraded past the pews. They paused in the arched doorway for the photographers, while the guests cheered.

Phyllis squeezed into the waiting car with damp-eyed Lela and her Earl. Ben and the two bridesmaids took the second one. Ginger and Lew climbed into the black limousine.

Leland Hayward would have to ask someone to transport him to the Ambassador Hotel.

For the duration of the half-hour drive to Wilshire Boulevard, Lela expressed concern that the hotel staff and the caterers wouldn't follow her explicit instructions. Earl and Phyllis, exchanging glances, took turns assuring her that everything would be handled correctly and according to plan.

The luxurious French Rooms overflowed with two hundred and fifty luminaries. Fred Astaire and his wife were present, so was RKO producer Pandro Berman. Phyllis, weaving through the throng, spied Ginger's former castmates—Claudette Colbert, Ruby Keeler, Andy Devine, and others.

An extensive selection of canapés was spread upon the food tables, including such delicacies as lobster, shrimp, caviar, finger sandwiches of chicken and anchovy paste, all the sophisticated fare that Ginger's character in *Professional Sweetheart* had longed to try. Waiters served highballs and cocktails—the Rogers household might be teetotal, but Lela didn't dare deprive Hollywood's hard-drinking denizens.

"They look like they stepped out of a fairy tale," Anne Shirley burbled. "What was the service like?"

"Exactly as she wanted it to be. Perfectly lovely." Phyllis studied at the couple, trapped in the receiving line of well-wishers.

"Where will they spend their honeymoon?" Betty Furness wanted to know.

"At the fancy hotel in Monterey. Their studios didn't give them much time off." Looking over at her flowers, which she'd deposited on the cake table, she said, "Tomorrow I'm going to the hospital to give Mary Blackford my bouquet. And a slice of wedding cake."

A stir across the room drew everyone's attention. Hedda Hopper, a minor actress, had cornered Louella Parsons. The two women resembled alley cats spoiling for a fight. Lela, attempting to make peace, bravely inserted her tiny body between the pair.

Of all the moments for a public spat, Phyllis fumed. Haven't they any respect for appropriate decorum?

When the combatants parted, she waylaid her aunt to ask, "What set them off?"

Lela, clearly annoyed, replied, "Hedda threatened to establish herself as Louella's rival in the gossip game, claiming she's got superior sources and won't be inventing stories or relying on studio publicists for information. Louella said something mean about Hedda's hat, an Adrian design. Hedda boasted of her friendship with Marion Davies, who the whole world knows is the mistress of Louella's employer. I've seen toddlers that were better behaved."

Waiters distributed glasses of champagne for toasting. Phyllis and Ben took their places with the wedding party to pose with Ginger as she sliced the cake. The Samson Sisters bakery had produced a three-tiered masterpiece, decorated with the couple's entwined initials and surrounded with swags of daisies. Perched on the topmost layer was a foot-high bride doll, its face modeled on Ginger's. She wore a replica of Glory the Purity Girl's wedding gown in *Professional Sweetheart,* and her veil was appliqued with miniature daisies like the one in the film. A miniature groom in his tux stood beside the cake. Bridesmaid dolls, smaller in scale, were dressed in the same colors as Phyllis, Janet, and Mary.

Phyllis, unlike her eager friends, hovered at the rear when all the hopeful single females assembled for the tossing of the bridal bouquet. She didn't want Ben to suppose she had matrimonial aspirations, when nothing could be further from the truth.

CHAPTER 31

Phyllis and Anne and Ben returned to the Ambassador Hotel for a gala benefit fundraiser for Mary Blackford. For weeks, the Puppets had worked hard to secure performers for a live radio broadcast. They peddled tickets and canvassed celebrities for contributions, collecting forty-five hundred dollars that would cover Mary's medical care to date, and the remainder could be put towards future therapies.

Mary, listening from her hospital room, received a personal message from headliner Will Rogers, another of her frequent visitors.

"Hello, Mary, darling," he twanged into the microphone. "How are you tonight? Gee, this is a wonderful shindig your friends have put together here at the Cocoanut Grove. Everyone I ever heard of is here! This is the first time I've ever been in this fancy place, but I promise you, dear Mary, next time I come here I'll bring you with me!"

The attendees responded with deafening applause.

Phyllis and Ben Alexander shared a table with Junior Durkin, her *Little Men* beau, his sisters, Anne Shirley, and Henry Willson. The blonde and lively Durkin sisters always addressed their brother by his given name, Trent.

Like him, they had performed professionally since childhood.

Gracie told Henry, "We don't want him to play juvenile roles after he's done with Franz."

"He's about to turn twenty," Gertrude added. "Too old to be billed as Junior."

"I swear to you," he responded, "for the picture he and Anne begin in the New Year, he'll be credited as Trent Durkin."

Phyllis, aware that she appeared to be younger than her actual age, didn't expect to be cast in mature parts any time soon. Although her role as Mary Anne, Franz's sweetheart, was a minor one, it was a welcome promotion from uncredited, anonymous extra.

While the band was taking a break, Anne and the Durkin girls made the rounds of nearby tables. Ben, primary organizer of the event, excused himself to confer with Will Rogers.

The pair seated across from Phyllis spoke softly to each other, their two dark heads separated by barely an inch. When Henry reached for Junior's hand to caress it, they shared an intimate glance.

Until then, she hadn't comprehended the nature of their relationship.

Had any of the Puppets Club members figured it out? Did Ben know? She wouldn't feel comfortable asking him. Homosexuality in Hollywood was tolerated, provided it was rigorously and artfully concealed from the public. Henry regularly escorted actresses around town, and periodically one of them would be identified as his fiancée. Junior was Anne's current crush, and from the way he'd been flirting with her, he appeared to reciprocate her infatuation.

"Hello, Phyllis." Katharine Hepburn placed a hand on the back of her chair.

"Hi, Kath." She stood up, thankful to have this diversion from life's complexities.

"Pretty gown."

"Ginger had to make room in her closets for all the ones in her trousseau." It was a diaphanous chiffon in her cousin's favorite shade of blue, sewn all over with silver bugle beads.

"Quite the star, Miss Rogers. Receives six thousand fan letters a month, according to Leland Hayward." Her faintly sarcastic tone indicated that Ginger's ascendancy at RKO was a sore point. "Haven't seen you around the studio lately."

"I was loaned to Mascot Pictures for *Little Men*. We're rushing to finish by the end of the month, for a Christmastime release."

"Who plays Jo?"

"Erin O'Brien-Moore."

"Too pretty. Not tomboyish in the least. What's your role, kiddo?"

"Mary Anne. I'm not in many scenes and have hardly any dialogue." She thanked Kath for coming in support of the Puppets' money-raising effort.

"I thought I should, even though I'm pooped after wrapping *Spitfire*. I'm past ready for Leland to take me home." With a glance at Henry and Junior, she added, "My agent and I aren't quite as, ah, chummy, as a certain someone is with his. You looked so lost and lonely, sitting here with those lovebirds."

Kath's remark, devoid of judgment or disapproval, confirmed what Phyllis had already deduced. But her description of the twosome as lovebirds was startling nonetheless.

Were they drawn to one another by reciprocal affection? Mutual physical desire?

She hoped Henry wasn't like those lecherous studio

bosses who chased after starlets, promising eventual promotions in exchange for momentary satisfaction. Manipulating a client that way—male or female—would be unethical. But Phyllis had experienced his method of dispensing favors as a form of payment. After she gave him her magazine article about Ginger, he'd arranged for her to play Mary Anne in *Little Men.*

She gathered up her gold cloth evening bag, Ginger's gift to her bridesmaids, and looked for Anne.

"What a week," she sighed while they waited for Ben and Junior to move through the line at the coat check window. "Ginger's wedding. Mary's fundraiser. Beginning a costume picture."

"Are your dresses nice?"

"Calicoes, mostly, with ruffles at the neck and hem and a bustle in back. I wear a black mourning gown for the funeral scene. I hate my wig, but my hair's too short to curl into ringlets."

"Before the boys come back," Anne whispered, "I've got to tell you what Junior said. He admitted that Henry talked him into bringing me tonight. But he wants to take me on a real date—just us. I really do like him."

"More than Tom Brown?"

"You know we aren't sweet on each other. He's like a brother. Anyway, Anita Louise is his girl. Again."

"For now. His fancy is fleeting. I know from experience."

Anne's brown eyes widened. "Did he break your heart?"

"Impossible. I don't fall in love like other girls do." She wasn't sure whether this was a curse or a blessing.

"Don't let Ben hear you say that."

Little Men opened to positive reviews, praised for its moral message and affecting performances from the youthful players. It was popular enough that cinemas held it over for a second week or longer. Phyllis hadn't expected to be singled out—her role was small, unconnected to the main plot—but newspapers and magazines printed her name in the cast list. All the advertisements promoted the romance element and featured a picture that showed her gazing raptly at Junior Durkin.

RKO's failure to capitalize on her prominence and provide her with significant roles convinced Lela that Phyllis should request termination of her contract. She untethered herself from the studio at the same time they left Dunklee Drive for a bungalow on North Crescent Heights Boulevard. This was the setting for a cocktail party her aunt hosted in her honor. Of the one hundred guests who were invited, the majority were film industry people that Lela felt should be informed about her niece's availability.

But in the aftermath, when the leftover food and the plates and glasses had been cleared away, Phyllis learned why her aunt was so desperate to push her into a job without delay.

"The time has come for you to get a place of your own," Lela announced, "because Earl Eby is moving in with me. I'm sure you understand how improper it would be for you to occupy the residence of an unmarried couple. To protect our reputations, and yours, you'd have to participate in all kinds of subterfuge and secrecy. He and I will do what we must to conceal the truth. But I can't ask that of you."

Phyllis felt her sense of security slipping away. Staring across at her aunt's implacable face, she asked, "Does Ginger know?"

"She soon will. Don't worry, dearie, I'm not shoving you out onto the street. You can start looking around tomorrow."

For the sake of household harmony, she tried to suppress her distress, annoyance, and panic over her impending eviction. Before going to bed, she pulled the newspaper out of the trash can and looked at the classifieds to get an idea of what it would cost to rent an apartment.

The next time she and Anne visited Mary at the hospital, she hid her despondency behind sunny smiles and exuberant giggles. While Anne rattled off the names of all the important producers and directors who had attended Lela's party, its honoree wondered which of them would provide salvation with a significant and well-paying film role.

Still bedridden, their friend no longer wore the stabilizing neck brace. "Except when I'm asleep," she told them, flashing her bright smile. "Next week, or the one after, I'll be discharged to an orthopedic facility for therapy. And then I'm going home!" She beamed up at Phyllis. "I've seen *Little Men*. Henry Willson and Junior Durkin and Frankie Darro borrowed a print and brought a projector and figured out how to point it towards the ceiling. You looked adorable. What's next?"

Sensitive to Mary's feelings about her interrupted career, Phyllis and Anne were reluctant to discuss their professional activities. But she always inquired, out of genuine interest.

"Universal hired me for a series of Sterling Holloway comedy shorts." She'd accepted because they sounded like fun. In future she needed to be pragmatic, basing her decisions on the remuneration offered.

Leaving the flower-filled room, she and Anne retraced their way along the hushed corridor. Phyllis felt a hand pressing on her forearm.

"You're not yourself today."

She couldn't deny it. "I hope Mary didn't notice. I was trying to be cheerful."

"What's wrong? Maybe I can help." Gently tugging, Anne drew her into the lounge where six months ago they had waited for updates on their friend's condition.

When they were both seated, Phyllis explained, "Lela thinks it's time for me to leave the nest." Unable to reveal her aunt's true motive, she added, "She wants me to become independent. And why shouldn't I be? I've got a three-picture commitment to Universal, and my freelance writing. I'm not worried about money." Not much. Not yet.

"But you two haven't lived in the new house very long. What does Ginger say?"

"I doubt she knows about it."

"Tell her. She must have plenty of bedrooms."

"Even if she offered to take me in, I wouldn't accept. She and Lew are practically honeymooners still. In this town full of struggling actresses, I expect I can find someone who needs a roommate."

Anne ducked her head, her straight brown eyebrows drawing together in a frown. Her dejected pose lasted barely a minute, and she lifted a radiant face. "You can live with me. I always wanted a sister, and my mother is so fond of you. Say yes!"

Deeply touched, Phyllis replied, "Not unless you let me pay my fair share of the rent. And the food bills."

"If you insist. See, I told you I could help!" Anne gave her a smacking kiss on the cheek. "Your aunt hurt your feelings, didn't she? I'm sorry about that. But for me, it's a dream come true. We'll put a second twin bed in my room and paint it white to match mine. We can pick out material for curtains for Mother to sew. And we'll invite our friends over for games. Think of all the fun we'll have!"

"Don't forget our joint birthday party."

"The first of many," Anne vowed, squeezing her hand.

CHAPTER 32

Luxuriating in her rare day of freedom from increasing responsibilities, Lela lazed in the bed she and Earl shared, pillows supporting her turbaned head. While showering, he sang something from one of her daughter's movies. His voice was excellent. She resolved to inform the staff in RKO's casting department about it. They needed to know.

Life was lovely. She couldn't recall a happier time.

Although she and Earl appeared in public as a devoted couple, only Ginger and Phyllis were aware that they lived together. He escorted her to restaurants and premieres. He mowed the grass around her bungalow and was a reliable and skillful handyman.

When RKO offered her a job as a scout, she'd negotiated for more responsibility. As director of the Young Talent Department, she managed a drama school and a small theatre, both housed in an abandoned radio station on the studio complex. Her productions would be filmed to serve as screen tests for her pupils—an improvement over those static camera tests that seldom captured a performer's charisma and ability. Her curriculum included lessons in deportment and poise and movement, all necessary to propel a promising player into a lasting career. She had high hopes for her special girls—Phyllis and Betty Grable and Lucille Ball. She had her eye on dear Anne Shirley for the ingenue in *Love is Laughing*, the inaugural production at her studio playhouse.

When experiencing a surge of guilt about foisting Phyllis onto the Shirleys, she reminded herself that she'd done her niece a favor by uprooting her from Oklahoma. Since then she had housed her, provided careful guardianship, and an enviable show business education. And now Phyllis was living with a companion almost the same age. Lela felt no qualms about entrusting her to Mimi Shirley, a perfectly proper Englishwoman, who had nurtured and chaperoned Anne through extreme hardship and the recent successes. She'd invested in two properties, a modest house purchased after *Anne of Green Gables*, and their current home on Alta Vista Drive.

Phyllis filled small parts at studios all over town and earned additional income from her articles for the movie magazine. Even though Ben Alexander was no longer her steady beau, they remained devoted to one another. She had a knack for turning broken romances into friendships.

Ginger's partnership with Fred Astaire had ensured the survival of cash-strapped RKO. In her spare time, she assisted Lew with his home movie productions. Lela worked with her son-in-law as co-producer and co-director for *Little Red Riding Hood*, his most elaborate effort so far. Although many scenes had been filmed in the backyard of the couple's Roxbury Drive house, the cast traveled all the way to Lake Arrowhead to shoot in a forest. Phyllis portrayed the title character, and Ginger appeared as a snow nymph. Ben, the wolf, had helped Lew edit the footage down to a reel and a half. The premiere screening had taken place during one of the regular game nights that Ginger and Lew hosted for their friends.

The telephone cut into her reverie.

"Mother! Thank goodness I found you!" Ginger's wail was piercing. "I tried your office and lots of others."

"I'm off today. What's the matter? Where are you calling from?"

"My portable dressing room. Please get over here, quick as you can."

"Why? What's the urgency?"

"Just come. I'm desperate!"

Her frantic plea was unusual enough to demand immediate action. Lela hurried out of bed, abandoning visions of a leisurely day reviewing scripts and assigning roles and making lunch, to let Earl know about her abrupt change of plans. She put on a suit—appropriate armor for what was presumably a tussle with the bosses—and covered her hastily arranged hair with a severe hat.

Her daughter's trailer was parked alongside the soundstages where an extensive series of Venetian canals had been created for *Top Hat.* Leaning against it was the bicycle Ginger used to transport herself around the lot. Lela rapped once.

Clarkie the wardrobe woman let her in. "Good thing you've come. Louise and I have never seen her like this."

The walls were painted a warm shade of pink, and peach-colored satin covered a chaise longue and the tufted chairs. The filmy pink fabric draping the windows and the dressing table mirror were held back with fluffy rosettes. The girlish, frilly décor was not at all to Lela's taste, but it demonstrated the studio's willingness to satisfy her daughter's every frivolous whim.

Ginger, in pale slacks and an untucked blouse, leaned against the vanity. One leg was extended, the foot swinging back and forth. Louise Sloan, her hairdresser, stood by with hairpins poised, to secure the broad braid wound around the strawberry blonde head.

"Tell Mother what's upsetting you."

"'Cheek to Cheek,' that's what. We're about to have our final rehearsal so we can film the number today. And they say they hate my gown." Ginger's foot stilled, and her body went rigid. "Bernie Newman designed it exactly as I asked him to. When Clarkie was bringing it here from wardrobe, the director called her over so he could examine it. Next thing I know, he shows up. Mark Sandrich stood right where you are now and told me to put on the white one from *The Gay Divorcee*. I pointed out that all the ladies in the audience will remember it. They pay attention to what I'm wearing on the screen."

"And the department stores sell copies of your gowns," Lela stated.

"Everybody will want this one." Ginger marched to the dress rack and removed the subject of the dispute. Feathers cascaded from the high neckline down over the bodice of the ice blue satin gown, and below the waist they trailed all the way to the floor. "Isn't it splendid?" Tugging at a hanger, she pulled out a limp length of pale chiffon. "Look, this was never cleaned or pressed. It's smudged with dirt."

"I don't understand Mr. Sandrich's objection to the costume you commissioned. Clarkie, please find him and ask him to come back. Sit down, dearie, and let Louise finish your hair."

Ginger was studying her elaborate coiffure with a hand mirror when the director responded to the summons.

"Nice to see you, Lela," he greeted her with cool politeness. "Perhaps you can persuade your daughter that her 'Night and Day' costume will read better on film than Newman's bird-like concoction. And it won't shed."

"Do you want me to wear the same shoes?" Ginger

inquired. "The badly fitting ones that were so small and tight that my feet bled all over them?"

Lela intervened, saying evenly, "The older dress is in an obvious state of decay. What's more, Ginger's fans will recognize it. And they'll question our studio's finances if she's seen wearing the same gown twice."

"I'm not the only one who voted against the blue one," he said defensively.

Glancing at the open door, Lela spotted a cadre of men hovering outside. Production staff. Studio executives. Reinforcements. The females were outnumbered.

"If the white is so unsatisfactory," Mark Sandrich went on, "Clarkie can find her something else."

Choosing her strategy, Lela produced a sly, false smile. "Yes, Clarkie, go and get a different costume from storage. Then Mr. Sandrich can find himself another girl to wear it. Come along, dearie." She beckoned to Ginger.

Staging a highly public walkout, she ushered her daughter through the soundstage, past the faux-Venetian facades and the gondolas bobbing on the watery canal. The doorman was about to open the giant portals when the assistant director caught up with them.

"Wait!" he pleaded, out of breath. "You can't leave, Miss Rogers. Mr. Sandrich is ready for you and Mr. Astaire to rehearse. Blue dress," he huffed.

Lela leveled her gaze at her daughter. "If you don't want to go back, you don't have to. Leland Hayward can deal with them."

"I'll stay. But if they change their minds again and nix my beautiful gown before shooting starts, I'm out. Stick around. You might have to drive me home."

"I'm not going anywhere."

They returned to the trailer. Lela helped her daughter into her costume, as she'd done during the vaudeville years. The smooth satin fit like a second skin, and the feathers trembled with every indrawn breath. It wasn't a very practical garment, even she could see that, but it looked divine when its wearer was in motion.

Ginger held out her bare arms so the makeup woman could slather on the greasepaint and apply a coating of powder to set it. "I'd bet anything that Fred started this controversy. He didn't want to make me mad by confronting me and found others to do it. Now I've got to go on the set and listen to him sing about how much he loves me. And dance with him like I love him back."

"Don't treat it as a rehearsal. Give it your all. Prove how essential you are to this picture. Convince those bullies that your gorgeous gown is crucial to your performance."

"That's a fact. It's never enough simply to keep up with Fred and match his steps. He's so proficient that I have to make myself just as visible. That's why I wanted all these fluttering feathers. And I've told Bernie Newman to stick glittery sequins all over my 'Piccolino' costume." Ginger's chin lifted. "For the past year I've been a trouper. No grumbling. No complaints. I've worked hard to overcome Fred's impression of me as a jumped-up chorus girl."

"Which you never were. You started out as a featured performer. Or the leading lady. Now you're the star."

"After today, they'll say I'm troublesome and temperamental," Ginger mourned.

"It's never unprofessional to stand up for yourself. They pay Fred a fortune. You earn considerably less than he does. It's time to make it clear to everyone around here that you won't be pushed around."

Ginger grinned. "Only on the dance floor."

Throughout the ensuing rehearsal, the atmosphere in the oversized soundstage was chilly. During filming, the dancing couple completed several takes. In between,

Ginger positioned herself on her tilted reclining board while the hairdresser tended the strawberry blonde tresses and Clarkie smoothed ruffled feathers.

The following afternoon Ginger asked Lela to go with her to view the previous day's rushes. As they entered the darkened projection room, none of the assembled executives or the director or the producer greeted them. Fred merely nodded, and dragged on his cigarette.

She didn't care. The sight of her lovely daughter floating across the screen in her chosen costume was affirmation that the Rogers team had scored a victory. Not one of these men could reasonably insist that "Cheek to Cheek" should be re-shot, nor could they argue that the feathered gown hadn't photographed exquisitely.

When everyone else departed, wordlessly, Lela saw that Ginger required consolation. "Never mind them. They know they've witnessed one of this studio's finest production numbers. Even if their arrogance won't let them admit that. Or credit you for it."

It was Phyllis who picked up the phone when Frankie Darro telephoned with news of another fatal automobile accident. She then had to inform Anne about the death of Junior Durkin, her frequent date and their close friend.

The head-on collision had occurred near the Coogan ranch near the border of Mexico. Jackie Coogan, the sole survivor, was thrown clear. His father, behind the wheel, was one of the three adults who had also perished. Henry Willson, a guest at the ranch, had remained behind—unwittingly saving his own life. Junior's untimely death preserved the name that the agent had hoped to erase; few press accounts referred to him as Trent.

"I can't believe it," Anne repeated as they awaited

information about the funeral. "Henry must be devastated. Junior was his most important client."

"Boy client," Phyllis corrected her. "You're his other favorite."

Tears streaming, her friend said plaintively, "He was going to be billed as Trent Durkin in the *Ah, Wilderness* picture. And if Mary hadn't been injured, she would've played his girl, the same part she did on the stage. It's all so sad."

The funeral service took place at Forest Lawn Cemetery's Wee Kirk o' the Heather Chapel. Henry's demeanor impressed and touched Phyllis, aware of the deeper feelings he secretly harbored for the actor who had shared his opulent new Beverly Hills home. During the eulogy, his grief was carefully modulated, and nothing he said indicated that he regarded Junior as anything but a close friend and gifted actor.

He was no less circumspect at a private memorial gathering of the Puppets gang.

Betty Furness murmured to Phyllis, "Junior and Henry reminded me of Cary Grant and Randy Scott. I was never entirely sure what was going on with those two, either."

Phyllis understood the implication.

"When they lived together, RKO fixed up Cary and me a lot. It was obvious we weren't going to become a serious thing, but we enjoyed each other's company. When the studio gave me good parts, I figured it was because I'd helped keep his public image above reproach."

Maybe, Phyllis mused, I could get good parts by becoming a homosexual movie star's pretend girlfriend. Except I'm not enough of an actress to be convincing. I prefer truth to fakery.

"When Cary married Virginia Cherrill, I thought maybe I was mistaken about him. But now she's left him."

"It doesn't necessarily mean he's—" Phyllis paused. "There are lots of reasons Hollywood couples get divorced."

In her current film, Phyllis portrayed a shy bachelor's determined, marriage-minded sweetheart. Everything about her co-star Sterling Holloway amused her. The combination of a wide grin, oversized, low-set ears that stuck out, and a head topped by a reddish-blond thatch made him resemble a cartoon character. His distinctive, high-pitched voice emerged from a throat that sounded as though it was stuffed with cotton from his native Georgia.

Unaffiliated with a single studio, he encouraged her to work whenever and wherever she could.

"Make 'em compete to hire you," he advised.

She held back a laugh to avoid hurting her earnest well-wisher's feelings. Producers were unlikely to battle over a bit player who, from the outset of her career, had portrayed flighty, flirty, fun-loving girls. All that repetition hampered her chances of winning a breakout role like the one Anne had secured. Whatever talent she possessed remained undiscovered and uncultivated. Buoyed by Lela's and Ginger's belief in her abilities, she'd come to Hollywood with hopes of achieving success. Familiar with the heavy demands that fame imposed on her cousin and Katharine Hepburn and Irene Dunne, and other top tier actresses, she doubted it would suit her. Not that she was likely to find out.

CHAPTER 33

When Phyllis joined the cast of *The Black Room Mystery*, a Boris Karloff thriller for Columbia Pictures, she welcomed the change from campus movies and short romantic capers.

"I'm a bridesmaid at the heroine's doomed wedding," she told Anne. "Yesterday I practiced sitting down and standing up in a hoopskirt. They're putting me in a beautiful wig of long loose curls, prettier than the one I had for *Little Men*. And I've got a gorgeous hat, a pointy sort of tricorne trimmed with ostrich down."

"Sounds lovely," Anne breathed.

"Today we're working at Forty Acres, in the foreign city section. I get to ride in a horse-drawn carriage."

Her romantic notions about that old-fashioned mode of transport were swiftly dispelled when she and the second bridesmaid and Marian Marsh, in elaborate bridal finery, jolted along a street lined with European style buildings. Villagers in festive Germanic garb flung flowers that thudded against the coach roof. The day was warm, and the actresses were packed into a confined space, wilting under their layers of satin and petticoats. Phyllis couldn't prevent her elbow-length gloves from bunching up in wrinkles. And the hoopskirt rehearsal hadn't prepared her for gracefully descending from the vehicle while simultaneously managing her voluminous gown and holding onto her bouquet. As she followed the ethereally lovely Marian, swathed in a lace veil, she tried not to flinch as the extras pelted them with blossoms and loose petals.

Boris Karloff was a pleasant contrast to his chilling horror film characters. Affable and warm-hearted, he complimented the trio of actresses on their beauty, in a courtly manner devoid of lecherous overtones. His sonorous voice was distinctly British.

After twice escorting the bridal party up the cathedral steps, a makeup woman patted his face with a tissue and powdered it. "I require greater cosmetic enhancement than you lovely ladies," the actor said jovially. "But compared to what I had to endure in the past, this is nothing. I've sat for ages while greasepaint was slathered over my face and bits of rubber were glued on. Two pictures as Frankenstein's monster. Then Dr. Fu Manchu."

"And the Mummy," Phyllis contributed.

The brown eyes gleamed. "Ah, yes. Nine hours in the chair. They smeared my flesh with clay and wrapped my entire head in linen and plaster, while I inhaled spirit gum fumes and gasped for breath. The entire mess was excruciating under the lights. Another two hours to remove it all." Beaming, he stroked his lean cheek. "As a nobleman, no scars, stitches, or gauze."

Later in the day, Phyllis filmed a solo scene of such brevity that she doubted it would survive the final cut. Rapping on a Gothic door, she summoned the bride to her wedding ceremony.

"Your ladyship, the Baron is waiting. Everything is ready."

The principal performers—those who characters had thus far survived the murderous nobleman's schemes—

assembled inside the soundstage for the highly dramatic scene in which his greatest deception would be exposed. Continuity and wardrobe personnel adjusted the bridesmaids' hats and hair and jewelry, and a makeup girl re-applied powder to their faces and freshened their lipstick. Phyllis and her fellow bridesmaid accompanied Marian Marsh as she proceeded serenely towards the altar rail, past the crowded pews. When the archbishop and priests completed their brief parts in the ritual, the dog handler and his charge made their appearance.

Karloff turned and said to Phyllis, "Our director claims this animal is more responsive to commands than actors are. Mind you, I'd be as obedient as Von if they rewarded me with four and a half pounds of meat each day. My dogs should be so lucky."

The laugh stuck in her throat when she spotted the dun-colored beast trotting towards them, his thick neck circled by a leather collar embedded with metal spikes. "Is he friendly?"

"When he's supposed to be. Because I'm his prey, I'm not permitted to treat him nicely. Even though the stuntman here will take my place for the attack." He stepped aside, making way for his impersonator.

The German handler and the director briefly discussed the dog's participation, which had been rehearsed previously. Everyone resumed their places. At the signal, Von charged forward and flung himself at the stuntman, knocking him backwards. The mighty jaws clenched on his left arm, protected by padding sewn into the sleeve.

The bride and bridesmaids reacted with expressions of genuine terror. Then the camera apparatus was moved to capture the shocked villagers in the congregation.

"Now, Karloff, we'll get a close-up of the hound lunging at you. You'll have to put on the padded jacket."

"Is no hound, sir," the aggrieved handler corrected.

Fondly he eyed the beast at the opposite end of the leash. "Great Dane."

Boris Karloff's dresser stepped forward and helped him replace his wedding coat with the one the stuntman had removed.

"All right, everyone."

"Quiet on the set," the assistant director called through the megaphone.

"Ready sound!"

"Ready!"

"Roll camera!"

"Rolling!"

A bell clanged.

When instructed, Von surged forward and sank his teeth into the actor's wrist, well below the protected portion of his arm.

Yowling in agony, Karloff retreated.

"Von, out! Sit!" the handler called. The dog obeyed.

"He got me! I'm bitten." Karloff plucked at his lace cuff. Staring at his wound, he groaned, "And bleeding."

Phyllis, seeing the red stain spreading over the white fabric, felt lightheaded. She gnawed the inside of her cheek and looked away.

The director called a halt and shouted for the doctor.

"He vas doing vat he vas told," the trainer said, bringing his charge to his side with a hand gesture. He tugged off his flat cap and scratched his bald head. "He's good boy. Professional."

"I'd best take myself off to the infirmary," the wounded star muttered.

"You're going to a hospital," the director told him. "The rest of you, stay as you are so we can shoot close-ups from different angles."

Boris Karloff was led away, to applause. Everyone cleared a wide path for the departing canine.

Marian Marsh murmured, "That monster gets paid more than a hundred dollars a week."

Phyllis was equally amused and appalled to learn that her own salary was significantly less than a dog's.

"My sister Jean is naming her baby after me," Phyllis told Lela and Ginger, when they met to rehearse scenes for Lew's next home movie.

Lela, the co-director, looked up from her shooting script. "Isn't it a boy?"

"Yes. Phillip. I don't know if her husband agreed with that choice, but he's no longer around to object." She held up her coffee cup so the manservant could refill it.

"They've separated? But they married the same week I did." Ginger's fingers tapped the surface of the patio table, counting out months between November and September. "They didn't have to get hitched out of necessity, either."

"Typical," Lela said on a sigh. "Women in our family have terrible luck with first husbands. And second ones." She added grimly, "In poor Virginia's case, third ones as well."

Phyllis rested her chin in her palm. "I don't intend to marry until I've found the kind of man I can spend my whole life with. Who'll stick by me forever and ever and ever."

"Amen," said Lela, hands pressed together prayerfully.

Observations of her cousin's marriage perplexed Phyllis. Ginger, constantly working, was seldom at home. She'd never been a wild child and didn't object to staying in at night, but she wasn't as dedicated a hermit as Lew. There were no obvious signs of significant dissension, or trauma—nothing that could cut deep enough to leave scars. Overdone meat and burned casseroles and a collapsed coconut cake could be laughed at—and easily avoided by hiring a cook or making restaurant reservations.

Their dog Rover ambled over and sidled up to Lela, who broke off some of her coffee cake and slipped it to him under the table.

"I saw that," Ginger said, peering over the newspaper.

Phyllis leaned down to stroke the floppy ears. "If she hadn't done it, I would've. My puppy is in danger of being thoroughly spoiled. I got him from the pound for two dollars. Best purchase I ever made."

"What breed?"

"We can't tell. We take him and Angel, Anne's Scottie, when we visit Mary Blackford—she adores them. She's thrilled to be home after all those months in the hospital and the rehabilitation center. She says she'll walk again."

"Well, blow me down." Ginger stared at the paper in disbelief. "She went through with it. Everyone assumed her engagement to someone else was a ploy to make her lover jealous."

"Who are you talking about?" Phyllis asked.

"Sylvia Sidney married a New York publisher." Ginger folded the section in half and shoved it across the table.

Lela glanced at the article before passing it to Phyllis.

In a posed photograph, the lovely movie star sat beside a dark-haired man whose face expressed intelligence and humor. "I wonder whether Mr. Cerf knows about her affair."

"He'd be the one person in the world who doesn't," Ginger replied. "Sylvia and B.P. never bothered to hide it.

Not from his wife. If Adeline still is his wife. They separate and reconcile so often, nobody can be sure."

Lela scoffed, "Adeline is a radical socialist and B.P. Schulberg has loose morals, like all the liberals. He's a Roosevelt man. A New Dealer."

"How could Sylvia abandon the head of Paramount Pictures to marry a man in the book trade? His name seems familiar, but I can't think why."

"Harold Ross," Lela supplied. "He and Bennett Cerf are great friends. Even though he always loses at backgammon or poker or whatever they play."

Phyllis said pensively, "I feel sorry for him, if he truly loves her. It sounds like he's being used. That's not fair."

"Time will tell." Ginger hopped up. "How about a game of badminton, Phyl? Doubles, if I can lure Ben and Lew away from their cutting and splicing."

"Sure." Phyllis drained her cup.

Lela intervened, saying, "Before you go, Phyllis, I want you to tell me all about that college picture you've just completed."

"Hardly anything to tell. I'm not part of the main story, just a comic subplot as Andy Devine's sweetie. His character is goofy and clumsy, and I'm annoyed with him all the time. Dodo Gates is my favorite role so far. I didn't even mind that I had to dye my hair a lighter shade." She tugged a golden-brown curl.

"It suits your coloring. How does *Fighting Youth* present the spread of communism on the campus?"

Pondering the question, she tried to recall. "A secret committee infiltrates the college football team. One of its leaders is a Russian spy working to undermine the United States Government."

"I hope there's no glorification of communistic propaganda. And don't tell me it's only a movie. What passes for harmless entertainment can carry dangerous messages if the screenwriter has an agenda."

"The spy is exposed. The heroine wins back her football star from the siren who schemed to convert him to her radical cause."

"Has there been a preview screening?" When Phyllis shook her head, Lela said, "I'll telephone Universal's publicity office and find out when it will be. They'll need informed people like me, knowledgeable about the insidious evil of communism, to fill out their comment cards. You should go with me. I'll tell you what to write."

"All right." It was best to agree with Lela whenever she mounted her political soapbox. Picking up her badminton racquet, she went to join Ginger and Lew and Ben at the net.

"It's our patriotic duty," Lela called after her.

CHAPTER 34

In the final days of her busiest moviemaking year, Phyllis returned to Twentieth Century Fox for a featured role in *Every Saturday Night.* She portrayed yet another silly girlfriend in yet another youth picture, but as a freelancer, any move up the casting ladder was welcome. The hot topic on the set was the apparent disintegration of Sylvia Sidney's hasty marriage to her publisher. The actress skipped a honeymoon for a location shoot at Lake Arrowhead, and her bridegroom had returned to New York.

"He's one of those East Coast intellectuals," Spring Byington told Phyllis when they were being made up. "A literary type. I met plenty during my Broadway days. They have a low opinion of motion pictures. And the people who make them."

"It didn't stop Mr. Cerf from falling in love," Phyllis was quick to point out.

"That was his first mistake. His second was marrying Sylvia. Mighty convenient for her and B. P. Schulberg, if this husband of hers prefers New York to Hollywood."

Phyllis recalled the newspaper photo of the attractive, dark-haired man with the pleasant smile. Her initial sympathy had increased with the news that he and his bride were living apart so soon after their wedding.

"You look like her," the older woman commented. "The shape of your face and your nose and mouth. Your hair is similar in color. Don't you part it on the same side she does?"

Phyllis regarded her reflection in the dressing table mirror. "If there's a resemblance, it's only physical. She's successful. I'm not."

"My dear, any actress with a paying job can consider herself a success."

Early in the New Year, Ginger and Lela traveled to the nation's capital to participate in President Roosevelt's birthday celebrations. Despite their fealty to conservative Republican doctrine, it was too great an honor to refuse. They returned with tales of White House visits and Ginger's command performance in the Oval Office—tap dancing for the President.

"He was so tickled, he gave me the script of his radio address," she said, showing the typed pages to Phyllis. "With a personal note written on it. Even though he's a Democrat, he's definitely a gentleman. And Mrs. Roosevelt was magnificent. At public events, when crowds swarmed all around us, she was so gracious and dignified."

"We met Frances Perkins," Lela added, "the Secretary of Labor. I deplore socialism and the union movement, but Mr. Roosevelt deserves some credit for appointing a woman to such an important government position."

After her momentary appearance in another period piece, Republic Pictures' production of a Gene Stratton Porter novel, Phyllis had no further film work in view. To pass the time, she composed articles intended for the major movie magazines. *Hollywood* accepted the one written from the perspective of Rover Ayres, one of Ginger's dogs, and scheduled it for the May issue.

Before Phyllis could visit the bank to deposit her paycheck, Ginger called to say she and Lew were separating.

"I need your help removing my things tonight. I've already found a furnished apartment."

When she arrived at the house on North Roxbury Drive, Ginger's cocker spaniel Michael came scrambling over floor tiles to greet her.

"He goes with me," her cousin said. "Lew keeps Rover. They're hiding out at his ranch. I hope Mother will take the cat. If not, the cook can—she feeds it."

Under cover of darkness, they made repeated trips to Ginger's temporary rental on Gregory Drive. In addition to clothing, Ginger took her tennis and badminton racquets, easel and art supplies, her movie camera, and a favorite backgammon board. She'd packed a box of framed photographs and filled another with record albums.

"I can't use all these dresses," Ginger said, gazing at the items piled on the bed. "Take whatever you want. Lew didn't like going out in the evening, he's so private and solitary. And unwilling to play second fiddle."

"To whom?"

"Me, because my career is on the upswing. And Mother, for being so involved with my personal and professional life. It's sensible to part now, he says, before our differences cause problems that get bigger and harder to hide."

Ginger had never alluded to this tug-of-war between husband and parent. Lew, an admitted pacifist, had surrendered to Lela, the stronger force. And by doing so, he proved that he was less committed to the marriage than Phyllis had believed when hearing him speak his vows.

"There's no other girl," Ginger said, answering the

question that hadn't been asked. "That would be awful, of course, but what's worse is his deciding he doesn't want me anymore." Her legs buckled, and she sank down beside the mountain of dresses. When she began to cry, softly, her little dog placed a paw on her slender, shapely calf. Looking up, she said unsteadily, "At least my marriage lasted longer than Sylvia's. Yesterday she got her divorce from the publisher." After Phyllis persuaded her to stretch out on the bed, Ginger watched her fold garments and place them in the bureau drawers. "I've never lived alone. Not ever in my life."

Was Ginger going to ask her to move in? She'd grown so attached to Anne and Mimi Shirley. What's more, she was reluctant to return to that place she'd previously occupied, deep within the shadow cast by the outrageously talented and enormously popular movie star.

"I'm dreading what will happen after we make our public announcement. Mother says I should spend the rest of the summer at our Malibu beach house, even though it's an awfully long drive to the studio." Pressing her fingers against her temples, Ginger said, "I've been so busy with work, and trying to hang on to Lew, that I let you down."

Phyllis swung around. "In what way?"

"I meant to help you get a contract."

"I'm doing fine without one. *Screenland* accepted my profile of Anne for their June issue. And I've got an appointment with Ted Magee of *Hollywood* magazine. His dad is Carl Magee, who used his fortune from inventing the parking meter to buy the *Oklahoma News*—the same paper that sponsored the student essay contest I won." Laughing, she added, "That, you know, was my real debut as a published author."

When Phyllis entered the startlingly young magazine editor's office, she hoped he wasn't going to pry into Ginger's marital situation. As far as she knew, the press was unaware of the couple's separation, unless an informer had somehow discovered they were living apart.

"Your dog story was terrific," Ted Magee told her after she was seated across from his cluttered desk. "Just the kind of insider information our readers crave."

"I don't have anything else to offer you," she said apologetically. "I sold my Anne Shirley article to *Screenland.*"

"I know. Like *Hollywood,* it's also a Fawcett publication, along with *Motion Picture*, *Movie Story*, and *Screen Secrets*. The combined newsstand circulation of our periodicals—the fan magazines and all the others—is nearing ten million copies. When I suggested to Jack Smalley, our managing editor, that we should hire you as a regular monthly columnist, he gave the okay. Interested?"

Her fingers clenched the handle of her purse in a spasm of surprise. "Very."

"You socialize with Henry Willson's crowd. Tom Brown and his society girlfriend. Ben Alexander, the guy who hosts that radio show, *Hollywood Talent Parade.* Nights at the Trocadero. Parties at the bowling alley. You're their chum, and can provide factual information about the youngsters in the picture business. Not that fictional pap the studio publicists feed us."

"Youngsters. Young stars. That could be my column's title: 'Hollywood Youngstars.' A play on words."

He grinned. "Perfect. Got a camera?"

She nodded. "I took all those photos of Ginger and Lew and their dog."

"It's a salaried position. I'll set things up with payroll. Any questions?"

"Would I be expected to always name names? That's not my style," she warned him. "I don't mind dropping hints, like I did when writing gossip for my high school paper. In some cases, I'd rather leave it to the reader to guess who I'm referring to. 'Which actress did this?' 'What leading man said that?' I'd make it a regular feature in my column."

"Fine by me," Ted told her. "We've got enough sharks tapping the typewriters in this town."

"Can I also write for your other publications?"

"Sure. We'd pay you by the piece for anything we decide to run. Send me the copy for your debut column by the end of the month, and I can get it into our July issue."

"I will. Thank you."

They shook hands across the table.

"Come with me," he said, getting up. "I want you to meet Smalley."

The affable managing editor was pleased to learn of the arrangement. "Welcome aboard," he said, "from one who's been with this company for ten years. I don't expect a girl as pretty as you will stay with us quite that long. As you'll soon discover, we don't give a damn what our writers look like, or how they spend their time when away from the typewriter. We just want them to submit peppy, readable stories." His monologue was interrupted when his secretary buzzed to say Captain Fawcett was phoning from Minneapolis. Picking up the receiver, he waved Ted and Phyllis away. "What can I do for you, sir? Calling to check up on your boy Gordon?"

All of Wilford Fawcett's sons, Ted explained as he walked her to the reception area, held executive positions in the family firm, working from Los Angeles or Minnesota or New York.

"You've heard of *Captain Billy's Whiz Bang,* I'm sure."

"The humor magazine? You bet. The boys in my grammar school liked to quote the jokes—dirty ones, to disgust us girls. The one I remember wasn't naughty at all. It went, 'Are you acquainted with Olive Oil? I'm her brother, Castor.' Or something like that. We thought it was hilarious."

"Unfortunately, its glory days are behind us. The final issue has rolled off the press."

Leaving the magazine office, she discovered that the light spring shower had stopped. Pushing back the hood of her raincoat, she decided to walk from Hollywood Boulevard to the Shirley house on Alta Vista.

"I wondered if you'd ever come back," Mimi said, a note of excitement in her voice. "Your cousin wants you to ring her back straightaway. She has important news."

Phyllis peeled off her gloves and dialed Ginger's number.

"You picked a fine time to disappear," her cousin complained. "Tell me you don't have anything in your appointment book for tomorrow morning."

"I don't think so."

"Good. Republic Pictures wants to test you for an ingenue role. In a western. With John Wayne!"

There was no greater contrast to the Sacramento Valley's dry and rugged landscape than the elegant Café Trocadero, the French-inspired nightclub where Hollywood's elite gathered. And Phyllis, for the first time, was entering it as a leading lady, a blonde, and a fan magazine scribe seeking print-worthy material.

She and Ben had arranged this celebration for Anne, recipient of her high school diploma. Tom Brown had brought Natalie Draper, the socialite he was dating regularly. Usually they opted for the Cellar, the downstairs cocktail lounge, but tonight they had reserved a table in the dining room favored by the famous.

"Tell them what you told me about your daily schedule," Anne prompted Phyllis.

"I can guess," Ben said. "A limousine delivered you to the set. In between scenes, you sat in your luxurious air-conditioned trailer, nibbling grapes while resting your feet on a satin covered hassock."

"How I wish," Phyllis answered on a sigh. "My morning call was for four-o'clock. I was barely awake when my makeup was applied. After putting on my costume—long skirt, lots of petticoats—we had a brief rehearsal. At eight, we started shooting. By nine, I was longing for lunch." Breaking into the laughter, she added, "And the director shot everything in one take—no second chances. If my lines didn't come out exactly as written, nobody cared as long as John Wayne could pick up his cue. Our entire shoot lasted ten days."

"Is that common?" Natalie asked.

"No!" the others chorused.

"My pictures take about four weeks," Anne replied.

"Longer than that, for Ginger's," Phyllis said. "Six to eight weeks, at a minimum. She and Fred have to learn their songs and record them for the playback. And they rehearse for about a month, perfecting those dance routines."

Winds of the Wasteland, the speediest of her films, had also been the strangest. The sole female in the main cast, she hadn't previously encountered any of the male actors from her time at RKO or Twentieth Century or Universal or Paramount or Mascot. She played the doctor's daughter from the East, reluctant schoolmistress in a struggling prairie town. Gradually her character's disdain for her rustic surroundings dissipated, along with her antipathy towards the extremely laconic and impressively tall John Wayne. Their slowly developing romance was overshadowed by schemes and fistfights and stagecoach chases.

"What's next for Hollywood's newest star?" Ben asked.

With a nod at her roommate, Phyllis said, "Over the summer Anne and I are going to write a musical set in the Old West. Tom's helping us. And I'll carry on with my—" She stopped herself, not yet ready to admit she'd started a novel. "With my monthly columns. I'm counting on all of you to supply juicy gossip about people you know. Otherwise I'll be forced to spill the beans about present company."

They knew it was an idle threat. She was circumspect about friends in general and her cousin in particular.

Ginger's antidote to sorrow over her break from Lew was building a massive house, a birthday and Christmas gift for Lela, who shared her nativity with the Lord Jesus. Their elevated three-acre lot in Coldwater Canyon offered a limitless view. On a clear day, Ginger boasted, Catalina Island was visible on the horizon. It was immediately apparent that "Mother's mansion" would possess features that the daughter considered essential: tennis court, swimming pool, projection room, and art studio.

"With separate guest quarters for your use," Ginger assured Phyllis. "Harold Ross can stay there when he visits us from New York."

For the time being, Ginger divided her time between her place in Malibu and Lela's bungalow. Earl Eby had moved out but continued as Lela's official escort and appeared in many plays at her RKO drama studio. Phyllis had fulfilled her aunt's repeated requests to mention him favorably in her *Hollywood* column, although as an obscure actor of thirty-three he in no way matched the designation "Youngstar."

She looked forward to reporting the success of Mary Blackford's therapy at the Milton H. Berry Institute in Van Nuys. Her friend could now move her head and partial mobility was restored to one arm. From gratitude to Dr. Berry and in support of his paralyzed patients, the gang of young performers organized a Christmas party benefit for his foundation. Will Rogers, Mary's devoted patron and beloved by the entire nation, had died last year in a private airplane crash in Alaska. Tom Brown succeeded him as master of ceremonies.

Phyllis, Anne, and another actress presented a lively rendition of "There's a Tavern in the Town." They received enthusiastic applause from the movie stars and moguls in attendance and more significantly, from the children undergoing treatment at the facility. After they took their final bows, Phyllis carried her floppy sunbonnet to a little girl in a wheelchair and tied it onto her head.

Stepping away, she discovered a man standing behind her. Introducing himself as Maurice Conn of Conn Pictures, he handed her his card.

"We're starting pre-production on a thriller. I'm waiting on the final script, but I can tell you that the plot centers on a sweepstakes swindle exposed by a journalist. I'm hoping to sign Frankie Darro as the newsboy. His sister, the reporter's sweetheart, is an aspiring nightclub singer. A Ginger Rogers type."

With her perkiest smile, she inquired, "Are you asking me to test?"

"No need. I liked you in John Wayne's movie for

Republic, the one before Universal snagged him. And I've heard you singing. As far as I'm concerned, that's enough of a tryout."

Her voice wasn't nearly as strong or as well-trained as her cousin's. But if he didn't care, she certainly wasn't going to mention it.

"When we're ready to discuss terms, how can we reach you?"

"Through my aunt. Ginger's mother. She's a talent scout at RKO."

She couldn't let this opportunity pass her by. If she won the part, it would prove to Lela and Ginger that their belief in her, and all the help they'd provided, hadn't been a waste. And the salary, whatever it might be, would augment her ever-fluctuating income. But this sudden stroke of good fortune, coming so late, was less meaningful to her than it might have been a year ago. Having determined her true calling, she was no longer wholly committed to the career her relatives had imposed on her. Her magazine columns had ensured her self-sufficiency, she'd begun work on her novel, and she was collaborating on a screenplay. Achieving that elusive success as a film actress no longer seemed as important to her as it had been.

PART III: 1937-1941

Phyllis Fraser, RKO player, is in New York on a visit to her aunt, Mrs. Lela Rogers, mother of Ginger Rogers.

–Motion Picture Daily, 1939

CHAPTER 35

The New Deal, deplored by Lela as a dubious and rampantly socialist program, had delivered minimal benefit to Oklahoma. Farm families, displaced by persistent drought and blizzards of dust, drifted away from rural areas and into the cities in search of work or government assistance. The desperate and destitute swelled the number of vagrants roaming the neighborhoods and begging for cash or sustenance.

Phyllis had returned to her hometown to celebrate her twenty-first birthday and to attend her two-year old nephew's christening. While there, she would promote *Tough to Handle,* Maurice Conn's shoestring production. Her castmate, juvenile heartthrob Frankie Darro, had predicted that her performance as a blonde chanteuse would make her as sought-after as Ginger was. Phyllis appreciated the compliment but was all too aware of her deficiencies as a songstress.

Before *The Daily Oklahoman* sent its reporter to the house to interview her for a feature article, Mama dyed her hair from stark blonde to a flattering shade of auburn.

"Should I refer to you as Helen, or Phyllis?" the newspaperman wanted to know.

"Phyllis, if you please." Her mother and sister now called her by that name.

Breezily she answered his questions about her life in Hollywood, the mutt she'd adopted, and the pet rabbits she and Anne kept. He wanted to know which movie role had been her favorite.

"I had the best time playing Dodo Gates, Andy Devine's girlfriend in *Fighting Youth,*" she told him. "He's lots of fun."

"Got a boyfriend?"

"Not one I can discuss publicly."

After she obliquely referenced a certain actor's devoted mother in the "Riddle Me This" section of her *Hollywood* column—naming no names—Carlyle Moore, Junior, had asked her out. They'd been seeing each other ever since.

"That beau of yours must be serious," Mama observed, watching her tear into the small box that had arrived from Los Angeles.

"He is," she confided. "Oh, look! He sent me one of his wood carvings. My dog in miniature." She held up her present.

"Do you feel the same about him?"

"Yes," she answered shyly, unaccustomed to discussing affairs of the heart with her mother. "But Mrs. Moore doesn't like me much. Or any of the girls he's dated since he signed with Warner Brothers. She tells him an actor's appeal to female fans depends on his staying single. Her late husband was a playwright, then a unit director for silent pictures. She performed on the New York stage and toured all over the country."

"Does her son live with her?"

"He rents a house." She said nothing about his occasional reliance on her to keep it tidy. "Sometimes he entertains the gang there. Anne and I help with the food and decorations."

"I suppose Ginger's still keeping company with her millionaire. Isn't he a Rockefeller?"

"A Vanderbilt. Last month Ginger and Alf threw a big party at the Rollerdome, the skating rink in Culver City. She got the idea after she and Fred performed a dance number on roller skates. So much preparation—she insisted on lots of jokes and silly games and enough food to feed an army. All the important people in Hollywood were there. Joan Crawford. Cary Grant. The Gershwin Brothers. Humphrey Bogart. *Life* magazine sent a photographer."

"You must enjoy all those parties," Mama commented, her tone wistful.

"I'm invited because I write for the movie magazines," she pointed out. "People hope I'll mention them in my column, or print their photograph."

In Oklahoma City, her Hollywood luster lifted her above the mediocrity that plagued her film career. On Friday night, Mama took her to WKY radio station for a live interview. She sang both of the songs from her forthcoming film, "Spring Will Make You Fall" and "What You've Got Is Love," repeating her recent performance on Ben Alexander's weekly variety show. She hoped her undiscriminating hometown audience would be more impressed by her renditions than her friend's national listenership had been.

She wrote long, affectionate letters to Carlyle, describing her reunion with Doris White and former classmates from Classen High, and expressed her eagerness to travel back to the West Coast.

When Jean brought her son to meet Phyllis, he prattled unintelligibly and seemed to enjoy her attempts to amuse him. He was a placid child, with the rounded face so prevalent among Owens descendants. Her sister struggled to support the pair of them and pay for the babysitter on her beautician's salary. But she was a thrifty shopper and a skilled cook, and proudly shared recipes with Phyllis.

On Sunday morning, she dressed her little nephew in his christening outfit, a miniature satin suit with a Fauntleroy collar that she'd purchased for him. During the service he sat contentedly in her lap, occasionally reaching up to poke her hat brim. She tugged off one glove for him to play with until it was time for the baptism. Although her mother and sister, as divorcees, had chosen this Protestant church, she felt nostalgic for the more formal rituals of Catholicism.

When it was time to depart, Phyllis politely concealed her relief. With each mile the train placed between her and her closest living relatives, her connection to them felt ever more ephemeral.

Anne collected her from the Pasadena railway station, and for the duration of the drive to the house on Alta Vista she detailed the schedule of festivities for her birthday celebration.

"Normally I'd be working on a Saturday, but luckily I'm free tomorrow. Some of the girls wanted to take me to lunch, but I said we should take cake and cookies and punch to Mary Blackford's. In the evening, our fellows are treating us to dinner at the Troc. And on Sunday, Natalie's having a picnic. I've been so busy shooting *Stella Dallas* that I haven't seen anybody since you left."

"What's Barbara Stanwyck like?"

"A hard worker and a terrific actress. I'm in awe."

Mimi Shirley received Phyllis with a gentle hug and a cup of tea. "Not a soul would guess you've turned twenty-one," she declared. "In show business, youth is everything, so take advantage of your girlish looks as long as you can."

Despite feeling travel-weary, she was up early to bake Anne's cake and a batch of cookies. Their party at Mary's lasted from midday till late afternoon. When Carlyle showed up at the Shirley house, Phyllis was practically drooping from fatigue. They had to wait for Lee Bowman, Anne's date, to arrive.

Over a late dinner of hamburgers and fries, the men cooked up a plan for an outdoor cocktail party at Lee's the following afternoon. They left the booth to circulate around the oak-paneled Cellar Lounge, inviting all their contemporaries—whether acquainted with them or not.

A picnic tomorrow, followed by another party, thought Phyllis in dismay. I'm so tired, I'd rather sleep the entire day.

"Who are they pestering now?" Anne wondered. "He must be an actor, he's so handsome. You're the gossip girl, you know everybody. What's his name?"

Phyllis, pressing pleats into her napkin, glanced at the dark-haired fellow with the deep cleft in his chin. "John Payne."

"Who's he with?"

"No idea. I don't know her." Feeling the effects of her French 75, a heady concoction of champagne, gin, lemon juice, and sugary syrup, she stifled a yawn.

When their dates returned, it was clear that they expected the girls to assist with their project.

Anne informed them that they had to look elsewhere for hostesses. "Natalie Draper expects us at her picnic."

A five-piece combo struck up "Night and Day." Carlyle stood up and pulled Phyllis to her feet. "Miss Fraser, this dance belongs to me." Square-faced, with full lips, he didn't tower over her like lots of men did. The top of his light-brown head wasn't much higher than hers.

As they swayed in time with the music, she leaned her head against his shoulder and closed her eyes. A mistake—she felt even drowsier and her mind seemed even more clouded by the alcohol.

He whispered in her ear, "I'm not waiting a minute longer to ask the question that's been on my mind from the day you left town. Will you marry me, Phyl?"

She missed a step, and her heel landed on his toes. "Sorry!" she gasped.

"Sorry that you won't?"

"No. I mean, yes." Don't think. Follow his movements. "I will."

Warm lips brushed her forehead. "I've been saving up for your ring. But I want you to choose, so I'll know you like it."

"Do you mind if I tell Anne? It'll be an unforgettable birthday present."

"Sure. I want the whole world to know! I can't wait to read all about our romance in your next column."

And just like that, she was engaged.

CHAPTER 36

The new day was an hour old when the girls climbed into their beds. Anne's excitement over Carlyle's marriage proposal gradually receded, and she drifted into slumber. Phyllis, awake and thoughtful and still slightly tipsy, was extremely weary in body but far too busy of mind. She feared the engagement wouldn't change Mrs. Moore's attitude towards her, or help her establish a rapport with her future mother-in-law.

In the morning she'd cable her happy news to Mama. She preferred to inform Lela and Ginger in person, and soon, but their hectic schedules were an obstacle.

Her aunt was directing a play at her studio theatre and teaching her film acting classes. She supervised screen tests, strategically presenting her most promising pupils to RKO's producers and directors. The release of *Shall We Dance,* Ginger's latest hit with Astaire, had cemented her fame. More determined than ever to take on non-singing, non-dancing roles, she was scheduled to appear in a comedy-drama about New York stage actresses in a boarding house. Katharine Hepburn—with whom she was reportedly feuding—had also been cast.

At mid-morning Phyllis reluctantly left her bed. She crept around the room collecting her clothes, careful not to disturb the sleeping Anne, and managed to dress in the bathroom without making any noise.

Going to the kitchen, she told Mimi, "Natalie wants us to bring sandwiches. If I don't wake Anne soon, we'll be late to the picnic."

"Do you mind going by yourself? She's worked awfully hard all week, returning so late at night, and never complained. You young people assume you've got unlimited stamina and wear yourselves out, but it's important to catch up on your rest. I'll make the sandwiches and pack them up for you."

Phyllis put on her dark glasses, shielding her eyes from the midday glare. She set out in her car, belatedly recalling it was overdue for a tune-up. Blooming jacarandas formed huge violet clouds on every street, and the fronds of pepper trees danced in the breeze flowing in from the ocean. The Drapers occupied a stately residence on Spalding Drive. If Carlyle achieved the stardom his devoted mother felt he deserved, he and Phyllis might eventually reside in a similarly enchanting neighborhood. The houses were attractive but not overly ostentatious, with velvety green lawns, exquisitely shaved shrubbery, and vibrantly colored roses.

The mystery site for Natalie's picnic turned out to be a short walk away, on the Beverly Hills High School playing field. Since graduating over a year ago, she had enjoyed the enviable privileges of a rich girl. She'd traveled to Europe with her mother's close friends Marion Davies and William Randolph Hearst and stayed in their Welsh castle. She appeared in department store fashion shows often enough to lend credence to press descriptions of her as a model. And she dated a popular young screen actor.

Smoothing the ruffled collar that circled her slender neck, she said, "I've told my mother I don't care about high society and being a debutante. I'm only interested in becoming Mrs. Tom Brown. As quickly as possible."

In this group of six, Phyllis counted four of his former flames, herself included. She wondered what Natalie knew about his prior romances.

"Are you two already discussing marriage?" Ida Lupino wanted to know.

"All the time. In between our spats."

Phyllis pitched a bread crust to a watchful sparrow. "What do you argue about?"

"Everything. Nothing. It doesn't matter. I'm desperate to be with him every minute he's not filming." Natalie's smile was beatific. "In the daytime. And even more at night. You know what I mean, Phyllis. You and Carlyle Moore have been going together for ages."

Instead of confirming her engagement, she equivocated, saying, "I'm his steady girl."

Ida leaned forward. "We all thought Ben Alexander would be the lucky man."

Unlike Natalie, Phyllis didn't feel ready for the intimate aspects of matrimony. She and Carlyle held hands at movie screenings, and when they were alone, they kissed a lot. There had been light petting sessions in his car, under cover of darkness. Engaged couples went considerably farther than that. But if he expected premarital sex, he was destined for disappointment.

I'm not going all the way until there's a gold band on my finger, she vowed. *And by that time, I'll be feeling just as passionate as the naughty girls in the steamy novels Anne and I trade with each other.*

"We can't stand waiting any longer," Natalie went on. "Whenever we're dancing slow and close, and Tom holds me so tight, all I can think about is—" Her eyelashes fluttered. "You know. That."

The girls giggled. Phyllis half-listened as they compared their boyfriends' romantic techniques. A mere twelve hours had passed since she'd accepted Carlyle's proposal, and regret was rapidly surfacing.

When her friends started packing up the uneaten food, Phyllis claimed the tastiest leftovers to take to Anne. But when she got home, her friend wasn't there.

Mimi Shirley's gaze rose from the shawl she was crocheting. "Lee Bowman has too many boys at his party, so he sent someone to pick Anne up. She wants you to join her."

"I need to start on my next column," Phyllis replied. A convenient excuse with the benefit of being true. She couldn't admit her reluctance to see Carlyle, who would be there.

Poring over her accumulated notes, she decided her mood wasn't conducive to formulating zippy descriptions of recent social activities. Instead she turned to the manuscript bearing the title *My Hollywood and Yours,* in hopes that it might distract her from unsettling thoughts about her future. The half-finished novel was a highly fictionalized account of her experiences and those of her friends. She resumed her depiction of a Garden of Allah bacchanal and was so absorbed that she was oblivious to her roommate's return.

Anne bounced into the bedroom. "You'll never believe what happened!"

Phyllis twisted in her chair. "Do tell."

"I met an amazing, wonderful man. John Payne. We saw him last night at the Troc. Remember? Well, when I got to Lee's, there he was—without a date. He walked right up and started saying such nice things about my performance in *Two Many Wives*. We went inside together and played some records on the Victrola. We like all the same songs! We talked and talked. I was chattering away and listening so closely to him that I forgot I had food on my plate. He accused me of being one of those girls who won't eat so she can keep a slim figure—just teasing. When I denied it, he told me I could prove it by letting him take me to dinner. We exchanged numbers. I don't know what I'll do if he doesn't telephone. I must be in love, because I've never, ever felt this way."

As her friend burbled on, Phyllis experienced envy's sharp bite. Anne had known this marvelous John for a single afternoon and was already roused to heights of emotion that she hadn't quite reached.

"You must've seen Carlyle."

Anne nodded. "He was mighty glum. You should've come over."

"Who else was there?"

"You know, I didn't notice. Nearly everyone had left the party before John and I got up from the sofa. He's so nice. I think he liked me, too."

Every evening that week Anne stayed home, ostensibly to study lines but obviously awaiting the call that never came.

"I can't bear it," she said when Friday was on the horizon. "I've got comp tickets to a movie preview at Grauman's. Should I invite him? Or would that be too bold?" She stared indecisively at the scrap of paper that he'd given her.

Before Phyllis could answer, first in the affirmative and then the negative, Anne darted towards the telephone table. Her finger hovered over the dial.

"Go on. Do it."

Her friend's face lit up the instant she was connected to the other party. With feigned assurance, she asked, "Am I speaking to John Payne? This is Anne. Anne Shirley. We met on Sunday at—oh, good. Yes, it was a swell party. Twentieth Century gave me passes to Tuesday's preview at the Chinese Theatre, and I wondered if you might like to go. Tyrone Power and Loretta Young." Anne fell silent, holding the receiver in a death grip. "Do you? I know, it's short notice," she said, her voice sinking. "Mmmm hmmm. I see. I'm sure we will. Thanks. You, too."

Studying the woeful face, Phyllis guessed, "He's busy."

"Another engagement. That's the word he used. I bet it's a date with that girl he took to the Trocadero. On my birthday." The brown eyes filled with tears.

"Don't assume the worst."

"You and Carlyle can have my tickets," Anne sobbed. "You've hardly seen him since the weekend. I hope you two didn't have a fight."

"Oh, no," she said airily. "Unlike Tom and Natalie, we get along. All the time."

Failing to lift Anne out of despondency and in need of cheerier company, Phyllis drove to Malibu for an afternoon of beach-walking and grown-up girl talk. After an amiable stroll along the shoreline, she and Ginger took bottles of soda from the icebox and spread a towel on one of the dunes. This was her chance to consult her cousin about those aspects of marriage she couldn't comfortably discuss with anybody else.

"You want to know what happens in bed?"

Phyllis shrugged off the question. "In high school we secretly shared a sex manual somebody found hidden in her mother's bureau. And I've read plenty of scandalous novels and magazine confession stories. I'm not too worried about the wedding night. But I don't want to have a baby right away."

"You can't. It takes nine months."

Phyllis flicked a handful of sand at her smirking companion. “You know what I mean.” Cheeks burning, she asked Ginger to inform her about the available and reliable methods of preventing conception.

“You can use a pessary. Or suppositories. He can wear a rubber sheath, or withdraw before his climax. But you shouldn’t rely on him,” Ginger warned. “You can’t even trust yourself. If you’re too excited, or tipsy, and he gets carried away, you might forget all about taking precautions.”

Phyllis tried to imagine herself overcome by arousal. Her toes curled, raking the grit beneath her bare feet.

“Has he tried to go all the way?”

“Sort of. If we do, he says, we’d have to get married. His mother wouldn’t be able to stop us.”

“But she’ll believe you trapped him into it.”

“I know. I’m tempted to tell her I’m a good Catholic girl, saving myself for the honeymoon.”

“I don’t think the really good Catholic girls use birth control, do they? When we go inside, I’ll write down the name of my specialist. She’ll fix you up. Adeline Schulberg established female clinics. Not just for married women, but unwed ones. Like Sylvia Sidney—who was Ad’s husband’s mistress.”

“She’s going back to Broadway to do a play,” Phyllis said. “Her publicist wants me to mention it in my column.”

“Maybe she’ll reconcile with the book publisher she divorced so fast,” Ginger said.

“After the way she ditched him, he won’t want anything to do with her.” Phyllis stood up and brushed sand from her shorts and backside and bare legs.

Facing her, Ginger said solemnly, “Don’t you worry if sex isn’t wonderful your first time. Or the second. It will be, eventually. With the right person.”

During her homeward drive, Phyllis wondered how many men, not counting her two husbands, Ginger had slept with. Her current love was RKO director George Stevens, newly separated from his wife.

The next day, a florist's van stopped at the Shirley house to drop off a dozen gardenias, accompanied by a note that made Anne glow with pleasure. John Payne's Tuesday evening commitment mysteriously evaporated, and they went to the film preview.

The first outing was followed by a nightly dinner date, regardless of how late Anne got home from the *Stella Dallas* set. Each week John sent her flowers—a dozen camellias, a cluster of orchids, a bouquet of lilies. On an afternoon when both were free, he drove her to the beach, and opened the subject of marriage. One evening around dusk, he arrived at the house with an armful of red roses and waited over an hour until Anne returned from filming her *Stella Dallas* wedding scene. Phyllis and Mimi left the pair alone, until they were called in to admire the ring on Anne's finger.

"I'll treasure it forever," she gushed to Phyllis later, shifting her hand to make the diamond chip sparkle. "A token of our engagement, he says, because he plans to give me a bigger stone but doesn't have it yet. Then he clammed up and didn't answer my questions. Wouldn't it be wonderful if you and Carlyle and Johnny and I had a double ceremony?"

"Or a triple one," Phyllis said, purely in jest. "If Tom and Natalie can stop fighting long enough, they'll tie the knot this summer."

As waves lightly slapped the hull of the yacht *Arbutus,* Phyllis tipped back her head to admire the pale curve of a waning moon. Catalina Island's distant shore was marked by star-like lights that twinkled in the darkness.

With a sigh, Anne leaned against John. "So romantic."

The passengers, summoned to the aft deck, arranged themselves in a semi-circle. Tom and Natalie, hands clasped, faced the vessel's captain.

"Go ahead, sir," Tom said. "We're ready."

Mopping his brow with a handkerchief, the man said to John, "You'll have to hold the flashlight closer." When the beam landed on the paper Tom had handed him, he read, "Do you, Thomas Edward Xavier Brown, take Natalie Draper to be your lawfully wedded wife? To have and to hold from this day forward, till death do you part?"

"I do."

"And do you, Natalie—"

"I do." Her left hand released Tom's so he could place the ring on her finger.

"By my authority as ship's captain, I pronounce you man and wife. Congratulations. Go ahead and kiss your bride." The officiant shook Tom's hand, saying, "I've never done this, you know, so let's hope I got it right. I can only tell you for sure that we were beyond the twelve-mile limit when we did the deed."

"It was perfect," Natalie gushed.

The captain and all the assembled witnesses signed and dated the paper.

After adding her name, Phyllis handed the pen to actor-songwriter Bert Kalmar, Junior.

When Anne returned the document to Tom, she marveled, "When you invited us to come along, you and Natalie were already planning an elopement."

"That's right. Months ago, when I asked Nat's dad for

permission, he said he wouldn't allow her to marry before she turns twenty. We couldn't wait two whole years."

"And Tom's parents don't think he's old enough to settle down." Natalie raised her hand to show off the gold band. "We've proved how wrong they all are. But no telling. This has to remain a secret until we decide to confess."

The captain returned to his duties in the pilothouse, and everyone else traipsed down to the galley to open champagne and toast the newlyweds. Phyllis, regarding Tom's choice of venue as a poor one, was unable to enter the spirit of celebration.

"This is the same yacht that collided with a steamship last year," she murmured to Anne. "The *Arbutus* accident was in all newspapers and on the radio. People were injured, and it almost sank."

Anne was winding a loose curl around her forefinger. "You can't be superstitious about such a happy event. We've all been hoping Tom would find his perfect girl. He's like a brother to me, and I want everything to be wonderful for him. For them."

Phyllis refrained from mentioning another source of disquiet, the persistent quarrels and arguments she and their friends had witnessed, and the countless break-ups and make-ups documented by the press. No couple got along beautifully all the time, she reminded herself. Still, she had to wonder whether Tom and Natalie were as prepared for the realities of matrimony as they believed themselves to be.

The girls, crammed into a shared berth, found themselves with extra room that night—Natalie was absent. Not until morning, when they converged on the galley to make breakfast, did she rejoin them. Under questioning, she blushingly admitted that she and Tom had consummated their marriage in one of the lifeboats.

Motor launches arrived at the yacht's mooring in Avalon Bay to transport its passengers to the island. The newlyweds stayed behind.

A swarm of Hollywood stars buzzed around Catalina, gambling in the popular casino and dining in restaurants and sunning themselves on the beach. Phyllis and her friends spotted Mary Pickford, Charlie Chaplin and Paulette Goddard, both Selznick brothers, and Claudette Colbert. After an early dinner, they boarded their motorboats and chugged across the water to the yacht. Tom and Natalie, tousled and tanned, asked about their activities. Nobody inquired about how they'd spent their hours of solitude.

At nightfall, when they heard the boom and blast from the island, the entire group assembled on the deck with their cocktails. Watching the multicolored sparks shoot upwards, arc gracefully down, and dissipate into nothingness, Phyllis couldn't shake her pessimism. She hoped the wedded couple's present elation wouldn't prove as ephemeral as the fireworks that flared against black sky and instantly vanished.

CHAPTER 37

After successfully directing a stage play in Baltimore and meeting with New York theatre managers, Lela returned to California brimming with plans. Her time on the East Coast had been productive, and after five years of polishing her co-written script of *The Funnyman,* she deemed it worthy of Broadway. But before pursuing that project to its desired conclusion, she would resolve unfinished business in Hollywood. Construction of the house in Coldwater Canyon was completed, but she needed to oversee the final decorative touches. And she would urge her niece to decide on a wedding date, if she wanted a traditional ceremony and not one of those speedy affairs before a judge.

"Most, if not all, the churches and chapels and hotel ballrooms and country clubs will be booked," she told Phyllis over lunch in the RKO dining room. "There's no hope of finding a suitable venue for June, but July is still a possibility. Ginger and I will handle everything, if you tell us what you'd like."

Phyllis raised her head to say, "Right now, my greatest wish is to break the engagement. Without hurting Carlyle. Nobody else can do that for me."

Lela reached across the table to clasp her niece's left

hand, still unadorned by a diamond. "Your chat with Ginger didn't put you off?"

"No. Not that."

"Then what's the problem, dearie?"

"The usual one. His mother. She doesn't like me. She blames me for rushing him into marriage. When he reminds her that she and his father eloped twelve weeks after they met, it makes no difference. She tells him he'll never be a movie star if he has a wife."

"Ridiculous! Most of them do, not to mention those who divorced and remarried. Carlyle is a supporting player. Warner Brothers may never put him in leading roles. You don't have to look far in Hollywood to find experienced actors who are better-looking than he is, who haven't a prayer of stardom. Actresses, too."

"And I'm one. That's another of Mrs. Moore's objections. I'm not successful enough to deserve him. She can't let her precious boy tie himself to a failure who will drag him down. She actually said that. The other day she threatened to leave Los Angeles and move back East. There's no point staying here, she says, if Carlyle means to throw away his career after all her sacrifices to help him. And because he's a playwright's son, she insists it's his duty to uphold his late father's legacy."

"What an appalling way to treat him. And you."

"He believes she'll calm down after the wedding. I know better. I'm a threat. An enemy. And Carlyle can't understand how hurtful that is. I'm not used to being disliked. I was popular in school. I've made lots of friends in Hollywood. So you see, I can't possibly marry him. And though his mother is the main reason, I realized I'd made a mistake almost as soon as I accepted his proposal. I'm not sleeping well. Every morning when I get up, I tell myself it's the day to be straight. But when we're together, enjoying ourselves, I just can't bring myself to do it. I'm still fond of him. But my feelings are tame compared to what Anne and Johnny Payne have. Or Natalie Draper and Tom Brown."

"I pity any female who marries because of the sexual thrill, only to discover it's not strong enough to carry her through better or worse. And with a mother-in-law like Ethelyn Moore, you'd have entirely too much of the worse. It's your prerogative to have second thoughts. Even a girl of twenty-one still has growing up to do. Explain to Carlyle that you can't and won't bear the responsibility of a rift with his mother. Tell him you'll never be content without her acceptance. But don't put it off any longer. Nobody gains by delay."

"I know."

Seeing that Phyllis would welcome a change of topic, Lela leaned back in her chair and said, "I expect Ginger and I will be living in the new house before she finishes *Stage Door.* You won't be surprised to hear they've given her a dance routine in one scene. A short one, with that teenager, Anne Miller, who surely lied about her age to get the part. Lucille Ball was cast as a smart-aleck actress, a wonderful showcase for her. Katharine Hepburn plays Ginger's foil. The less said about her, the better."

"Is it true that Kath leaned out of a window and poured a glass of water on Ginger and her fur coat?"

"It's debatable whether her intent was malicious. She told everyone she was fooling around."

Horse-faced Hepburn was entirely too fond of her reputation for eccentricity. From the moment she arrived at RKO she'd queened it over the lot, until Rogers and Astaire caught the public's fancy, eclipsing her and delivering profits that rescued the studio from financial ruin. Hepburn's *Sylvia Scarlett* was a box office disaster. The producers of *Quality Street,* an insipid period piece, and in all likelihood another flop, offered various excuses for delaying its release. How many failures would it take to convince the bosses that their favorite wasn't worth the fortune they paid her?

The rumor mill churned out predictions that Ginger, always more concerned about the quality of her role than the placement of her name, would get top billing. Miss Hepburn, greatly offended by the prospect of demotion, was reportedly making a grand fuss.

As an RKO employee, mother of Ginger and mentor to Lucy, Lela was present whenever they were filming. Her girls held their own against Hepburn, unquestionably a strong and skilled actress. Greg La Cava, the director, encouraged them to contribute ad lib dialogue. Ginger, in the character of a cynical wisecracker, had a particular gift for well-timed jibes—mostly directed at the patrician Katharine. She behaved impeccably on set, furnishing quantities of cake for the four o'clock tea party her prickly co-star hosted for all the actresses. Their only catfight—so far—was the scripted one between their characters.

A pity, Lela mourned, that Phyllis wasn't also a resident of the film's Footlights Club boarding house. Any part, even a small one, would lift her spirits as she prepared to break off her engagement.

Early in July, two weeks before the birthday and housewarming party, she took her niece with her to check progress at the house on Gilcrest Drive. She steered the car past the towering retaining wall embedded in the cliff and followed the steep and winding driveway to the deceptively modest dwelling, faced and fenced with fieldstones. This outward simplicity concealed the fact that it consisted of multiple levels and sprawled across the hilltop. It was designed to take advantage of an unobstructed view of the canyon below and Beverly Hills beyond.

Every possible convenience was provided for her tennis-mad daughter. Workmen were smoothing the *en tout cas* court, an all-season surface that was the most comfortable to play upon. It was surrounded by light fixtures attached to poles, so matches could continue after nightfall.

She and Phyllis climbed the broad steps leading to the blue-tiled pool. The front edge of the cabana awning flapped in the breeze.

"You should've brought your suit."

Gazing at the rippling water, Phyllis replied, "Ginger ought to have the first swim."

"She did, the day the pool was filled. Come along to the house, and I'll show you how we've decorated it."

Out of her strong sense of patriotism, Lela had advised Ginger to adopt an Americana theme. The sturdy drop-leaf tables and straight-backed chairs were made of maple or oak, and the sofas were upholstered with chintz. A braided rug filled the space in front of the fireplace, and antique brass-handled implements were hanging on either side. Lela led Phyllis to the cavernous playroom downstairs, with ample room for the ping-pong set up and a billiard table.

Indicating the window alcove, she said, "I've commissioned a soda fountain that will go right there. A real one. It's being constructed off-site and will be assembled before we move in. I'm giving it to Ginger as a surprise birthday present. You know how she loves her sundaes and banana splits and floats and milkshakes. She'll be able to make and serve them to you and all her friends. But I'll have to abstain, because I'm reducing. I've taken off twenty pounds," she boasted.

The tour concluded in the kitchen. "We'll hire a cook, of course. I've been gathering references. And I found a groundskeeper who works in this area. He put in the front shrubbery and the flowering plants."

Lela filled a shiny kettle with water. While the tea was steeping in the pot, she placed cups and saucers on a tray and carried it to the dining room, painted a dramatic shade of plum. After reviewing her handwritten list, Lela tucked it into her purse and gave Phyllis her undivided attention.

"Did Anne and John set their wedding date?"

"Not yet. Everyone was so preoccupied with Fourth of July plans. Tom Brown chartered a yacht for our holiday excursion to Catalina Island."

"That must have been nice. After Anne settles into her new nest, what becomes of you? I suppose Mimi will be glad to keep you on as a boarder."

"I'm already looking for an apartment of my own. I'm able to save half my salary from the magazine, and some of what I've made as a freelancing actress."

"No regrets about Carlyle Moore?"

"Not a one. His mother was so afraid I'd want him back that she sent him off to New England. She let a Cape Cod summer stock company have one of his father's plays, provided they cast Carlyle in the lead."

"I heard you've been seeing the younger Bert Kalmar, the lyricist's son."

"It's the least I can do, after he saved my life. Not that I remember much about it. We were doing relay races in his parents' pool. I was underwater, going so fast that I messed up a turn and conked my head on the ladder. Knocked myself out cold and sank to the bottom." Phyllis shuddered. "If Bert hadn't spotted me, I would've drowned. He hauled me out and revived me."

"A fine start to a romance."

"Oh, he's not a boyfriend. He's my collaborator. We're writing songs for *Look Out Below,* another movie musical Anne and Tom Brown and I were scripting. Before she got engaged to Johnny, and Tom became inseparable from Natalie Draper." Phyllis opened her satchel and pulled out a bundle of papers bound with a thick rubber band. "Here's our opening number."

Lela put her reading glasses back on and scanned the score. When she finished, she nodded approval. "A promising effort. When you finish, I want RKO to take a look. Maybe they'll offer to buy it—for Ginger to star in."

CHAPTER 38

The Browns and the Drapers, concerned about the validity of a shipboard wedding, soon found out that the eloping couple's union was unlawful. The State of California required an official marriage license. Tom, deprived of his bride, promptly obtained the necessary item in Pasadena and arranged for a judge to perform a second ceremony. Making the best of it, his in-laws announced that a formal church ceremony would take place in the autumn.

While she and Phyllis dressed for Ginger's birthday party, Anne said, "After what happened to Tom and Natalie, Johnny is determined to do things properly. He means to apply for our marriage license well in advance so we'll be ready if we decide to marry at short notice. You and Mother will be our witnesses. Henry Willson is giving me away. Until I met Johnny, he was the most important man in my life. Since he's been my agent, I've had so many successes. I'm sure he could help you, too."

"He did. Once." Rapidly diverting from a subject she'd rather not pursue, she said, "Did you choose your wedding date?"

"I'm hoping we can have our ceremony a month from now, and sneak away for a short honeymoon. It all depends on when Paramount schedules Johnny's picture with George Burns and Gracie Allen. I've no idea what RKO has planned for me."

Ginger's grand house, built for entertaining, was large enough to accommodate a large crowd of the same performers whose social activities and love lives Phyllis recorded in her magazine columns. A sizeable sampling of influential producers and important directors and studio executives was present—the result of Lela's influence, she surmised.

She located her cousin in the playroom, standing beneath her soda fountain's red-and-white awning, as she enthusiastically demonstrated its features. The oval-shaped marble counter featured a row of gleaming taps connected to containers of ingredients. The ice box unit was stocked with various flavors of ice cream, and the miniature refrigerator contained milk and whipped cream and eggs. Jars of chocolate sauce and fruit jam and all kinds of nuts were lined up on a shelf.

"I'm not a proficient soda jerk yet," Ginger announced, "so I called in reinforcements from the nearest drugstore!" She beckoned to a pair of young men. "Okay, everyone, place your orders. And you're all entitled to a piece of chocolate cake."

Phyllis wielded the knife, placing each slice on a white china plate rimmed with turquoise and silver, and handed them to Lucille Ball for distribution. Ginger's spaniel monitored the proceedings, watching closely for any scrap that might fall to the blue-tiled floor.

When all the guests were served, Ginger approached the cake table, licking a speck of frosting from her finger. "Can I borrow you for a moment, Phyl? Lucy can take over."

Phyllis went with her to the staircase, and the din

receded with their ascent. Halfway up, they sat down on the same broad step.

Cupping her chin in her hand, Ginger heaved a sigh. "Twenty-five years old. Incredible."

"I bet you've done a movie for each year of your life."

"More than one. Counting *Stage Door,* in post-production, it's thirty-five. Or thirty-seven." Ginger shrugged. "Something like that. But that doesn't include all those early shorts and two-reelers. Lately it's been one picture after another after another. Work, work, work. That's why I'm demanding all the unused vacation time RKO owes me. I'm planning a lengthy trip, incognito, to a remote spot where I can let my hair down and be outdoors all day long. I want complete privacy. George Stevens recommends the Canadian Rockies, for horseback riding and fishing and hiking. Not quite Mother's idea of a swell time, and anyway, she can't get away from the studio. I want to take you."

"I like hikes. And horses. I love to fish. When do we leave?"

"Three, four weeks from now. We'll go to Seattle, maybe spend time with our Aunt Inez, board the boat to Vancouver and explore it before we take a train to Banff. I can have an automobile shipped up there ahead of us—as *car*-go," Ginger joked. "The convertible will be perfect for sightseeing. Everyone who visits Lake Louise comes back marveling at its magnificence."

It occurred to Phyllis that even if she could get away, the timing of this trip might coincide with Anne's wedding. Later, when she and her friend were in the kitchen wiping crumbs from the plates, she raised this possibility.

"Johnny and I will wait till you get back," Anne declared. "Like Ginger, you need a holiday, and it sounds like a great adventure. I've had one international trip in my life—that day you drove me down to Tijuana, Mexico, because I wanted to be able to say I'd been in another country besides this one."

"I'd hate to miss your bridal shower."

"Don't give it another thought. Having you as my bridesmaid is all that matters." Anne followed up this assurance by saying, "It seems backwards for a girl to have her shower after her wedding, but we should throw one for Natalie. She didn't have a trousseau. I can get the names of her high school crowd from Mrs. Draper, and we'll put together a guest list for a ladies' luncheon. On the terrace at the Beverly Hills Hotel."

"We should also invite Ida Lupino and Betty Grable and Betty Furness. The Durkin sisters. And Mary Blackford."

"Of course." When Anne reached up to push back a dangling curl, her new engagement ring sparkled.

Phyllis seized her hand. "Let me see that diamond again." The stone, over four carats, was a Payne family heirloom.

"When Johnny gave it to me, and told me about all the jewelry and antiques his parents will send us, I couldn't believe it. I worry people might think I'm marrying him because of his rich family. But honestly, when he proposed I had no idea." She carried the coffee cups and saucers to the sink for the butler to wash.

Anne provided Phyllis with three tickets the *Stella Dallas* preview. Ginger took this opportunity to try out the black wig she planned to wear during their trip to conceal her identity. She sat by herself in the back row of the cinema, far from her mother and Phyllis.

Lela, pleased with her protégée's performance, said afterwards, "Anne is strong in her scenes with Barbara Stanwyck—no small feat. Mark my words, she'll be nominated for the Academy Award. As I expect you to be, dearie," she told Ginger. "For *Stage Door.*"

"If anybody from our cast is recognized, it'll be Katharine Hepburn," Ginger predicted. "The Academy loves her."

Phyllis, aware of her cousin's longing to receive the Oscar, wouldn't know who to root for if both Ginger and Anne were in contention. Kath already had one.

The majestic Banff Springs Hotel, designed to resemble a French chateau, sat in a low basin surrounded by soaring peaks. The driver who had collected Ginger and Phyllis at the railway station pulled up before the front awning. Half a dozen bellhops stepped out into the rain, followed by the hotel manager, who showed them to their suite with great ceremony. When he parted the thick curtains to reveal a vivid rainbow painted onto the pale gray sky, he did so with the air of one who had prepared it for them. All the luggage trucked over from Vancouver was already unpacked, and their clothing, pressed by the laundry staff, filled the closet and bureau drawers.

Unfortunately, the hotel's luxuries did not include the privacy and anonymity Ginger desired. People loitered near the entrance and filled the lobby, hoping to catch a glimpse of the visiting star, or request her autograph. Her initial appearance in the dining room caused such a commotion that she and Phyllis agreed that subsequent meals would be delivered to their suite.

In order to evade the curious eyes of other guests and interested locals, Ginger roused Phyllis hours before sunrise. They washed and dressed, and summoned bellhops, to carry gear—fishing rods or golf clubs or art supplies or camera equipment—to the convertible that had preceded them via train. They sought out secluded lakes, encircled by mountains and screened by evergreens. They golfed in the faint morning light on grass wet with dew, in view of moose and elk. Later in the day they went horseback riding, returning at dusk. Spying journalists detected the cousins' routine and doggedly tracked their movements. They reported the number of fish the movie star caught—none, on the first outing—the distance her golf balls traveled, and how often she defeated her opponent when playing ping-pong in the hotel's game room.

Hollywood realities intruded. Because Ginger still owed them a picture, Warner Brothers sent her a script. She received a phone call from her agent and a telegram from Pandro Berman, her producer at RKO.

"He's extremely pleased with the final cut of *Stage Door,*" she informed Phyllis. "And he's now willing for me to work up original comedy bits for *Having Wonderful Time.*" Spreading butter across a toasted crumpet, she asked, "Are you listening?"

"Yes." Phyllis stuffed their dwindling collection of unused film rolls in the camera bag.

Ginger put down the telegram and picked up a letter. "Mother is talking to RKO about putting you under contract again."

"I can't imagine why. She insisted that I free myself from the one I had."

"Because she believed you'd receive better roles elsewhere, and more money. But you're not working at all."

"I'm writing. That's work."

Disregarding this response, Ginger went on, "If she and I join forces, we're certain to prevail. I rarely ask for favors."

"No? As I recall, you're the one who persuaded them to delay *Vivacious Lady* until Jimmy Stewart gets well."

"Because he's the best actor for the part."

"And you're sweet on him."

"What if I am?" Ginger picked up her glass of orange

juice, and before drinking said, "To tell the truth, I'd jump at the chance to perform opposite anybody who isn't Fred. I've begged Pan Berman to give me a break from musicals, and my message is finally getting through."

"I thought you wanted dramatic parts. Your next two pictures are romantic comedies."

"But I won't be singing and dancing. When the right script comes along, I'll fight for it. Hard."

"Remember when you visited me in Oklahoma City, years ago? You were dying to be in musicals. Now you're allergic to them. And to Fred."

With a shake of her strawberry blonde head, her cousin replied, "Neither of us expected our screen partnership to become permanent. After his sister Adele quit their act to marry her English lord, Fred was determined not to end up as one half of a team again. If we don't go our separate ways soon, the studio will keep us dancing together till we're both old enough to sashay into that New Jersey rest home for aged actors."

A mental image of geriatric hoofers made Phyllis laugh.

"I'm not joking. Fred and I have heaps of fun working together. I think he's wonderful. But like the characters we portray, we're so different. Conflict is necessary in a light script with a happy-ever-after ending. Off-screen, it's problematic. He's changed a lot since our Broadway days. His wife is a society lady who doesn't care for show people. His brother-in-law is a duke's son. His suits are specially tailored in London and shipped over. He invests in racehorses. I suppose he still regards me as the lesser artist. But even if I'm not the best dancer or the best singer in Hollywood, I'm the one who's popular with the public."

"You are," Phyllis agreed.

"Which is why," Ginger said on a triumphant note,

"RKO will take my advice and cast you in *Vivacious Lady* and *Having Wonderful Time.*"

As the organist played, heavy black curtains parted to reveal a casket almost obscured by flowers, outnumbering the arrangements at Peg Entwistle's sparsely attended funeral five Septembers ago. Today Phyllis was haunted by lost friends. Peg, with all her beauty and talent, driven to suicide by despair. Charming Junior Durkin, whose darker secrets were buried with him. Courageous Mary Blackford, lying beneath the lily-covered coffin lid in the chapel's Mary Baker Eddy Room.

Seated with newlyweds Anne and John, she pondered the sad coincidence that her friend's funeral was taking place on the third anniversary of the automobile crash. September, the cruel and cursed month that altered Mary's life, had also ended it.

This is one gathering that I won't write up for *Hollywood* magazine.

"At my bridal shower," Anne whispered, "she told us Dr. Berry was so pleased by her progress. She showed us she could move her arm, just a little bit, and she was so excited. Her mother mentioned fainting spells, but Mary didn't seem concerned."

Phyllis was surprised that this rite was being led by a female Christian Scientist. A curious choice, given the denomination's aversion to medical intervention—from which Mary had benefitted. And what, she wondered, were the teachings on death and the afterlife? Reluctant to embark on a religious conversation with Lela or Ginger, she'd never asked them about it. She held fast to her understanding of God and Jesus and the Holy Mother and the saints. Her morality had been formed by the Catholic concepts of mortal sin, repentance and redemption, heaven and hell. Despite her failure to attend confession or mass, the religion of her formative years proved durable, but unlike her aunt and her cousin, she didn't trust prayer alone to cure illness or injuries. She'd always depended on the healing powers of physicians and surgeons.

In his heartfelt eulogy, Henry Willson spoke of Mary's brief but vibrant life, her boundless optimism and valiant spirit, and the cheerfulness that readily won hearts. He acknowledged the significant financial support the actress had received from celebrities and funds raised through the ceaseless efforts of her tightknit group of friends. He described how the Puppets had faithfully transported her to football games, cinemas, parties, and picnics.

After a psalm and scripture reading, the congregation sang "O Gentle Presence," inspired by a Mary Baker Eddy poem. As Phyllis half-sobbed "Thou love that guards the nestling's faltering flight, keep thou my child on upward wing tonight," her streaming eyes were drawn to Mrs. Blackford's bowed head. At the conclusion of the hymn, Henry escorted the bereaved mother from the chapel. It was hard to tell which of them was nearer collapse.

Anne gripped her husband's arm as they descended the steps of the Spanish-style building. "A lovely tribute. Quite moving."

Phyllis nodded, not trusting her voice.

They watched the pallbearers load the casket into the hearse.

In a few days, she and Lucille Ball and Florence Lake would travel in her cousin's wood-paneled station wagon to Big Bear, where studio carpenters had constructed a lakeshore Catskills summer camp for *Having Wonderful Time*. Battered and bowed by grief, she doubted that her time on location would match the movie title.

CHAPTER 39

"Your place is lovely, dearie," Lela approved. "You've done well for yourself."

Phyllis had leased a furnished garden apartment in the Andalusia building on Havenhurst Drive, a stone's throw from their former dwelling in the Garden of Allah. Her large living room, with vaulted and wood-beamed ceiling, compensated for the compact kitchen and a tiny bedroom. Cats were the only pets her landlord permitted, so she'd consigned her devoted mutt to Anne's tender care.

She took Lela to her portion of the shaded terrace, where she'd set out a light lunch.

"Can you afford this place? Because if not—"

"I can. Thanks to Ted Magee and Jack Smalley, who promoted me to society editor at *Hollywood.* And to Ginger, for re-establishing me at RKO. I'm so flush I can cover Mama's travel expenses when she comes to visit."

"We'll take her to the studio to watch Ginger in action. And she can meet the hair stylists and makeup artists. Will she arrive before I leave for New York?"

"Yes." Phyllis scooted her chair out of the shade and into a pool of sunshine. "What does Ginger say about your relocation plan?"

"She'll be too preoccupied with work to care that I've gone away. Like you, I'm declaring my independence. High time I shed the dreadful 'stage mother' label." Resentment overlaid the resignation in Lela's tone when she added, "Whatever success the performers I train and coach achieve, or the excellence of the screen tests I supervise, here in Hollywood I'll always be known as Ginger's mama. In Manhattan, where female professionals are accepted, I can burnish my reputation as playwright and producer. But I've got another motive for making this move."

Phyllis listened politely to the familiar complaint about how drastically Los Angeles was changing—and not for the better. The European immigrants continually flooding in, fleeing fascist regimes, brought their different notions of art—and morality. They influenced politics, reinforcing Lela's suspicions that their distinctly un-American sympathies had crept into too many screenplays. She mistrusted the writers more than the studio bosses. Louis B. Mayer, for instance, upheld conservative values and espoused proper virtues.

"But the executives' private behavior doesn't always match their public pronouncements," Phyllis reminded her.

"Nonetheless, I applaud their determination to preserve and promote patriotism and speak out against the rampant socialism of the Roosevelt administration. Don't think I'm surrendering. Oh, no. I'm taking the fight to New York."

Lela soon voiced the question she must have been withholding ever since she crossed the threshold. "Are you seeing anyone special?"

"I go out with anybody who asks, if he's nice. And hasn't got an interfering mother."

"I cannot believe Carlyle Moore got married so soon after you broke off your engagement."

"One of life's finest jokes," Phyllis replied with a smile. "Mrs. Moore packed him off to the Cape Cod summer stock company to get him away from me, and he promptly eloped with another actress. I sincerely pity her. Not for marrying Carlyle, but for having a mother-in-law like that."

Not long after their visit, Lela returned to spend the afternoon with the sister she hadn't seen for seven years.

"You've certainly kept your looks," she commented after their embrace.

"A necessity, in the beauty trade." Mama returned the compliment, saying, "No wonder the columnists say you could be Ginger's twin. But you're a great deal thinner than you used to be. How do you manage it?"

"Coffee and cigarettes," Phyllis volunteered. "She rarely eats."

When her mother handed around recent snapshots of her toddler grandson, Lela smiled in recognition, saying, "A round-headed Owens descendant. Looks like he'll resemble our papa when he's grown."

"Phillip's more even-tempered," Mama declared thankfully. "Good as gold. I take care of him when Jean's at her evening job. I feed him supper and put him to bed. And I'm quite happy to care for him whenever he needs me. As you know, when my girls were his age, they lived with our parents so I could go wherever I could find work." After a pause, she said, "If Ginger had a child, it might've saved her marriage."

Lela directed a skeptical glance at her sister. "And how did that help us with ours?"

Mama was amenable to every plan devised for her entertainment. Phyllis and Lela showed her around the RKO soundstages, introducing her to the starriest employees. She sat in the canvas chair with Ginger's name stitched on the back and watched Ginger and Beulah Bondi film a comic scene in a railroad car.

Impressed by the luxuries of the Coldwater Canyon mansion, she declared, "The magazine photos don't do it justice." While taking tea on the terrace, in view of the pool and tennis court, she asked, "Do you have time to enjoy all of this?" Her hand swept outward in an encompassing gesture.

A grimace accompanied Ginger's reply. "Not enough. Maybe I will in the future. Leland, my agent, is renegotiating my contract. Bigger salary, an easier schedule."

Showing great restraint, Lela failed to take one of the petit fours from the plate Phyllis passed to her. "While you're on the coast, Virginia, you should take the train to Seattle to see our sister Inez. She lives in a charming log house on a lake, with mountains all around. She was thrilled by a visit from Billie and our nephew Lee when they came West. I'd pay your fare."

"Better hold onto your money, you'll need it all when you're living in New York. I can't extend my stay. I'm a working woman."

"As are we all," Ginger murmured. "After we finish our snack, I'll show you my art studio. I've made a sculpture of Mother."

"A whole statue?" Mama asked, eyes wide.

"Head and shoulders," Lela explained. Succumbing to temptation, she speared a miniature cake with her silver fork.

When Ginger continued the tour, Phyllis helped her aunt carry the tea tray and plates to the kitchen.

"Thanks for spending time with Mama."

"I trust she's enjoying herself."

"She says so. Yesterday she saw the magazine office, and last night we went to a club. It must be strange for her to see the way I live. After all the years we've been apart, she's forgotten how to mother me. Or doesn't know how." Tipping the wet tea leaves into the waste bin, she concluded, "She's ready to get back home to little Phillip. And the salon. She misses Oklahoma City."

"I can't think why. You never did."

After setting the empty teapot on the counter, she turned to Lela. "If you and Ginger hadn't taken me away and brought me here, my life wouldn't have been half as interesting."

"We couldn't bear to let all your promise go to waste." Lela wrapped the remaining petit fours in waxed paper, saying, "Once I'm settled in New York, I'll send for you. I'm sure you'll love it as much as Ginger and I do."

"You won't try and turn me into a Broadway star?"

"I'm absolutely certain I could, dearie. If you let me."

The bird of paradise plant, a prominent feature of the Andalusia courtyard, wasn't displaying as many multi-colored spikes as it had during summer and fall. Even in December, the bougainvillea trailing up the apartment building's white stucco walls produced purplish-red-petals. Phyllis carried her suitcase down the steps and past the perpetually green ferns and palms surrounding the central fountain. A tiled pathway led her beneath a curving arch to the twin garages where residents stowed cars and golf clubs and paraphernalia. In five minutes—and he was always on time—her fiancé would pick her up.

She was the latest to catch the matrimonial fever that had struck her friends over the past year. Several weeks ago, she'd announced her engagement to cinematographer Henry Freulich. Today they were embarking on an out of town trip together, appropriately chaperoned.

Next month, when they returned from their New York honeymoon, she'd leave this charming oasis for his bachelor rental near Toluca Lake. He'd commissioned blueprints for the house he planned to build on a lot on North Crescent Heights Boulevard. Next April their Beverly Hills home would be the setting for a triple celebration. Henry's birthday was the day after hers, and Anne's was two days after his.

Florence Lake, who regularly appeared in Ginger's films, had played matchmaker. Her brother was Dagwood in the *Blondie* films at Columbia Pictures, where Henry was a director of photography. At thirty-two, he was already a film industry veteran. He'd quit high school to work as an office boy at Universal Pictures, where his late father had been portrait photographer. His Uncle Roman, after shooting publicity stills for Columbia, had received a promotion to scene writer. Henry's most significant credit as cameraman was *It Happened One Night,* one of her favorite movies. And he was a world-traveler. Magazines had published the photos he'd taken during his tour of European countries, and he'd visited China and Singapore and Japan.

Before meeting him, Phyllis had given up any hopes of lasting love and commitment. Henry's maturity—he was thirty-two—and his seriousness appealed to her. He was gainfully employed in a stable profession, and he'd earned the respect of his peers. He worked in the picture business, but he wasn't a performer. Best of all, he didn't much care whether she continued acting or gave it up in order to concentrate on her writing. Which she was tempted to do on a daily, almost hourly, basis.

The vehicle that halted in front of the entrance gate wasn't his. It belonged to John and Anne.

When Henry hopped out, she said, "I thought we were driving to Bear Lake by ourselves."

"Change of plan. You don't object to sharing the back seat with me, I hope."

She reached up to flick his hat brim with her forefinger. "You know better." His recent haircut exposed ears that stuck out even more than Clark Gable's used to.

After he squeezed her case into the crowded trunk, he helped her into the car.

Anne twisted around to blow a kiss. "We're going to have such fun! I hope there's lots of snow, to make it feel like a real old-fashioned Christmas. The house we rented for the week has a fireplace. We'll be so cozy."

Taking Henry's hand, Phyllis said, "You Easterners miss your winter, don't you? Aunt Lela says the best thing about New York at this time of year is being able to wear furs comfortably. Unlike here in California."

"I haven't noticed that the weather makes any difference to you," her fiancé commented. "Or your Cousin Ginger. I'm guessing the furriers sell as many coats and stoles in Hollywood as they do in Manhattan. Maybe more."

"Betty Furness and her husband—our other Johnny—will join us tomorrow morning," Anne said. "They're supposed to be bringing Tom and Natalie. Unless—" After a pause, she concluded, "With those two, you never know."

During the summer, shortly before their first anniversary, the Browns had separated. Natalie spent a month at her parents' house before reconciling with Tom. Although neither specifically stated the cause of the rupture, it hadn't fully healed. Despite her parents' opposition, or possibly to provoke them, Tom had decided Natalie should become an actress. Phyllis had accompanied her to Columbia Pictures for her screen test, filmed by Henry. But not a single casting director had offered her a role.

Phyllis, after working as a glorified extra in Ginger's

recent pictures, had completed a string of minor parts at Twentieth Century—a secretary, a cashier, and a florist's assistant. *Everybody's Baby* was her third film with Hattie McDaniel, who reminded her of Clara Willingham, Mama's former housemaid. The black actress had confided that Mr. David Selznick would be testing her for Scarlett O'Hara's servant in *Gone with the Wind.*

Because Anne knew Hattie from *Stella Dallas,* Phyllis shared this news, adding, "This week he plans to burn the city of Atlanta, out in Culver City."

Henry nodded. "He'll feed the flames with all the old sets and scenery littering Forty Acres."

"That's where I got started in pictures," Phyllis reflected. "A brief scene in an Eddie Quillan comedy for Pathé. I was fifteen."

Anne turned again to ask, "Will you take Henry to Oklahoma City to meet your mother and your sister?"

"Not enough time off," Henry explained. "Right after Christmas, *Blondie Meets the Boss* goes into production. We won't wrap till late January."

"Our wedding will be as simple as yours," Phyllis told her. "Lela's not here to arrange an elaborate one, and Ginger's too busy to be involved. But we'll have Henry's uncle and cousin. And maybe his mother, if she returns from Europe in time."

Theirs would be a civil ceremony, because the Freulichs were Jewish. Phyllis hadn't told her mother. Lela, who very likely had figured it out, must also have guessed that the members of Henry's family were registered Democrats. If these facts didn't matter to Phyllis, they shouldn't bother anybody else.

John spoke up. "I read in the paper that Mrs. Rogers might follow you and Henry to the altar. With J. Edgar Hoover, of all people. Any truth to that report?"

"He takes her out when he's in New York on FBI

business," Phyllis replied. "I suspect she welcomes the publicity their relationship brings. She's always been adamant about never getting married again."

At the Market Stop in San Bernardino, Anne and Phyllis purchased everything necessary to provide meals for their crowd. While the butcher wrapped up their order of sliced ham, minced beef, frankfurters, ground coffee, milk, butter, and ice cream, they visited the bakery counter for sandwich bread, pies, and sugar cookies.

"Those jelly rolls look delicious. We'll take a dozen," Anne told the white-coated woman behind the display case.

Phyllis and Henry made room on the back seat for the paper sacks of provisions. For the final hour of the journey they sat even closer, his arm around her shoulder and her elbow lodged against his thigh.

"It'll be like old times," Anne enthused, "working together in the kitchen. Remember how we used to roast a leg of lamb for our boyfriends?"

"And we served that silly candlestick salad," Phyllis contributed. "With whole bananas standing on end. And I baked my pumpkin tarts."

"After impressing the fellows with one fancy home-cooked dinner, we made them take us to nice restaurants."

Falling temperatures had frozen the pools of melted snow in the winding roadways. Each time the car skidded, Phyllis held her breath and leaned hard against Henry. Anne got muddled when comparing her written directions to the map. Recovering from several mistaken turns, John found the gravel drive that led to an oversized chalet. He and Henry took care of all the luggage. Anne and Phyllis stowed their groceries in the icebox and cupboards. Then they went through the house, switching on lamps and turning on wall heaters.

"Each married couple has a bedroom," Anne

announced, "and there's one for our single girl. Her fiancé gets the rollaway in the den." With a sympathetic glance at Henry, she said, "I hope it's comfortable."

"I never have trouble sleeping," he assured her.

While their men stacked logs in the living room's stone fireplace, Anne and Phyllis prepared a hearty spaghetti supper. Everyone pitched in to clean up afterwards, and they gathered around the fire to toast marshmallows. Wife and husband eventually retired to their quarters, leaving Phyllis and Henry cuddling on the big sofa.

A session of heated kissing ended when she gently extricated herself from his embrace and climbed the stairs alone to her room. As she quickly replaced her garments with warm flannel pajamas and thick socks, she wished they could remain a foursome.

By mid-morning, the additional two married couples arrived. Zipping themselves into their warmest winter gear, Natalie and Betty built a snow family while their husbands engaged in a friendly snowball battle. Phyllis and Anne retreated to the kitchen to confer about lunch, leaving Henry and John playing checkers at the fireside. In the afternoon, some members of the party pulled toboggans and sleds out from under the porch and set out in search of a snowy hillside. After dinner and marshmallows, John scrounged up a deck of cards for poker.

Phyllis, suffering from chills, had difficulty concentrating on the game. Later, despite the blankets she piled onto her bed, she was still shivering.

CHAPTER 40

On her third day in the mountains, Phyllis woke up with a throbbing head. She felt a burning rawness at the back of her throat and at breakfast discovered the agony of swallowing. Her nose was so stuffy that she was no longer able to enjoy the scent of pine and cedar that hung in the chilly air. She mentioned none of her ailments, except to warn Henry about the dangers of kissing.

Bravely she set forth with their friends to Barney's, the nearest nightspot, where the men drank beer and the ladies—except for Phyllis—sipped cocktails. Her brandy-laced hot toddy induced drowsiness, but at bedtime she felt so feverish that she wasn't able to sleep.

In the morning, Anne came to her room to check on her. She struggled into her clothes and went downstairs for a morning meal she doubted she'd be able to eat.

"You're not going anywhere today," her friend declared. "I won't, either. I'm nursing you back to health."

"No," Phyllis croaked. "I'll manage. You should go."

"You know I don't ski."

"But you'll enjoy watching Johnny and the others."

"Tom and I can stay with her," Natalie volunteered. "I brought my knitting, and he's got a police drama script von Sternberg sent him. Honestly, we don't mind spending the day indoors while everyone else is out in the freezing cold, sliding down mountains."

"Speak for yourself," Tom shot back. He shoved his chair back from the table and stalked out.

An embarrassed and oppressive silence descended. Betty Furness broke it, either by accident or design, dropping her fork on the wooden floor.

Natalie's shining head dipped down, then swiftly lifted, revealing a stony face. "He was desperate to win me back. Mother warned me I'd regret giving in, but I believed his promises to behave better. As you see, he's the same beast he's always been."

Despite the trouble she had speaking, Phyllis was moved to offer comfort. "His grumpy and temperamental spells don't last. And he's always sorry afterwards."

Natalie drew a shuddering breath. "You're all so kind, and I'm grateful. But there's nothing any of you can do to make things better."

The skiers invited Tom to go along, but he remained at the chalet. He carried his script to the living room and sat down to scribble notes on the pages. Natalie settled nearby with her knitting but put it away when he complained that the click of her needles distracted him.

"I'll be in the kitchen," she told Phyllis, pointedly ignoring her spouse, "chopping vegetables for soup."

"I'll help."

"Keep those germs to yourself," Natalie replied, smiling.

To ward off an oncoming chill, Phyllis went upstairs to get a heavy wool blanket from her room. She rummaged in her purse for her notepad, flipping the pages till she found her outline for a short story. Settling into an armchair on the staircase landing, she tried to compose the opening paragraphs but was so comfortably cocooned that she dozed off.

Raised voices from below jolted her awake.

"You're a spoiled brat," Tom raged. "I'm sick to death of it."

"Not as sick as I am of being bullied," his wife shot back. "It's bad enough that you treat me like dirt when we're alone, but you do it when we're with our friends. I can't stand it anymore."

"What's that supposed to mean?"

Phyllis could see them but they hadn't noticed her. She hated to eavesdrop like this, but if she left her chair they'd see her. That would be awkward for everyone.

"We came to this beautiful place," Natalie went on, "to have fun. You've done everything you possibly can to ruin it for everybody."

"You accepted the invitation. Not me."

"Because I expected you to behave like a civilized human being. And tolerate me for just one week—or pretend to. My mistake."

Crossing to the staircase, he called, "You hear that, Phyl? Mrs. Brown has actually admitted to an error in judgment."

Natalie wiped her eyes. "Leave Phyllis out of this."

"You assured me I'd get red carpet treatment when we visited the Hearst estate, that Marion Davies would adore me. Far from it. You told me that if we married, you'd be the happiest girl in the world. We all see how that turned out. Oh, and you promised me your stuck-up parents would accept me as their son-in-law. Nope. Hasn't happened. Never will."

"How is that my fault?"

Tom moved to the hearth and picked up the poker. After stabbing at the logs, he brandished it in Natalie's direction. "God alone knows what I ever saw in you. I should've stuck with Phyllis. Or Anne. Or Betty. Any of the really nice girls."

"They're luckier than I was. Each of them ended up with a decent, caring person. And I hope I do, too. Someday."

This time it was Natalie who stormed off. She came charging up the stairs and shut herself in their bedroom.

Phyllis jumped up from the chair so fast that she tripped on her blanket, stumbled, and narrowly avoided a fall. Going to the couple's door, she rapped softly.

From the other side, Natalie said, "Go away."

"It's me," Phyllis rasped. She rattled the knob. "Please, let me in."

When she crossed the threshold, she found Natalie perched on the rumpled bed. "Now you see why I left him last summer. After the holidays, I'll do it again. The bitterness, the insults make my life an absolute hell. You want to know what's worse? Some days he won't even speak to me at all, like I don't even exist. You saw it yourself, Labor Day weekend, at the beach. When we're having good times—and there are some—I can't imagine living without him. After we fight, I wonder whether I can ever be happy again. I suppose I still love him. But I'm so mad right now that if I still had that vegetable knife in my hand, I'd carve him into pieces."

"She threatened to kill him?" Ginger turned away from her dressing room mirror.

"Nobody else heard," Phyllis clarified. "Just me. And she didn't mean it. Don't say anything about this to anyone. Promise?"

"I can keep secrets." Ginger pressed a powder puff to her brow. "You'd be amazed by the things I conceal from you."

Phyllis reclined on the chintz-covered chaise longue,

enervated by the malaise that had come back with her from Bear Lake. Her gaze roamed from one elaborate embellishment to another—drapery swags, ruffle-edged pillows, gilded picture frames. She was lying beside a pair of red-lipped boudoir dollies in frilly, fancy gowns. One had brown hair like hers, and the blonde resembled Ginger. When decorating her future home, she would not copy her cousin's preferred style.

Staring up at the ceiling, she said, "Yesterday Natalie told me she's moving out of their Van Nuys house. She wants to get an apartment, if her parents pay for it. Or she'll live with them." She eyed the scripts stacked on the side table and leaned over to pick up the one on top. "*Little Mother.* Will that be you?"

"Only on screen."

"Good thing. If you want a baby, you need a husband."

"Technically, I've got one. Lew and I aren't divorced yet. Have you and Henry talked about children?"

She nodded absently as she leafed through the script. "When does production on this masterpiece begin?"

"Nobody seems to know. After Fred and I are done with our impersonations of Vernon and Irene Castle, I'm visiting Mother in New York." Ginger closed the box of powder and stood up. Plucking the long chiffon sleeves of her dancing costume, she asked, "What do you think? Mrs. Castle had to approve the design. It's a copy of one she wore a quarter of a century ago."

"Very nice."

"While I'm rehearsing you should read the whole screenplay, so you can give me your opinion. Like Mother does."

"My eyes hurt."

Still, she felt duty-bound to carry out Ginger's request. Plowing through page after page of dialogue, she found nothing endearing about the characters or amusing in their situation. Her cousin returned to find her nodding off—and she still hadn't reached the climactic scene.

"Did you finish it?" Ginger inquired, holding her back erect so the wardrobe woman could unfasten her gown.

"I didn't need to. Polly doesn't strike me as the challenging dramatic role you've been begging for."

"Maybe not. But I like Buddy DeSylva, and it's his first time producing. Garson Kanin will direct. Every actress eventually gets her chance to be upstaged by an adorable tot. I'm no exception."

When Clarkie carried away the Irene Castle costume, Phyllis said with conviction, "This picture isn't worth your time. You should turn it down. Lela would agree with me."

"If you're sure."

"Positive."

Ginger phoned the studio operator and asked to be connected to Mr. DeSylva. During their conversation she stated her reservations about the material, liberally quoting Phyllis.

"He wants to discuss it with me in person," she said, hanging up. "You've got to lend me your support. Expect an invitation to a very select gathering."

On a drizzly January evening, Phyllis was obliged to exchange dinner table small talk with the producer and the director whose pet project she had condemned. After dinner, down in the playroom, they bombarded her with questions, correctly identifying her as the source of Ginger's misgivings.

"What don't you like?" asked Buddy DeSylva.

"The entire storyline. Isn't it supposed to be a comedy? And it needs a better title."

Garson Kanin rubbed the bald space that extended

from his brow to the crown of his head. "How about *Baby Makes Three?*"

"No, no, no," Buddy objected. "We're sticking with the motherhood concept." He leaned towards Phyllis. "Everything depends on the performances, honey. Ginger has perfect timing, she'll draw the laughs. There's plenty of farcical business with the baby. How about we perform a scene for you?"

Kanin shook his head. "You're no actor, Buddy. Stick to producing. And song-smithing."

Ginger was already on her feet. "Let's do it."

Their impromptu performance was hilarious. Phyllis couldn't contain the giggles that were scorching her throat.

"All right," she gasped, holding up both hands. "It plays funnier than it reads. Ginger, may I please have another serving of ice cream?"

Her cousin tossed aside the bolster representing the abandoned infant and crossed to her canopied soda fountain.

Buddy DeSylva sat beside Phyllis. "I swear, honey, *Little Mother* is a sure-fire hit. You've got to be my date at the preview screening, so I can see you laughing like a goof all the way through to the end. How about we put you in the picture? I bet you'd like that."

Drawing back, she said, "I won't be available." Before he finished shooting his movie, she would be Henry Freulich's beaming bride.

After her guests departed, Ginger warned, "Watch out for Buddy. He's got a wife."

"And I have a fiancé. Henry would be here tonight if he didn't have to spend his evenings at Columbia Pictures with Blondie and Dagwood."

For days her persistent sore throat and constant cough kept her homebound. By the weekend she felt somewhat better, so she invited Henry to Sunday dinner. Their main course, she decided, was an opportunity to try a Polish recipe his mother had sent all the way from Warsaw. After Mrs. Moore's enmity and distrust, she was grateful for the warm affection she received from Henry's relatives, in Hollywood and overseas.

Throughout the meal he spoke of the increasingly dire situation in Europe. Germany's Nazi regime had annexed Austria in the spring, and autumn brought the seizure of the Sudentenland in Czechoslovakia. He feared Poland; homeland of his parents and other Freulich immigrants, would be the next to fall.

"Dad returned as often as he could, to visit my grandmother and my aunt. Sometimes I went with him. And after he—" Henry's voice faded away. He rarely referred to the father who had committed suicide two years ago. "When my mother was widowed, she went back. I'm urging her to leave."

Phyllis said, "I hoped she might make it back for our wedding. But if we get married this month like we've planned, I don't suppose it's possible."

She expected him to stay long enough to look over her recent photographs—his Uncle Roman had offered tips about light settings and shutter speed. Then they would listen to Walter Winchell's broadcast and snuggle during the music program that followed it. But he told her he couldn't linger.

Frowning, he said slowly, soberly, "You won't want me to, when you've heard what I came here to say. I've put it off too long, and that's not fair to you. To either of us."

A premonition made her shiver all over, uncontrollably. This wasn't the chill that preceded a fever, but an icy symptom of dread.

"You're having second thoughts. Is that it?" She read

the answer in his expression. "I see." But she didn't, not at all. "Since when?"

"That holiday house party with your friends. I went for a peaceful, relaxing week in the mountains. Instead, I got too much Tom and Natalie drama. And a whole lot of actor and actress chatter."

"I didn't enjoy myself either," she acknowledged. "Stuck in bed half the time, with this awful cold that never quite goes away."

"It made me think about my parents, and all that went wrong with their marriage. Dad was tireless in his work—probably to escape troubles at home. Maybe to distract him from the despondency that he eventually succumbed to. My mother felt neglected. She was." Shaking his dark head, he admitted, "I'm a lot like him. Which is the best way of saying I'm not the right man for you."

What he meant, but couldn't bring himself to tell her, was that she was wrong for him. And there wasn't anything she could do to change that.

"You're a terrific girl, Phyllis. I don't want you to be mad at me. I already feel bad, and that would make this even worse."

"I'm not," she said. "If you wouldn't be happy, I can't be either."

But I do love you, she cried silently, so much. And I can't stop, simply by wishing I could.

In a gesture of acceptance, she found her way to the coffee table and picked up his hat. He took it from her, his face revealing mingled guilt and relief.

Striving for lightness, she told him, "I turned down a proposal once. And I've broken off an engagement. It's tough, isn't it?"

He offered her a faint smile. "Thanks for understanding."

She went with him to the door. "What will you do about the lot on North Crescent Heights?"

"The blueprints for the house are finished. I expect I'll proceed with construction. When my mother returns, she can live there with me."

Dredging up a feeble response, she said, "A nice arrangement. For both of you."

And I'll stay here at the Andalusia. A sick and sorrowful spinster, all alone. Surrounded by shattered dreams.

No, no, no, she corrected herself.

That would be a betrayal of my proud Owens heritage, and all the strong, brave women of our family. Mama, widowed once and twice divorced, unbowed by fate's unkindness. Ginger and Lela, so devoted to one another and their careers that they remain resolutely and contentedly single.

She, too, was an independent working woman, determined to prove herself just as capable and confident. Even though she would spend the rest of this night in tears.

Recovery from heartbreak, Phyllis could attest, was more prolonged and painful when the sufferer was simultaneously afflicted by ill-health. Swallowing was so great a torture that she hardly ate anything, not that she had an appetite. A trip to the doctor resulted in a double diagnosis of walking pneumonia and tonsillitis.

Ginger was so deeply entrenched in Christian Science that Phyllis asked Anne to transport her to the hospital.

"At least it's a short stay," she observed. "When I was a kid, I spent months in a children's ward." The removal of her tonsils would leave no visible scars, unlike all those repairs to her shattered leg.

At the scheduled time, a gurney rolled her into an operating room, permeated with that sickeningly antiseptic smell she remembered. Her heart raced at the knowledge of what was about to happen. She saw the tray of shining instruments. A stark light beamed down upon her.

A man shrouded in a surgical gown held up a rubber mask with a trailing tube. "When I place this over your nose and mouth, breathe regularly and count backwards from ten."

Opening her eyes, she saw a misty, white-gowned figure hovering over her and blinked to clear her vision. A young woman, pretty and blue-eyed, bent over the bedrail. A loose lock of golden hair slipped from her starched peaked cap.

"Peg." The name formed in her mind but would not emerge. The pain in her throat was unbearable. She felt nauseous.

"Can't talk," she mouthed, gesturing at her neck. The fog in her brain was lifting, and panic poured in.

"Don't worry," the nurse soothed her. "It's normal. You must keep completely quiet until you've healed."

Her eyelids drooped, shutting out the face that was so similar to her dead friend's.

Suppose her voice never returned? If she could no longer be an actress, after striving to fulfill an ambition she had willingly adopted, she would have wasted seven years—almost a third of her life. She might have gone to college and trained for some useful profession, like teaching. Or she'd be a librarian, surrounded by stacks of books, with access to all the literature and accumulated knowledge in the world.

Buried deep beneath her fear, a seed of relief was sprouting. She wouldn't mind being freed from the career that, over time, had become a bearable form of bondage.

Before sinking into sleep, she marshalled one vague but coherent thought: I'll still be a writer.

Every morning, she received a glass of fruit juice. Twice a day she struggled with a bowl of warm broth. The addition of strawberry gelatin cubes to her limited diet was unsatisfying. Her tummy was in constant turmoil. Each time she stepped onto the scale, the nurse pursed her lips and shook her head.

"Eighty-two pounds. Even for a little thing like you, that's worrisome. If you go much longer without solid food, you'll waste away."

Confronting the square of mirror at the sink, Phyllis saw that her cheeks lacked color and had lost fullness. Her dimples were less obvious, even when she forced a smile.

Anne, her daily visitor, was never at a loss for words, so the inability to converse was immaterial. In her idleness and silence, she was desperate for books that could distract from the pain and draw her out of despondency. One day she passed her friend a note: *Please bring me cheerful stories to read. Not too funny. They say I shouldn't laugh.*

She was discharged to continue her recovery in the Shirley-Payne household, where her former dog kept her company while her hosts were working at their respective studios. And when Phyllis returned to her Andalusia apartment, Anne stopped by as often as her schedule allowed. She delivered vats of soup and foamy milkshakes from Schwab's. She arranged the get-well cards along the windowsills and discarded faded flowers from the bouquets sent by friends. Phyllis was touched to the point of tears by the one from Henry Freulich and his Uncle Roman. A stream of telegrams had arrived—from Lela in Manhattan, from Mama in Oklahoma City, and from Hollywood performers too busy to put pen to paper.

Before departing for New York, Ginger foisted her revised *Little Mother* script on Phyllis.

"I really don't think she should play Polly," she whispered to Anne, who emerged from the kitchen with a glass of ginger ale and a bowl of consommé. "Even in a supposedly straight role, they're making her dance. She enters a jitterbug contest because she needs the prize money."

"What's the story?"

"A department store salesgirl who lost her job sees a woman deposit an infant on an orphanage doorstep. When she picks it up to soothe its crying, the director assumes she's its mother—and unmarried. The store executive hires her back and gives her a raise so she can afford to keep the baby. She insists it's not hers, but nobody believes her. Her employer's dad assumes he's the kid's grandpa. And the plot descends deeper and deeper into farce."

"Stop talking and eat. You're supposed to be studying the *Sorority House* screenplay. I don't want you ruining our scenes together."

Phyllis choked out a feeble giggle that almost didn't hurt.

When Ginger returned from the East Coast, she was shocked to find Phyllis so pale and frail.

"I'm taking you to Palm Springs to restore you to health. You don't look like you have the strength to hold a ping-pong paddle. A week in the sun and hearty food will do you a world of good. In no time, I'll have you horseback riding and swimming."

By the conclusion of their desert holiday, Phyllis was feeling a great deal better. Her welcome home present was a term contract from RKO. In addition to appearing in *Sorority House* with Anne, she'd serve as Ginger's stand-in while *Little Mother* was filming. She had difficulty mustering enthusiasm about it. After nearly seven years of toiling in Hollywood, and various ups and downs, she'd traveled a full circle back to the same place where she'd started, as an anonymous bit player.

CHAPTER 41

"Is it correct, Miss Fraser, that you accompanied Mr. and Mrs. Brown when they eloped?"

Phyllis nodded. Remembering the attorney's instruction to speak her answers, she said, "Yes, sir. We were on a yacht, sailing to Catalina Island. I didn't attend their second ceremony. The legal one." She glanced at the judge, whose eyes were half-shuttered.

Natalie was seated behind the plaintiff's table. Her black coat dress, exquisitely cut, flattered her model's figure, and red lipstick contrasted with her ivory complexion.

"At any time during the past year did you observe the sort of mistreatment Mrs. Brown has described to the court?"

"I was present on certain occasions when he belittled her. At nightclubs and the bowling alley and parties. And our Labor Day weekend beach party when Tom—Mr. Brown—didn't speak to her at all. Not once. It was embarrassing for her—and the rest of us." She mentioned the Christmastime incident at Big Bear. "I saw him pick up the fireplace poker. But he didn't strike her," she hastened to add.

"Please describe to the court what you witnessed on New Year's Eve."

"In the middle of our celebration, he told her he regretted their marriage. That she shouldn't have agreed to marry him."

"Does Mr. Brown drink to excess?"

"I've known him for five, six years and have never seen him drunk."

"Are you aware of any acts of physical brutality?"

Even though she knew this question was coming, it distressed her. "None."

"What is your assessment of Mrs. Brown's present state of mind?"

"She's depressed. Anxious. So much that she turns down modeling assignments and screen tests."

"Thank you, Miss Fraser. Your honor, I have no further questions of this witness."

After a brief recess, the judge granted the interlocutory decree, on the grounds of spousal cruelty. The dissolution of the Browns' marriage would become final at a later date. Natalie maintained her impassive expression as she glided past the newspaper reporters and cameramen, her white-gloved fingers gripping her velvet clutch purse. Descending the front steps of the courthouse, Phyllis wished her hat shielded her face. She worried that Tom would hold it against her when he saw the press photographs of her at Natalie's side.

Her fondness for him was deeply ingrained, and her supporting role in Natalie's domestic drama felt like a betrayal of that longer friendship with her husband. She regarded Tom as a brother, just as Anne did, and the likelihood of a permanent rupture pained her. But, as she knew only too well, his words and actions had driven his wife away. And he wasn't contesting the divorce, even though he professed to love Natalie, who claimed to love him still—despite everything. Each of them had accepted that they simply couldn't get along or live together harmoniously.

No Hollywood marriage for me, she vowed when she and Natalie climbed into the attorney's vehicle. *Never again will I allow myself to develop serious feelings for a man in the film business.*

The interest and passion that so often sparked on soundstages or remote location or nightclub dance floors rarely proved to be durable. As she'd seen with Ginger and Lew, disparity between spouses—when one achieved greater fame and received a higher salary than the other—was an acid that devoured and destroyed love. The demands of film work and the grueling schedules it imposed kept couples apart, increasing the risk that one party might stray.

And the alternative to matrimony?

A solitary home life. Relying on family members and friends to save her from self-absorption. Peace of mind.

With plenty of time to write.

By the time she'd torn off five pages of months from her calendar, Phyllis had accrued a bank balance substantial enough to support her for the rest of the year whether or not she accepted future offers of film work. She could therefore afford to divide her time between writing magazine articles and developing her ideas for fictional works. She reviewed an early novel draft, written in the heady days when success as an actress had seemed so tantalizingly within reach. But her perspective had changed.

At great personal cost, she'd obtained sufficient material for a tragic saga. Two broken engagements—three, if she counted the unaccepted proposal from Buddy Parsons. Three dead friends. Countless professional setbacks. Failure to find true and enduring love.

Unwilling to commit herself to a lengthy, demanding project, she embarked on a series of satiric short stories with Hollywood settings. She parceled out incidents from her own history to one plucky heroine, who dodged death multiple times. She survived a gas explosion, being struck down by a delivery van, an earthquake, and a near-drowning in a friend's swimming pool. Her movie star boyfriend believed she was his lucky charm, the key to all his successes, and tried desperately to keep her from harm.

She sent her collection of tales to Lela, her critic and champion, and in return received helpful comments leavened with assurances that she was destined to make a sale. Phyllis typed up clean copies to submit to *Liberty* magazine and steeled herself for potential rejection.

Shortly after she got back from the post office, Ginger telephoned with an invitation to a Pasadena preview screening.

"For what?" she wanted to know.

"My baby movie. And yours. Flo Lake is going with me, and so should you."

"Why? To find out if they've edited me out of the New Year's Eve celebration in Times Square?"

"You were hopping around with David Niven, so you needn't worry. Lots of important studio people will be there. In fact, Buddy DeSylva said he looked forward to seeing you again. I've been complaining about the title, and now that Louella Parsons has denounced it, he's agreed to make a change."

"All right, I'll go."

Florence Lake drove them in her car as a ruse, to prevent the press from spotting the picture's star. Ginger huddled in the back seat, disguised by a flaming red wig instead of the black one that seldom fooled the columnists or their spies.

As they reached the outskirts of Pasadena, Flo told Phyllis. "Next month I'm paying a visit to New York, to see friends and check out the latest Broadway shows. And I'll sniff around for radio voice work. Your cousin planned to go with me and spend time with her mother, but RKO won't extend her vacation time."

Behind them, Ginger muttered, "The bosses are making sure I earn every dime of the raise I got with the latest contract."

"I'd love to see Lela," Phyllis said, "and her fancy Central Park apartment."

"You ought to go with Flo," Ginger encouraged her. "Let me pay your way. I owe you that much for showing me how to hold a baby without making it cry."

"I'll think about it."

Flo parked a block from the cinema. The threesome crept stealthily inside. Ginger and Flo chose seats in the back row.

Buddy DeSylva waylaid Phyllis. "You promised to sit with me," he told her.

"Did I? When?"

"I haven't forgotten, even if you have." He grabbed her hand.

She ended up sandwiched between him and director Garson Kanin.

"Don't judge too harshly," Buddy murmured, his lips disconcertingly close to her ear. "It's not the final edit."

"All right." He was an important producer at RKO, and it would be uncivil to slither away from him.

"You've got the sweetest smile I've ever seen," he told her during the opening scene. "I'm going to write a song about it."

The woman seated in front of them turned her head to shush him.

When the mechanical toy ducks appeared on the screen, her giggles were drowned out by uproarious laughter from the audience. During production she'd sometimes watched the rushes, but seeing the film in edited form was a revelation. As the star's stand-in, she'd moved about the set while the technical crew worked out placement for their cameras and lights and microphones. Multiple infants portrayed Johnnie, and the expressive Bert had been her favorite—and the director's. Even though baby-wrangling hadn't been included in her job description, she'd often volunteered to cuddle the youngest members of the cast. She was among the New Year's Eve revelers, cavorting with a visibly uncomfortable David Niven, desperate to work his way through the crowd separating him from Ginger.

When the screen went blank, she apologized to the producer for misjudging the script.

"You can make it up to me," he replied. "Let me take you to dinner. I know the perfect place. Very private."

Where none of his acquaintances—or his wife's—would spot them. "Thanks, but I can't."

"Jealous boyfriend?"

"Like Ginger—and Polly—I'm a bachelor girl."

His broad brow creased. "*Bachelor Girl.* A pity I can't use it for the title. I'm still determined to highlight Polly's accidental motherhood."

"How about *Bachelor Mother?*"

"Say, that's good! For that, you deserve two dinners, at a minimum."

"You're under no obligation whatsoever, Mr. DeSylva. Consider it a gift."

"Buddy. C'mon, say yes."

Grasping at the best available excuse, she told him,

"I'm about to pay a visit to my Aunt Lela. Before long, I'll be leaving for New York City."

"What a coincidence." His grin flashed in the half-light of the auditorium. "So am I."

"Where's the kid?"

"At the theatre." Lela tipped the cream jug towards the teacup Harold Ross held out. "With Buddy DeSylva."

"I wonder what the hell she sees in him."

"She's seeing the city. The World's Fair. Baseball games at Yankee Stadium. Carriage rides through the Park. Matinees and lunch dates. But she doesn't let him take her to nightclubs unless I go with them. He has a wife in California. She goes out with other men, of course. Any attractive new girl in town finds herself in demand. And Hollywood actresses are by far the most sought after."

Harold sipped his tea. "This would taste a hell of a lot better with a tot of whisky."

"You know I don't keep liquor around."

"From what I've seen at the Stork Club, somebody taught your little one to drink. When are you bringing her to my place in Stamford? Why not this weekend?"

"Buddy gave us tickets to something. And Phyllis wants to shop for a suit to wear on Monday, when she starts her summer job at McCann Erickson."

"I guess I shouldn't be surprised you convinced them to hire her." Harold's hand plowed through his shaggy head in a characteristic gesture.

Lela fluttered her fingers dismissively. "No convincing required. I showed Stuart Ludlum her clips from *Hollywood* and *Photoplay*. She's assigned to the radio advertising department, writing copy for a face cream account. I'm hoping they'll keep her on."

"They could put her in their print ads. As a model."

"She's no longer interested in posing. Or performing."

For years she'd honed and faceted and polished her niece, striving to produce another sparkling Hollywood diamond. Although Phyllis was by no means a failure, she hadn't approached the kind of success Ginger, or the actresses in Lela's squadron of protégées, had achieved. Anne Shirley had earned an Academy Award nomination for Best Supporting Actress. Betty Furness played lead parts at MGM and elsewhere. Lucille Ball was getting feature roles at RKO.

"Your Phyllis reminds me of Sylvia Sidney. Her face. Her hair."

Lela considered this comparison. "There may be some similarities in their appearance, but not in temperament. Phyllis doesn't believe in extramarital affairs. Or divorce."

"Poor Bennett. That was a heavy blow. But even when he was so depressed over being dumped, I couldn't whip him at backgammon. Your niece claims to play the game. Bring her to Connecticut so I can find out if she's any good. I always lose to Ginger."

"She sometimes loses to Phyllis."

"I wish you hadn't told me," he said dolefully. "I hoped I'd get lucky against a wide-eyed innocent."

Lela picked up the heavy crystal lighter and held it to her cigarette. Standing at her broad picture window, she looked out on the green swathe of Central Park and the jagged array of buildings to the south.

Her building occupied the site of the former Century Theatre, on the west side of the park between 61st and 62nd. The two-bedroom apartment, situated in one of its distinctive double towers, was bathed in sunlight during the morning hours. The sunken living room was large enough to accommodate a dining table, but for their lunch and dinner she and Phyllis favored restaurants frequented by show business people. Ginger took care of the rent, and all other living expenses.

For exercise, they strolled across the park to the Madison Avenue shops. Phyllis could spend hours wandering the art museum, and yesterday she'd explored the collections of bones and skulls and rocks and curiosities in the Museum of Natural History.

"Does the kid play poker?"

Lela turned away from the view. "She does. I can't personally attest to her prowess, but I don't doubt she can hold her own. Unless you like surprises, Harold, don't ever underestimate Phyllis."

CHAPTER 42

Each weekday morning Phyllis dressed with care, gulped her breakfast, and trotted off in the direction of Columbus Circle station to board the subway train. For some twenty blocks she hurtled underground, emerging at the 42nd Street stop. From there she walked for ten minutes or so through Bryant Park, past the imposing Public Library, to the McCann Erickson offices at 40th and Madison. Buddy DeSylva had warned her not to append "Street" or "Avenue" to the traffic-clogged East-West and North-South thoroughfares, or she'd be taken for a rube.

Throughout her life she'd envisioned New York City as it appeared on film, a collection of skyscrapers in shades of cinematic gray. She'd been startled to discover the variety of colors—golden and silver towers pointing towards a pure blue sky dotted with bright white clouds. Thick grass carpeted the parks, and the tree branches bore deep green leaves. The residential buildings were constructed of brownstone or granite or red brick.

The advertising agency had inserted her into a corner in one of its less populated offices. Her desktop was just wide enough for a typewriter. She could use all the drawers except the one reserved for the illustrator of the all-important Flit insecticide and Essomarine engine oil accounts. She had yet to meet this invisible character.

One damp morning when she was almost late, she leaned her umbrella against the cloakroom wall and hastily hung her coat. Grabbing her rain-spattered satchel, she raced to her chair. It was occupied by a lanky man who had shoved the typewriter aside. He was sketching on a piece of agency letterhead.

"Good morning," she greeted him. "I'm Phyllis."

"Pleasure." He extended a large hand. "Ted. Did they bother to tell you I keep stuff in this desk?"

"You're Mr. Geisel."

"Most of the time. Whenever I'm here."

She tilted her head. "And when you're not?"

"Dr. Seuss, author."

"Really? What sort of books do you write?"

"The ones that don't sell very well," he replied. "Illustrated tales for kids, with rhyming text. However, at the moment, I'm cooking up something in prose, for grown-ups. Later this year, Random House will publish *The Seven Lady Godivas.* My silly pictures of naked ladies overcame Bennett Cerf's better judgment." Ted gathered up his worn-down drawing pencils. "You can have your desk."

"I just need my clipboard and a sheet of paper. I write radio ad copy." With a self-deprecating shrug, she added, "I try to."

"For which program?"

"*The Career of Alice Blair,* brought to you by Daggett and Ramsdell cold cream," she said, in the singsong tones of a radio announcer. "I'm new to advertising. And New York. I live in Hollywood."

"Ludlum mentioned that we had a movie star in our midst."

"He was pulling your leg. But I do work in pictures—

that is, I did. RKO. Twentieth Century Fox. Warner Brothers. Universal. Columbia Pictures. Minor studios, too."

"I can't get enough of California. My wife Helen and I would live there, if we could."

"I was a Helen, too, before my cousin changed my name. She's Ginger Rogers. A real star."

"And how! I hope you're enjoying our fair city."

"I haven't missed Los Angeles at all since I arrived here," she responded truthfully. "New York is constantly in motion, even late into the night. Neighborhoods to explore, each with a character of its own, inhabited by people from every country in the world. I feel like I've reached the heart of the universe." Her chin rose when she said, "If you've always lived here, you can't understand how exciting it is to someone like me. I grew up in Oklahoma City."

"I'm from Springfield, Massachusetts. My horizons were broadened in Hanover, New Hampshire—I'm a Dartmouth man—and Oxford University in England." He pulled out his drawer to rummage through a stack of pages covered with drawings and slogans. He took out a slender hardcover book and presented it to her. "For you. A study in the benefits of observation and the powers of imagination."

She examined the cartoon drawing on the cover of *And to Think that I Saw it on Mulberry Street.* Handing it back, she asked him to inscribe it for her but didn't admit that this would be her only autographed book. She'd always disdained collectors of signed film star photos, not seeing the point of them, but an author's signature was something special, a keepsake to be cherished.

Ted hunted for an ink pen and uncapped it. On the flyleaf he swiftly outlined a peculiar creature that wasn't a duck or a horse, but a delightful combination of both.

Beneath it he scrawled, *For Phyllis and Helen, who are one and the same. What a pleasure to meet a most personable dame! From Ted (Dr. Seuss), of the lower drawer, to a top-drawer colleague. July, 1939.*

That night she proudly showed off her prized possession.

"Very nice, dearie," Lela said distractedly. "Now hurry out of that suit and into the pretty dress you got from Bonwit's. Harold is picking us up at six, and you know how he hates waiting. We're celebrating tonight."

"What's the occasion?"

"Our change of address. Today I inquired about renting an available suite at the Madison Hotel. Two bedrooms, and a living room every bit as large as this one. It has a kitchenette, which is all we need. And daily maid service. We'll still be close to the park. You can take a city bus straight down Madison to your office. Or a taxi. And the rent is less than I pay here."

That Ginger pays, thought Phyllis, but refrained from pointing that out. "I want to contribute something to our living expenses. I make two hundred a week at the agency."

"And you're worth every dollar," her aunt declared.

"I wonder if my boss thinks so."

Creating radio ads was proving more difficult than she'd expected when she accepted her position. She'd given up her Pond's cold cream for Daggett and Ramsdell's version, so she could accurately extol its attributes, a forty-five-cent investment that so far paid minimal dividends. Women purchased their beauty products for finite reasons—price, perceived results, and habit. She struggled to come up with fresh ways to entice them into purchasing more, or lure them away from a competing brand. But because the Pure Cold Cream had been on the market for three decades, there couldn't be a female alive who was unaware of its existence.

Each weekday at airtime, she went to the coffee room to hear the WOR broadcast of the fifteen-minute episode. After the theme music, consisting of interminable high-pitched humming, a female announcer with a pseudo-British accent read out the copy Phyllis had labored over. She'd borrowed a favorite line from Wordsworth as an introduction to her description of a woman's hectic activities. After that, she detailed the supposed benefits of cleansing with Daggett and Ramsdell Pure Cold Cream.

Alice Blair, her program's main character, was an aspiring actress who left her small town for Manhattan—a plot device familiar from countless Hollywood movies. In no time at all, she landed a clerical job at a publishing house, headed by a man whose interest in her might not be entirely altruistic. Phyllis noted that certain aspects of her present existence matched the heroine's. But Alice's desk faced a window overlooking a New York street, whereas she confronted a wall. And Alice didn't have to share hers with somebody else.

At the end of her working day, when she joined the throng of humanity moving up and down Madison Avenue, Alice's lines from the radio script rang true.

They aren't just people. I see a story behind every one.

On a blazing hot mid-July day, Phyllis sat at the wheel of her aunt's jaunty convertible, searching for town line signs posted along the Merritt Parkway. Raising her voice over the engine's growl and the whooshing wind, Lela described the rural serenity of Harold's house beside the Rippowam River.

"Is my playsuit too casual?" Phyllis asked her. It was

red gingham, its short skirt covering the bloomers, and her pumps were printed with a similar checked pattern. The red scarf tied over her head was supposed to keep her hair from blowing into a tangle.

Lela, impeccable in pale linen, her face shaded by a straw hat, assured her she looked perfect for the occasion. "You're the picture of summertime. Harold likes for his guests to feel comfortable. And he makes sure they're amply supplied with alcohol. If you don't want to drink hard spirits, you can decline. He'll act like he's offended, but pay him no mind."

"Who else will be there?"

"Nobody but us, I assume. Slow down—we've almost reached Long Ridge Road. That's our turn. We're getting close." She directed Phyllis to a wooded lane running parallel to the river.

The woman who opened the front door of the rambling gray clapboard house informed them that Mr. Ross had gone down to the riverbank, where the air was cooler.

"Mrs. Rogers, you and Miss Fraser will share a room," she said apologetically. "The gentleman from the city will be staying overnight as well. He's supposed to arrive in time for dinner. After you settle in, you're to join Mr. Ross. I'll bring cold drinks—you ladies must be parched. And if you want me to press any of your things, place them on one of the beds."

They went upstairs to a bedroom with an angled ceiling. Lela blotted her face and reapplied her lipstick at the mirror hanging above the bureau. Phyllis ran a brush through her mussed hair and smoothed the creases from her overskirt. Together they left the house and followed a pathway to a grouping of high-backed wooden armchairs.

Their host greeted them enthusiastically, and Phyllis received a paternal kiss on the cheek. "Blistering day, isn't it? Have a seat, make yourselves at home. Well, Miss Gingham 1939, what do you think of my place?" Harold's long arm shot out.

"Wonderful," Phyllis said.

They answered his typically masculine inquiries about the length of their drive and the traffic they encountered along the way. A native of Utah, this towering figure of the literary scene was a curious combination of Western directness and Manhattan elitism. His deep devotion to both Rogers women extended to Phyllis, and she'd grown accustomed to his contradictions. In all her years of reading *The New Yorker,* she'd never imagined becoming friends with its formidable founder and editor.

When he asked what they'd been doing with themselves, Lela described the *Bachelor Mother* premiere at Radio City Music Hall. "We were the guests of honor. The lady columnist for the King Features Syndicate interviewed us outside the theatre."

Harold turned to Phyllis. "Steer clear of Walter Winchell. One of my best writers is determined to do a profile on the conceited bastard, and maybe I'll let him. It won't be flattering. How could it be?"

Lela replied tartly, "His comments about Ginger are almost slanderous. He's itching to write about her affair with George Stevens but doesn't quite dare. I hope and pray his innuendo flies right over the heads of his readers."

"Better hope he doesn't get wind of the kid's friendship with DeSylva." Harold's thick lower lip protruded as his gaze shifted to Phyllis. "Is that masher still chasing after you?"

She was saved the trouble of replying by the crunch of wheels in the driveway.

"Oh, good," Harold said, rubbing his palms together. "He's here."

The man coming down the path was tall, with a pleasant face that was mysteriously familiar. He was dressed as casually as Harold, in a sports shirt with loose trousers and brown saddle oxfords.

"Ladies, I present the great Bennett Cerf. Publisher *par excellence.*"

"Nice to see you again, Mrs. Rogers."

"This is Lela's niece, Phyllis. I told you she'd be here."

The man smiled at her, his brown eyes warm and soft yet simultaneously probing. Maybe his vision was poor. He held dark-rimmed spectacles in his left hand. Looking up at him, she realized why she recognized him. He was Sylvia Sidney's former husband.

"Hello," she managed.

"Our little gingham girl is a refugee from Hollywood," Harold was saying, "trying her luck on our turf. She's a backgammon player. Maybe you'll be brave enough to take her on. I hear she's pretty good."

Bennett Cerf took the chair across from hers. "Suits me. Harold is poor competition. He always loses."

The housekeeper brought a tray, glasses of beer for the men and lemonade for Phyllis and Lela. Conversation was centered on the oppressive weather and the chances of a change before the weekend ended.

"Too damn hot for tennis or badminton," Harold grumbled. "But there's plenty of time for a swim before we eat. I hope everyone brought bathing suits."

"Phyllis did," Lela said. "Go and put it on, dearie."

Dubiously she regarded the pool of water, its depths obscured by the shade cast by towering trees. Her near-fatal accident in Bert Kalmar's pool had made her wary of venturing into unknown depths. And she didn't want to muddy her brand-new swimsuit. Maybe Harold would be satisfied if she dipped her feet.

When she got up, Bennett Cerf bounded out of his chair. "I need to get my bag and briefcase from the car."

He stepped aside to let her go ahead of him on the pathway.

"You aren't allowed to work while you're here," Harold called after them.

As she continued towards the house, she could hear footsteps gaining on her, then the question, "How do you keep busy when you're not bent over a backgammon board?"

"Radio advertising. At McCann Erickson."

"If you don't mind my saying so, you don't look old enough."

She whirled around, throwing herself off balance. "I'm twenty-three, Mr. Cerf. Care to check my California driver's license?"

He grinned down at her. "I'll take your word for it."

They parted in the driveway. She left him striding towards the sleek, new-style Cadillac parked near Lela's sports car.

She went upstairs to the guest room with the twin beds. Unfastening the row of tiny buttons on the front of her romper, she shucked it off. Her green and white seersucker bathing suit, purchased days ago at Peck and Peck on Fifth Avenue, had a knee-length matching coat, lined with terrycloth. After years of wearing Ginger's hand-me-downs, nice as they were, buying clothes with her earnings was both a pleasure and a point of pride.

Bennett Cerf exited his room at the very moment she left hers. Because he was still fully dressed, she felt overexposed despite her modest outer wrap. As he came towards her, she acknowledged him by inclining her head, the only part of her body that seemed capable of motion. She ought to move out of his way, except she couldn't manage it.

Not even when he moved in closer. Or when the dark head swept down, and his smiling lips pressed against hers.

She stepped away, too shocked to speak. Seemingly of its own accord, her open hand delivered a hard slap to his cheek. Then she turned and fled.

His laugh, low and warm, followed her along the hall.

CHAPTER 43

"Bennett Cerf made a pass at me." Phyllis belatedly disclosed her secret while driving back to the city on roadways choked with the automobiles of the other weekend refugees.

"When?" Lela asked.

"About fifteen minutes after Harold introduced us. You sent me inside to change. He followed me."

"You appeared to enjoy his company," her aunt observed. "Deep conversations. Backgammon games. Strolling together at sunset."

"This morning before breakfast he asked if he could take me home."

"To his place? The nerve of the man!"

"Ours. The Madison. I told him I'm your chauffeur." Before carrying her suitcase to their car, he'd asked for their telephone number. And she'd given it to him.

"Putting the two of you together was a silly scheme of Harold's. I have no idea whether he's matchmaking in earnest, or teasing his friend, because he thinks you resemble Sylvia Sidney."

Her sunny mood dimmed. "I don't look a lot like her. Do I?"

In retrospect, she realized her slap had been an

extreme reaction to his kiss. That awkward beginning hadn't doused the spark of mutual attraction. She pondered the unsettling possibility that Bennett's attentiveness had been prompted by her supposed resemblance to his former wife.

On Monday she returned to her desk in a brighter frame of mind than she'd left it on Friday. Her country weekend had reinforced her kinship with Alice Blair, whose boss was a handsome New York publisher keen to pursue her. Mr. Ludlum had explained that the smooth-talking Mr. Newman's interest in his secretary would lead to scandal and potentially wreck Alice's reputation in her hometown. But his seduction attempt would unfold slowly. To keep the avid audience tuning in, a radio serial scriptwriter was required to maintain interest and suspense.

She perched on her chair, pencil in hand, determined to produce the finest copy she'd ever written. Before writing a single word, her eyes fell on the telephone.

I should've given Bennett the switchboard number. If he calls me at the Madison and Lela's not there to answer, he might give up.

She dialed the hotel operator and asked if anybody had left a message for her.

"Nothing for you, today, Miss Fraser. Three calls for Mrs. Rogers. Mr. Ross. Mr. Hoover. Mr. Hannagan."

Steve Hannagan, Lela's current beau, was a renowned publicist and promoter. When in the city, he was a permanent fixture at the Stork Club, which honored him by bestowing his name on his favorite dishes and drinks. He straddled the continent, serving clients from New York to Hollywood, and various places in between. He represented the big racetrack in Indianapolis, Florida's Miami Beach, and a ski resort opening in Sun Valley, Idaho.

For two whole days she waited impatiently for Bennett Cerf to phone.

"It makes no sense," she complained to Lela as they dodged each other in their kitchenette. "At Harold's he hardly ever left my side."

"You sound like you want to see him again."

"I do. Oh, I know he's lots older than I am. And a very important person. I'm just—me. But we seemed so simpatico." She slid her spatula under a half-cooked grilled cheese sandwich and flipped it. "Couldn't we give a dinner party? Six people—three women, three men. Flo Lake. Mr. Hannagan. Harold. Us. And Bennett Cerf."

"I'll order a rib roast from the butcher. We'll need to buy potatoes." Lela's busy fingers shredded a chunk of iceberg lettuce. "And I'll make my stuffed avocado salad—if there are any to be found. We can finish with a delicious dessert from that bakery we like. I'll look over my appointment book."

Before they settled on a date and time, Bennett Cerf telephoned.

"A nice couple I know, who happen to be from Los Angeles—like you—asked me to supper and contract bridge afterwards," he told her. "I'm supposed to find myself a partner. I hope you can help me out."

Her knowledge of bridge was limited to the fact that it was extremely complicated, and her ignorance would sink her chances of impressing him. His West Coast friends would be older, as brilliant and urbane as he was, putting her at a disadvantage. As much as she longed to see Bennett again, his invitation posed too great a risk.

"I wish I could accept," she told him, and meant it. "But I can't."

"Sorry about the short notice. Next time?"

"That would be great."

She put down the phone, certain that he was already

asking somebody else. One of those sleek, sophisticated Manhattan women she'd seen shopping at Bonwit Teller by day and sipping cocktails at El Morocco at night.

Why does it bother me so much? I don't really know him well. But oh, how I want to . . .

She reached for the phone again and dialed Florence Lake.

"Flo, do you play contract bridge?"

"Sure. Why do you ask?"

"Last weekend I met a bridge player, and I like him. A lot. How long would it take you to teach me?"

The actress laughed. "Let's find out."

On Saturday morning, Bennett contacted Phyllis again, proposing a late afternoon visit to the World's Fair and dinner at one of the international pavilions in the Government Zone. Although she'd toured the site often enough to become familiar with its wonders, she was irrationally excited about returning with him.

They went in the gleaming Cadillac that offered every imaginable comfort. She didn't question him about last night's card party. She judged it safer to ask America's supreme editor to recommend books.

"You'll have to give me some clues about what you like."

"Quality novels by contemporary authors. Serious stories. And humor."

"I can heartily and enthusiastically, but not objectively, endorse any number of Random House titles." Keeping his eyes on the street, he said, "According to your aunt, you're a fiction writer yourself."

"I've submitted short stories to *Liberty*. And *Col-*

lier's. No sales, but I have a growing collection of friendly rejection letters."

"That means it's simply a matter of time till you're discovered," he replied.

"Lela says that, too."

When they arrived at Flushing Meadows, he parked opposite Fountain Lake.

After he turned off the engine, he looked over at her and asked if there was anything she particularly wished to do or see. "We could start with Elsie the cow standing in her living room. I pegged you as a milk drinker the moment I set eyes on you."

"I'm twenty-three, as I told you when we were at Harold's."

"Easy to forget. You look like a teenager."

"That didn't stop you from kissing me." She looked up in time to catch his abashed reaction.

"I was feeling fresh. I couldn't help myself. You're so irresistibly cute. Then, and now."

"It seems to me that a man your age—whatever it might be—would have developed self-control."

"I'm north of forty." Swiftly he added, "But not far north."

They embarked on an aimless wander along Rainbow Avenue, so committed to conversation that they were oblivious to the attractions. Phyllis had already seen all the landmarks. On prior visits she'd marveled at the spiky Trylon, so tall that it seemed to stab the sky, and had gone inside the globular Perisphere. At the edge of the Lagoon of Nations they came to a sudden stop, chatting away, oblivious to people whose progress they blocked. A typically blunt New Yorker pointed out their error in no uncertain terms, using extremely salty language.

They decided to dine in the Hungarian Pavilion, because neither of them had previously done so. After viewing the exhibits of Herend porcelains, Bohemian glassware, and lace, they entered the restaurant section.

Studying the menu, Phyllis commented, "Little Hungary in Los Angeles serves many of these dishes. One night when I was there, Hedy Lamarr left her table and sang folk songs with the gypsy band. I didn't frequent the fanciest places, unless I went with Ginger. Or when my friends and I were celebrating."

"Did you know Sylvia? You must've heard about us."

She nodded. "When you got engaged, your photo was in the newspaper."

"And when we divorced." He peeled away his glasses. "We genuinely believed our marriage would work. But I couldn't leave New York. And she needed to carry on with her career."

"Harold Ross thinks I look like her." Phyllis looked up from her goulash. "Is that why you kissed me?"

"Hell, no. You're adorable, and I'm impulsive. If I'd known Harold meant to introduce me to an exceedingly young babe who supposedly resembled my former wife, I wouldn't have gone anywhere near Stamford. I avoid reminders of Sylvia. She wounded me. Deeply."

His vulnerability was even more attractive to her than his self-confidence.

"And, I'll have you know, he paid dearly for my presence and my time. I extracted his promise that his rag would review three Random House books. He had to agree in advance to play backgammon with me. He always bets high and never wins."

"You and I didn't play for money."

"That would've been ungallant. Your salary is a fraction of his." Bennett tugged at one of his shirt cuffs. "Tell me about your job. In advertising, I mean. Not movies."

"I sit at a battered desk all day, staring at a wall, thinking up ad copy for face cream. The agency people seem nice. Interesting. Or quirky. Ted Geisel is my favorite, but he rarely shows up at the office."

"He's my author. I'll publish anything, everything he produces. That man is a genius. I gather he makes a pile of money doing those clever ads for Flit bug spray and Schaefer beer."

"That's what I've heard, too. But he says he'd rather spend his time writing children's books."

"The one he just turned in to me is definitely not for kids. It's full of naked women."

"He told me."

Later that week, he picked her up at her office and took her to dinner again. This time they went to the popular French Pavilion, a multi-level restaurant that could accommodate hundreds of diners. The *maître'd* escorted them to a window table overlooking the lagoon.

Phyllis sampled the French wine Bennett selected and expressed the approval he was obviously waiting for. "You've probably been to Paris."

"My first visit was in '24. I lodged in a Left Bank *pension,* run by a pair of remarkably rotund landladies. My pitiful French reduced them to hysterics. As my language skills improved, so did the breakfasts they served me. In '32 I went back, to meet James Joyce. I wanted to put out the American edition of *Ulysses.* We went to court over it, and by a miracle we prevailed. And it was worth all the trouble and effort and expense, because that book was the making of Random House. Scandal and litigation—the best kind of publicity."

She was curious about the celebrated authors and poets and playwrights he knew and had published or intended to publish. The names tumbled out—D.H. Lawrence, Eugene O'Neill, William Saroyan, Gertrude Stein, George S. Kauffman, George Bernard Shaw, William Faulkner. He discoursed at length, quite passionately, on a variety of topics. His famous wit, natural and unstudied, was immensely appealing. But his boyish enthusiasm, which had so charmed Phyllis at Harold's, contrasted with his reputation for cosmopolitan sophistication.

She started the meal with chilled melon, and for her entrée ordered the trout because she remembered enjoying it during her Banff holiday with Ginger. Choosing a dessert proved quite difficult, the options were so enticing. She requested Désir de Roi, which turned out to be stacked profiteroles topped with ice cream and drizzled with chocolate sauce.

For their third date, Bennett took her to the Stork Club. This, too, was familiar territory, from prior visits with Buddy DeSylva, or Lela and Harold.

The doorman guarding the famous portal unhooked the solid gold chain to admit them. Proprietor Sherman Billingsley came forward, hand outstretched. Bennett's popularity and prominence were obvious to her as they made their way to the main dining room. Women held lacquered fingers to scarlet lips and blew kisses as he passed their tables. The gentlemen rose to shake his hand or came over to pound his shoulder. Walter Winchell, heading for the cocktail bar, stopped short and stared at them so intently that she suspected he was mentally composing a paragraph for his column. Phyllis realized that Bennett had made a significant and very public acknowledgment of their budding relationship.

Sherman Billingsley sent vintage champagne to their table, and personally hand delivered a small box wrapped in silver paper and tied with a shimmering ribbon. Opening it, Phyllis found a bottle of Sortilège, the intense perfume produced by the fabled French house of Le Galion.

"Only the best for an Oklahoma girl," he declared. "I

grew up in Enid. Got my start as an entrepreneur bootlegging in Oklahoma City."

Several of Bennett's table-hopping acquaintances accused him of robbing the cradle. His annoyance was obvious as he repeatedly and defensively stated that his date was of legal age, even if she didn't appear to be.

One fellow, who had clearly imbibed too freely, stumbled over to them. "Good going, Cerf. Bet I know what cocktail this little darlin' likes best." He leaned over and winked at Phyllis. "Between the Sheets."

"Go to hell," Bennett growled.

He lapsed into a rare silence, fidgeting with his bread knife.

Phyllis reached out a hand to still the frantic motion. "Don't let anybody spoil our evening."

His head came up. "I should've known showing up with a girl your age would make waves. Lucky for me that Harold is in California, or there'd be no end of his self-congratulation. I hope he stays at your cousin's house for a long time."

"He's supposed to go to Reno so he and his wife can get divorced."

"And she'll be marrying his replacement straightaway—without skipping a beat. At least I was spared that Nevada indignity. Sylvia filed in a Los Angeles court. For years I've kept my distance from actresses," he declared soberly. "But here I sit, with another one."

"I'm a copywriter," she clarified.

"While you're in New York. Someday you'll head back to Hollywood to make movies."

He sounded as though he'd be sorry.

"I'm through with the picture business," she insisted. "Either I was a lowly extra, or my parts were very minor ones. I did have a couple of leads at Poverty Row studios, but my characters existed merely to show the male star's softer side and didn't affect the plot. I never got a chance to play the kind of sparky, witty girls that suit Ginger so well."

"I can't understand that. You're one of the sparkiest and wittiest creatures I've had the pleasure of knowing. You've now proved my suspicion that those movie men are idiots."

"I've always believed my finest performance was in the stage play my aunt directed. Like my friend Peg, I liked the presence of a live and responsive audience."

"Is she one of your studio pals?"

Phyllis hesitated before answering. "Peg Entwistle was a Broadway actress. RKO signed us at the same time. After using her—or misusing her—they didn't renew her contract. She committed suicide."

"Poor girl."

"She had an apartment in Tudor City. I thought that was a funny name for a New York neighborhood. After I went to a preview of the Charles Laughton film, I imagined the residents wandering the streets dressed like Henry the Eighth and his six wives."

"Not quite so colorful, but unique and picturesque. I'll take you there so you can see."

When asked if she wanted coffee, Phyllis boldly offered to make it in her kitchenette at the hotel. After they walked up Madison Avenue, a river of gleaming headlights, Bennett grasped her hand. As they halted at a crosswalk and waited for the signal to change, he pulled her close. Feeling his breath against her cheek and his arm at her waist, she realized how easily she could fall in love with him.

But I shouldn't, she reminded herself. I'm heading back to Hollywood when summer is over.

The office grapevine carried news of her romance with one of the city's eligible bachelors. The chilliest of the stenographers, who clearly envied her position as copywriter, began to thaw. Maybe she believed Phyllis could help her into a job at Random House.

On a day when Ted Geisel stopped by with a sheaf of cartoons, she described her latest outing with Bennett. The illustrator was asking her which Bronx Zoo animal she'd liked best when her desk telephone rang.

"Mr. Ludlum needs to see you right away, Miss Fraser."

"Summoned by the boss?" Ted said. "Tell Stuart I'd be extremely glad to hand off my Flit account to you."

"I'll accept," she said over her shoulder, "provided you keep writing all the copy and draw the pictures."

She hoped this meeting was the preliminary to a meaningful assignment, one that might keep her in New York longer than she'd originally planned—or forever. She'd submitted spec scripts for *Meet Miss Julia,* the new serial about an elderly boarding house proprietress and her lodgers, and earned an extra one hundred and fifty dollars for the one that went into production. But her optimism evaporated when she saw her supervisor's unsmiling face.

"I won't keep you long. But you should sit." Stuart glanced down at some papers. Looking up, he said, "We were aware that you were an advertising novice when you came aboard. You're an experienced writer, and we figured you'd be able to adapt your skills to our client's needs. Unfortunately, that isn't happening. You're a delightful young woman, and it's a pleasure having you here. That's why I'm so sorry to tell you we're terminating your employment at McCann Erickson."

Leaving the agency—or staying—wasn't a decision she'd have to make herself.

Mustering a smile, she said, "This job was for the summer, you said so from the start. I'm grateful to you for taking a chance on me. To tell you the truth, I'll be glad to give up Daggett and Ramsdell cold cream and go back to my Pond's."

"If I had another position that was suitable, you could stay on with us. But you lack the advanced secretarial skills of our typing pool. You did a fine job with your Miss Julia episode. When you get back to Hollywood, you should carry on with that movie script you told me about. Or finish your novel. Maybe your boyfriend will publish it."

But he won't be my boyfriend, she thought in anguish, if I'm living on the other side of the country.

That night, after conferring with Lela, she decided there was no point in delaying her journey to California. The next day, during her lunch hour, she cabled the girl who had sublet her place at the Andalusia, announcing her return. She devoted her remaining days at the office to wrapping up her assigned tasks, and at week's end, removed her small collection of personal items from her desk. She wrote a farewell note to Ted Geisel and placed it in his drawer, her final act before leaving the building.

When she arrived at the apartment, Lela presented her with a train ticket printed with tomorrow's date.

"A luxury roomette was available, so I booked it for you even though it leaves so soon. And I've asked the concierge to have your suitcases taken out of storage and brought up." Handing over an envelope, she added, "This was waiting at the front desk when I returned. The hotel operator took a message from Bennett Cerf."

He didn't yet know she was leaving town. All week he'd been busy with sales meetings, and every evening was devoted to an important visiting author. Although he'd given her his number at the Random House office, she'd never used it.

The switchboard connected her to his assistant, who put her through at once.

His familiar voice twanged through the line. "Good day, Miss Fraser. I'm happy to report that after this evening I'll be free from all commitments and able to devote my attention to you. Start thinking about what you'd like to do this weekend."

Without preamble, she blurted, "I was fired."

"Well, that's not so bad, is it? You weren't terribly keen on copywriting."

"I called to tell you goodbye." Her voice wobbled when she added, "Because I'm going back to California."

An extended silence ended with a curt, "When?"

"Tomorrow."

"Where are you right now?"

"At the Madison. Packing."

"I'll be right over."

"Oh, Bennett, I don't think—"

He'd already hung up.

When Lela heard that Bennett was on his way, she put on her hat and gathered up her gloves and handbag. "I'm off to the market to pick up something nice for our supper. Do you think he'd like to join us?"

"He can't." She was grateful to Lela for finding an excuse to remove herself.

Bennett arrived laden with literature. He set an armful of books on the dining table and removed his fedora. "I thought you might like to read these on the train. All the latest offerings from Random House. Including an anthology edited by yours truly."

"Thank you."

"Is that the best you can do? Come here."

His embrace was equally comforting and agonizing. He kissed her, for a long time. She didn't slap him.

"Now don't you go running around in front of those

Hollywood fellows in that cute red gingham number. Promise?"

"I'll leave it here. For when I come back."

CHAPTER 44

Uncertain whether her Hollywood exile would be temporary, Phyllis pounded out feature articles and composed lengthy letters to Bennett, who responded in kind. There were, she discovered, advantages to courtship by correspondence. She shared her thoughts on the books she'd devoured during her train journey, starting with his volume of short stories. He was every bit as charismatic—and as challenging—on paper as in person. After two months of intense written communication and regular transcontinental telephone conversations, their lighthearted social relationship of July and August moved inexorably towards an all-consuming romantic affair.

Making an effort to re-establish her former social life, she found that certain members of her circle had settled into domesticity. She relied on Ben Alexander to squire her about town, to the popular places where she could meet prospective interviewees. Whenever they went out, she dabbed her Sortilège perfume on her collarbone and wrists and wondered whether Bennett would be dining at the Stork Club that night with some unknown rival. Jealousy was an unfamiliar emotion, and she disliked its strange power.

She'd always prided herself on her pragmatism in her

relationships with men. Not getting engaged to Buddy Parsons because she was too young. Relinquishing Carlyle Moore when his mother became an obstacle to a happy marriage. Accepting, hard as it had been, that Henry Freulich didn't want her for his wife. But no amount of objective reasoning was sufficient to dispel her strong conviction that Bennett Cerf could be the ideal partner she hadn't really expected to find.

She didn't require additional proof that her destiny would be decided in Manhattan, but it came in a telegram from Lela, alerting her to Stuart Ludlum's plan to re-hire her for an entirely different job. This was her cue to divest herself of the bulk of her possessions. She sold her car to a friend and surrendered her apartment and donated heaps of clothing to actress friends. New York fashions, like its weather, were different from those of Los Angeles. She would need fewer lightweight garments and a lot more tweed and wool.

Sorting through a box of photographs and old newspaper cuttings, she came across the diary she'd kept during her earliest weeks in Hollywood. She cringed at the immaturity and naivete revealed in its pages, and decided it wasn't worth preserving. She also discarded autographed movie star glossies but kept the best of the candid photos she'd taken—her cousin on the tennis court, Anne with the dogs and her Johnny, Ben Alexander hosting his radio show, Mary Blackford in her wheelchair. Another box held a sixteen-millimeter print of *Little Red Riding Hood,* produced and directed by Lela and Lew Ayres, starring Phyllis and Ginger and Ben. Perhaps Bennett would get a kick out of seeing it.

Near the bottom she discovered the personal horoscope cast for her when she was assigned to RKO's ill-fated *Thirteen Women.* Curious to discover whether she was entitled to the one hundred dollars Irene Dunne promised her castmates if any of the predictions came true, she examined the faded type. The assessment of her personality and temperament was startlingly acute, she realized. At sixteen, had she known herself well enough to be aware of it? Probably not.

Nothing stirs you like a clean slate, the promise of a new day, and a fresh start.

That was certainly true.

Her eyes skimmed paragraphs describing her positive and negative traits, seeking the section on love and sex.

While easily aroused, your passion is lasting. You enjoy sex more than most, when the act arises from true love and romantic attachment . . . In partnership you demand loyalty and are impatient with disloyalty . . . You generally have a strong idealistic streak . . . When you have a love affair, you will enjoy it most fully, and your relationship with your partner will be perfect.

Ginger and Anne were bemused by her abrupt decision to move permanently to Manhattan for a position with the same firm that had so recently dropped her. She assured them that her assignment, editing and producing radio shows, was a promotion from the drudgery of copywriting. They'd heard the name Bennett Cerf often enough to draw accurate conclusions about her primary motive for accepting Stuart's offer.

Accompanied by the suitcases of clothes and possessions she'd elected to take with her, Phyllis reprised her springtime journey from Los Angeles to Chicago to New York. In choosing her reading material for the eastward migration, she selected books that she believed the illustrious Mr. Cerf would want his lady friend to read. She jotted down her reactions and opinions, which she was eager to share with him.

Her heart hammered at her first view of skyscrapers,

pointing towards a brilliantly blue sky—a happy omen, surely.

After Phyllis had unpacked and settled herself into the familiar suite at the Madison Hotel, Lela announced that before long she'd be making her way back to California.

"I always intended to divide my time between Manhattan and Los Angeles. I prefer to avoid northern winters. And I feel a great need to be with Ginger for the holidays, now that she's no longer involved with George Stevens. I'm afraid she might decide to reconcile with Lew. After all this time, they still haven't finalized their divorce. You shouldn't have any difficulty finding a place to live," Lela said airily. "Plenty of working girls around town would be glad to have you splitting the rent with them."

Yet again her aunt's change of plan required Phyllis to hurriedly find another home at short notice, and this time she'd be left stranded in a vast city she hardly knew. "I'll get in touch with Ethel Korn," she decided. "Hattie Carnegie's niece. She used to model at the shop, with Lucille Ball, until she decided to switch to acting. She wasn't getting movie parts, so she came back here to work for her aunt. A tiny blonde creature. Nice. Respectable," she added, anticipating a question that her aunt would inevitably ask.

She looked forward to living among a group of females close to her age. Her only New York acquaintances were Lela's friends and contemporaries, like Harold, and the McCann Erickson folks. And Bennett.

Settling into her job as story editor, she was determined that her tenure would be lasting. Working closely with two female writers, she refined their scripts and checked for alignment with the long-range, thirteen-week plot. After obtaining Stuart Ludlum's approval of the material, she conferred with producer Carleton Alsop. Her duties expanded to include scheduling the players and providing their copies of the script. During production, she assisted Carleton by keeping track of the elapsed time, ensuring the correct placement of the client's commercials. They recorded five fifteen-minute shows in a day, the entire weekly broadcast output, on vinyl disks that were shipped out to the radio stations.

Her cast was top-notch, experienced and thoroughly professional. Joseph Cotten was on Broadway, co-starring with Katharine Hepburn in *The Philadelphia Story.* Martha Scott, lauded for her portrayal of Emily in *Our Town,* was under consideration for various Hollywood films. Josephine Hull, who played Miss Julia, the elderly boarding house owner, had recently finished a lengthy and successful run in *You Can't Take it with You.*

Bennett took Phyllis out to dinner several times a week. On weekends they returned to the World's Fair, less crowded than it had been during the summer. The menu at the French restaurant had changed with the season. Nowadays Great Britain's pavilion was extremely popular, a demonstration of support in the wake of that country's war declaration against Germany. Bennett took her to bridge parties, where she exhibited skills acquired from Flo Lake and Buddy DeSylva and her theatrical friends. On Sunday evenings, they were Stork Club regulars. Sherman Billingsley showered her with presents—a charm bracelet, a necklace, a gold pen. Her date received ties and cufflinks embedded with tiny diamonds, and bottles of rare and well-aged whisky.

"Did you finalize things with the girls at the Southgate?" Bennett asked when they glided off the dance floor.

"Not yet. During tomorrow's lunch break I'll walk over to East Fifty-fourth. I like the building and the location. Close to the river, and a ten-minute taxi ride to the office. In springtime, if the agency keeps me that long, I can walk."

Even though she wasn't greatly concerned that Stuart would fire her again, she saw no harm in voicing that extremely remote possibility to Bennett. If he feared she might make her way back to California, he was smart enough to figure out how he could tie her permanently to his city. And to him. That night, before falling asleep, she replayed their dinner conversation, pondering what deeper meaning and serious intent might lie beneath certain exchanges. For all his busy-ness and responsibilities, editorial and social, he seemed to crave her company. He'd introduced her to his father, a clear indication that she had become important to him.

Even though *The Philadelphia Story* was reportedly a sell-out, Bennett managed to acquire tickets. According to Lela, Katharine Hepburn had commissioned the play and partly funded its production in hopes of repairing her film career after being labeled "box office poison."

One November night Phyllis witnessed the star's post-performance arrival at the 21 Club. Kath wore her customary slacks, prompting aggrieved eyebrow-raising by certain members of the conventionally-dressed crowd.

"Hello, kiddo," she greeted Phyllis in a typically offhand fashion. "What a treat to meet another member of the RKO sisterhood."

"I no longer belong," Phyllis admitted.

"Wasn't sure I did, either," her friend replied, "after all those flops of mine. My play is such a hit that the studio brass is asking Leland Hayward when I'll be available for a film version."

"That's no surprise," Bennett commented. "You're the toast of Broadway."

"As I intended to be. Mission accomplished," Kath concluded with a broad wink.

"Behave yourself while I'm away," Lela cautioned Phyllis before climbing into her waiting taxicab. She was bound for Grand Central Terminal to board the Twentieth Century Limited. "Don't let that suitor of yours get the wrong idea about you."

"He won't," Phyllis assured her. "Oklahoma wholesome, he calls me. And he refers to the Southgate Apartments as my convent."

Their cheeks met in a mimed kiss, to avoid lipstick marks. Phyllis waved until the vehicle vanished, absorbed into the early evening gloom. Drawing the front of her thick fur coat closer, she decided it was too cold to walk from the Madison to her apartment building. The doorman hailed a cab for her. Rush hour traffic slowed its progress, and she frantically checked her watch—did she have enough time to change for her movie date with Bennett? They would drive across the river to a cinema in Brooklyn, to see Ginger's latest, *Fifth Avenue Girl.*

"She adores Manhattan," Phyllis told him in the car afterwards. "The real one, not the version created by RKO, or the section at Paramount where she goes to shoot New York street scenes. Most of her movies were set here—*Stage Door, Bachelor Mother, Romance in Manhattan, Fifth Avenue Girl.* Lots of others. I wish she had time for a visit."

"So does Harold. He's crazy for her. Always has been."

When she learned a one-bedroom ground floor apartment at the Southgate had been vacated, she informed her roommates that she'd decided to take it for herself. She preferred privacy when her gentleman caller called.

One evening as she and Bennett drank coffee in her

living room, she noticed he was fidgeting with a loose shirt button.

When it came off, he said, "Looks like a visit to my tailor is in order."

"I'll sew it back on." She got up and went to the cupboard for a needle and thread and scissors.

"Am I supposed to undress for you?" he asked when she rejoined him on the sofa.

Her cheeks got hot. "That will not be necessary. Remove your jacket—nothing else." When she plucked the fabric from his chest, her knuckles brushed against warm skin and hair that tickled.

"Don't stab me."

"Keep still, and I won't."

She was in no rush to complete her task. Close as they were, she needed to be even closer to him, enfolded and merged. Her entire body felt lit from within, and she was fired by the absolute certainty that she would be sublimely happy spending the rest of her days with this man. Meeting his rapt gaze, she saw that her clear conviction was reciprocated. She also sensed that neither of them was prepared to articulate this explosive surge of mutual feeling.

Daunted by the prospect of a solitary Christmas, unable to celebrate with relatives or close friends, she persuaded her mother to pay a December visit—and meet Bennett. Her place wasn't large, but she could give up the bed and sleep on the sofa where she enjoyed cuddling with the man who had won her heart.

As tour guide for Mama's first time in New York, Phyllis made sure she saw the significant landmarks, treated her at the Automat, and invited her to a recording session at McCann Erickson. Before the holiday, they attended an afternoon screening of the spectacularly successful *Gone with the Wind*.

Dabbing her eyes during the final credits, she said,

"My friend Anne Shirley tested for Melanie. I love her to bits, but she would've been all wrong. Olivia de Havilland was perfect. She and Vivien Leigh definitely earned an Oscar nomination. And the statue."

"Clark Gable reminded me of your stepfather," Mama said.

Bundled in their furs, they shopped at Hattie Carnegie, where her former roommate Ethel sold them dresses and applied the employee discount. Before leaving town to ski in the Adirondacks, Bennett escorted them to the Stork Club and 21 and El Morocco. Harold Ross was no less eager to look after Lela's sister. He invited Phyllis and her mother and another pair of holiday "orphans" to spend Christmas week at his Stamford house, where she discovered that her irascible friend was a tender parent to his little daughter Patsy, adoring and adored.

Bennett had volunteered to collect them on New Year's Eve, but he arrived two days early. Flattered, Phyllis regarded this as a promising sign of his devotion.

As usual, he was the victor in every backgammon game with Harold. Their host had a habit of gambling with increasing recklessness as his cool-headed opponent's winnings accumulated.

Looking up, Bennett's brown eyes searched for Phyllis. "In February, I am making my annual visit to the Bahamas with friends. Another game or two, and I'll win enough money to pay your way. How would you like to go with me?"

Mama stiffened. "Not without a chaperone."

"Never fear, Mrs. Nichols. No harm will come to your precious girl. I'll reserve separate berths on the Orange Blossom Special. On the train and at the Nassau house, we'll be accompanied by an older married couple of pristine reputation. What say you, Mam'selle Fraser?"

"She says yes," Harold answered for her.

CHAPTER 45

Phyllis suffered no lack of imagination, but she'd hadn't expected to find herself in the land of fragrant citrus blossoms and lavender jacaranda trees within months of deserting it. After years of struggling for show business success in Hollywood, through a startling twist of fate, she'd actually achieved it in New York City. And here she was again—an actress no longer, but the co-producer of a radio drama that was broadcast nationwide, every weekday.

Like many a Broadway smash, *Our Town* was destined for the silver screen, with Martha Scott reprising her stage role. Joseph Cotten's stage performance in *The Philadelphia Story* had piqued the studios' interest. They decamped to the West Coast, and McCann Erickson transferred production of *The Career of Alice Blair* to a Los Angeles facility. When Carleton Alsop found out the leading lady was dating makeup man Perc Westmore, he was no longer willing to supervise the radio show from New York. And because Phyllis had extensive Hollywood experience and valuable professional connections, he brought her with him.

Although Ginger and Lela invited her to stay with them, she was occupying the guest room at Anne and

John's house on Evanview Drive in the Hollywood Hills. She had a joyful reunion with the dog that had formerly been hers, and was saddened to learn the pet rabbits had reached the end of their pampered lives. Because the expectant mother was reluctant to drive herself, she voluntarily handed over her car keys to Phyllis.

"It's like old times," Anne said one afternoon as they sat together under the backyard trees, heads bowed over their knitting. They weren't making infant clothes today, but items to be auctioned on behalf of British War Relief. Anne, daughter of an Englishwoman, was actively supporting the cause.

"Not really," said Phyllis with a laugh. "You've got a husband. And a baby on the way. And I'm sort of promised to a New Yorker. I hoped he'd propose while we were in Nassau, but the tropical warmth couldn't melt his doubts."

"About you?"

"He's afraid I'm too young for him, and he's too old for me. Instead of receiving a diamond ring as a souvenir of our ten-day vacation, I took home a box of seashells and beach glass. After dropping me at my apartment, he rushed off to dress for a dinner date with another female. I was livid."

"No wonder. What did you say to him?"

"Not a thing. I took desperate measures. I started seeing someone else, a nice fellow I knew from my RKO days. Bennett got the message right away. Now I'm waiting for him to figure out that we belong together. Not simply for weekends in the country with friends, or at a resort, or dinner and dancing at the Stork Club."

"But you're here. And he's there."

"Ed McCann and Stuart Ludlum assured me that this is a temporary assignment."

Anne put down her needles to place her hands on

either side of her round tummy. "You have to stay till the baby comes. You're its godmother. And the longer you're separated from Bennett, the more he'll miss you, and want to marry you. Does your aunt approve of him?"

"Very much. She doesn't even mind that he's Jewish. From Lela's point of view, his only deplorable characteristic is being a Democrat. Who adores President Roosevelt."

"When I ran into Ginger at the studio, she showed me the engagement ring Howard Hughes gave her. Five carats, she says. Her mother must be planning a big wedding."

"Not just yet," Phyllis said, and made no further comment.

Howard Hughes, no longer entangled with Katharine Hepburn, had convinced Ginger to conclude her long-delayed divorce from Lew Ayres, insisting that his personal lawyer should handle all the legalities. That he'd had an ulterior motive was perfectly clear to Lela, deeply concerned about her daughter's involvement with Hollywood's notorious lothario. Phyllis, recipient of her aunt's frequent complaints—in person or by telephone—was similarly troubled.

"How can he always know in advance when she'll have a day off from work?" Lela wondered aloud when Phyllis visited her at the Coldwater Canyon house. "He calls at a shamefully early hour of the morning, demanding that I wake her up to go on one of his cockamamie excursions. He flew her across the desert in his airplane to show her the wildflowers. And all the way to San Francisco for lunch. He's teaching her to sail. They golf together so often that she's just about good enough to take on Fred Astaire."

Aware that top actresses were Howard's favorite prey,

Phyllis pointed out, "He's a love-them, leave-them type. Maybe the romance won't last."

"There's nobody else left for him to leave her for. He's had Katharine Hepburn. Bette Davis. Olivia de Havilland. Her sister, Joan Fontaine. Hedy Lamarr. I hate for Ginger's heart to get broken—again—but the sooner he moves on to someone else, the happier I'll be. A multimillionaire film producing daredevil aviator is not the sort of son-in-law I want. I have to remind myself she isn't legally free to marry for another year. A lot can happen in that span of time." Lela smoothed the hair at the back of her neck. "Honestly, worrying about you girls is taking years off my life. I do hope God can keep up with all my prayers."

She was still airing her many concerns when the studio car dropped off her daughter, who had spent the day on the *Lucky Partners* set with co-star Ronald Colman.

"We've been talking about your fiancé," Phyllis informed Ginger, to see how she'd react.

"Did Mother tell you he plans to build me a bigger house with an even better view than this one?"

"Big, bigger, biggest," Lela commented. "Just like a Texan. You have plenty of choices for a marital home. His Muirfield estate. Or this house, which suits you so well."

"But it's your name on the deed. You pay the taxes, and all the bills."

"With the money you've earned. I could never live here on my own, it's too much for me. And I'll continue to spend part of the year in New York."

Ginger turned to Phyllis. "Did I ever tell you that Howard proposed to me years ago? It was after Mervyn LeRoy let me down by marrying Doris Warner, and before I fell head over heels for Lew. He wants to take care of me. And he's already so rich and so famous, I don't have to worry he's after my money or using me for publicity."

"When will you announce the engagement?" Phyllis asked.

"Not any time soon. Howard prefers to keep it private as long as we can. He's on his way over right now. He wants to drive me to his mountaintop property so I can see it at sunset."

The moment she was out of earshot, Lela muttered, "I suspect that rascal is keeping quiet about their marriage plans because he's got another girl on the string and doesn't want to mess up the arrangement. He crooks his finger at Ginger, and off she goes. I live with her, and rarely see her. Won't you stay for supper? I'd be grateful for the company."

Phyllis accepted her aunt's invitation. Throughout the meal she listened noncommittally to a diatribe on the present political situation, domestic and international.

"The Roosevelt administration is socialist to its core. The liberal mindset has permeated movie scripts, and I'm certain the majority of the foreigners working here are Reds. I'm not convinced Britain and France are up to the job of subduing Hitler and Mussolini and all those hateful fascists. But the Communists are worse, with their collectivism and their anti-capitalist propaganda."

Phyllis speared an orange section in her fruit salad. Since coming to California she'd heard less talk about the warring nations than she did in New York. Was it because there was a whole continent plus a vast ocean between Los Angeles and Europe? Bennett and his friends, especially his Jewish brethren, deplored America's neutrality despite Germany's aggression against longtime allies. In shocked murmurs, they exchanged reports obtained from their relatives and friends overseas—evictions, the wanton destruction of property, atrocities and mass murder committed in concentration camps.

She and Lela were drinking their coffee on the veranda, enjoying the cooler air that arrived with dusk, when Ginger reappeared. Her mood was less ebullient than when she and her fiancé had departed. She described his newly acquired spread as vast, with a panoramic vista of the hills and Lake Hollywood and the city.

"I'd like to see it," Lela said, "and Phyllis does, too, I'm sure. Tomorrow you can drive us there in that fancy station wagon Howard gave you. Why he wanted to replace the perfectly good one you already owned, I can't imagine."

"It's mighty rugged up there," Ginger hedged. "Are you leaving, Phyl? I'll walk you to your car."

Night was closing in. On the horizon the distant lights of Los Angeles glittered like stars scattered upon the earth.

"Howard bought that Cahuenga Peak property to please me—over a hundred and thirty acres. I don't know how to tell him that I don't want to live there."

"Why not?"

"The spot he plans to build on is so close to the Hollywoodland sign. I'd always be reminded of your friend, the girl who jumped." She drew a labored breath and swiped at her long hair—dyed dark for her film—as if brushing away memories of Peg Entwistle's tragic end.

The script on Anne's side table was stamped with the Twentieth Century Fox name and logo. Phyllis picked it up and read its title. "*For Beauty's Sake*. Does RKO know a rival studio is trying to poach their star?"

"It came for Johnny, and he's turning it down. Too

lightweight, with a silly plot. The male lead is an astronomy professor whose aunt dies and he inherits her beauty emporium. Her will stipulates that he has to manage it successfully in order to receive her fortune." Eyes bright, Anne chirped, "You know all about salons. Your mother works at one."

"Always has."

"I'll get Johnny to tell Lew Schreiber you're available. He handles casting. You should be in this picture."

Whenever her best friend formed a plan, she could be as dogged as Lela in carrying it out. Phyllis was therefore not at all surprised to be offered the part of a college girl, an exact replica of the many insignificant roles she'd filled in the past.

Bennett, a careful planner, overcame time zone differences to talk with her by telephone. Their conversations alternated between the serious and the silly. He wanted to hear the details of her working day, requiring concrete evidence that she had a valid reason for remaining on the West Coast. Phyllis tended to focus on the emotional aspect of their relationship.

"You keep saying you're crazy about me. And telling me how adorable I am. It's nice to hear. But I need to know what you're feeling."

"Bereft," he answered. "Deprived."

"Because?"

"You're not here. I miss you."

"Why?" She went silent.

"Phyllis? You still there? I can't hear you."

It was worth another try. "Bennett, whenever I say 'I love you,' all I hear in return is, 'That's great, honey. That's perfect.' Maybe there's something you could add."

"Well, to start, you're my favorite person in the entire world. Brilliant. Funny. Charming. So pretty that when we're together, I can't take my eyes away."

"You've missed my point. Completely."

Suddenly he was the quiet one. Then she heard his voice, pitched low, almost whispering, "I do love you, Phyllis. I. Love. You. Cross my heart. Does that make the situation clearer?"

"It'll do. For the time being." Having extracted his declaration, she could share her news. "Twentieth Century Fox has cast me in a picture."

"What?" There was no mistaking his dismay. "You can't be serious."

"My character even has a name. Julia." She relished this rare and welcome chance to tease New York's great jester. Her motive wasn't malicious, but she wanted him to worry—for a short while—that her stint in Hollywood would be extended.

"My scenes are shooting later this month, at Griffith Park Observatory. On a Saturday, so there's no conflict with my radio show."

"But you disliked being an actress." His accusatory words buzzed in her ear. "You said so, lots of times."

"The part won't stretch my acting abilities. It's small." Smaller than she cared to reveal. She'd receive a day player's rate and most likely wouldn't be credited.

Lela and Ginger, who had instigated and supported her career in film, were both so preoccupied with Howard Hughes that they received the same announcement without comment or congratulations.

According to Lela, Ginger was having second thoughts about marriage.

"He's suspicious about how and where she spends her time when they're apart," Lela explained during a phone call. "And because he seems to know an awful lot without being told, she worries that a detective is following her and reporting her movements to him. Or that he's wiretapped her phone. And he obviously wants to get rid of me. Always asking when I'm leaving California and offering to fly me to New York in one of his airplanes. I won't budge. I'm staying right here, to protect my darling girl."

Curious about her cousin's complicated romance, Phyllis invited Ginger to meet her for lunch at Al Levy's Tavern. After a prolonged wait, she accepted that her cousin wasn't showing up and ordered a turkey sandwich. Her afternoon recording session proceeded without a hitch, and after finishing up her paperwork, she drove herself to the Payne house. Ponce, the manservant, informed her that Miss Shirley was napping, and that Miss Rogers had called and insisted that she get in touch immediately.

"I'm so sorry I forgot our lunch date," Ginger said. "I'm at my wits' end, and I don't know what I should do. I've got to tell Mother, and she'll say she warned me, and—"

"Take a deep breath. And another one. Okay, now continue. Slowly."

"Howard's cheating on me. He parks his tacky old car outside a certain starlet's bungalow. In broad daylight. And sometimes at night, when he's supposedly working late at his company, and I'm waiting for him at Muirfield. A friend of mine has seen him coming and going."

"I'm on my way over."

"Not now. Here's Mother—she just got home. I'm scheduled for a press interview tomorrow morning but I'm cancelling it. Can you come then?"

"I'll get Carleton to rehearse Martha Scott by himself. He'll think I'm doing him a favor, giving him all that time with his sweetie."

She sympathized with her cousin's plight, but her thoughts remained centered on Bennett. He had his eccentricities and was accustomed to getting his way in all things, either through power or charm, and his control over his temper faltered at times. But he was a decent man, genuinely kind and thoughtful. And she enjoyed every minute in his company. She relied on his frankness. And she missed him so much, never more than when consumed by a family crisis.

In the morning, she drove up along Coldwater Canyon to the mansion perched high above Gilcrest Avenue. Lela must have been watching for her, because she opened the door before Phyllis reached it.

"How is she?"

"Demon-possessed. The rat telephoned this morning, demanding that she drive him to the dentist. She refused and hung up on him."

"Where is she?"

"Upstairs."

Ginger's luxurious bedroom was littered with all the gifts she'd received from her betrayer. The jumble on her bed included scarves, lingerie, and a mink cape. She was emptying the contents of a jewelry box onto the coverlet.

"I'm giving it all back," she said through gritted teeth. "I can't wait to dump everything on his doorstep."

"Let me drive you to Muirfield," Phyllis told her. "You're in no state to get behind the wheel."

Ginger opened her fist and dropped a rainbow of gemstones into a plain paper sack. She tugged at her huge emerald engagement ring, grimacing when it rasped her knuckle.

The telephone rang.

"If it's Howard again, I don't want to speak to him. Ever."

Phyllis picked up. "Miss Rogers's residence."

"Put her on."

Repaying masculine bluster with feminine tartness, she replied, "She isn't taking calls at the moment."

"Tell her it's Noah. She knows me. I work for Mr. Hughes."

When Phyllis mouthed the name, Ginger frowned and shook her head.

"I told you, she can't come to the phone."

"I don't believe you. Listen, lady, this is an emergency. A few hours ago, Howard was in a car accident—head-on collision. He's out of surgery and asking for Miss Rogers. Seventy stitches to his face, and he's lucky he didn't lose his eye. Get her to Presbyterian Hospital and don't delay."

Phyllis broke the news to Ginger, who thought hard for a minute before saying, "Let's go."

During the half-hour journey, Ginger poured out her pent-up fury over Howard's attempts to exert total control. He wanted to manage her career and choose her scripts and plan her vacations. He was determined to pry her away from Lela. He restricted their phone calls when she was with him at Muirfield.

Without any explanation, Ginger handed her bundle to a startled hospital receptionist and asked directions to Howard's private room. She went in alone, abandoning Phyllis in the corridor with Noah Dietrich, his right-hand man.

"If she'd taken him to the dentist like he asked, this never would've happened. He's a terrible driver."

Avoiding the stranger's steely, accusing gaze, she didn't bother to reply.

Within minutes, Ginger exited—without the paper bag—and slammed the door, drawing stares from the medical staff. Her heels clattered against the polished floor.

"That's done," she announced. "All over. Finished." She turned and marched down the hallway.

Hurrying to catch up, Phyllis asked, "How did he look?"

"Like a mummy. With white bandages wound all around his head."

"What did he say?"

"He was dopey from medication. He mumbled it was my fault he had a smash-up. By hanging up on him this morning, I upset him so much that he crashed into that other car. When he paused for breath, I threw the jewelry on the bed and told him I found out he's sleeping with someone else. I said I never want to see him again. He made sad puppy dog eyes and started crying."

Lela, greatly relieved, decided it was safe to return to Manhattan.

"He bludgeoned her pride," she said to Phyllis on the way to the train station. "Comfort her. Watch out for her. Keep that weasel away from her. Oh, and when I see your publisher, I'll let him know you've been pining for him."

"I am," Phyllis said fervently.

"His long-distance telephone bills are going to be immense. A good thing he's rich."

One bright and breezy Saturday morning, Phyllis joined a bevy of day players at the Twentieth Century Fox studio to have her hair set and her makeup applied. She was hurried into a dark dress suit and given a hat before boarding the studio bus to Griffith Park.

Phyllis was scheduled for two scenes being shot in reverse order. She stood near the observatory dome while ingenue Marjorie Weaver flirted with handsome newcomer Ted North. After a couple of takes she was told to stay close by until called for her next appearance, with the rest of the girls from the fictional St. Vincent's College.

She spent her free time walking the circumference of the viewing platform, pausing at the various lookout points. One of them, she soon discovered, faced the Hollywoodland sign. The white letters, rising from the low-growing vegetation, gleamed bright in the midday sunshine. Confronting the summit where Peg had chosen to die, pushed to its edge by unfulfilled aspirations and broken dreams, Phyllis felt a familiar ache.

Her own lack of success had ceased to trouble her. For the most part, she'd enjoyed her years as a baby starlet under contract to RKO, and her freelancing days at lesser studios. But despite her competency and her persistence, she'd performed just two leading roles. By then, the small surviving measure of her ambition had already waned.

"Come back, ladies!" the assistant director bellowed through his megaphone. "We're set up to shoot your arrival."

With a valedictory glance at the stark and storied symbol of her past, Phyllis turned and crossed the plaza to complete her final performance.

CHAPTER 46

Ginger was determined to use her ten days of vacation between completing re-takes for *Lucky Partners* and her pre-production activities for *Kitty Foyle.* Phyllis agreed to go with her to Yosemite, overcoming her reluctance to leave Anne when she was so close to her due date. Carleton Alsop granted her request for a holiday but required her to work madly almost to the moment of her departure, scheduling voice actors for the upcoming recording sessions.

She was filling a suitcase with casual wear when Anne's contractions started. John bustled his wife into his car and rushed her to the hospital at top speed. Phyllis and Mimi Shirley sat vigil with him in the waiting room, until, after a protracted labor, Anne delivered a six-and-a-half-pound girl. Phyllis was able to beam at tiny Julie Anne Payne through the infant nursery's glass window, but cuddling her goddaughter would have to wait until she returned from her trip.

Conscious of surfacing maternal feelings, she went to the hospital entrance where Ginger would pick her up. The duplicitous Howard had ordered Hughes Tool Company to repossess her station wagon, taking back his gift. She promptly purchased a new model, now packed to the brim with luggage, her art supplies and easel, camera bags, board games, puzzles, and a backgammon set. Her cousin's hair, dyed medium brown for *Primrose Path,* was colored even darker for her upcoming portrayal of Kitty Foyle. Ginger expressed her hope that this change would prevent recognition by her fans.

"Fred Astaire's partner is a blonde. And I'm not."

"Don't you miss dancing with him?" Phyllis wondered. "Even a little?"

"When we wrapped the Vernon and Irene Castle picture, I was teary, I admit. But now I'm able to prove myself as a dramatic actress. Mother and I made the writers revise the *Kitty Foyle* script—several times. We're almost satisfied."

"What was wrong with it?"

"Too bleak. In the novel, she's unwed and pregnant and gets an abortion."

The territory at the edge of the city, Phyllis noted, had changed during the years since her arrival early in the Depression. Paved roads covered the former scrubland, and new houses were springing up where shantytowns and flimsy tents used to be.

Ginger's effort to avoid the mob of fans that she'd encountered during their Banff vacation was successful. Their rental cabin was sufficiently secluded, and it offered easy access to mountain trails, lakes, and streams. They cooked hot dogs for supper and spent the rest of the evening in close study of walking maps.

During their hike to a distant waterfall, Ginger wanted to know why Phyllis hadn't yet mentioned Bennett.

"I'm being sensitive to your state of mind."

"I'm over Howard, I assure you. You wouldn't believe how many actresses got in touch to tell me what a heel he is. Or which ones."

"I was a Hollywood gossip columnist, remember? I

heard plenty of unsavory rumors about him that I didn't dare print."

"I'd rather talk about your beau. Mother says he's wealthy and distinguished."

"She's right, but those aren't the qualities that score highest with me. He's a gentleman. He's considerate. With a wonderful sense of humor. He has a gift for telling jokes, and it's a point of pride."

"The life of the party type?"

Phyllis nodded, adding, "He can be serious, too. And confident without being arrogant. He's competitive, but can shrug off losses. His calm demeanor conceals an explosive temper, but after the big blast he goes right back to being genial and polite. And he's thoroughly devoted to his publishing house. He likes to socialize with authors and singers and actors and playwrights. Bennett seems surprised by how well I fit in his crowd. But in Hollywood I was accustomed to being around people a lot more famous. His city friends—especially their wives—were always pulling me aside to ask when we're getting married. I wish I knew."

"If you're so compatible, what's he waiting for?"

"Before he married Sylvia Sidney, he was a very popular New York bachelor. The divorce enhanced his prominence, and it went to his head. He loves attention, and the chance to perform. I knew when he started to fall for me—even though he was seeing other women. It wasn't long before he gave them up. He stepped out on me, just once, right after our Nassau trip. It was a dinner date, perfectly innocent. But I made it abundantly plain that fidelity is the high price of my affection. It's one he's willing to pay."

"You're fortunate. I suppose you'll give up your job as soon as you marry."

"Heavens, no. I wouldn't be content with a wholly

domestic life. I'm not the type to sit around the house waiting for my husband to come home from the office. I look forward to settling down with Bennett, and setting up our household, and being hostess to his interesting friends, and all that. But I'll always need to work. I want to. And he likes that about me."

"Where does he live?"

"In the Navarro building. It's a custom designed apartment with a park view. His dad, a widower, lives upstairs. Gustave is a darling."

"Good thing. You're a rare woman, accepting an in-law as a near neighbor."

Phyllis lifted her binoculars to follow the flight of a large raptor. "A hawk!" she cried. "With a fish in its mouth! Over there." She gestured towards the woods.

Ginger pointed her camera lens at the treetops.

After a week of nature walks and fishing excursions and afternoon swims in icy lake water, they loaded their luggage and paraphernalia into the station wagon and began their trek back to Los Angeles.

On her first day back in the production office, Phyllis was marking time on the recording script when Carleton Alsop interrupted her.

"Ludlum's on the line. For you."

She put down her pencil and picked up the phone. "Good afternoon, Stuart."

"It's still morning here, Phyllis. Hope you had a relaxing holiday in the hills."

"You bet I did. Is that what you called to find out?"

"No. Ed McCann and I are waving the white flag, surrendering to your Mr. Cerf. He keeps calling one or the other of us, asking why in hell we're keeping you out there. To shut him up, we have to get you to New York. You're going to work on the *Alice Blair* scripts from here. And we want you to produce *Ask Miss Julia*."

Her triumphant smile was reflected in the glass pane of the recording booth. "Sounds like I'll soon be packing my suitcases again. Mustn't keep my Mr. Cerf waiting."

"We'll wire you the plane fare—another of Cerf's demands. The trains take too long, he says. Put Carleton back on, will you? We've got to figure out all the damned details."

She transferred the call to the producer and hung up.

All right, Bennett. Here I come. Get ready for a serious conversation about our future.

He met her at the new airfield in Flushing Meadows. Before she descended the metal staircase, she spotted him waiting at the terminal building door. He hurried out to throw his arms around her, lifting her off the hot tarmac.

"God, I missed you. You're not escaping me again."

When he returned her to solid ground, she said calmly, "It wasn't an escape."

"I've accepted an invitation to a country house weekend. The place is in New Jersey—the nicest part. My hosts want me to bring my girl. How about it?"

"If you can convince me that I'm the only girl you had in mind."

He responded to her quip with a smacking kiss. "No doubt about that."

They had to wait for the luggage to be unloaded from the airplane's hold. Bennett paid a porter handsomely to cart her suitcases to his car and handed over a generous tip.

By all rights she should be tired after hopscotching across the country, repeatedly descending so the plane could refuel, and bumping up again through the clouds. But his nearness revived her energy, and his firm clasp on her hand inspired hope that the expected and longed-for proposal was forthcoming.

"You bought the Buick," she commented while her things were stowed in the trunk, "instead of another Cadillac."

"You wanted me to."

Encouraged by this proof of her influence, she patted his arm. He helped her into the passenger seat. When he lowered the top of the convertible, she removed her hat so it wouldn't blow off.

Throughout their journey to the adjacent state, she was breathless with anticipation, certain that at any moment he would pop the question.

He didn't.

The topic of matrimony never came up at all during the leisurely rural weekend.

Or when he drove her to the Ritz Tower on Park Avenue, where Lela occupied a typically stylish suite.

I'm not bringing it up, Phyllis vowed. The man does the asking. Even when the answer is a foregone conclusion.

Her aunt counseled her to be patient. "A typical case of cold feet."

"But we've been dating pretty seriously for a whole year. Almost."

"And half that time you've been in California. My goodness, you should hear Stuart Ludlum's description of Bennett's desperate campaign to get you back here. He wouldn't make that kind of effort if he meant to leave you dangling. He must be waiting for the right moment."

"He's already missed plenty of perfect ones."

For an entire week, she alternated between frustration and amusement as they dined and danced their way across Manhattan, followed by coffee and kisses in Lela's suite.

Harold Ross stopped at their table one night at the Stork Club to extend an invitation to his house in Connecticut. She consented, hoping that at some point during a weekend of endless games of backgammon, interspersed with lively but friendly arguments between her beloved and his friend about recent magazine articles and book reviews, she might become engaged.

She regretted the decision when they discovered that their host was stuck in one of his cantankerous moods. Not uncommon—Harold required many hours beside his riverine paradise to recover from the pressures of editing *The New Yorker.* Phyllis unpacked her garments, including the green seersucker swimsuit and robe she'd worn the first time Bennett smooched her.

Raised voices from down the hall indicated that a masculine debate was already in progress. She checked her hair in the mirror, touched up her lipstick, and turned the door handle, prepared to referee.

Harold stood on the threshold, grinning broadly. He seized her hand and bent down to gently kiss her forehead.

"Congratulations, my dear. Bennett shared your happy news."

"What news would that be?"

"About getting hitched. It'll be the wedding of the year."

She stiffened, and said in a taut voice, "Excuse me. I need to have a word with my—my betrothed."

She marched down the corridor and met Bennett as he was coming out of his room.

"What mischief are you up to? Harold's gone misty-eyed. Did you just tell him we're getting married?"

"I had to. He yelled at me. He was ranting about the trouble of putting us in separate quarters when we stay here. He's got just the two guest rooms, and if we're using them, he can't invite anybody else for weekends. Preferably somebody he could beat at backgammon. He was going on and on. To shut him up, I declared my honorable intentions."

"And that's the *only* reason?"

"We'll discuss it later."

"Nothing to discuss." She gave him a peck on the mouth. "It's a wonderful idea. I can't wait to tell Lela. And my mother. And Ginger. And Anne."

"No need to rush into it," he insisted, on a note of panic. "What's the hurry?"

"You're not getting any younger. I'd rather not wait till I have to push you up the aisle in your wheelchair."

"Aisle? Are you saying we've got to marry in a church? I'm Jewish."

With her sauciest smile, she replied, "We can discuss it later."

"He *still* hasn't proposed," Phyllis said from behind the stack of radio scripts on her desk. "As soon as we left Stamford, he tried to back out."

"But you stood your ground," Lela approved.

"I sniffled a bit and explained that if we don't marry, my heart will be broken and I'll never be happy again. I was teasing, but he was in such a state of dread that he couldn't tell. We've decided the ceremony will take place on the nineteenth."

Relieved to have the matter settled at last, Lela opened her fountain pen again and held it over her notepad. "Let's get down to business. The location?"

"It can't be a church. Even if I wanted a Catholic service, no priest would perform it. He's Jewish, and he's divorced."

She frowned. "A courthouse is dreadfully impersonal, it functions like an assembly line. Bennett is famous, far beyond New York. You were a movie actress. Trust me, we can improve on a common county judge." Her pen hovered over the paper while she considered. "I'll ask Fiorello LaGuardia"

"The mayor can marry people?"

"He has that authority. And it solves the problem of a venue. He's working from the summer City Hall, out by the World's Fair site."

"Let me find out what Bennett thinks."

Lela continued jotting notes to herself during the engaged couple's brief telephone conversation.

"He says speaking our vows in front of Mayor LaGuardia sounds dandy."

"I'll get in touch with His Honor's secretary. Then I need to talk to Sherman Billingsley about reserving the Stork Club's big room for your engagement party. Harold will be my co-host. Now, about the theme. I'm thinking we should tie it to Ginger's *Lucky Partners* picture. We can invite well-known twosomes."

"Who?" Phyllis asked. "McCann and Erickson?"

"Definitely," Lela said, writing the names. "George Kauffman and Moss Hart. Richard Rodgers and Lorenz Hart."

"Edgar Bergen and Charlie McCarthy. Burns and Allen. The Duke and Duchess of Windsor." After a pause, Phyllis added, "Ginger and Fred."

"If only we could," she said regretfully.

"I was joking."

"You've given me an idea. I'll have their photographs printed on posters and hang them all around the room." She made another note.

"You could invite Franklin and Eleanor Roosevelt.

They're New Yorkers, and the President's campaigning for re-election. Bennett would love it."

"Not on your life!" Lela retorted. "Do be serious. You haven't even decided what you'll wear, and having a smart suit made up takes time. Sophie at Saks designs beautiful things. And Sally Victor can make a hat to match. I'll book the appointments."

When the chosen date proved inconvenient for the mayor, the happy couple moved the wedding up by two days. Lela alerted the catering staff at the Ritz, the site she'd chosen for the reception, and told the dressmaker she had less time to finish making their wedding attire and formal gowns for the engagement party.

On the eve of the ceremony, Lela had the satisfaction of filling the Stork Club's event room with prominent people. In every corner a folding screen displayed the partner posters, which received comments and compliments. Sherman Billingsley, making the rounds of the club, popped in to present Phyllis with a solid gold powder compact, its lid encrusted with tiny diamonds. After the reception, many guests migrated to the main dining room, where Lela and Harold and their honorees sat down to dinner.

Out of consideration for Harold's dislike of Walter Winchell, Lela had left him off her invitation list. The two men's mutual detestation resulted from an extensive and unflattering Winchell profile *The New Yorker* had recently published in installments.

The head waiter came to their table and handed Harold a note. After glancing at it, he passed it across the table.

Bennett put on his glasses. "The sheer gall of them."

"Who?" Phyllis asked.

"That bastard Winchell. And Sherman. This is an eviction notice."

Lela stood up and beckoned to the man who had delivered the message. "Frank, tell your boss I want to see him. Immediately."

Harold pushed his chair back from the table and doubled over in laughter.

"What on earth is so amusing?" she demanded.

"Everything," he gasped. He grabbed his napkin to blot his streaming eyes.

The club's proprietor ambled over. "Sorry, Harold. I don't want to kick you out, but Winchell is forcing me to. Please understand that I've no choice. You've got to go. And he says I can't let you back in. Ever."

"Don't be ridiculous," Lela snapped, as Harold succumbed to another fit of mirth. "It's the height of incivility to banish him, when we both spent a considerable amount of money entertaining significant people. I tell you, if Harold goes, we all walk out. You can send Winchell the bill for our dinners. And the reception." Placing a hand on Harold's shoulder, she added, "If not for him, there wouldn't be an engagement. Or a wedding."

Bennett cleared his throat. "The fact that I'm mad about the girl also had something to do with it."

"You never did propose," Phyllis accused him.

"What's more," Lela persisted, "I'll tell Ed Sullivan how you let his rival bully you, and he'll put it in his column. Louella Parsons was here earlier, blowing kisses to Harold. She looked like she was starving for meaty New York gossip. She's nationally syndicated, and after she writes up this disgusting incident your club won't be as attractive to celebrities as it is tonight."

Sherman Billingsley raised both hands in a gesture of surrender. "All right, all right. Finish your meal. But don't hang around afterwards. I can't afford to offend Winchell. Nobody can."

Lela sat down. Flashing a glare at Winchell, observing

them from his established location, she muttered, "How I wish I might give that vile serpent a piece of my mind. And I would, if this weren't a family celebration."

Phyllis addressed the table at large, saying, "He'll regret getting on Lela's bad side. She was a Marine."

Bennett lifted his champagne glass. "To militant females. Heaven bless them. And may we never be so unfortunate as to stir up their wrath."

CHAPTER 47

From force of habit and professional necessity, Ginger was an early riser. On the morning of the wedding, she telephoned Phyllis to offer best wishes.

"I wanted to be there. If I could, I would be," Ginger insisted. "But since I'm in every scene of *Kitty Foyle,* there's no way the director can shoot without me."

"I know," Phyllis replied. "We understand."

"It feels strange, knowing you're about to become the wife of a man I've never met. I don't suppose you'll be bringing him to California any time soon."

"I doubt it," Phyllis acknowledged. "But after your picture wraps, you'll be visiting Lela, won't you? How is it going?"

"All right. I think. I hope. One columnist was quite savage. She accuses me of darkening my hair to copy Hedy Lamarr—even though hers is black and mine plain brown—and hates the way I have it styled. Oh, and in her opinion, I'm overly ambitious, unqualified to take on this important role. I guess I'm supposed to remain a blonde song-and-dance comedienne forever."

"Don't let it get you down."

What a reversal this is, she acknowledged. A bride's

cousin should be soothing premarital jitters instead of expressing her own. "Do you ever see Fred these days?"

"Sure. Not often, but we always have laughs when we run into each other. I'm crazy about the man. I can be at ease in his company, now that I don't have to dance with him every single day. Say, here's my studio car coming up the driveway," Ginger announced. "Must dash, or I'll be late for makeup." Smooching, smacking kiss sounds were followed by a breathless, "Love you!"

"Love you, too."

Holding the silent phone, Phyllis realized that she benefitted from Ginger being stuck in California. She'd rather not compete for attention on the most significant day of her life. The bride should be the only star at her wedding.

Her fingers were twitchy as she worked the buttons of her custom dress suit, fashioned from light wool in a flattering shade of medium blue, and attached the mink half-stole to her shoulder. The same fur decorated the brim of her hat. When it was in place, she sent the hairdresser to her aunt's room.

When Lela emerged, her golden tresses were arranged in an elaborate half-up and half-down coiffure that replicated Ginger's from *Fifth Avenue Girl*. She wore a small black hat with dramatic veiling, and a black dress designed to show off her trim figure.

Stepping out of the hotel, Phyllis was relieved to see that the weather was fair, and not overly hot.

"Lela's prayers must be responsible," she murmured to her bridegroom when they met in the waiting area outside the mayoral office.

"You look terrific. Doesn't she, Pop?"

"Pretty as a picture," Gustave Cerf responded, bestowing a fond and fatherly smile.

Bennett's uncle nodded. "Gorgeous."

With shaking hands, her bridegroom pinned a large corsage of orchids and fragrant lily of the valley to her lapel. She held up her own trembling fingers to show him, and they both laughed.

Lela, moving as regally as a queen on her coronation day, approached the door, turned around, and announced, "The matron of honor is here."

Confused, Phyllis said, "I don't have one." Then she saw Anne Shirley standing on the threshold. As they embraced, she asked, "How did you get here so fast? Yesterday, when we spoke on the phone, you were in Los Angeles."

"I flew, silly. On the overnight plane. I've come straight from Mayor LaGuardia's airfield. Johnny sends love and best wishes. Julie Anne, too. Or she would, if she could articulate instead of gurgle. I brought photographs to show you."

"Come and meet Bennett."

She and Anne were chatting with the three Cerf men when Bennett suddenly said in an aggrieved tone, "Where's my groomsman? If he was late leaving Stamford and we have to delay the ceremony, he and I are finished."

Lela's chin jutted out in displeasure. She offered a pithy criticism of the unreliability of the male species when the missing person barged into the anteroom.

Bennett marched over to him. "What held you up?"

"The gendarmes spotted my hunting guns lying across the back seat of my car—I'm taking them to the city for cleaning. They wouldn't let me pass through the gates until they confiscated my weaponry." He struck a pose and loudly declared, "I assure you folks that this is no shotgun wedding. These two are pure as the driven snow. Lela and I made sure of that."

Mayor LaGuardia was the last to appear. "Let's get this show on the road."

When the mayor asked Phyllis if she took Bennett as her lawful wedded husband, she said she did. He put the question to Bennett, who gave the same answer. Harold presented the gold wedding band and she held out her hand, fingernails ceremoniously lacquered rosy red. The ring went on easily.

"By the authority vested in me by the laws of the great State of New York, in this County of Queens, I pronounce you man and wife. Don't blame me for anything that happens." He shook Bennett's hand and kissed Phyllis on the cheek.

Startled by the brevity of the proceedings, she asked, "Is that all? We're lawfully wed?"

He scrawled his signature on the document an assistant handed him and passed the pen to the witnesses. "You are now." With that, he withdrew to his office to carry out more pressing official duties.

A fleet of cars conveyed everyone to Midtown for the private sit-down luncheon at the Ritz Tower. During the reception that followed, Lela ushered Phyllis and her husband past a sea of mostly familiar faces to a table supporting their four-tiered wedding cake. She spotted newlyweds Carleton Alsop and Martha Scott. And Flo Lake, her traveling companion during her initial train journey to New York and her bridge instructor. Stuart Ludlum represented the McCann Erickson agency. Bennett's business partner and his wife were there. A cluster of playwrights and a gaggle of novelists had gathered at the back of the room.

Lela stage-managed the wedding party into position—matron of honor, the groom—tucking his glasses into his coat pocket—the bride, and the groom's father.

She took her place in the group and passed Phyllis a silver slicer before signaling to the photographer.

Phyllis felt Bennett's hand cupping her elbow as she cut the first piece. Her diamond engagement ring and the gold band glistened as the camera flashed.

Placing the sliver of cake on a napkin, she stared at the date imprinted on it.

September 17th, 1940.

This day, she realized, will forever be one of celebration. Miraculously, magically, in a month shadowed by many past sorrows, she'd attained the ultimate joy.

Turning to Bennett, she rose onto her toes and fastened her lips to his.

On a particularly damp and chilly Monday, Phyllis dodged the puddles a recent record-breaking rainstorm had deposited on the sidewalk. She was on her way from her office to the Ritz Tower, her folded copy of *The New York Times* under her arm. The entertainment section contained the list of Academy Award nominees for the films of 1940. Ginger, temporarily residing in Lela's apartment, was a contender.

"You're going to win that Oscar," Phyllis predicted.

Ginger sank back against the sofa cushions. "When Leland Hayward called to tell me the happy news, I told him the Academy is playing a mean joke on me."

"How so?"

"Katharine Hepburn, Joan Fontaine, and Bette Davis are also in the Best Actress category. Can't you recall a certain common connection we all have?"

Phyllis glanced at the page, seeking the answer. "Howard Hughes. You had an affair with him, and so did all the others. Except Martha Scott."

"Every one of them is a critically acclaimed actress. Experienced in dramatic roles. In Hollywood, I'm still regarded as a singing dancer. I'm not liking my chances."

Phyllis fought hard to stifle a yawn. In this third month of pregnancy, she was constantly counting down to the next nap. "Less than two weeks till the awards ceremony. Where you'll take possession of your golden statue."

"Stop talking about it, or you'll put a jinx on me."

"Lela says she might play your mother in the next picture."

"It's not much of a part, and you know she'll want to make a big splash. I've asked RKO to come up with something better for us. That's enough show business talk—I'm trying to have a vacation. How was your honeymoon?"

"In brief, the American history lesson I never wanted. After brushing the rice off our wedding clothes, we went down to Washington—in Bennett's new car. One of J. Edgar Hoover's drivers drove us around all the monuments, and we went inside the important government buildings. My bridegroom decided he had to visit every battlefield in the vicinity. Gettysburg. Manassas. Yorktown. I saw the Blue Ridge mountains, pretty enough but not nearly as magnificent as Yosemite or the Canadian Rockies. We went inside Luray Caves, which I hated. And wandered around Williamsburg. We stayed at a beach hotel. We had a minor accident that banged up our automobile."

"What an adventure."

"Some of the time we quarreled," Phyllis admitted. "Testing each other. Learning to speak honestly about our feelings and frustrations without causing pain."

"And the marriage survived," Ginger marveled.

"Somehow all the strife strengthened it. When we got

back, our lovey-doveyness inspired Bennett's dad to reveal the existence of the secret lady in his life. And now they're married. We spent Christmas together, and had a tree and a turkey. Pops gave me a doll in a miniature cradle—hint, hint. He didn't know I was already pregnant, and neither did we. But it wasn't long before Bennett and I could tell him he's getting the grandchild he longs for."

"Do you want a girl or a boy?"

Phyllis shrugged. "We'll be delighted to meet whoever comes."

"You're positively radiant. Pregnancy is a great beautifier. Not that you needed one."

"I'm ridiculously content. My husband is marvelous. Our friends are fascinating. I'm learning so much about the book business. And I've got a swell job in the radio division."

"No regrets about giving up your film career?"

"None. I remember how you used to tell me about the excitement of New York, all the interesting people and nightlife and culture. Peg Entwistle felt the same way. Even before I got here, I realized how limiting it was for me, striving for the limelight."

Ginger got up and crossed to the window, the fabric of her wide-legged slacks billowing with each graceful step. "All these years since that girl died, Mother and I have kept a secret from you. A conspiracy, you might say. I've prayed about it a lot, because I've never been as certain as she was that we did the right thing." Abruptly she turned around. "Every time you mention Peg, my conscience cuts me. I can't stand it any longer."

"If confession will bring comfort," Phyllis said, "you should tell me what you mean." She clasped her hands in her lap and eyed her cousin expectantly.

"An anonymous woman discovered Peg's body. Remember?"

"I do now." A minor, forgettable detail in that major and memorable tragedy.

"I had no idea she was missing on the morning I drove to Beachwood Canyon to hike the hills. It was such a hot day, but I was determined to get up to the ridge, all the way to the Hollywoodland sign. When I did, I found your coat on the ground, and the black pocketbook with the suicide note inside. I started looking around, terrified of what I might discover. After I picked up a high-heeled shoe, I saw her body. Way, way down. In a ditch. I'll remember that till my dying day."

Looking down, Phyllis saw that her fingers had involuntarily clenched.

"I didn't know what to do," Ginger continued. "I carried all the things home—to the Garden of Allah. Mother said that involving myself with a scandalous suicide would be bad for my career. I hadn't been in Hollywood very long, and I was trying hard to get established. So were you. I begged her to let me contact Peg's family, but she wouldn't listen. You know how she is. She hid the coat and purse and shoe in the trunk of our car. After dark, she drove to the nearest police station and left them outside."

"Who made the telephone call?"

"Mother made me do it. She didn't want to lie and claim she'd found the body—it would be a crime, she said. I told the desk clerk I'd seen a female body on the mountainside. I didn't give my name. Or Peg's. We believed she'd be identified right away. Only she wasn't. The next day we took you to the beach, so you wouldn't see the newspaper story, or hear about the mystery girl on the radio. But that's exactly how you found out. I felt terrible about it."

The thick fog that had formed over the past nine years

suddenly evaporated, revealing stark memories. Sand and sea. Shock. Sorrow.

Ginger drew a ragged breath. "Since then, Mother and I have never spoken about what we did. We made a pact not to. I was so shaken. After Peg lost hope and took her life, I worried that I'd drawn you into a profession rife with hardship and rejection. We worked you so hard, Mother and I. Dance lessons, and acting classes, and screen tests. We wanted you to succeed as an actress. Otherwise, your spirit might have been broken. Like Peg's."

"Her money had run out," Phyllis said tonelessly. "I wanted to pay her way to New York, so she could make a fresh start. She felt very strongly that she belonged here."

"Please don't be angry with me. Or with Mother. Faith and prayer can solve every problem and alleviate all kinds of suffering. I've always believed that and always will. God forgives me, I know that. But you're the only person on this earth who can absolve me of this guilt I've borne for so long."

Phyllis left her chair and moved to the window. "I wish you'd told me, back then. It would've saved you years of agonizing. I was never in danger of succumbing to despair like Peg did. After she died, I was even more determined to seize every opportunity that came my way. I felt so grateful to you and Lela for taking me away from Oklahoma, and I still am. Both of you were models of confidence and female self-sufficiency. Whether you meant to or not, you taught me the value of working hard and making careful choices and learning lessons from mistakes." She squeezed Ginger's hand. "When you sent me here, to stay with Lela, you transformed my life all over again."

"Your gain, my loss. I miss having you nearby," Ginger confessed. "Ever since we were little, you've been my sister and my best friend."

"You've got Lela," Phyllis reminded her. "I know she'll be sitting with you at the Academy Awards when the master of ceremonies calls out your name as Best Actress." She returned to the sofa to retrieve her belongings. "Walk me back to my office. Our agency moved into a big new building not far from here. The fresh air will do us both good."

"Very cold air."

"We have fur coats."

"I dislike being conspicuous."

"I want you to be. I'm extremely proud to be seen with my favorite movie star."

Arm in arm, they covered the blocks between the Ritz and Rockefeller Center. Ginger drew stares of recognition, of course, but New Yorkers were accustomed to seeing celebrities and none of the passers-by accosted her.

I've never minded being identified as Ginger's cousin, Phyllis reflected, or as Lela's niece. On my wedding day, I acquired another treasured label—Bennett Cerf's wife. Loving him and being loved by him is a reality that far exceeds my dreams of happiness.

Her journey from actress to magazine columnist to copywriter to radio show producer proved her tenacity and adaptability and resilience, qualities necessary in her marriage to a man of boundless energy and achievement. And to a mother, which she would become in a matter of months.

Those characteristics were just as essential to a professional writer. In the long-ago days when she'd scribbled stories and poems and mailed them to Lela, she'd recognized her true calling. Her unsuccessful quest for stardom had been a diversion. She was finding her way back to the right path—the months and years ahead would reveal its rough spots and smooth sections. As her baby increased in size and vigor, so did her nascent ambition to create literature with lasting value and significance. She would focus her initial efforts on the entertainment and education of young children, the ones who couldn't yet read and those who were beginning to learn.

Someday, she promised herself, the name Ginger had given her would grace the spine and cover of a published book.

EPILOGUE: 1947

I can't exaggerate what a wonderful girl she is.
~ **Bennett Cerf**

"Hold it higher, Mrs. Cerf," the *Daily Oklahoman* photographer instructed Phyllis. "Got to show off the title."

"Can't you read? She's Phyllis Fraser. It's printed right here," Bennett growled, his finger stabbing the volume in her hand.

"He's more than a husband," she explained. "He's my publisher."

"And you're not just another author," he stated. "You're an editor, too."

Smiling, they posed beside the table displaying their output—three of her books, three of his.

For the duration of her hometown visit, Phyllis would overshadow her nationally famous spouse. Many customers streaming through the bookshop doors introduced themselves as Classen High graduates, or Mama's friends. After signing her professional name on the flyleaf of their purchases, she added "Helen Nichols" in parentheses. One former classmate brought along a glamorous glossy publicity photo from her distant RKO starlet days and asked her to autograph it.

Gazing ruefully at a picture taken over a decade ago, she commented, “I don’t look like that anymore. Six and a half years of marriage, plus two little boys, can change a girl.” She was still shedding extra pounds gained while pregnant with Jonathan, now nine months old, and a few left over from carrying Christopher, who was five.

“You don’t look different to me. I remember how you and Doris White ran all around the school, collecting gossip to put in the newsletter. We were so excited when you moved to Hollywood to be in the movies. How’s that cousin of yours? Do you ever see her?”

“Ginger visits New York occasionally, when her mother is there. After we leave town, we’re heading to California to stay with them. Bennett hopes to interest the studios in his writers’ novels.”

Not only would she return to Los Angeles as a published author. She was also an editor at the *Book of the Month Club*, a columnist for *Newsday*, and the co-creator of puzzles and cryptograms for the *Saturday Review of Literature*. Marriage to Bennett provided an entrée into publishing, she couldn’t deny it, but over time she’d established a professional reputation independent of his. Her black and white photographs of Random House authors appeared on their book jackets—she was credited for the portrait of Ayn Rand, an early acquaintance from the RKO wardrobe department. With the advantage of household staff and the boys’ nanny, her various literary endeavors were compatible with her domestic life. Bennett’s position, and his love of society, meant that even her busiest working days were a prelude to a dinner party or a night on the town.

A well-dressed stranger came forward with a daughter about Christopher's age. The woman picked up the alphabet and counting book.

"Can you sing the ABC song?" Phyllis asked the child and received a shy nod in response. While the mother examined *The Story of Dimples and Cock Sure,* she made her pitch. "It's a drawing book as well as a storybook. My son loves it. Because activity books are engaging and educational, they stimulate a child's mind. And with a parent's supervision, they can foster interaction and bonding."

"I'll take it. And these." The customer gathered up both Little Golden Books, *Mother Goose* and *This Little Piggy*. "My husband would like this." She added *Great Tales of Terror and the Supernatural,* the anthology Phyllis had co-edited, to her stack.

While they chatted, Bennett was wandering through the shop, seeking confirmation that Random House titles were well represented on its bookshelves.

Her years of living with that strong-willed gentleman had increased her assertiveness. On leaving the bookstore, he asked for the car keys. She refused to give them up.

"Sorry, darling. You'll get lost—again. When will you stop being so obstinate and listen carefully when I give you driving directions?"

Last year Mama had married again. She and her fourth husband, Austin Clendenin, housed and cared for twelve-year-old Phillip, Jean's son. A modest studio apartment, they said, was too small for two people, and one of them a growing boy. The arrangement made Phyllis wonder whether her sister shared her enjoyment of motherhood, or her ability to cope with its occasional difficulties and frustrations.

Backing the car away from the curb, she said, "We should call home and find out how the boys are doing.

It's a shame they didn't come with us to meet their grandmother and their aunt and their cousin."

"They aren't the right ages for a trip as long as this one," he replied. "And I like having you all to myself for a change—until Ginger and Lela and Anne crowd me out of the picture." Studying the city buildings, he sat up straighter. "Say, I've remembered that bet we made. The one about oil wells on the state capitol lawn. I won't believe you until I see them with my own eyes."

"Prepare to pay up."

She was glad to see the prosperity that had come to the region during the world war and since the restoration of peace. Her memories of Oklahoma City during the Depression hadn't included these busy downtown stores, or all the military bases that had been established, or the new factories on the edge of town.

As she followed Lincoln Boulevard, the familiar dome appeared in the distance. So did the tops of the oil derricks.

"I'll be damned."

Rounding the corner, she eased the car into a space right across from the north-facing façade. "Unlike you, I never exaggerate to improve a story."

He reached for his wallet and whipped out a ten-dollar bill. "I can't spare this, you know. You outsold me today."

"You should've expected it," she teased. "I'm the one who grew up here. Console yourself with the fact that all those book profits go to Random House. Minus my royalties, which will be added to our household account. Partners for life. Partners in publishing."

"The luckiest partners on the face of the earth," he declared, leaning in to kiss her. "And that's no exaggeration."

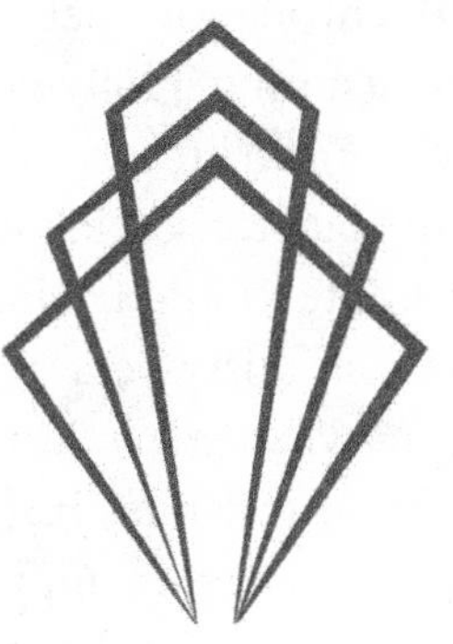

AUTHOR'S NOTE

By any measure, Helen Maurine Brown Nichols, best remembered as Phyllis Fraser Cerf Wagner, was a remarkable person. Throughout her journey from Oklahoma schoolgirl to aspiring Hollywood starlet to wife and mother to New York literary fixture, her warmth, sense of fun, and intelligence served her well.

Phyllis was fortunate to find lasting love twice during a long life. During her thirty-year marriage to Bennett Cerf, she was a renowned New York hostess in addition to her professional pursuits. Her sons, Christopher and Jonathan, inspired her to champion educational and entertaining children's books, and became her collaborators. Her dress sense, dating from the Hollywood years, helped her become a Manhattan fashion icon whose chic ensembles were highlighted in the social columns. In the 1950s she was a television quiz show participant, appearing a couple of times with Bennett on *What's My Line?* and as a regular panelist on *Down You Go*.

She didn't intend to marry again after Bennett's death. Four years later, after a lengthy period of companionship and courtship, she was wed to Robert F. Wagner, fellow Catholic and former mayor of New York City. He predeceased her in 1991. In 2006, she suffered complications from a fall in the five-story brownstone where she and both husbands had welcomed celebrities of the literary, broadcast, film, political, and diplomatic realms. She was ninety years old.

The New York Times obituary charted her life of accomplishment: "A newspaper and magazine columnist, movie actress, publisher, writer of radio soap operas, advertising executive, and civic fund-raiser, she lived at the center of Manhattan social life, entertaining successive generations of the city's artistic and political elite. . . . As a hostess and occasional confidante, she hobnobbed with the most famous people of the day, including Frank Sinatra, William Faulkner, and Truman Capote."

Her commitment to the development of children's reading skills and Bennett's love of television were legacies received by both of their sons. Christopher Cerf was a *Sesame Street* creator, supplying music and lyrics and voice over, and he worked on *Electric Company* and other programs. His songs have been widely performed by non-Muppet artists. Jonathan Cerf served as President of the *Harvard Lampoon* magazine, was also involved with *Sesame Street*, and co-authored *Big Bird's Red Book*.

Bennett, a proud graduate of Columbia University, deposited his papers there and was interviewed by that institution's Oral History Project. His recollections later appeared in book form. After his death, in 1984, Phyllis also participated in a series of audio recording sessions, recounting the details of her life and her varied careers, but the transcript of these tapes was not published. In her responses to the interviewer's questions, she occasionally muddles her chronology, which I have corrected by cross-checking newspapers and movie magazines and film shooting schedules. She reveals a great deal about her cousin and her aunt, including their carefully concealed intimate relationships with men. Her commentary provides a rich and detailed record of show business and publishing from the 1930s through the mid-1980s.

Ginger, whose illustrious career is extremely well-documented, won her only Academy Award for *Kitty Foyle*, shortly after her New York visit in February of 1941.

Lela, who eventually portrayed Ginger's on-screen mother in the *Major and the Minor*, continued as her daughter's chief advisor and *de facto* agent. A staunch Republican and avowed conservative, she co-founded the Motion Picture Alliance for the Preservation of American Ideals and was an energetic anti-Communist crusader. In 1947 she testified as a friendly witness before the House Un-American Activities Committee (HUAC), identifying what she believed to be Communist themes in screenplays and offering up names of alleged party members. Her condemnation extended to Random House authors and editors, resulting in a temporary rift with the Cerfs. At her death, she was eighty-six years old.

After her late RKO successes, Ginger moved from studio to studio, earning an ever-escalating salary. In 1949, she reunited with Fred Astaire for *The Barkleys of Broadway*. In common with the majority of Golden Age stars, her opportunities declined in the 1950s, as the studio system was dismantled and television came to the forefront. She returned to the Broadway stage as Dolly Levi in *Hello, Dolly*, and toured worldwide.

In 1991, she published a memoir, *Ginger: My Story*. She mentions taking her pretty cousin Helen back to Hollywood and inventing the name Phyllis Fraser, but her date for the Oklahoma City visit doesn't coincide with the factual record. Her book contains numerous errors and omissions, some of which I rectified in this fictional account. She spent her last years quietly, hobbled by increasing weight and persistent ill-health, but holding fast to her Christian Science beliefs. She died in 1995, at the age of eighty-three, and her ashes were buried with

Lela's in Oakwood Memorial Park in Chatsworth, California.

Peg Entwistle was signed by RKO at the same time as Phyllis, and both were cast in *Thirteen Women*. Although the nature of their interactions during or after production is uncertain, Peg's role was reduced, and Phyllis landed on the cutting room floor. The promising young actress leaped to her death from the Hollywoodland sign on September 16, 1932. This event and her motivations have for decades inspired mythology and misinformation. Her biographer, the late James Zeruk, Jr. carried out thorough and painstaking research in his effort to present her true and unvarnished history, in *Peg Entwistle and the Hollywood Sign Suicide*. Filmmaker Hope Anderson devotes particular attention to Peg, with filmed interviews of her brother and her niece, in her documentary *Under the Hollywood Sign*, though her primary focus is the development and preservation of Beachwood Canyon as a residential district.

No evidence exists identifying Ginger Rogers as the hiker who located Peg's discarded belongings and spotted her body. Or that Lela delivered the coat, purse, and shoe to the police station in Hollywood. Of course, there's also no proof that they weren't involved—in fiction, anything is possible. The anonymous female tipster's refusal to give her name to the authorities, and her desire to avoid publicity, implies that either she was an actress or a notable person with a connection to the film community. Interestingly, a decade after these events, Lela wrote a mystery novel featuring Ginger as heroine, in which she discovers the body of an unconscious person.

According to Peg's brother Milton, shortly after she ended her life, RKO sent her a letter offering a role in an upcoming film. It's conceivable that she would have been considered for *Little Women*, having previously played

Amy March on Broadway. The day after Peg's funeral, the *Los Angeles Times* and other newspapers reported that Phyllis Fraser had been cast, but after George Cukor took over the production, he assembled performers of his choosing.

Throughout her life Phyllis crossed paths with many famous people, but her work with Ted Geisel, her former desk mate at McCann Erickson, was particularly notable. Even before they co-founded the early reader imprint Beginner Books at Random House, he'd achieved mass popularity as Dr. Seuss. Their first literary collaboration was *The Cat in the Hat*, and the rest is history. Their editorial clashes were legendary, leading to a professional rupture and some hard feelings.

Successful Cerf matchmaker Harold Ross, an early member of the Algonquin Round Table, the famously obstreperous yet beloved editor of *The New Yorker* magazine, carried out his duties until his death from a cancer operation at fifty-nine.

Anne Shirley and John Payne divorced shortly before their daughter's third birthday. Her second husband, screenwriter and producer Adrian Scott, was a victim of Hollywood's blacklist; their marriage ended when he decided to move overseas. Later she married Charles Lederer, nephew of Marion Davies, William Randolph Hearst's mistress.

As an uncredited actress, Natalie Draper appeared in several movies and later had a featured role in *Forever Amber.* She married twice after her divorce from Tom Brown, who remarried once. He received the *Croix de Guerre* and the Bronze Star for valor as a World War II paratrooper, continued making movies, and had a consistent career in television.

I'm immensely grateful to my friend Paul Brogan, for the hours he spent sharing his personal recollections of

Ginger and Lela, of Katharine Hepburn, and of others who lit up the screen during Hollywood's Golden Age. And to Austin and Howard Mutti-Mewse for their remarkable reminiscences of the famous and the unheralded players of that era.

In addition to the Gallica Press crew, I extend heartfelt thanks to Bev at BKR Editing for developmental assistance, to Erin at Hook of a Book for her stellar proofreading skills, to Michelle at Melissa Williams Design for stylish formatting, and to Deborah of Tugboat Design for the perfect cover.

Like any writer, this one depends on the support and the understanding of the people in her life.

My mother and my late father, constant readers who read to me constantly in my formative years, are entirely responsible for my love of books. Their encouragement and their enthusiasm for my progress as a writer has been a great gift.

In recent years, I've been especially thankful for my dear friend and writing companion, novelist Virginia Macgregor, who was at my side in spirit or in person in the earliest stages of *The Limits of Limelight*, then moved into my neighborhood before it was completed. I will forever treasure the hours talking through our projects and working on them together.

The greatest measure of credit and gratitude goes to my husband, who for so many years has steadfastly endured the vagaries of my creative life, as a devoted presence through the creation of fourteen novels.

ABOUT THE AUTHOR

MARGARET PORTER is the award-winning and bestselling author of more than a dozen works of historical fiction. A former stage actress, she also worked professionally in film, television, and radio. Other writing credits include nonfiction, newspaper and magazine articles, and poetry. She and her husband live in New England. Information about her books and other aspects of her life and career can be found at www.margaretporter.com.